BAD GIRL

MICHELE JAFFE

BALLANTINE BOOKS • NEW YORK

A Ballantine Book
Published by The Random House Publishing Group

Copyright © 2003 by Michele Jaffe

www.ballantinebooks.com

Library of Congress Catalog Control Number can be obtained from
the publisher upon request.

ISBN 0-345-46498-2

Manufactured in the United States of America

Cover design by Michael Harney
Text design by Julie Schroeder

First Edition: July 2003

10 9 8 7 6 5 4 3 2

To Dan. For not changing the locks.

There is nothing either good or bad
but thinking makes it so.

—William Shakespeare
Hamlet, Act II, Scene ii

CHAPTER 1

She couldn't get the sign out of her head.

CLAIM YOUR OWN BAGGAGE.

It hung over the luggage carousels at the Las Vegas airport, huge letters. It seemed disingenuous, she thought, for a city like Las Vegas where people came to leave the baggage of their lives behind.

CLAIM YOUR OWN BAGGAGE.

No. She wouldn't. Defiant, she had left her bag there. Marched out of the airport and left it to circle around and around on the carousel, her underwear, three sample tubes of lipstick, two favorite T-shirts, a pair of jeans, a photo in a silver frame, and a young girl's jewelry box, all neatly packed. Her luggage, her past, abandoned.

As if it were that easy.

The next day she was back at the airport, offering the clerk at Lost and Found a lame excuse, a smile. He handed her the bag and it seemed to have gotten heavier overnight. By then she had already begun to realize what was now, three months later, painfully clear. That no matter what you do, how many possessions you sell off, how often you move, how much therapy you pay for, your baggage will always be waiting for you to claim it.

By then she had begun to realize why she had come to Las Vegas. Why she had to come.

Be good, she heard her father's voice say.

And saw the sign, CLAIM YOUR OWN BAGGAGE.

It's not always as easy to be good as you want, Daddy, she thought as she sat in her car across the street from the house.

Every thirty seconds the clock on the dashboard made a tiny clicking sound. Be good. Click. Claim your own baggage. Click. Saabs had to be the only car in America that didn't have a digital clock in the dashboard, she thought. She had only been sitting in front of the house for ten minutes this time but the clicking was starting to drive her crazy. Click, click, click, like a metronome, flipping her back and forth between present and past.

Be good.

Click.

Claim your own baggage.

Lights were on in every window of the house, almost. Shadows moved in front of the one in the bottom right-hand corner, the den off the living room, a tall silhouette, the oldest boy, and a shorter, rounder one.

The mother.

Behind the shadows the air flickered, like someone had turned on a TV. Probably they were watching it together as they waited for the boy's brother and sister to get home. The older boy was about fourteen, his younger brother eleven. He was at his clarinet lesson. The sister was fifteen. She went to the gym Mondays, Wednesdays, and Fridays and didn't get home until 5:30 P.M. As soon as she did, they sat down and had dinner. Together. Sometimes Dad joined them too, but not tonight. He was working late. Big business dinner. He'd worn his fanciest suit to the office that day.

For a moment the woman in the car wondered what would happen if she rang the bell and asked if she could join them for dinner. They did not know her, they were complete strangers to one another. At least, they knew nothing of *her*. She knew all about the Johnson family. Quick sketches of their faces covered the pages of the pad on the seat next to her. Despite herself, she could not stop watching them.

Be good.

Click.

Claim your own baggage.

A man strolled by on the street walking a fluffy white dog, and his eyes met those of the woman in the car. He looked familiar, she thought, then realized it was not *him*, it was *here*. Everything was familiar here, this was the curse of her baggage, what she needed to free herself from. The man with the dog was the icon for everything she came to purge, everything she couldn't escape.

Hands tightening on the steering wheel, she watched the dashboard clock click one more time. The little brother got dropped off, music under one arm, clarinet case sticking out the top of his red and blue Spider-man backpack. He used his key on the small gate next to the driveway, closed it carefully, stepped over the hose the exterminator left there to finish the job the next day, and entered the house by the side door. The door went into the back hallway, the woman knew, next to the laundry room; farther down was the kitchen. She could see them all in her head.

Ten clicks of the clock later, a beige Jeep Wrangler pulled to the curb opposite and the sister got out. The woman in the Saab watched the girl go through the gate, and into the house the same way her brother had. She had perfect thighs.

She was not as careful as her younger brother, though, and the gate didn't close all the way. It hovered slightly ajar, an invitation. Come on in. Pay us a visit. See our perfect home from the inside. Carve out a place for yourself in our family.

Don't do it! the woman's head screamed. *Leave now. Be good. Now isn't the right time.* She glanced at the clock and saw that was true. Not the right time. She had to get to work. It was almost the dinner hour. She started her engine and pulled out, heading toward the Strip.

CLAIM YOUR OWN BAGGAGE.

But she'd be back. She wasn't done with the Johnson house yet.

CHAPTER 2

"Man, you trying to bore me to death?" Roddy Ruiz asked, shaking his head. "I tole you already. I kidnapped her, brung her in through the back door, had sex with her, then, like, killed her when I was done."

"Why did you kill her?"

"She was giving me some trouble, like I said, *cabrón*. Why do you keep digging at me, man?"

"What kind of trouble, Roddy?" Detective Nick Lee asked. "We need to get the details down."

His partner, Detective Bob Zorzi, offered, "Did she challenge your manhood?"

Roddy's eyes narrowed, hard street stare style. "You wanna talk about my manhood, *hijo de puta*? You take these cuffs offa me I'll show you—"

Detective Lee said, "Just tell us what happened."

"Chinaman, you tell your partner there ain't no problem with my *manhood*. That bitch, she was sat-is-fied. She was begging for it. That big dick asshole of her boyfriend, he don't know nothing about pleasing a woman. That's what she tell me. She say 'oh papa please take me.' Them white women, they love a little Mexican love taco. Why you think they call me Hot Rod?"

Chicago "Windy" Thomas, new head of the Las Vegas Metro police department's criminalistics bureau and thoroughly exhausted mother of a six-year-old just over the stomach flu, leaned her forehead against the cool one-way glass panel, half to get a closer look at the suspect in the interrogation room, and half to calm her raging headache. She had only been in her position for two weeks, had only been in Las Vegas for a month and a half, but she thought she could recognize Roddy. Not him so much as something inside him. Insecure boys playing at being tough men shared characteristics no matter where you went.

Roddy Ruiz's file said he was fifteen years old, which in street years made him about forty-five. He looked eleven. He was small, with big ears, brown eyes, close shaved dark hair, and a faint line of fuzz on his upper lip and chin that Windy was sure he'd call a mustache and beard. No parents, lived with his uncle. He'd refused a lawyer, confessed to murder, and now leaned back in his chair, tapping his white K-Swiss sneakers on the floor to the beat of a song in his head, moving his shoulders. There were large rust-colored stains on his jeans and Tommy Hilfiger T-shirt where he'd tried to wash blood off, but they didn't seem to bother him. He was a badass, his unconcerned posture said, nothing they could do to the Hot Rod that he wasn't ready for.

The two detectives were jumpier than Roddy, from lack of sleep and excitement. To Windy, even the stenographer who had gone in with them looked smug, like the cat who had swallowed the canary. They'd caught Roddy less than forty-eight hours after he attacked and killed the daughter of a California billionaire in the bathroom of a tiny Las Vegas apartment while his uncle watched the Shop At Home Channel in the other room. Less than forty-eight hours was a good capture time, made better by his confessing it up front, and the cops knew they could count on a lot of accolades from the higher-ups, not to mention a lot of attention from the media. The Shop At Home Channel had been founded by the girl's father, it was how he'd made his billions, and no news executive around the country could resist the irony—although they used the word tragedy—that if it had not been on the television in the next room, Roddy's uncle might have heard something and been able to save the girl. Even the national networks had sent crews, so there were more than the normal handful of reporters hanging around the press room, ready to make this week's heroes out of the men who had worked the case.

They deserved that, the attention, the praise, Windy thought. Everyone deserved it. Everyone should feel important and special. It was the lack of those feelings that created individuals who could beat a billionaire's daughter to death and then pose her pornographically in a bathtub. No, attention and praise were good, which was why Windy felt like crap about what she was about to do.

She took a deep breath, slid the manila folder from the ledge in front of the one-way glass under her arm, and knocked on the door of the interrogation room.

Four faces turned to her as if annoyed by her intrusion.

She thought she heard Detective Zorzi mutter, "crap" under his breath when he saw her. "How can we help you, ma'am?" he asked, trying to be polite but really, she thought, to remind her who was in charge.

The suspect whistled low, leaned back in his chair, and spread his legs wide under the table. "You shouldn't have, officers. A stripper, all for me. And they say the cops are assholes." Roddy licked his lips appreciatively. "Honey, you tell 'em to get these cuffs offa me and we can get the party started *right*."

Out of the corner of her eye Windy saw Detective Lee almost choke with embarrassment. "She's not a strip—"

Ignoring him, Windy walked over to the table and sat down facing Roddy.

"Mr. Ruiz, I'm Chicago Thomas," she said. "I'm here to save your life."

The first thing Roddy noticed about her was the way she pronounced her name, Thomás, with the accent on the last syllable, trying to act like she was Latino. Bond with him. Man, these cops must think he was dumb. He took her in, caramel-colored hair, light green eyes, and sneered. "You trying to get down with me, *mamacita,* saying your name all slick like that, act like from my 'hood? You think you're J. Lo? What part of Mexico you from, honey? You know, Texas don't count." He winked, man to man, at the detectives but they just stared at him. Cop bastards.

"My family is from Chile," the lady cop said. "But I was born in the States."

"What kind of a name is Chicago?"

"The name of the city where I was born. What kind of a name is Roddy?"

"A sexy one." Roddy winked. "They call you Chicago? Or just Chica?"

"My friends call me Windy."

"No shit. I used to have a dog named Windy. On account of him farting all the time."

Windy looked at him wide-eyed. "Really? You'd be amazed at how many people have that same pet. Now tell me about yourself. Where were you born, Roddy?"

"Man, I was born the day I saw you."

She smiled, but more like a mom would. Made Roddy nervous. Then she said, not to him, but to the detectives, "I'd like to have Mr. Ruiz's guardian here for this, please. That's his uncle, I believe?"

"No need to involve Mr. X," Roddy told them. "I got my shit under control myself." He leaned across the table. "You sure you ain't a stripper, lady? You could make good money, you know, tits and face like you got. You dead sexy even if you got a fucked up name. Now I know this club, I can set you up, me and the manager, we—"

But the dirty blonde wasn't even looking his way. "Please bring in Mr. Xavier," she repeated. "I believe I saw him in the west hallway."

Roddy watched as the taller detective left the room. Man was at least three times the size of the lady, but there he went, doing what she said, and not taking his time about it either. She must have some power, something, to get him hopping like that. He looked at her more closely. She was wearing a gray business suit, all the cops wore suits, *idiotas*, trying to look professional, but hers was something a little special. Sort of cool and classy. Underneath she had on a shirt like a man's that buttoned down the front, gold with white pin-stripes, the top two buttons open, and a tie, but not wearing it like a man, wearing it inside the shirt, sort of like a scarf, so it was sexy. Roddy had to hand it to her, the woman could dress. She looked like something out of one of the fancy magazines with the foreign sounding names, *Elle* or *Glamour*, that he looked at while Mr. X was getting manicures. Finally he said, "You a lawyer or something, lady?"

"No."

"A judge?"

"No."

"Then how you gonna save my life? You got super powers? See through walls and shit?"

"Yes. As a matter of fact, I do."

"Yeah? Prove it." He stood up, showing her his jeans. "Tell me what I got on under my pants."

"Blue-and-white striped boxers. Now please, Roddy, sit down. You are making the detective nervous."

The expression on Roddy's face when she told him what color underwear he was wearing was better than Windy could have hoped, but when he followed that up by covering his crotch with his hands, so she wouldn't be able to see his "love taco" with her X-ray vision, Windy thought she might have to step outside to keep from laughing. Only Bob Zorzi's return kept her there, and kept her from telling Roddy that according to the crime scene reports, he owned a total of five pairs of underwear, all of them blue and white striped boxers and that she'd just been making an educated guess.

Hector Xavier, the man Detective Zorzi escorted in, was medium height, in his late thirties, and confident, maybe a little cocky, judging from his walk. That could be useful, Windy thought. Hector had been Roddy's legal guardian for five years, and the way Roddy looked at him, it was clear to Windy that he pretty well idolized the man. Hector and Roddy had been hiding out together since the murder, and when the cops caught up with them it was Hector who had convinced Roddy to tell the truth. He had a pencil mustache, a mouth full of gold, and a sharkskin suit whose lapels would have pleased a Mafia don of the 1960s, once it got a good pressing. It looked to Windy as though he, like Roddy, was still wearing the clothes he had left home in when they went into hiding. His white silk shirt, no longer crisp, was unbuttoned to the middle, showing a large gold cross against a muscular, hairless chest. He looked his ward over carefully, then put his hand on his shoulder and said, "You okay, Hot Rod?"

"Yeah, Mr. X," Roddy replied, struggling to regain his cool tone. "Doin' fine."

"Good." Hector sat down next to Roddy and asked, "We got a problem here, officers?" He gave Windy a smile with his mouth of gold. She wondered how much a set of teeth like that cost.

"Just a little one," Windy assured him, returning the smile. Unless you counted having your ward confess to a brutal murder. She opened the manila folder, started taking out shiny color photos and sorting them on the table.

"You showing us girly pictures?" Hector asked, looking around hopefully at the male cops for a reaction. Out of the corner of her eye, Windy saw Hector wink at Roddy and mouth, "Don't worry."

She got the photos in the order she wanted, gathered them together and tapped their edges against the table, evening them. She looked up and asked no one in particular, "It's getting warm in here, isn't it?"

Hector and the two cops squirmed a little inside their suit jackets, as if her mentioning it had raised the temperature in the room.

Hector said, "Is this gonna take a long time?"

"No. But you should get comfortable."

He slipped off his Mafioso jacket. "Okay, what is it? What are those?"

Windy laid the pile of photos on the table, facing Hector and Roddy. "We might get to them later, if we need them." She watched Roddy recognize the corner of their overfurnished living room in the top photo: sofa, TV in the black lacquer entertainment center, matching coffee table. Doorway to the left going to Hector Xavier's office. Some of his confidence seemed to flicker. "I'm going to tell you a story," she said. "Feel free to interrupt me, but if I were you, I'd wait until the end." She was talking to both of the men across from her, but her gaze stuck to Roddy. "Danielle Starr came to your apartment at around eleven thirty in the morning. She'd come to pick up a brick of heroin her boyfriend Fred had contracted with Mr. Xavier for, and she carried a shopping bag full of bills. Roddy, you were watching TV when she rang the doorbell, so you let her in and told her to wait on the couch while you got your guardian, Mr. Xavier. When you came back, she had flipped to the Shop At Home Channel. I suspect she told you that her father owned it, made some kind of small talk. She was nervous, this was the first time Fred had trusted her as a courier, and that wasn't all. He had sent her out with five thousand dollars less than he owed. He'd told her to do whatever she could to make Mr. Xavier satisfied, buy him a few days to come up with the rest of the money."

Windy's eyes went to Hector, who was looking around the room, bored. "She made you that offer when you took her into your office. Being a sensible businessman, you decided to take her up on it. You'd been expecting to do business and you were dressed for it, wearing a suit, but that wasn't a problem. You slipped off your jacket, got comfortable in your desk chair, opened up your pants, and told her to get on her knees. She did what you wanted, started sucking, but for some reason it just wasn't happening. You couldn't stay hard."

"Aw man, this is bull*shit*," Hector said. But now he looked at Windy. She'd found that any man would get excited, pay attention, if you started talking about his private parts, even if you said derogatory things about them. Inexplicable but true.

Windy used this magic power to hold Hector's gaze. "What did she do, Hector? What was her mistake? Did she say something wrong? Something about the Snoopy statue on the desk inhibiting your performance? Did she laugh at you? Your pants are down around your ankles and she's laughing at you? Humiliating you? So you decide you'll show her. You take the bronze statue of the Snoopy playing golf and you hit her with it once, here." Windy pointed to the crown of her head. "That doesn't shut her up, so you do it twice more. She slides onto the floor, but you're not done yet, you hit her in the chest with the statue, breaking her rib cage, and across the nose. She most likely died of the fourth blow, when her ribs punctured her lungs, but I don't imagine you care about that. Then, when you had shown her good, you look up and see that the door to the office is partway open, that there is someone standing, watching between the door frame and the hinges." Windy glanced at Roddy, then back to Hector. "You call him in and get him to carry Danielle's body into the bathroom before she bleeds all over the rug. He hugs her to him, close, only letting one of her feet drag on the ground, trying not to make a mess. He puts her in the bathtub and is going to leave her there, but you tell him to pose her. Set her up, make it look like she's touching herself. No—you have a better idea. Take the Snoopy statue and shove it up inside her. You want to humiliate her, even after she's dead. Make it so everyone knows what a whore she was."

Windy's gaze rested on Roddy again, who was watching her as if hypnotized. "But you couldn't do it, could you, Roddy? When Hector turned his back, you moved Snoopy so he was lying next to the girl. You were covered in her blood from carrying Danielle, but you hadn't killed her, and you felt bad about it. You locked yourself in the bathroom with her and turned on the water, so Hector wouldn't hear you throw up. Then you sat down next to the bathtub and cried. When you got up, you—"

"No," Roddy said, his first word, voice higher now than before. Talking not to Windy, but to Hector. Pleading. "I didn't. She's lying, man. I didn't. I didn't cry, man."

Hector ignored him. "Shit, lady," he drawled. "That's a fine story you got. Like I got a problem with my equipment, got to beat a girl to death to get a hard-on. You want to try it? Right here? I'll give you a ride you won't forget."

Windy's eyes did not leave Roddy. "What did Hector say to you, Roddy, to convince you to take the fall? Did he tell you you'd be tried as a juvenile, out in a few years? That's not true. They are going to ask for you to be tried as an adult. You could go to prison for the rest of your life, no parole. Did he say that if you confessed we wouldn't ask too many questions? Did he point out that you're a good talker and cops were dumb, we'd believe anything? That you'd get in and get out, just like that, and then he'd be waiting for you? You'd be a real man? You have no record, Roddy, you've never been inside. You can't imagine what it's like."

Roddy said, still not looking at her, eyes only for Hector, "I didn't cry, man. You got to believe me, I didn't cry."

Hector shook his head. "What are you trying to do to the boy, lady? It's not good enough for you that he confessed? Shit. Know what you should do? You should go, get yourself a typewriter, write a novel. You got one hell of an imagination. You say I did this? Killed this bitch? Where's the proof? I beat the bitch to death? Okay, show me some blood. Show me some gore." Hector stood up, spread his arms. "Look at my shirt. Same shirt I was wearing that day. Not a spot of anything."

An electrical jolt ran through Windy, a bolt of excitement. Oh Hector, she thought. You should learn not to brag. Not make it too easy for me. She said: "When a person is beaten to death the way Danielle was, the blood does not explode out. It gets on the object that is used to do the beating. When the object is swung, droplets of blood fly off of it." Windy rolled up one of the eight-by-ten crime scene photos so it formed a cylinder, like a club made of paper. She held it in both hands. "If this is the weapon, the person doing the beating would go like this." She raised the cylinder with both hands over her shoulder, then brought it down hard on the table. "Danielle was hit five times. The first time the killer hit her might not draw blood. The second time a little, the third more. Each time he pulled his arms back to take another swing, blood flew off the weapon. But not onto his chest. The killer would not have blood on the front of his shirt. He'd have it here." Windy held the makeshift club over her shoulder, showing where it would go when she drew it into position to strike again. "On his back."

For a moment the interrogation room was completely still. Hector standing there, his arms outstretched, showing how clean he was. Detectives Lee and Zorzi staring, transfixed, at his back.

Then Hector did a crazy dance, trying to see over his shoulder, trying to turn his shirt around, twisting, and Windy saw what she knew would be there. Hundreds of small red circles, medium velocity blood spatter, cascading down from his right shoulder, the shirt looking like it had been hit with a half empty can of rust-colored spray paint.

The detectives were just coming out of their trance when Hector lunged across the table and tried to strangle Windy. "The bitch is crazy, man," he yelled as Detective Lee pried his fingers away from her neck. "She's crazy. No way she knows that stuff. On my back. Bullshit. No way. Unless—"

Hector's eyes got crafty and at the same time took on a weird sheen, making him look a little nuts. They darted around, fast. "You've been watching my house. The feds, they got cameras in my house. That's illegal. I got rights. I want a lawyer. I'm not saying anything else until I get a lawyer. This is America. Ain't no one got the right to have cameras in my house. You been filming this, filming me. I'll sue all of you. I'll—"

Windy got up from the table, the electricity gone. She moved to the door, feeling like her joints were made of lead, knowing that no one in that room liked her, wondering why she had done it. If the truth was worth it. Two good detectives would feel humiliated for having made a mistake and would blame her. Hector's lawyer, if he was any good, would find a dozen forensic experts to argue with her in court. And Roddy, Roddy who she'd saved from life in prison—

As the door closed behind her she could still hear him saying over and over, "I didn't cry. I swear, man, I didn't cry."

She looked at her watch. It wasn't even lunchtime. She wanted to go home and snuggle into bed with her daughter, Cate, and watch cartoons. Forever.

"That was quite a performance," a voice to her right said. Took a deep breath, exhaled it. "You shouldn't have had to do it, though. The detectives never should have taken Roddy into custody given the evidence. But it was still impressive."

Windy turned her back to the one-way glass window to look at the man who had spoken. He was tall with medium-dark hair, cut short, sharp blue eyes, a small indentation in his chin that could have been a scar, and a platinum toothpick at the corner of his mouth. His face half in shadow made its planes more pronounced. His jaw was tight.

"I wouldn't blame it on the detectives," she said. "They were working under pressure and they did the best they could with the information they had. It's not really their fault they made a mistake. The problem is with the way the system is set up here."

"What is wrong with it?"

"There's too much ranking going on, too much competition. Homicide, sex crimes, the forensics teams. No one wants to share information because everyone wants to take credit for catching the bad guys. Get the head of the Violent Crimes Task Force—the big boss's—attention."

"So this is his fault?"

"Not exactly. But he's the only one who can fix it. Make everyone work together, encourage a collaborative environment, not competitive. My crime scene team practically had to fight homicide detectives to get into the apartment. That's wrong. They can help each other. They've got to. It's the whole point of having a violent crimes task force. It's been shown that cases can get cleared 50, even 80 percent faster if cops and criminalists work together, rather than in competition. The head of Violent Crimes needs to make that happen. And fast. Otherwise he isn't doing his job. And then there's—"

The man put up a hand to stop her. "Before you go on, I think it's only fair for me to introduce myself. I'm Ash Laughton. The, ah, head of the Violent Crimes Task Force." He waited for her to be surprised, embarrassed. He had a little speech ready, to show there were no hard feelings.

She said, "I know."

He did not have a speech ready for that. "You know?"

"Of course. Why would I bother to say all of that to someone who can't do anything about it? Or would you rather I just complained behind your back?"

"No, I—" Ash paused, thought about it. "No. I definitely wouldn't."

She scrutinized him with eyes the color of light green jade, and said, "I think you mean that. Good. We'll work together fine."

As if she'd been interviewing him.

Now she was frowning. "Were you just passing by, or did you come to make sure I was doing my job?"

Amazing. Putting him on the spot, now, making him feel like he had to explain himself. Who *was* Windy Thomas? Ash shook his head. "Actually, I came to ask you for your help. I've got a crime scene I need your advice about."

They were joined at that moment by an African-American man about Ash's age but a good two inches taller than he was. The man had high cheekbones, light brown eyes, and short hair done in corn-rows across his head. He wore an enamel yin-yang symbol on a leather cord at the open neck of his golf shirt.

"Chicago Thomas in person," he said, giving her a smile and his hand. "I'm Jonah Priestly. It's a pleasure to meet you. You come with a solid gold reputation."

Windy liked his handshake, powerful but relaxed. "Everyone calls me Windy."

"Like the dog," Ash put in. He kept his face deadpan for two beats before his mouth curved into a grin.

Windy had no idea how rare that was, but Jonah did. He watched, enthralled as Windy started to laugh at a joke apparently between herself and Ash, and said, "Yes. Just like the dog."

"Jonah is the administrative officer in charge of the task force," Ash explained. "As well as being our liaison with the press, the rest of the police department, and the mayor. He lets me think I'm in charge, but the truth is, he pretty much runs things around here."

"Yeah, sometimes I let Ash come in, feel useful. Keep his ego intact. But I kick him out when he starts to get annoying." Then, getting serious and saying to Ash, "Have you told her yet?"

"Told me what?"

"We've got a murder," Ash explained to Windy. "The crime scene is a bloodbath. This killer—from the level of violence I'd say this wasn't his first offense."

"A serial killer?" Windy asked.

Ash nodded. "That is what we are afraid of. I want to run his MO through the Violent Crimes Apprehension Program database at Quantico, but with the way the scene was left, I can't even ascertain enough to even start filling in the VICAP form."

No crime scene visits, Bill had insisted when Windy first brought up taking the job in Vegas. Okay, babe? You'll just stay in the office. I don't want to have to worry about you anymore. His finger had traced the scar between her breasts, seduction and warning at the same time.

Right, she had agreed. No crime scene visits. But this was an exception. Different. She could already hear herself making the excuses. A serial killer, Bill, everyone has to—

"We just got the crime scene photos," Ash said. "We were hoping that you could look at them, tell us what you see."

Photos. Reprieve. Windy nodded. "Of course. Is the body in the photos as well?"

Ash and Jonah exchanged glances. Ash said, "Bodies." Pause. "Yes. Or parts of them."

Windy turned and stared through the one-way glass in front of her. She'd forgotten about Roddy and Hector, sitting there in the interrogation room, quiet, leaning away from one another, waiting for lawyers. Roddy had his head on the table, his feet not tapping out a beat now. Windy had an urge to go back in there and stay. The two of them looked banal, sensible compared to what Ash's tone suggested she was about to face.

"How many people did he kill?" she asked, still looking at Roddy and Hector.

"Four. Mother and three children. The Johnson family."

CHAPTER 3

Flying into Las Vegas six weeks earlier, Windy's daughter, Cate, had looked out the window of the airplane and said, "Look, Mom, they have house farms here." From the sky, the desert bloomed with rows of newly constructed homes (always "homes" in the advertising, Windy noticed, never the more sterile sounding "houses"), the dark asphalt roads running between them looking just like plow lines in a field. Cate was still getting over her disappointment that instead of the "farm fresh" chateau she had fallen in love with from a newspaper ad—"Eight bedrooms, Mommy! And four fireplaces and, Mom, what's a b-k nook? And a breakfast nook and an o-v-r-s-z-d spa perfect for adult entertaining"—Windy had taken a bungalow (three bedrooms, no nook or spa, one fireplace, fake) in one of the few older neighborhoods in the city. The Johnson family had lived in another of those neighborhoods, the fancier version, in a house Cate would have loved despite its age. Set behind a low metal fence but right at street level, the house had the façade of Versailles, a bowling lane, an indoor/outdoor pool, five fireplaces, and six bedrooms. Eight thousand square feet of opulence, three thousand of which were now soaked with blood.

The Johnson family—Carol, Doug, and their three kids, Doug Junior, Norman, and Ellie—had been living there for three years, since Doug Senior was transferred to Vegas by the bank he worked for to oversee their casino investments. Doug Senior himself had found the bodies of his wife and children when he got home from a business dinner that turned into drinks, that turned into a visit to Olympic Gardens, one of the larger strip clubs in Vegas. At least, that was where he thought he'd been. He had stumbled in through the side door at around 5:30 A.M., trying not to wake anyone, and tiptoed up the back stairs into his bedroom. He hadn't noticed the puddle of blood spanning the hallway, but he could not miss the corpses of his wife and children sprawled in the middle of the king-size bed, their heads in their laps, staring at him.

As the only member of his family to escape being murdered, the beneficiary of a large insurance policy on the lives of his wife and kids, the possessor of a moderate cocaine habit he'd been hiding from his family, and the owner of both the pairs of shoes that matched the two sets of footprints found at the crime scene, Doug Johnson Senior made a great suspect. Luckily for him, he was also a good tipper, and the lap dancer he'd favored at the Olympic Gardens remembered him well.

"The lap dancer, Greta, said Mr. Johnson was a real gentleman," Ash told Windy when they were in his office. "He showed her pictures of his wife and kids from his wallet. And was definitely at the club until five, which means he has an alibi for the time of the murders."

The Violent Crimes Task Force offices were at the far end of a cluster of single-story brown stucco buildings in a vaguely Spanish style that the police department had moved into five years earlier. On one side of them was the building housing the DNA and documents labs, on the other the criminalistics department. Immaculate grass and impatiens grew between the buildings, giving them a pastoral look that belied what went on inside. There were no exterior markers announcing that this was part of the police department, and the people who worked there liked to keep it that way. The sign in front of the complex still read DENTAL CENTER, the legacy of the former occupants.

Ash's office had beige striped wallpaper topped with a blue flowered border and the walls showed faded squares where a dentist's diplomas had once hung. It was almost identical to Windy's in the criminalistics building, except that her wallpaper had large ferns stenciled on it, and while her window had a nice view of the parking lot, his window looked out at grass. Seniority, she figured. But neither of them was really thinking about the view.

Windy's eyes strayed over the crime scene photos as she listened to Ash's report on Mr. Johnson's alibi. When he was done she nodded, saying, "This killer isn't just a husband out to collect insurance money. This is something more. Someone with immense rage against women and the idea of family. Probably abused by his mother as a child." She looked up. "Sorry, that is all obvious. And hardly helpful for VICAP since 90 percent of killers fall into that category. I'm just thinking out loud."

"Keep going. I'm getting every word."

She started laying the pictures out in deliberate piles on his desk, then moving them around. After a few minutes she stopped abruptly and squinted.

Ash said, "Have you found something?"

"I don't know. I can tell you what he did, where he went, to a point. After that—there are gaps. He did something, and took something. I don't know what yet." She stared at the photos, shook her head, returned her attention to Ash. "Okay. First, you asked about the murder weapon. It's not just a knife, it's a cleaver, six inches long, and three inches wide. A specialty piece, like chefs use. The same for all four victims."

"How do you know?"

Windy spread out four photos, pointed at what looked like a spot to Ash on the first one. "You can see the imprint of it here on the sheets in the master bedroom. He slit Mrs. Johnson's throat in the bed, then put the knife down for some reason and it left this mark. It has a hole in the top corner of the blade, for hanging it, and the handle appears to have some kind of pattern or texture which is visible here, here, and here. Each time after he cut them, he put the knife down. I wish I could figure out why. According to the crime scene report, the knife does not match any in the house, which means the killer brought it with him. I would have suspected as much anyway because they found pieces of a white thread on Mrs. Johnson's body that they could not match anything in the house. I think it came off whatever the killer was using to carry the knife in."

"That's good," Ash said, writing it down. That was the kind of thing the VICAP database was useful for matching.

"There's more. He knows how to use his weapon. Somewhat of an expert. His cuts are clean and sure. That means he's strong, too. One swipe, no evidence of sawing."

"Practice," Ash said.

"Or profession."

"Right. A chef. A butcher. Someone who uses a knife in their work. I'll send that to VICAP too."

"He did not break into the house but was let in by Mrs. Johnson, I think at the back door. It is hard to tell since Mr. Johnson used the same door to come in and smeared the prints. But it does mean that he is presentable, at least enough to get her to open the door."

"Unless Mrs. Johnson knew him."

Windy nodded. "Yes. I would say that she either knew him, or he threatened her as soon as he was inside."

"I'll buy that, but why?"

"How else would he have gotten her to go quietly upstairs to her bedroom with him so he could kill her there, without alerting any of the kids? Of course, they were all in their rooms, the daughter listening to her stereo, loud—" Windy pointed to a photo of the girl's room, with the stereo volume knob swung all the way to the right. "—the youngest son practicing his clarinet—" Photo of a knocked-over music stand with a clarinet lying next to it on the floor. "—and the middle son—" Windy didn't finish, just let her finger rest on a close-up of a computer screen with an animated image of a shot-up dead body in the corner, a set of headphones dangling from the side, and the words GAME OVER across the middle.

"That's quite an epitaph," Ash said. "Do you think he knew that all the kids would be distracted, or was he just lucky?"

Windy shook her head. "I can't tell. Whichever it was, he got Mrs. Johnson into her bedroom, killed her there, put on a pair of her husband's shoes, and then went down the hall and killed the children."

"Calm. Organized. Deliberate."

"And with some understanding of forensics, knowing we could use his shoe prints. He did each victim in their own room and then moved them all into the master bedroom and left them on the bed there together. Does that mean the bedroom has some significance for him? There is no sign of any kind of sexual assault, which is unusual but not unheard of in these cases, although it could make his use of the bedroom as his mortuary more telling. And here's another interesting point: he moved the bodies almost right away, but it was only later—maybe even a few hours later—that he put the heads in place. I'll send a request to have them swabbed inside and out. Maybe Trace can find some evidence of something that will give us a clue to what he was doing with them in the interval."

"My vote is for arts and crafts. I'm sure whatever we learn will be heartwarming," Ash said. "Anything else?"

"A few things I can't explain. Has Doug Senior been taken around the house to see if anything is missing?"

"He went through it earlier, fast, and didn't see anything but we've sent him back over now that the bodies are gone to look more carefully. Why?"

Windy held up a photo of Mrs. Johnson's dressing table. It was covered with black-and-gold-cased lipsticks, three crystal bottles of perfume, different pots of moisturizer, a box of Kleenex, a hairbrush, everything scattered around, a mess. All of it, and the mirror behind it, spattered with blood. Windy's finger rested on a spot near the front corner of the table. "There is no blood here," she said. "That means that there was something standing in this place, something that appears to have been round or octagonal. I'd like to know what it was. Probably a powder container or a jewelry box or something. Also ask if the table has been moved at all."

Ash made a call to the detective who was at the Johnson house with Doug Senior. "Mr. Johnson says he can't remember. There may have been some pearls. The last time he saw them was on her dressing table. He's not sure if the furniture has been moved."

"Ask him if his wife wears a wedding band," Windy said.

Ash relayed the question. Hung up. "Yes. Why?"

"Because there isn't one on the body in this photo."

"Do you think the killer took it as a souvenir? Jewelry?"

Windy shrugged. "Possibly. We'll need to search more but you could add that to the VICAP profile." She stretched her arms over her head and worked her neck back and forth. "I'm exhausted. I'm afraid I'm sort of out of useful information too."

"You've given us a good place to start, and several leads for—"

Jonah interrupted him, knocking once then opening the door of the office to say, "Gerald, incoming. Line one."

"Didn't you tell him I was in a meeting? Or out with hepatitis?"

"You being ill would give him too much pleasure. Plus he said it was urgent. Crucial. Used some of his other favorite words. You've got to take it."

"Who is it?" Windy asked. "Do you want me to go?"

"It's the mayor, Gerald Keene," Jonah said, "and he wants to talk to you too." He sat down in the empty chair at the end of Ash's desk and looked at him. "Ready?"

Ash nodded, and Jonah hit the blinking button on the phone

console. "I have Detective Laughton and Chicago Thomas of criminalistics for you, Mayor."

The mayor's voice yelled out of the phone, "How the hell could
you let the Snoopy Killer go and say that Danielle Starr was involved in drugs?"

Ash gestured to Windy, who said, "Roddy Ruiz is not the
Snoopy Killer and I said Danielle Starr was involved with drugs because it's true."

"*True*," Gerald Keene repeated, making it sound like a bad word.
"Let's be sure we both agree on what that means. From where I'm
sitting, what is true is what will hold up in court. Will your evidence? I've got the sheriff here with me, your boss, and he says he's
not sure from looking at the photos. Think about that, Ms. Thomas.
Is it worth ruining a family's life for something that won't hold up?"

"It's not *my* evidence, it is *the* evidence. And what family is it
ruining?"

"The Starrs. The parents of the dead girl. I have to tell you, they
find your conclusions distressing."

"Why?"

"Naturally they would rather believe their daughter was a good
girl who was kidnapped and raped, than that she went to that place
on her own and got down on her knees to broker a drug deal."

The word "naturally" made Windy queasy. "Why would one be
better than the other? Danielle is dead either way."

"The Starrs have a position to maintain in the community. The
idea that their daughter was involved in things like drugs . . ." The
voice trailed off before adding, "You understand."

Windy wanted to say that she didn't, but she did. She understood that having your daughter kidnapped and raped by strangers
lifted the blame squarely from your shoulders. It was an accident,
could happen to anyone. Whereas having a daughter who ran away
from home and took up with a drug dealer could raise distasteful

questions about who was responsible for her leaving home, and what, if anything was done to stop it. It opened the range of who-did-what-to-whom considerably.

Windy was not going to give the Starrs an inch. "I'm afraid I have to stick by my description of what happened. Nothing can change the fact that Roddy Ruiz didn't kill that girl, that she went there as a drug courier, and that she was not kidnapped. This is not a question of writing the best ending. This is a question of justice and truth."

"You are positive? That boy, Roddy, said he wants to do the time, and the family would prefer that too. It's your word against his confession. Did you hear me, Ms. Thomas, I said *confession*. I'm not asking you to lie, I'm just asking you to be sure of what you saw. And Roddy won't get life in prison. He'll still be young enough when he gets out to have a go at things."

Have a go at things. Like maybe he'd take up polo. Windy un-clenched her jaw to say, "And in the meantime the real killer goes free?"

"And in the meantime, everyone is happier."

The customer is always right, Windy told herself, a mantra drilled into her from childhood. Don't make waves. Don't disagree. Do what you are told.

But sometimes the customer doesn't know what is good for him. She said, "Perhaps you have a point, Mayor. Perhaps that would be better. And letting Roddy take Hector Xavier's place in prison would avert a major territorial war between the drug dealers of Vegas."

The mayor's voice came through louder, like he'd moved closer to the speaker. "What are you talking about?"

Ash caught Windy's eye, just a glance, but it said a lot. It told her he knew where she was going, and that he was amused. He mouthed, "May I?" and she nodded, yes, go ahead. Then leaned back in her chair to watch.

"I believe Ms. Thomas's point is that while putting Roddy in jail won't really shake anything up, taking Hector Xavier out of circulation would make the drug traffic in Vegas much harder to control," Ash said. "With him gone, his empire would disperse and we'd have to waste men watching a dozen dealers instead of one main one. So leaving him in place is probably wise. Since Hector Xavier is the drug kingpin of Las Vegas."

They heard the mayor say, "What the——" and then the click of the mute button followed by silence. But Ash didn't need the sound track to picture the discussion taking place in the mayor's office, the man and his aides trying out different headlines: VEGAS DRUG KINGPIN BROUGHT DOWN ON MURDER RAP versus BILLIONAIRE'S DAUGHTER KIDNAPPED, MURDERED IN LAS VEGAS. Not that hard a decision.

Another click and the mayor was back. "Ms. Thomas," he said, his voice polite, congenial, "you and your evidence have convinced me. The sheriff concurs. We have no choice but to go ahead with the Hector Xavier prosecution. He is guilty, and he must pay the price. See to it that the case against him is airtight. We've got to get this dangerous kingpin—and killer—off the street."

Jonah hit the OFF button, and the three of them in Ash's office started to laugh.

Ash looked at Windy. "That was the most fun I've had in a long time."

She had to agree. It was the same sensation that came with unraveling a hard mystery. The thrill of letting someone talk themselves into a corner of their own making, of playing the game well, and winning. The thrill of being good at something.

Her cell phone rang, and as she reached for it, she realized it was almost dark outside, making it past six. Dammit. Somehow being good at one thing always meant screwing up something else.

She said, "Excuse me, I need to take this," to Ash and Jonah and they heard her voice change, get softer, apologetic as she answered. "Hi honey. Yes, I know. I'm really sorry, I lost track of time. No, I'm leaving now, so I'll definitely be home for dinner. Oh, is that my punishment? Fine. But only half with pepperoni. Okay, I'll be there soon. I love you too. Bye."

She hung up and faced them. "I'm sorry about that. I didn't realize it was so late."

"No problem. You've been a tremendous help, Windy," Ash said. "We'll feed everything you learned from the Johnson crime scene photos into VICAP and see if we get any hits."

"Let me know."

"Of course."

Windy was glued to the spot. She had done everything she could, both for Roddy, and with the Johnsons. But she'd tasted the excitement of an investigation again. The urge to stay was almost narcotic.

It's not your job, she reminded herself. You promised, promised Bill, promised yourself that you would not work weekends, that you would stay in the office, that you would not get too involved in investigations. The job would be the How and the What of the crimes, not the Why. No interrogations, no stakeouts, no late nights at work poring over transcripts, talking strategy. She ran her fingers over the silk tie she was wearing, Bill's tie, worn to remind her of him, of her commitment to him. She was going to stay safe and sane, work normal-person hours, have a real life. That was why she had taken the job in Vegas. She would make time for her and Bill to be together, time for the family. She would make those her priorities, being a good mom, a good wife.

"Are you sure there's nothing else I can do tonight?" she heard herself asking again. Pathetic. The tie did *not* feel like a leash, she told herself.

"Nothing," Ash assured her. "And it sounds like someone is expecting you for dinner."

"You're right." Cate was waiting for her. That was worth going home for. She said, "Good night." Paused at the door.

Cate would be in bed by nine and Bill wasn't coming until the next morning.

Turned back. "Could I take the crime scene photos home with me? I might see something useful."

"The mayor had better get over his hard-on for the word kingpin," Jonah said when Windy had gone.

"No way. It's the only chance we have against him."

"Hardly seems fair. I mean, the man is outnumbered with you and Ms. Chicago Thomas tag-teaming him. I have to say, I like her."

Ash pulled a Twinkie out of his bottom desk drawer, offered half to Jonah and then ate it himself when Jonah made a face. "Yes," he said, chewing, "I think she'll work out okay."

"Sure," Jonah agreed. "She seems competent. And sweet."

"Competent? You should have seen her in the interrogation room. She wasn't competent, she was brilliant. And I wouldn't exactly call her sweet."

Jonah made a pretend gun of his right hand, closed one eye, aimed at Ash and said, "Gotcha. I just wanted to make sure you still had a pulse. When the most you can say about a woman like that— one who can do loop-de-loops around the mayor *and* looks the way Windy Thomas looks—is 'she's okay,' it makes me want to call medical and have them check your vital signs."

"There are people who would like your job."

"None you could tolerate. And none who could whip your ass at racquetball without breaking a sweat."

"I was playing left-handed."

"You were slow."

"For a man who does yoga five times a week you're not very Zen."

"For a man who just got back from his vacation, you have no sense of humor," Jonah shot back. "Or did you forget to pack it when you came home four days early? Can't even take a vacation like a normal person. And Zen has nothing to do with yoga."

"It wasn't a vacation. I was visiting my mother."

"In Bermuda."

"Best way to ruin a tropical island is let my mother live there."

"So it was bad?"

"Yep." Ash inhaled the last of his Twinkie. "I'd rather talk about something else. Like what you know about Windy, for example."

"Hey, look who dropped in. Its Mr. Subtle, long time no see, man."

"Are you done?"

"Yeah, I'll catch up with him later. All right, dossier on Chicago 'Windy' Thomas. Her last job was as acting sheriff in Larks County, Virginia, for three years. It was supposed to be temporary until they found a real sheriff, but she did such a good job they stopped looking."

"Why did she decide to come here?"

"No information available. I do know she didn't apply but was recruited when they decided to give the job to a civilian instead of a commissioned officer."

"And before Virginia?"

"Before that she was with the FBI in their crime lab for six years. She left when her husband died."

"She's a widow?" Ash sat forward, interested now. "Then who was she talking to on the phone?"

"She *was* a widow. She's engaged now."

"Ah. Know anything about him?"

Jonah kept the smile off his face. "Nope. I'll ask around, see what I can find out."

"There's no rush. Its not important."

"Oh, no. Of course not." Jonah stood up. "Listen, Shandra and I have reservations at Nobu tonight. Why don't you come with us?

That way you can eat something that was cooked rather than manufactured and enjoy our charming company at the same time."

"Twinkies are not manufactured, they are *extruded*," Ash corrected. "And thanks for the offer, but I can't. I have a date tonight."

"Bring her."

Ash's eyes went to the top of his desk. "I can't."

"I thought you were all done with that. Spending your nights sneaking into cheap motels with married women who are only interested in you for the sex."

"Why, when you make it sound so exciting?"

Jonah got to the door and paused. "I'm glad you're back. Even if you are a pain in the ass."

"Ditto."

Ash watched Jonah walk past his window toward his parking place, guessed how long it would take him to get to his car, added ten minutes, then left his office. Instead of driving to the Wrong Way Inn, the establishment that Cissily Longstrap enjoyed frequenting when her husband was out of town, he drove home and called her cell phone to cancel. "I'm sorry," he said, "I've got too much work. Yes, maybe another time. I'd like that."

Shut up, he warned the voice in his head asking why he was lying.

He stripped down to his jockey shorts, put a CD in the player on his stereo and turned it up as he mixed his paints. Golden brown, soft pink, deep gray. Pale, jade green. Ash had been painting since he was in his teens, entirely self taught, and, he was the first to admit, entirely without talent. It was the activity, watching the colors spread across the canvas, sometimes forming images, usually only blobs, that he liked, not the product. He never displayed any of his paintings, never hung one. They were just for him, something selfish but therapeutic.

He'd been painting intensively for two hours when he realized the CD he'd picked was *Chicago's Greatest Hits*. First canceling—without regret—a date with a perfectly lovely woman who would never demand anything of him aside from pleasure and discretion, and now this. *Oh brother, are you in trouble,* Ash told himself.

But he didn't turn the music off.

CHAPTER 4

"I'm telling you, all those contestants, every last one of them, is what you would call an Alien Life Form."

"No way, Gregory. The Miss America pageant is not some E. T. plot to infiltrate Earth. You're out of your mind on this one."

"You sure? Then tell me, where on this planet have you ever seen women who look and act that way for real? And they've got that crazy look in back of their eyes."

"Look, if aliens are smart enough to get here all the way from space, you really think they'd try to take over wearing high heels? You know women complain how hard those are to walk in."

The two men lounged against the barred windows of Cash Flow Pawn-It Open 24 Hours like they'd been there forever. It was almost midnight. One of the streetlights was broken and the other was fifteen feet away, so they were mostly in shadow. They weren't paying attention to the woman in the green car parked alongside them.

Across the street, on the second story landing of the Sun-Crest Apartments, a light came on outside the door of number five, filling the hallway with a lemonade yellow glow. It was immediately ringed by bugs. A door closed quietly, and a few moments later a tall man appeared, head bouncing as he jogged down the stairs.

Gregory waved at him. "Hey, Maximillian, how're you doing?"

The man paused, keys out, at the door of a clean Dodge with a dent in the rear fender. "Fine, Gregory. And you?"

"Doing great out here. You off to the hospital?"

Door of the Dodge open now, the man nodded, held up an Elmo lunch pail. "You know it. Got my provisions. Time to get my nose to the grindstone."

"His wife and kids pack him a snack every night," Gregory explained to his companion as the red Dodge farted away. "Car needs a new muffler, but they're saving every penny. Boy is going to be a doctor one day. He told me one time, his girls, they fight about who gets to choose the lunch box daddy gets to take to work with him. Like it's a prize for them, whoever gets to do it. Man with a family like that is lucky."

The woman in the green car parked at the curb with the windows cracked took that in. That was interesting about the lunch pails. She would bet the man felt stupid walking into work with an Elmo lunch box but did it anyway because he loved his daughters. Or maybe he left it in the car, emptied it out before he went home, lying to keep them happy. Maybe he ate hot dogs from the cafeteria during his shift.

Hot dogs. The woman pressed a button and the car window shut, silencing the men outside and closing out the smell of hot dogs from the all-night convenience store on the corner which had been making her stomach rumble. She was not hungry, she told herself, drumming her fingers on the steering wheel to cover up the sound of the clock.

How long had she been sitting there outside the Sun-Crest, the building still with its sixties style facade? She didn't even know, but she had covered six pages with drawings. She put aside her sketch pad now to watch as the light outside of apartment five went out, like someone inside was waiting to be sure Maximillian Waters had gotten off okay. Next the light in the front room went off, and after a beat, a fainter light in the window beside it came on. A bedside lamp, the woman thought, pretty sure that's the master bedroom.

The Waters family was careful about electricity, careful not to waste it, not like the Johnsons, lighting up their whole huge house as if it were a Christmas decoration. Electricity was expensive and the Waterses were trying to keep costs down, four of them living in that small apartment in the old building while Mr. Waters did his residency at Sunrise Medical, saving what they could to pay off his student loans. It was a grind, but he had always dreamed of being a doctor, and the dream was close now. He just wished it didn't keep him away from his family all night.

That was okay with the woman in the car, though. She liked watching them best when he wasn't there to interfere with her thinking. When it was just Mrs. Waters—Claudia—and the twin six-year-old girls, Minette and Martine, no father. Sometimes she imagined the three of them—the girls—snuggled up together in the parents' bed, watching television or maybe playing a game. Life. She remembered playing it with her dad when she was little, entertaining him by drawing pictures of what she thought all her children would look like. Then, when she was older, getting stoned and playing the game with Trish. They would sit around, get a really good buzz on, and make themselves hysterical building families in the little plastic cars that were the game pieces, hers always the green one, Trish's always red, Trish getting the munchies when they were halfway through, eating chocolate chips and peanut butter off a spoon. Trish always tried to get her to eat some but she knew better. All those empty calories.

The way the game was played, everyone got a car, and you filled it with these tiny plastic people, who looked like pegs, that were supposed to be your family. Carried them around like baggage. That part was cool, but what the woman hadn't liked was that the winner was the one who at the end had the most money. Was that really what Life was about? *Yes,* Trish had said, ruthlessly jettisoning husbands and children in pursuit of money, so at the end she was alone in her red car, flush with cash, on her way to Europe to paint and screw men with sexy accents. The green car was filled with happy kids and a perfect husband. Trish usually won, by the rules of the game, but the woman had always felt like she was the one who really understood life.

She thought about Trish now, living in a modest house in L.A., raising her two kids, supporting her husband, happy. Thought about herself alone in her green car. Not alone, exactly—there were always the knives.

Thought about what it would be like to go in and join the Waterses. She pictured herself walking into their apartment, going through the front room, through the bead curtain that goes *shush shhhush shhhush*, into the master bedroom. Pictured the twins scooching up the bed to make a place for her, letting her choose the game piece first. Pictured their mother coming in and saying, I'm sorry, there's no room for you, you're not wanted here. You are a worthless tramp. A bad girl. You deserve to be punished.

She was so tired of feeling bad.

The *put put put* of the red Dodge coming back jarred her out of her thoughts. Sweaty, palms clammy, she watched as it pulled up outside of the apartment and Maximillian got out, running. He must have forgotten something. It was that simple. He was back fast, a stethoscope swinging from his hand, in the Dodge, gone, less than three minutes passed total.

But to the woman in the car, it was a sign. Like her daddy, she was superstitious. Her mood was ruined. She unclenched one hand from the steering wheel to start the engine, and drove off.

She would have to come back another time. A time when she could be sure that Maximillian wouldn't be around to get in the way.

CHAPTER 5

Sometimes when Windy woke up in the morning she thought she could hear Evan moving around in the bathroom. Humming to himself under his breath. The drawers opening one after another as he looked for the toothpaste, never able to remember where it was although it had been in the same drawer for four years.

She'd put it in the same place in the new house too, out of habit, even though Evan would never look there. Never be there.

Bill had scolded her, reminding her that the toothpaste belonged in the second drawer. Bill always knew exactly where everything he wanted was.

Windy did too, it was part of her job to notice things. She had stayed up late the night before, looking at the crime scene photos from the Johnsons' house, reading the lab reports, noticing. Feeling that she was missing something. But really there was only one thing in the world whose location she cared about and at that moment it came bouncing through the door of her bedroom in orange and blue pajamas.

"Mommy!" Cate sang as she leaped across the bed and into Windy's arms. "Guess what?"

Windy hugged her daughter, giving herself one self-indulgent moment to take in the scent of newly awakened six-year-old girl and think there was nothing better on earth.

Windy loved her daughter more than was healthy, she knew, and couldn't stop. Cate was magical to her. Not just because she reminded her of Evan. She reminded her of why it was good to breathe.

She looked like her father, had his same huge blue innocent-looking eyes, with the same sparkle of mischief lurking back inside of them. The same desire to try everything. Windy's hardest task as a mother was not to keep Cate too close, smother her. When Cate said, "Don't worry, I've done it a million times before," like an echo of her dad, Windy had to clench her hands at her sides to keep from holding her back, bite her tongue to keep from shouting, "Don't say that. Don't ever ever say that."

She was determined not to share her fears with Cate. She knew how easy it was to learn from your parents because she had learned it from hers, fear born of too much love. Windy had grown up as the only daughter of two immigrants who escaped from Chile with their shoes and their lives. They would never talk about what they had left behind, would not even allow their daughter to grow up speaking Spanish. They worked hard so that she would have every-thing she needed to be a real American girl. And they were careful, careful of everything, because they loved her so much and wanted to keep her safe.

She remembered one afternoon when she was eight and the family had gone for a drive, stopping on the way home at a Buick dealership. They went because her parents had just opened their fourth dry cleaning store and her dad decided it was time for her mother to have her own car. It was an open secret that Magda Thomas didn't want one, that she never went anywhere without her husband, and that Bertino was really buying it for himself, but everyone played along because it made him happy. While her par-ents looked, Windy wandered over to the edge of the dealership where they'd set up a little fair, bales of hay, blond women wearing braids and cowboy hats. For a dollar you could ride on the back of a fat old workhorse that they led around a fenced area, one of the blond ladies holding him by a rope, never going faster than a walk. Windy turned around to ask her mom for a dollar but she didn't have to. Her mother's eyes made it clear that the horse was Something to Stay Away From. Other things on that list included:

> Public swimming pools
> Empty lot behind Karen's house
> Press in the back room of the dry cleaning shop
> Convenience store two blocks down
> Fast cars
> Boys
> Strangers
> Other people's business
> Ouija boards
> Water fountains
> Beef jerky (you didn't know what was in there)

Windy let Cate ride a horse the first time she asked, and when she got off and said, "It was kind of boring, next time I want to go faster," Windy vowed she would let her. She was not going to pass her fear on to her daughter like a congenital blood disease. Not going to pass on lessons about how to be a "good girl," never drawing attention to yourself, never getting angry, never disagreeing, always giving in to every argument, even if it hurt. Her mother pointing to the sign that hung over the counter in each of their now ten dry cleaning shops, reminding employees THE CUSTOMER IS ALWAYS RIGHT. An adage to be remembered in all parts of life: for good girls, someone else is always right.

At work, Windy could get caught up in the infallibility of the evidence and forget those lessons. She wondered if that was part of the attraction. They were a lot harder to shed in her personal life, some part of her still believing that no one would love her if she spoke her mind. The Customer Is Always Right.

She had sworn that while she might have live with rules like that, Cate would not. She was going to share with Cate all the lessons she'd learned from Evan. About the pleasure of laughing without stopping, of making a fool of yourself, the thrill of taking risks. Evan had made her hum inside. His life was like a pageant, always in motion. And she was the audience, applauding, admiring, cheering, exhilarated merely by proximity.

She could see Evan smiling down at her and Cate lying under the umbrella on that perfect Hawaiian beach, glistening like a rare fish in his wet suit. "Don't worry, honey, I've done it a million times," he'd assured her. The clouds are way out, he went on, charming, there's nothing to worry about. What kind of day for windsurfing would it be without *wind*?

Windy and windsurfing, his two passions. Ha ha ha.

Windy and Cate, dozing on the beach all afternoon, waiting for him. Waking up when the wind got bad. Sitting up, Windy all night, with the Coast Guard.

Evan's body washing up three days later, thirty miles south. The Coast Guard officer saying, "I swear, ma'am, he was smiling. What more could you want?"

I want my life back! she had wanted to shout. *I want my life back the way it was.*

For six months that went around and around her head like the chorus of a bad love song as she drowned in a whirlpool of grief. And then one day she realized it wasn't right. She did, she wanted her life back, she missed Evan like she was missing half of herself. But she also wanted more. She saw other ways the love song could go, other refrains. She could follow the story line to a place with someone who shared being a grown-up with her. Someone she could count on. Someone whose idea of an appointment did not involve a four-hour window in either direction. Someone solid. Someone who would never ever make Cate ask, "Did Daddy go away because I did something wrong?"

Someone who would never make Windy ask herself, "Did he go away because I wasn't exciting enough?"

"Mommmm, are you paying attention?" Cate, three years older, wonderful, self-possessed, was demanding now. "You haven't guessed what!"

"Okay, what?"

"The monster trucks are coming to town!"

"Monster trucks?"

"Yes they're big big big! Can we go to see them? Please?"

"Why do you want to see monster trucks?"

"Because I haven't seen them before," Cate answered, the most obvious thing in the world. "If we get our tickets now we can get a special pass and go and see them up close."

"Wow," Windy answered. "That sounds really great."

"That's what I said," Brandon pronounced from the doorway. "And with pretty much the same tone."

Brandon was, as he would unabashedly and accurately say, the best thing that had happened to Windy and Cate in years. When they had decided that Windy should take the job in Las Vegas, Ella, the woman who had been baby-sitting Cate since she got her first teeth, announced that she couldn't go with them. But she had a nephew who lived in Vegas who was twenty-six, studying to be a decorator, and great with kids, she assured them, because he was the second oldest of eight. He was a little different from the rest of the family, but he and Windy would get along fine.

"A little different" had turned out to mean that Brandon was gay. He was also smart, trustworthy, wonderful with Cate, and a good cook. Between design courses he was teaching himself Spanish by watching Mexican soap operas, and was good enough to speak to Windy's mom on the phone when she called, although Mrs. Thomas was stunned by some of his expressions. For the cost of room, board, and a tiny stipend that was less than a day care center, he was installed in the third bedroom of their house, on call all day and the occasional nights, if Windy asked ahead. He appeared in the doorway now in jeans and a T-shirt covered with a Hello Kitty apron, brandishing a spatula.

He waved it at Cate. "Come along now, Miss Minx. Someone has to dress for soccer practice *and* eat her French toast in less than forty-five minutes. And someone else has to get ready to meet her boyfriend at the airport. Or had you forgotten that Bill's flight arrives in about an hour?"

Bill. Bill Henderson had turned out to be the someone Windy had been searching for. When she met him she stopped making up stories of how her life could go next, stopped feeling like she was swimming against an impossible current. Her only fear now was that Bill would wake up one day and realize she did not deserve him.

"I know when his flight gets in," Windy insisted without conviction. "Eleven fifteen, right?"

Brandon stood in the doorway, shaking his head. "Ten forty. What you would do without me is anyone's guess. I hope you remembered to make reservations somewhere good tonight for a little romance because the Minx and I are going out on the town."

"Where are we going?" Cate asked.

"It's a surprise, honey," Brandon told her. Looked seriously at Windy. "Where are *you* going?"

"I don't—"

Brandon sighed. "I'll get you a reservation at Prime. *You'll* like it because it looks like an art deco brothel and Bill will like it because everyone will be in business suits. He'll feel right at home. Now come on, you two, breakfast is ready."

"Why can't we have breakfast in bed, like princesses?" Cate asked, the way she had every Saturday since they arrived in Vegas, and every Saturday morning Brandon explained that princesses did that only because they were lazy, and the two of them started their regular argument. When it came to the part where Windy was supposed to agree with Brandon he looked at her but she didn't say anything. She seemed to be about a million miles away.

Brandon said, "Isn't that right?" prompting her.

But Windy, whose mind was stuck on the phrase, "breakfast in bed," said, "You go on. I've got to make a phone call."

Ash heard the words "Really, go on, honey, I'll be right there," when he answered his cell phone, then Windy's voice saying, "Hello? Ash? Did I wake you?"

Yes, he wanted to say. Last night about three A.M. a dream about you woke me up. And when I couldn't get back to sleep I came to the office and have been sitting here reading reports about dead people to try to get you out of my head. Said instead, "No. I'm at my desk. Is something wrong?"

"I think I may have something. About the Johnsons' killer." She hesitated. "I'll need access to the crime scene, and a technician. With leuco crystal violet and a sprayer."

"Leuco crystal what?"

"Leuco crystal violet. It fluoresces with blood like luminol, but it will work better in this location. I'm sure we've got the makings for the mixture in the lab there. Can you arrange it for me? Have that and someone there to open the door in about an hour and a half?"

"I'll be there myself. What is it?"

"I'm not sure. Hopefully I'll know when I get there."

Ash picked up on something in her voice. "You sound concerned. If we don't find anything, that is okay. Likely, even."

"I wish that were true."

"What do you mean?"

"Not finding anything would be a blessing," Windy said. "It's what I think we are going to find that I'm afraid of."

CHAPTER 6

As soon as he spotted her, Bill picked Windy up in his arms and swung her around, like a scene from a movie. Everything with Bill was like that, picture perfect. It had been, from the first day they met, stranded at an incredibly dull cocktail party. He had played the part of the gorgeous blond stranger swooping in to rescue her from an excruciating conversation with an oily man who thought he was going to get her to come home with him. Both she and Bill, they discovered after about a minute, had been brought to the party by mutual friends, knew no one else, not even the hosts, and wanted desperately to leave. She reminded him of someone, he'd told her that night over drinks and then dinner, someone he couldn't quite remember. He spent six months of serious dating trying to place who it was, and then, boom, one day he got it— she reminded him, he said, of the woman he wanted to spend his life with.

He put her down now, kissed her on her forehead. "You look wonderful, babe."

They were standing in front of a bank of chrome and neon elevators between the two luggage carousels, their designated rendezvous place. Bill always told you precisely where to meet him, even if you were just going to the bathroom.

"You too," Windy said. He was strikingly handsome, too good

looking for her, she thought. When they first started going out, just his smile could make her knees weak. "Sorry you had to wait. I went up to the gate but you were gone."

"I thought only passengers got through security these days and I was rushing to see you."

She flashed her Metro Police ID. "One of the perks of the office."

"I love a woman with a badge," he said, giving her that smile, one arm covered with his trench coat, the other slipping over her shoulder. "Come on, let's go get some breakfast. Something healthy to wash the taste of airplane coffee out of my mouth." He started walking.

Windy cleared her throat, and he stopped, instinctively knowing something was wrong.

"Is Cate okay?" were his first words.

How could she not love a man who asked about Cate first?

"Cate is fine. It's just—"

"Work," he finished for her, setting his bag down between them. She watched him struggling with his face. "You have to work today, don't you?"

Windy's mother's voice ran through her head, scolding, don't draw attention to yourself, don't have arguments, smooth out the rough edges, *never* fight in public. "Only for a little while. I figured you would be tired, want to sleep. You just got off the red-eye." She reached for his cheek. "You won't even miss me."

He held his hand over hers. "You would not understand how much I've been missing you."

"I'm sorry. Its just that there is this killer who murdered a whole family and he—"

He interrupted her with a finger to her lips. "Shhh. Tell me tonight at dinner. The way I see it, the faster you get to work, the faster you'll be home with me. That's all I care about."

She tried to put all the gratitude she was feeling in her smile. He had every right to be furious with her and he wasn't. "Thank you."

"You're worth it. Now go on. I'll take a cab and see you at home later. Hurry."

Driving to the Johnson house, Windy wrestled with her guilt over working. Over wanting to work. She thought about how she would phrase her apology that night at dinner, how she would spend the rest of the weekend just with him, and Cate, show him how she could really concentrate on his needs—*their* needs. Sometimes she focused on the wrong things, got caught up in her job. But not anymore and not this weekend. This weekend would be for them. Once she finished with the Johnsons.

She had just figured out what she would wear to dinner, the dress Bill bought her for Mother's Day that she hadn't worn yet and his favorite underwear, when she pulled up outside the Versailles-esque mansion. Ash was leaning against a chrome sports car eating onion rings and talking to a heavyset man in his mid-fifties with curly dark hair and a dark mustache. Windy had seen him around the criminalistics department, but had not met him yet. She thought his name was Jack, John, something like that.

"Ned Blight," he said, holding out a hand.

Not auspicious. "Nice to meet you, Mr. Blight."

"Call me Ned, Ms. Thomas. You are, after all, my boss."

For a moment Windy wanted to get back in her car and bang her head on the steering wheel. She did not need this, not today, with Bill waiting for her, not the "boss" thing. The way Ned said the word it was a challenge, a test, to see how she reacted, Windy knew. She'd had the luxury of forgetting that being young, female, and in charge made people uncomfortable after the first few months of her three years as sheriff in Virginia, but Vegas was bringing it back. She knew she would eventually win Ned's respect just by working with him, over the next few months. What she needed today was merely his help. Rather than react she said, "Great, Ned, call me Windy. Did you bring what I asked for?"

"Detective Laughton said you wanted leuco crystal violet. Are you sure you didn't mean luminol?" With the tone in his voice he might as well have added "little lady."

Windy was determined not to be provoked. "Yes. LCV is easier to use, and comes out better in photographs. I'll show you. Besides, luminol can fluoresce with traces of bleach, and where we're going to be using it there's a high chance that bleach was used as a cleaning product."

"You thinking of the laundry room? Off the back door? We ran the whole place, didn't find anything in there," Ned told her, a little smug.

"No. The kitchen."

Ned shook his head. "Why?"

"Because there were no crime scene photos of the kitchen."

"Well, yeah," Ned said, getting defensive now. "We didn't do the kitchen. There didn't seem to be any point. There wasn't any sign that anyone was in there."

"That's what we need the LCV for."

Ned's expression was stubborn and skeptical. "I don't get it. Why?"

"Because there was a greasy, animal substance found in Mrs. Johnson's hair and a few brown crumbs near Doug Junior's head."

Now Ash spoke. "What does that mean?"

He'd asked Windy, but it was Ned who answered. Ned, in a tone of awe. "Bread and butter."

"Right," Windy said. "I think our killer had breakfast with the Johnson family."

CHAPTER 7

Ned only brought two respirators, so Ash stayed outside the kitchen while Ned and Windy worked. They started by
closing the shade over the window to make the room darker, make
it easier to see any signs of fluorescence. Windy sprayed a section
with LCV and Ned followed with a camera, ready to get photos of
anything they found. If blood had been present, even if the killer
had tried to clean it up, it would show up as a purplish violet fluorescence. Working from the hall door into the kitchen they meticu-
lously covered every inch, the sound of the faucet leaking *drip drip
drip* the only thing in the silence. They had gone over about a third
of the room before they began to find what they were looking for.

First they found the handprints, on the handle of the refrigerator, on the door, and on the jam jars inside. Around the center of
the jars, on the label, as though he'd grabbed each one and studied
the different flavors, trying to decide. Only one jar had any smudges
on the lid, indicating he'd taken the top off.

"Your killer likes strawberry jam," Windy poked her head out
the door to say to Ash in the hallway.

"I'll include that in the report."

Next they found small traces on the drawer pulls under the
countertop. "He was looking for the cutlery tray," Windy said, nar-
rating. "No, wait—" The Johnsons had two drawers of cutlery, one

with plastic handles, for casual dining, and the other silver plated. The killer had opened the drawer with the plastic handled ones but kept looking. "He used one of the sliver plated knives, treating himself right." A smear of blood showed how his hand had hovered between the butter knives and the steak knives, such a conundrum. Windy looked around and spotted a butter knife in the drying rack next to the sink, alongside a small plate. "He washed up when he was done," she said, nodding in the direction of the sink with her chin. "How considerate."

"Yeah, a real Mr. Clean," Ned said but any aggressiveness in his tone was for the perp, for being so damn tidy and making his clues hard to find, not for Windy. They were solid colleagues now.

They followed more drips of blood around the floor, more hand and finger prints—unidentifiable because the killer had been wearing gloves. They had been tracing his path, working their way around the kitchen for four hours, when they got to the white Formica table that sat off to one side in what Cate would call the b-k nook. Windy sprayed the LCV solution on half the table and turned to do the other half.

That was when Ned Blight started retching and Ash came running into the room.

"What happened?" he asked. "What—"

He stopped and stared at the tabletop. There were four purplish-violet circles glowing on the surface of the table.

"Those are neck marks. He brought their heads down with him," Windy explained, shooting pictures. "Put them on the table so they could watch him eat." She lowered the camera and faced Ash. "I think you should put that in your VICAP report. It seems fairly unique."

Ash couldn't speak for a moment, only nod.

Ned stood up, taking deep breaths. "You knew that was going to be there, didn't you?" he asked Windy.

"I had an idea we'd find something like that."

"Shit." Ned shook his head. Took off his respirator and wiped his mouth on the back of his hand. "Shit, I've been in this job twenty years and it can still get to me." He looked at Windy and now there was admiration. "It's true what they say about you. You *are* a witch."

"I just look at the evidence," she said, the same response she always gave.

Ash was observing them, thinking, she sure bewitched Ned. That man would follow her to the end of the earth now.

"I think the most important thing isn't that he did this, but that he cleaned it up," she said. "He left blood all over the house upstairs, but down here it's spotless."

"He didn't want us to know about it, or at least, not right away," Ash said.

"Yes. It was something extra he did, some special secret part of the ritual."

"The kind of thing that could help us identify him."

"Hopefully." Windy's voice was not optimistic. Her eyes fell to her watch and she grimaced. It was six o'clock. Bill was going to kill her. She was surprised he hadn't called her cell phone a dozen times, then realized she'd left it in her purse in the other room. The way she used to when she was out working in the field. The way that infuriated him.

She looked around the kitchen, a mess of equipment and chemicals. It would take at least half an hour to clean up. Ash caught her anxiety, said, "Why don't you take off? We'll clean this up. You look like a woman with plans."

She started to say, "You're right," but stopped when Ash's phone rang.

He answered it, listened for a few seconds, then said, "Excellent. Great work. I'll be right there." When he hung up he looked at the phone for two beats, then at Windy. He said, "They got a man trying to sell Mrs. Johnson's pearls."

"Is he—"

"It turns out," going on, smooth, only his tone betraying his excitement, "that he'd spent the last four days with complete access to the Johnson house and property. He is their exterminator."

Ned Blight whistled. "Their exterminator. Papers will be joy riding with that one. Won't even have to make up a nickname."

Ash nodded, still looking at Windy. "They wouldn't have found him if you hadn't thought to ask Mr. Johnson about any missing jewelry."

Both Ash and Ned watched her shrug the compliment away. "That's my job. Where did they catch him?"

"Good Life Pawn-n-Go," Ash told her. "They've got him in an interrogation room right now. Do you want to participate?"

Yes! Yes she did. More than she had wanted anything besides Cate's good morning in a long time. But she had somewhere to go. A dinner date to keep. And interrogations were not her job. Finding the evidence, that was what she was good at, *all* she was good at.

Bill was waiting for her.

Ash answered before she could. "I'm sorry, I forgot that you've got to be somewhere. Plus you've already done more than everyone put together already. Forget I asked." He gave her an adrenaline-charged smile.

"You'll do better without me. But call me if there's anything— if you have anything I can help with."

"Of course," he said over his shoulder and they heard his footsteps going fast down the driveway. Windy was almost dizzy with envy.

"Why don't you go home to your family and I'll finish up here," Ned said when Ash had gone.

"No. That's not fair."

"Go on, boss," he insisted, using the word "boss" naturally now, without thinking about it. "I've got nobody waiting on me and you do. Let me take care of it."

———

    The woman in the green car parked outside of the Johnson house watched Windy come down the walkway and get into her Volvo station wagon. She seemed distracted and in a hurry. But she looked like she knew something. Something important.

    The woman in the green car decided to follow her home.

CHAPTER 8

"He's innocent," Jonah told Ash, eyes wide, pointing with his head to the man in the interrogation room. "Doesn't know a thing about any murders. Or anything, for that matter. One of those guys who brags about his bench press record being twice his IQ."

The exterminator had a beefy build, with a boyish face, longish wavy hair, and the air of someone accustomed to being told he was "hot." He looked like a man that most women would not hesitate to open the door to.

Ash wondered if Windy would agree.

He turned his attention back to Jonah. "Anything else?"

"Been with Pest Packers 'They Send Your Pests Packing' for ten months. They say he is good, no complaints. Name is Anthony, Anthony Solomon, but his friends call him Tony or The King. Not after Elvis, after the one in the Bible."

"Get someone checking the addresses of the other properties The King serviced. I want to know if there were any burglary complaints filed in the weeks after he'd been there. And if they are all alive."

"Got it."

"Has he called a lawyer?"

"Waived his rights. Man's innocent, I tell you."

"What a surprise. An innocent suspect caught red-handed. What about his house? Find any other merchandise there?"

"The address he gave is his mother's place. We've got a team tossing it right now. But there's a woman in reception claiming to be his girlfriend." Jonah half smiled. "I think she's been watching too much *Law & Order*. She's demanding conjugal visitation rights in the holding cell."

Ash and Jonah stood shoulder to shoulder, watching the exterminator. "Does he look to you like someone who might want to brag?"

Jonah nodded. "Someone who might respond well to one of our shows? Yeah, I'd say so. You want to do it in the conference room? Take all the files out of my drawers again and spread them on the table before bringing him in, make it look like a command center, big investigation underway looking for him?"

"Exactly. And grab all the memos the mayor has sent in the past month. The ones we keep meaning to read." There had to be four or five boxes of them by now, each of them labeled URGENT AND CONFIDENTIAL in red capital letters on the top. Ash frequently wondered if Mayor Gerald Keene's plan to Clean Up Crime In Las Vegas simply involved blanketing the city in paper and having everything come to a stop like a snow drift. "If all that isn't impressive looking, drag in any box from the supply cabinet that isn't obviously labeled 'cleaning supplies.' "

Ash headed back to his office as Jonah made for the kitchen where he routinely "stored" the mayor's dispatches on top of the refrigerator. Jonah had been a beat officer in the Los Angeles Police Department until he was discharged over discipline problems, which meant, when Ash checked out the official file, "regular insubordination to a superior officer and remarkable inability to follow orders as given." Seeing that, he had hired Jonah as his assistant on the spot.

Ash believed in genuine teamwork, the kind that hierarchy

stifled, and he had all those boxes of mayoral memos to show for it. Mayor Gerald Keene liked to keep things tidy and organized, from the precise pyramid structure of his administration to the perfect crease in his khakis. His predecessor, who had established the Task Force and appointed Ash, had been a flamboyant and beloved figure, who had stepped down to pursue a lucrative career as a liquor spokesperson. Gerald seemed to have groomed himself to be almost exactly the opposite of that man. Where the previous mayor was spontaneous, fun loving, and occasionally irreverent, Gerald was a picture of serious sobriety. He looked like a soap opera version of a mayor.

Ash figured he was a decent enough man, but he made the mistake of believing his own press. It did not hurt that he was dating his press secretary who, it was rumored, wouldn't even let him feel her up if he didn't make the front page of one of the local papers. Ash was wondering what he got for national coverage, the kind a high profile serial murder case would garner, when his phone buzzed, Jonah telling him the conference room was all set.

Inside, the table was stacked with paper and there were boxes piled on the walls.

"Impressive," Ash said. "I think we're ready. Bring Mr. Solomon in."

Instead of looking around as he reached the door, Tony Solomon marched over to the table Ash was sitting behind, banged his palms on it and said, "I've had enough of this crap treatment."

"Sit down," Ash said, directing him to a chair with his eyes.

"I don't have to do anything you say, you piece of crap policeman. I can—"

"Sit down."

Tony sat. Now he looked around, chewing the inside of his cheek. "What is all this shit?"

Ash stared at him, admiring his wide vocabulary. Adjective: crap. Noun: shit. Nice.

Tony narrowed his eyes in the direction of three boxes of mayoral correspondence marked EXTREMELY URGENT. "That my file?"

Tony was distinctly edgy, but Ash couldn't tell whether from excitement, fear, or coming off some kind of high. He said, "You realize this is an official interrogation, Mr. Solomon?"

"Call me The King. What are you called?"

"Detective Laughton."

The eyes, brown, puppy dog-ish, came to Ash. "Hey, you're the boss, aren't you? Hey," Tony said, leaning back in his seat, "I must be pretty important. All this shit about me, now you here." He grinned, liking it, and tightened his biceps.

Ash made himself nod. "Yes. Mr. Solomon, we are investigating the murder of Carol Johnson." They had done their best to keep the dead children out of the news and so far it was working. "Since you spent the last week at the Johnson house, we thought maybe you could assist us."

"That other guy said I was under arrest."

"Well, you were caught selling stolen jewelry but maybe, you know, if you give us information . . ." Ash left it vague.

"Those pearls weren't stolen."

"Really? Why don't we start with that, then. How did you get them?"

"You want to know? I'll tell you. Mrs. Johnson *gave* them to me."

"She did?"

"You bet." Tony's eyes sparkled and Ash had a strong feeling he could guess what came next. "In exchange for 'services rendered.' I could have had more too."

"You went to bed with Mrs. Johnson," Ash said, trying to sound impressed.

"Sure did."

Ash could tell Tony wanted to talk, but he was only going to do it if he could be assured of an appreciative audience. "How did you get in? To the house, I mean."

"That? Easy. Mrs. Johnson was lonely, you know. She would open her door to anyone, postman, FedEx guy in his truck. She was looking for a man to talk to. All week she would come out and offer me lemonade, try to make small talk. She liked me. Then one day she came out in these short shorts and asks me if I'd noticed a green car across the street. I tell her sure, maybe, because I knew it was just a line, and she says she thinks someone is watching the house and is scared. So I offer to, you know, comfort her. All alone, the kids at school."

"She took you up on your offer?"

"Took me up on it? She practically dragged me up the stairs to her bedroom. Couldn't get me there fast enough." The biceps flexed again, twice.

"You had sex with her in the master bedroom?"

"For like three hours. Some guys, you know, they're into the floor, a bathtub. But an older broad like that, you got to go for comfort. She was scrawny too, you know, always dieting." Ash could tell Tony was warming to his theme. "Yeah, bony like. So I—"

"I'm sorry to interrupt, Mr. Solomon, but we're going to have to ask you for a hair sample."

"What?"

"To check against the hairs found on the sheets. And fingerprints."

Now, for the first time Tony looked wary. "I don't—no."

"Just to eliminate yours from the killer's in the bedroom. It's routine."

Tony cleared his throat. "You won't find mine."

"It would be hard to go at it in a bed for three hours without leaving some trace."

"Not me. Maybe for you but I'm young, see. I still got all my hair." He pulled on his, hard, to demonstrate.

Ash smiled at him, open, friendly. "Then one less piece won't matter to you."

"I'm not saying another word without a lawyer."

Ash traded his smile for confusion. "What are you telling me, Tony? That you didn't go to bed with Mrs. Johnson? Is that why we won't find your hair there?" Tony looked poised to say something but Ash went on. "Because if that is what you are saying, it means you lied and stole the pearls. Either you were in bed with Mrs. Johnson and she gave them to you and you are innocent and we'll find hairs like yours there. Or you didn't go to bed with her and you stole the pearls, and we won't find any hairs that match yours. If that's the case, we'll have to consider increasing the charges. If you're lying, you should tell me now."

"Increasing the charges? To what?"

"Murder, Tony."

"I want a lawyer."

"Okay. But it's almost ten. No one will come out tonight. You'll have to wait until tomorrow. Except tomorrow is Sunday. That means you'll probably have to wait until Monday. But I bet you won't mind. Strong guy like you, you'll be fine in the cells. Popular."

Tony opened his mouth again, decided to settle for a glare, and shut it.

"Why don't you think about how you want to play this for a while. Really examine all the options. I'd suggest coming clean, but that's up to you. I've got some work to take care of in my office, but there'll be an officer outside the door and he'd be happy to come get me if you decide you have something to say."

Ash pushed his chair away from the table and went through the door. Walking slowly down the corridor to his office, he felt worn out by the Tonys of the world, all that macho posturing and muscle flexing. When he was seventeen he'd taken his GED exam and left high school early, packing his possessions into an old pickup truck and driving around America. He worked at anything that would pay him, never staying anywhere longer than three months, and watched people, trying to figure out who he wanted to be. He had his heart broken twice, his arm broken once, lost a few hundred dollars playing pool and then won back several thousand. By the time he entered Harvard the fall after his eighteenth birthday, he knew how to fix a carburetor, how to hit the corner pocket off the rail every time, how to break up with someone gently, and how to program a computer. It was the last skill that earned him a fortune, $30 million when someone bought the rights to software he'd written for fun, but he valued the others more highly. He had been a beat cop when the program sold and everyone expected him to quit the police force, retire on a yacht somewhere. Instead, he'd bought a new car with a really complicated engine and worked harder to make detective. Computers could never be half as interesting as people.

Some people, anyway.

Back at his desk, he reached for his phone and was dialing before he knew what he was doing. By the time his brain stepped in, the phone on the other end had rung twice.

He hadn't realized how much he'd been looking forward to hearing her voice until a man's answered, a recording, saying that Windy and Bill were not available and asking him to leave a message at the beep.

Based on the voice Ash's brain supplied a picture of Bill that was a little too flattering, then stepped in with a quickie slide show of what "not available" might mean. Pitching his own voice low— yeah, right, he was tired of macho posturing—Ash asked Windy to call him at her convenience, that he had some questions about the case, then hung up.

He spent three and a half minutes assassinating "Bill" in his mind. Asked himself what the hell he was doing. And got back to work.

CHAPTER 9

"Cate is sleeping curled up with the Soccer Barbie you gave her. It's obscene how much she likes it," Windy said to Bill as she came into the bedroom. "Who was that on the phone?"

"Don't know, don't care. There is no one in the world I want to speak to that is not under this roof right now. And that," he said, taking a sip from a high ball of scotch, "is what I call heaven."

It was a simple statement, but it was also a warning to her, not to check the messages, not to look. The night was for them.

Windy moved toward him and ran her fingers up his tie. "I think you should slip into something more comfortable," she said. There was something about Bill that made it okay to say corny lines like that, that made them seem romantic, not idiotic. Her relationship with him was like a photo album filled with perfectly composed moments—*snap*—captured for all time.

Bill put his index finger under her chin now, tilting her lips toward him. "What are you thinking about?"

"Us. You. How good you are to me."

Snap. Close-up of a passionate kiss.

Snap. Distance shot of four bodies in a puddle of blood.

She pulled away from Bill fast.

"What's wrong?" he asked.

"Nothing. I just had an idea." She knew before it was out of her mouth it was the wrong thing to say.

He took a step backward, and sat down on the edge of the bed. "You were thinking about work." Crossing his arms over his chest now, looking at her with disappointment. "Were you thinking about it all night? When you were pretending to enjoy my company?"

"No. Not once tonight. It was just right now—"

"While we were kissing. Doesn't do much for a man's ego." His shoulders sagged.

"I'm sorry. The kissing was wonderful. Everything tonight has been wonderful. That's what made me think of it. It's so perfect, and I was feeling so lucky, and it made me think—" She could tell she was losing him again. "Never mind. I am so sorry. It is just that there is a man out there destroying families, and I feel like I have a responsibility to try to catch him. I feel guilty about not working."

"Guilty? What about your responsibility to the people in your life?" Bill shook his head. "Dammit, I did not want to have to do this tonight. I just wanted to have a nice evening with you. What a fool I was. I bet you would give anything to check the messages right now, see if there is some work you can do to get away from me." There was frustration in his voice but also a touch of anger, a touch Windy almost never heard. That was when she realized how much she had really hurt him.

She had to make this right. "I don't want to be anywhere but right here." He shook his head, not buying it, and she went on, almost begging. "What do you want me to do? How can I make you believe that?"

"I don't know." He stared straight in front of him, avoiding her. "Or actually, I do. I want you to keep your promise to me. To us. I agreed to move to Vegas, to change my whole life, because I want to be with you. Because you promised your hours would be more predictable, controllable. You said that here we would be able to have a regular life, without you tearing out of bed in the middle of the night to look at crime scenes and dead bodies. But now I have to wonder." His eyes came to her. "Is it really going to be different? What happens if I move here next month to make a family with you, but you're always too busy? What kind of life is that for us? What kind of life is it for Cate?"

Windy saw everything she had been building so carefully for the past year, all the stability, the even keel, the security, slipping away from her. She grasped for it. "That won't happen. This is just a hard period, with us being apart and only getting to spend weekends together. Not to mention being in a new city. After a move, there's bound to be a period of adjustment. Add to that, a big case." She looked at him steadily and said, "I promise you, we will make this work. I will not be too busy."

"I want to believe that. I want to believe I matter to you as much as your work."

"You do."

She reached for him but he stayed just out of range. "How am I supposed to know that? How am I supposed to believe that I'm not going to play second fiddle to your job here the way I did in Virginia? A job, I might add, you don't even need."

Windy went cold. "What are you talking about?"

"Look, I think it's very noble of you not to want to touch the money you inherited when Evan died, but be honest about it. You don't *need* to work. You work because you want to."

"That's not true. I'm not doing it because it's noble. I'm doing it because I don't want the Kirkland money. It's not mine. It was Evan's, and, when she turns twenty-one it will be Cate's. But never mine. By the time Cate inherits it, I want her to understand how important it is to work at something and care about something. To help people. And how can she understand any of that unless she sees me doing it? I don't want Cate to grow up the way Evan did, without role models and careless."

"Have you ever wondered if you use your work as a way to

avoid having to be close to people? Help them, yes. But when they don't need help, it's as though you don't know what to do for them."

Windy opened her mouth to object, then slowly closed it. Bill had a point. It was what her relationship with Evan had been like. Helping, him depending on her to make his life run, pay the bills, do the laundry, run the house, the grown-up stuff. With Evan being needed and being loved had been synonymous.

But not with Bill. Bill who was upset because he wanted to spend more time with her, because he loved her that much. Bill who traveled a lot but always came back. Bill not needing her, just wanting her.

He was right, she didn't know what to do with that. It was too precious. It overwhelmed her.

She said, "Maybe that's the problem. Maybe you're too well adjusted and I'm trying to give you a complex so I can take care of you." Her tone, light, almost joking, made Bill look at her.

"You're doing a good job," he said, trying to sound gruff. But a slight dimple in his left cheek gave away the unwilling smile lurking there. He took a deep breath and reached for her, pulling her onto his lap. "Babe, I love you so much. I just want to take care of you. Protect you. I'm so afraid of losing you."

"You won't. You can't. And my job for the rest of the weekend is to make you forget any of this happened."

"That won't be easy," he said with mock gravity.

She untangled herself from his arms, stood up with her back to him, said, "I'll just have to work very very hard," and let her dress fall to the ground with what she hoped was a suggestive shimmy.

"Yes you—Oh."

She had spent twenty minutes earlier that night rummaging through the silk and lace lingerie she liked to find the underwear he preferred, plain white Jockey for Her panties, white, unadorned Maidenform bra. By the time she found them they had almost missed their reservation, but no dinner in the world could have compared with the expression on Bill's face as she turned toward him now. The look he gave her was one of naked, almost desperate desire, the kind most women never glimpsed past the age of sixteen. He would not remember the mistake she had made, not remember her distraction.

Any woman in her right mind would be thrilled that her boyfriend found her sexy in the plainest things, her therapist in Virginia had told her when she brought it up at one session. It showed he loved her for who she was.

Evan had liked her best naked.

"Oh, Windy," Bill said, more of a sigh than a breath as he dragged her to him, sending them tumbling onto the bed. "Oh babe, you are amazing."

She closed her eyes and willed herself not to think of that other bed, soaked in blood. Not to think of that other family, of what she thought she'd discovered about their killer. Just think of Bill, who loved her for who she was. Which was more than she deserved.

CHAPTER 10

At 2:30 A.M. Windy couldn't stand it any more. She slipped on the pale green Chinese silk robe with the embroidered cherry blossoms on it that Cate had picked out for her last Mother's Day—"So you can be like a queen and I can be a princess"—went across the hall to check on Her Sleeping Highness, and then padded downstairs to her desk in the corner of the living room. She picked up Ash's message and dialed his work number, expecting his voice mail.

He answered on the first ring. "Ash Laughton."

"Ash, it's Windy." There was a pause so she added, "Windy Thomas. You know, in criminalistics."

"I know who you are," Ash's voice told her, amused. "I was just surprised to hear your voice. It's not exactly business hours."

"What are you doing at your desk?"

"What are you doing calling in? It's Saturday night. You are supposed to be off having fun."

"I am. Was," she stuttered. Paused. "I think I have difficulty letting go of work."

"I hear that's terrible problem. I wouldn't know personally."

"I'm sure. Are you planning to spend the entire weekend at the department?"

"No way," Ash said, insulted. "I'll go home for, oh, maybe forty-five minutes. But even when I'm here, it's not all work. Right now, for example, I'm making a sculpture out of the paperclips and Jujubes on my desk."

"I'm sorry to be interrupting such an important task. I can call back tomorrow."

"That's okay, it was time for me to take a break. What can I do for you? Do you always return calls around three A.M.?"

"Sorry. I thought I would just leave a message. I woke up with an idea."

"Tell me about it."

"No, you first. What's your question?"

"Is there any way a man and woman could have sex in a bed and have one of them not leave any trace evidence behind, no hair, no skin, no semen?"

Windy wondered what her mother would say if she knew the conversations her daughter considered normal. She asked, "Were the sheets washed?"

"No."

"That would be nearly impossible. Why?"

"That's what our exterminator, Tony, claims happened. He's got this long story about Mrs. Johnson being scared because a green car had been parked across the street and was watching the house so she turned to him for comfort. One thing led to another, the comforting turned to a tumble in the master bedroom, and afterwards she gave him the pearls as thanks or blackmail, you choose. Either way there's no evidence to support it."

"Why would he lie about that?"

"To cover up something. Stealing maybe. Now he's playing mute."

"Do you think he's the one?"

"I don't know. He's got a rap sheet about as tall as me under another alias, but it's all petty stuff, theft, fencing, a little drugs. Nothing like murder. We're holding him over the weekend to see if we can get something out of him, but I'm not counting on it. I'm still going to have a bunch of photographers covering the memorial service."

"When is it?"

"Monday morning."

"You think the killer would show up at the Johnsons' funeral?"

"Possibly, to see how much interest there is."

"I see. So you're pretty much giving up on the exterminator's story? The whole thing?"

"Not one hundred percent. Why?"

"Well, a suspect like that, who's dealt with the cops before, wouldn't he usually mix truth with his lies when he is embellishing? To make it easier to keep straight? Maybe, given that, we could follow up at least the part about the green car."

"Is there something in particular about that?"

"No, I don't—no. It just seems like a strange thing for him to have made up."

"I'll have my men canvass the neighbors again. What was your idea?"

"Do you have the lab reports and crime scene photos from the bedroom there in front of you?"

"The photos, yes. I can get the reports. Why?"

"I keep thinking that there had to be a reason he put all the bodies in one room, beyond simply shocking Doug Johnson Senior. At first their placement looks haphazard, mostly because the daughter and one of the sons are leaning forward. But that could have happened after he left, before rigor set in. If you imagine them sitting up instead, the way Mrs. Johnson and Doug Junior are, then you get a sort of tableau."

"Like a family picture," Ash said. "You think he was posing them."

"More than posing them. I have this feeling that he might have put himself in the picture too. I don't have the files here, so this is

really only a hunch. Before using it, you should check about indentations on the comforter between Doug, Junior and Norman. That's
where I think he went because there is a gap there. And also check
for hair on the wall behind that place."

"How would he see himself?"

"In the mirror attached to Mrs. Johnson's dressing table. I
couldn't quite tell from the crime scene photos, but I think the table
had been slightly moved. It looked like there might be two sets of
indentations in the carpet. I caught a shadow of them when you first
showed me the pictures and couldn't make anything of it but it
started me thinking."

"I'll take a look at the lab results and call you if we find anything. It would suggest that the reason he cut off their heads wasn't
just pragmatic, so he could enjoy their company at breakfast, but
also because it allowed him to depersonalize the victims when he
posed them. So he could picture any faces he wanted on top of their
bodies."

"True. And scary. I feel more and more like this is just the beginning. As though it's only a matter of time before this head case
kills again."

"I'm sorry," Ash said, sounding like he was choking. "Did you
say *head case?*"

Windy's hand went to her mouth. "Oh. Oh, brother. My mind
must have—I didn't mean—"

But it was too late. They were both laughing, the only antidote
to the sickness of what they were working with. "That was awful,"
Windy said, trying unsuccessfully to stop giggling. "I can't believe I
said that."

"Want to share the joke?" a voice asked from the door and
Windy looked up, saw Bill there, and froze. The urge to laugh van-
ished. "I've got to go, bye," she said, hanging up fast.

"What was so funny?" Bill asked again, coming into the room.

Windy held her robe tight around her, not wanting to meet his eyes. She had let him down and she knew it and she hated it—hated the feeling, hated herself for doing it. "Nothing. It was about the case we are working on. I just said something stupid."

"I doubt that. You are not stupid."

Windy felt like someone was squeezing her heart. "It was an accident. I'm sorry if I woke you up."

"It was your absence that woke me up. And then I heard you laughing. It's been a long time since I heard you laugh like that." Bill's tone was more wistful than angry.

"I'm sorry. I couldn't sleep and I had an idea and—" She didn't know what words should come next so she looked up at him.

Relief washed over her as his face broke into a bemused smile. "There is no stopping you, is there?"

She shook her head, one time, hard. Then got her lips apart enough to say, "I—I'm sorry, Bill. I'm incredibly sorry. I think there's something wrong with me."

"There's nothing wrong with you, Windy," he said, holding her against him. "I think you're just so used to turning to work for all your fulfillment, that it doesn't occur to you there could be another way."

She burrowed against his chest, wanting to be as close to him as possible, as close to the security, the solidness, he offered.

"No, there's nothing wrong with you," he repeated, stroking her head. "At least, nothing that a little supportive attention from the man who loves you can't fix. Just—can we try not to do this tomorrow? Try to make Sunday a real day of rest? A whole day with no work? Just you being a mom and me being a dad and Cate being Cate?"

"Yes. Of course. The bad guys are just going to have to live without me until after your flight leaves on Monday."

"That's what I like to hear."

CHAPTER 11

The desk clerk in the ER at Sunrise Hospital did not have time for this kind of shit.

"We just want to be sure he'll be able to be there," the voice on the other end of the phone was saying through the static.

"Fine."

"You know, it'll be their third child and—"

"Okay, that's just great." Who cared if some resident he'd never heard of was having another child? A baby shower. Not his problem. His problem was the guy bleeding all over the waiting room. The desk clerk said, "Whose schedule did you say you were looking for again?"

"Maximillian Waters's. When does he work this weekend?"

"He just got off. That means he's . . ." The clerk flipped back and forth between the pages of the schedule. Someone had screwed them up again. "He'll be back on starting at eight P.M. Sunday night."

"And when does he finish?"

"He pulled the long shift. He's on all day Monday straight through to four A.M. Tuesday morning."

"Home at four A.M. Tuesday. Thanks. Don't tell him, though. You know, keep it a secret. Will you? It's supposed to be a surprise."

The clerk laughed at that. As if he'd even remember the call in another ten minutes.

CHAPTER 12

Sunday passed into Monday for Ash in a blur of crumpled coffee cups, stale M&Ms, Pedro's Special Tacos from the place down the street, and "I'm not talking until my lawyer shows" declarations from Anthony Solomon. The exterminator looked better than he did, Ash had to admit when he finally went home Monday morning to shower and change for the memorial service.

It was an almost excruciatingly beautiful day, the kind that happened in Las Vegas maybe four times a year. Blue sky, light wind carrying the scent of desert sage, the mountains crystal clear around the valley. Ash wore sunglasses and tried not to walk stooped over and sideways like an underground creature seeing sun for the first time. The crowds at the funeral were enormous, including, inevitably, a half dozen camera crews. He was scanning the trees for his own photographers when someone brushed against him and he looked down to see a familiar face.

"Hi, Mr. Policeman," the woman said. "I thought I might see you here." She reached up and took the platinum toothpick from his mouth to give him a fast kiss on the lips. The toothpick had been a gift from her when they were involved a year earlier, to replace the wood one he'd always had before that.

He and Bobbie Casio had remained friends after their affair

ended and he was still a firm admirer of hers. "Hi, Bobbie. How is my favorite member of the Mafia?"

"Wife of a member of the Mafia. And you tell me. How do I look?"

"Beautiful as always," Ash said, meaning it.

"Really?"

"You know how stunning you are, Bobbie."

She gazed up at him with a look that was probably more vulnerable than she meant it to be. "You are the only man I know who can look sexy and taste like gummy bears at the same time. I miss you, Ash. I didn't realize how much until now. Have you missed me?"

"It's good to see you, Bobbie."

"Flatter me some more."

"What are you doing here? How did you know the Johnsons?"

"Carol and I played tennis together. Don't look so surprised, I can do 'suburban housewife' with the best of them. And Carol was one of the best of them. A neat woman. This is terrible. Just awful. I hope you get the man."

"We will." He paused, said, "Do you think Carol ever had any affairs?"

"I hardly think this is the place to discuss it, Ash."

"Come on, Bobbie. It could be important for my investigation."

Bobbie gazed over Ash's shoulder, squinting into the distance as she thought about it. "I think she was fascinated by the idea, but I doubt she ever did. She might flirt a little with the tennis pro or the pool man, but that was all. She was very timid. And, deep down, I think she was also romantic, you know, believed in marriage, happily ever after. So I'd have to vote no."

"Thanks."

"You're welcome." She scrutinized his face for a moment with her smart eyes then said lightly, "Don't believe what I said before. Funerals have a lousy effect on me. I don't miss you at all."

"I know."

Bobbie gave him a long look and headed back into the crowd, to her husband, Ash imagined, and then stopped thinking about her at all. He shaded his eyes with the program of the memorial service that had been shoved into his hands, eight pages of poems and letters and prayers, raking his gaze over heads of the three hundred people there. He caught sight of three of the four police photographers, sought the fourth, and found him up a tree. Good, all angles. Their photos would be scanned through a computer running the face recognition software he had invented to see if they got any matches to any known felons. He spotted at least two well connected mobsters, one of them Bobbie's husband, and kept his eyes moving. The only person he did not look at was Doug Johnson, the father of the dead family. He had glimpsed the man earlier and was horrified by what he had seen. His face was set like a mask that kept slipping, and beneath it Ash saw raw pain.

Ash dropped his eyes instead to the program. The front was a photo of the Johnson family on vacation, sitting on a rock outcropping, all smiling. In this context it was horrible to look at, a testimonial to loss. He remembered one of his first collars, a guy named Moochie Lopez, defending himself from a murder charge saying, "Why am I going to kill a guy that's got nothing worth dying for, man? It's like robbing an empty house." Moochie knew what he was talking about, Ash thought, his eyes uncontrollably returning to the crumpled figure of Doug Senior, a man who'd had everything worth dying for. With all those cameras and press vans around, the guy looked like a spokesmodel for grief and guilt together.

Around Ash, three hundred voices began to intone the Lord's prayer, a chilling sound against the silence of the day. *Our Father, who art in heaven.* His brain stuck on the first two words, repeating them over and over until they formed themselves into the question that had been nagging at him all morning: Did Doug Senior get left alive by accident or on purpose?

Ash took a longer look at the picture on the program and saw something he'd missed. Something crucial. With a sinking feeling in his stomach he realized he'd found the answer to his question.

CHAPTER 13

Windy dropped Cate at school, Bill at the airport, then broke a few laws speeding to work. She drove with all the windows open, amazed at how warm it was in October, thinking that Las Vegas was a pretty nice town. For a few minutes, she felt a degree of contentment and control that she had not experienced in a long time—so long she hadn't even realized she had been missing it. Moving here was a good idea. It would work out. Everything was going to be fine.

Walking down the corridor to her office, she saw how wrong she had been. A good-looking man with dark hair graying at the temples stood thumbing through the new copy of *Journal of Forensic Science* that had been left on the mail table outside her door, as if he had been waiting for a while. His clothes were well cut and carefully pressed, his hair neat, his shoes spit polished. He wasn't a cop. That meant most likely he was a lawyer or a process server. An enemy.

"This is incredibly cool," he said, slight southern flavor to his voice, holding up an article about maggots. The picture he had his finger next to showed a guy's face covered with them.

"They are doing amazing things with entomology," Windy agreed. Most people didn't think it was even vaguely cool. Bill banned her books and periodicals from the bedroom because of "those horrifying photos." And every time she went to visit her parents she still had the same conversation with them. It started in her mother's voice: How can you do a job where you look through other people's dirt?

It's not dirt, its evidence. Besides, you work with dirt all the time at the dry cleaning place.

Her mother's lips pushed together so hard that the color went out of them and you could only see the lip liner saying, I don't know, Chicago. Is not a job for a nice girl.

Windy shook her head now, her mother's voice sounding more and more like Brandon's imitation as the days she refused to return her phone calls added up, and said to the man outside her office, "Are you waiting for me?"

He gave one last look to a different picture, this one of arterial blood spray on a wall going up and down like hills in a Chinese landscape. "Yes. Sorry." Putting the magazine down now, giving her his hand and a friendly smile. "I'm Hank Logan." They shook and he dipped into his pocket for a business card, extending it toward her.

" 'Vegas Loves Kids' program of the Department of Juvenile Services," Windy read. That was the mayor's pet program, which would mean that Hank Logan was one of his inner circle. His hands were extremely well kept, nails short and well manicured, the sign of a man with time and money to take care of himself. A political appointee. Definitely an enemy. "What can I do for you, Mr. Logan?"

"I've been assigned the case of Roddy 'Hot Rod' Ruiz," he told her. "I've got some questions to ask you. Can we talk in your office? For privacy?"

"Of course," Windy said, wanting to say instead, why not just draw and quarter me right here. If the mayor was sending someone over to take an interest in Roddy's case, that likely meant he had changed his mind and was going to pressure her again to change hers about the crime scene. The Starrs, the girl's parents, must have some power.

Windy unlocked the door of her office and let him go in ahead of her.

Hank Logan looked around intently, taking in the blood spatter velocity chart she had hanging on the wall, the stacks of carpet sample books lined up on the bookshelf. His eyes stopped on a foam mannequin with a knife jammed in its belly.

"That how criminalists get their frustrations out?"

"It belonged to my predecessor."

"If up here is anything like downtown at our offices in City Hall, there isn't a lot of money in the budget for redecorating. Or even decorating." Glancing now over the calendar of a woman wearing a lot of lip gloss and a bikini sitting in a golf cart, the head of the club between her legs, not commenting on it, which Windy appreciated. It was another leftover from the former chief Windy kept meaning to get rid of but had started writing appointments on and hadn't managed to find a replacement for yet, reminding her of how unsettled she still was.

His eyes ended up finally on the snow globe Cate and Brandon had made as a present for her, her first day of work, the only thing of hers in the office. "Be careful out there, kid," a balloon said out of Cate's mouth, the photo glued over a postcard of the Vegas skyline.

Hank Logan chuckled at it. "How old is she?"

"Six going on thirty."

"Ah, about the same age as my daughter. It's nice to have such a good reminder of why we do this, isn't it?"

"Especially since I have a feeling you are here to make me feel like I did the wrong thing with Roddy," Windy agreed.

He sat in the chair she motioned him toward, shaking his head. "I can put your mind to rest on that. Roddy has been released and will stay that way. But I am here at the mayor's request, and to be honest, what he really wants is for me to spy on the Violent Crimes Task Force, using Roddy as a lever. Nothing would give him greater pleasure than to close the Task Force down. I think he's wrong about that—don't quote me, but I think he is intimidated by Ash Laughton. To tell you the truth, I don't care to get involved in his politics. I agreed to be his leg man because I wanted to work on Roddy's case. Dismantle the system from within."

Windy exhaled, just realizing how tense she'd been. She said, "Why are you telling me this?"

"I don't want to be a political pawn, and I don't want to waste your time. I think you and the Task Force have enough on your hands without some second tier functionary messing around."

Windy looked at him. "You don't sound like a political appointee."

"Damn. I've been working on my oily speeches too."

Windy had to laugh at that. "What can I tell you about Roddy?"

Hank got comfortable in the chair. "I think he's a kid with a lot of potential, but I am having a hard time getting him to open up. He won't talk at all about what happened that night, some sort of code of silence. I've tried explaining that it's privileged, that if he tells me it won't be useful against his guardian, Hector, only it might help him but he won't budge. I read the reports but there were a few things I didn't understand about what happened in the apartment and then afterward. I am looking for a way to reach this boy."

"What do you want to know?"

"It wasn't clear from the report—did Roddy hear what was going on? Or did he see it?"

"He watched it. From behind the door." Windy went on, telling him about the entire event in detail, taking pleasure in having such a good audience. He asked a few astute questions and when she was done he sat quietly, nodding to himself.

Finally he said, "That explains why he keeps showing up at that house, hanging around outside."

"What do you mean?"

"Sometimes people do that, to work through their memories of an incident, consciously or unconsciously. I think Roddy is still confused about what happened and he's trying to make sense of it, and the only place to do that is where the action took place. It's a crazy world, isn't it, where a boy is embarrassed *not* to have killed someone. Death doesn't mean anything to him, it's just a sign, a way to say fuck you to a world he feels like rejected him. Excuse me," he said, hand coming to his mouth. "Sometimes my language isn't what it ought to be."

"No problem. Do you see a lot of kids like Roddy?"

"Unfortunately I do. My specialty is abuse, and when you see that, you see kids whose values are topsy turvy. They become numb inside, and then can't feel anything for anyone else either, so taking a life and taking a sip of beer amount to about the same thing. Maybe even the same rush. With Roddy I feel like there's still hope. That's why I wanted to talk to you—if he really was crying over the body of the girl, showing some emotion, that's a positive sign."

Windy admired and envied his optimism, forgetting he was a political plant. "I hope so. How long have you been in social work?"

"I was in private practice for a while before moving here to Vegas two years ago. I joined the department because I was tired of listening to men wonder why their wives weren't satisfied with the Mercedes, the floor-length mink, and the diamond tennis bracelet and kept demanding things like fidelity. I figured if I worked with kids maybe I could deal with those problems before they started." He smiled, disarmingly. "Is there anything else you want to know about me? I could take you to dinner some time and give you a complete rundown."

Windy felt herself blush. "I would enjoy that, Mr. Logan but—"

"You're not interested. You're coming out of a bad relationship. You don't date men with receding hairlines."

Windy laughed, despite herself. "Your hairline isn't receding."

"A little on the sides."

"Actually, I'm engaged."

"Congratulations. But the dinner invite still holds. Or lunch. Just as friends."

"Thanks. That would be nice."

He stood to go and Windy realized she was a little sorry. His interest—interest in her work—had been refreshing and his enthusiasm, optimism, were infectious.

"It's been a pleasure meeting you, Mr. Logan."

"Please, just call me Logan. Everyone does."

"Call me Windy."

They were shaking hands when Ash appeared at the door. The two men looked each other over in a way that made Windy think of lions. Before she could introduce them Ash stuck out a hand, saying mechanically, "Ash Laughton."

"Hank Logan."

"He's with the Department of Juvenile Services," Windy put in. "Working on Roddy's case." Not saying he was supposed to spy on them. The machismo was thick enough in the air as it was.

Ash nodded, not really easing up. "Is there a problem?"

"Not yet," Logan said. "See if we can't fix the boy up." He looked at Windy. "Thanks for the help. You have my card. Call me if you think of anything else. Or if you're just hungry."

"Thanks."

Ash watched the man leave, wondering what the hell that meant. The woman was engaged. And if she weren't—

She was.

He turned back to face her, said, "I wanted to give you the good news myself," and was rewarded with her undivided attention.

"We got the green car?"

"Not quite that good. I found our killer's artistic inspiration." He dropped the program from the memorial service on her desk. It landed next to the crime scene photo of the Johnsons' bedroom.

Windy had to swallow a lump in her throat before she could talk. The parallel between the two was unmistakable. "He posed the bodies to look like this photo. He purposely recreated this scene."

"And the place you told me to look for evidence? Between the two sons? It's the place the father filled in the picture."

Windy looked at the crime scene photo more closely. "This photo was standing on the bedside table. He was making the picture real. I guess we can deduce that he purposely struck when Doug Johnson was out. Less competition."

"Exactly what I was thinking. Which means he is trying to take the place of the father."

"Fill his shoes figuratively as well as literally." Windy tapped two fingers on the top of her desk, impatient with herself, feeling like she was missing something. "We know for certain that he felt at home at the Johnsons' house or he would not have stayed long enough to pull a stunt like this."

"True. It almost seems like he's playing a game. A game about control, controlling the family, controlling his environment."

Windy's eyes met Ash's. "He's not going to stop after this one."

"No, I don't think he is. But what worries me even more is that he's going to get better at his game each time he plays."

"Which means for him to get the same thrill, next time will have to be worse."

There was a long pause. Ash broke it, trying hard to sound hopeful, saying, "Unless we have him in custody right now. It could be the exterminator. I'll go have another chat with him. I think I can break him."

"Yes. That's a great idea."

As Ash left, Windy wondered which of them was lying more.

CHAPTER 14

　　　　The red silk dining room of the Paradise Lost Café was mostly empty, just one couple lingering over a soufflé and a group of businessmen studying the tips of their cigars as they debated whether to go out to a strip club or have the girls sent to their rooms. It was after midnight and in the prep area their waitress leaned against the wall, careful not to crush the white-feathered wings of her uniform, and downed her tenth espresso of the night, willing the stragglers to leave so she could have a cigarette.

Eve Sebastian, the marquee chef and half owner of the restaurant, sat in her office off the kitchen, putting her knives away. The night had started out crappy with two of the prep staff calling in sick, and gotten worse when a short circuit in the sprinkler system flooded the kitchen during the dinner crush.

"I never want to go through a shift like that again," Reiko Mars, the assistant manager of the restaurant, said, coming into the office and dropping into the hardwood chair next to Eve's. She slid off her mules and rested her feet on the desk. "When the sprinkler system went haywire, I thought things were bad. But then when Matt and Johan started going at it and refused to put their knives down . . ." She shook her head. "I keep expecting someone to come and tell me we had the *New York Times* reviewer in the dining room tonight. That would be the icing on the cake."

Eve rested her fingers on the hilt of a carving knife and tried to bring out a smile. The office was small and she had purposely chosen the furniture to be uninviting. She was not comfortable having people near her except in the kitchen. She especially hated the way Reiko put her feet up, made herself at home. She worked not to stare at Reiko's ankles, perched so casually on the edge of the desk.

"Hopefully tomorrow will be smoother," Eve said, trying to be polite but also encourage the woman to go.

"We'll have the hotel maintenance staff look at the sprinkler system. Disconnect it if they can't fix it before dinner tomorrow. We don't want a repeat performance."

"No." Eve's fingers tapped against the blade of the knife.

"Are you feeling all right? You seem sort of distracted."

"I'm just tired."

Reiko leaned forward. "Do you need help with the knives?"

"No, thank you," Eve answered, too harshly by the look on the other woman's face. She forced another smile. "It's bad luck to have someone else clean your knives."

"You chefs are so superstitious," Reiko said with a laugh. She slid her feet off the desk and stood up. "Well, I should get home."

Yes, Eve thought. Leave me alone.

But the woman didn't move. Instead she pointed to the flowers on top of the filing cabinet. "You are so lucky to have a man who sends you flowers every week. How romantic. That Barry of yours must be great."

"Harry. He is. Well, see you tomorrow."

"Bye."

Eve watched her go through the door and could see the fat dimples on her bottom. She looked instead at the flowers, which did not make her feel better, then at the framed picture standing beside them. It showed a man and a little girl, holding hands. The man was wearing a bowling shirt with the name EDDIE S. stitched over the pocket. His eyes crinkled as he smiled at the camera, a cigarette dangling from the corner of his mouth. Around the wrist of his free arm was a thick gold bracelet with a horseshoe on it, and the index and middle fingers of his hand were crossed. He always crossed them in pictures, for good luck he said. The little girl was wearing a gold necklace with a #1 DAUGHTER charm. You couldn't see it in the picture, but Eve knew it was there. She still had it, carried it in her change purse.

There had once been another person in the picture, on the other side of the girl, but the only sign of her now was hidden under the thick frame, a tiny corner of a floral print dress. It had taken Eve several tries before she managed to trim away the image of her mother without ruining the composition. Sometimes if she stared long enough, she thought she could see the hem of the dress creeping out from under the frame, as if the woman was still trying to steal his attention. Trying to say, "See, I won in the end. You had to leave and I'm still here."

He loved me the most, she wanted to scream. He loved *me*.

Stop it, she warned herself. Thinking about her mother always made her hungry. The office started feeling claustrophobic, like it was going to collapse on her, too many voices, too many memories. She had to get out of here. Carefully folding up her knife case, she slipped it into her purse, picked up the vase of flowers, and locked the office. On her way to the exit she paused just for an instant at the door of the dark kitchen to breathe in its familiar smell of cleaning products, stainless steel, and blood. Her kitchen. She loved that smell.

She remembered the time she'd brought Harry there, to seduce him. Long after closing time, just the two of them with only the task lights on. She remembered the way he looked laid out naked on the metal counter like a slab of meat, waiting for her. A slab of meat with an erection. He had liked her enough then. He'd sent her flowers the next day, telling her he loved her, and every Monday after that.

But two months after that he'd changed his mind. Two months later he had asked her to meet him at his office because they needed to talk. Instead of sitting in the armchairs with her, like he did in the past, he had her take the chair with the itchy ice blue upholstery on the other side of his desk. He smiled at her, the way he smiled at the people he worked with, his clients. Then he tented his fingers and said, "This isn't going to work out. I'm sorry, Eve. You have too many issues."

That had happened three weeks ago. The first Monday the flowers didn't come, she thought she would go out of her mind. So she solved the problem by sending them to herself. No one needed to know about it. About her failure.

She hadn't thought it could get any worse but it did. That afternoon, as they were setting up for dinner, he had called to congratulate her on a write-up about her restaurant in the local newspaper. He had asked how she was. How business was. If she was seeing anyone. Her heart had stopped, thinking that maybe this was it, he was going to say they should get back together. Maybe she had been wrong. So she'd told him the truth. "No. Are you?"

And he had said, "Sort of. It's not serious. Not yet anyway."

She locked the door of the restaurant and headed toward the employee parking lot. *Not yet anyway* seemed to echo in the sound of her footsteps on the concrete as she walked to the far corner where she always parked. She dropped her bag into the back of her green car on top of the pile of wedding magazines there, but kept the knives with her up front, along with her sketch pad, something she had started doing recently. It helped her feel composed, in control.

Only she did not feel in control now. *Not yet, anyway.* She reached into the glove compartment and pulled out a fresh box of her favorite candies. Sitting with the doors locked and her seat belt on, she unwrapped the chocolate flavored squares and put them in her mouth, chewing each one eighteen times.

Three weeks earlier, when Harry told her she had too many issues, she had figured out a way to solve that problem. She would confront her issues, she decided, say good-bye to them. And then she would say good-bye to Harry.

The clock in the dashboard clicked. She glanced at it and saw that it was one in the morning. That meant Dr. Waters would still be at work for at least three hours.

She knew what she had to do. Putting the remaining two squares of Ex-Lax in her mouth, she gently touched the knife case on the seat next to her, and started the car. The tears began as she drove out of the parking lot onto the street outside. Raining down, blurring her vision. Please, she wanted to stop the car and scream at the pedestrians in the crosswalk when she braked for a yellow light. *Please someone stop me.*

But no one did. The light changed. The car raced forward.

CHAPTER 15

The ringing of the phone woke Windy Tuesday morning. Her mind unconsciously ran through its normal diagnostic exercise—Cate was in bed, her parents were—

The case.

She was wide awake by the time she picked up on the third ring. The hands on her Big Bird alarm clock said it was just before five A.M.

"Hello?"

"Windy? Ash. I'm sorry to call so early."

"There's been another murder, hasn't there?"

"Yes. I know you're not on duty right now but I thought—"

"Where is the crime scene? I'm on my way as soon as I pull on some clothes."

"I was hoping you'd say that. I already sent a car to pick you up. It's going to be a crush and I want you there as soon as possible. They should be at your house in about five minutes."

"Where's the exterminator?"

"We still have him in custody."

So he was innocent. At least of this killing. And of the Johnsons' if the evidence said they were done by the same person. "Oh, brother."

"You read my mind."

———

The street in front of the Sun-Crest was swarmed with police cars and cordoned off with yellow crime scene tape and orange cones, press vans parked right up against the tape. While cameramen unfurled their snaking cords, a local anchorman dropped Visine into his eyes and an anchorwoman touched up her lipstick. It was like a carnival, complete with flashing lights and an air of expectation.

"Welcome to hell," Ash said, coming over to Windy as she wrestled equipment out of the trunk of the criminalistics sedan.

"How did the press get on this so fast?"

They ducked under the crime scene tape together. "I can't even think about that right now but if I had to guess I'd say that either we have a leak, or the mayor was in bed with his press secretary when the news came across the police scanner. Neither is very appealing. And not your problem. I've set up a command post over there, in front of the pawn shop, but you've got complete authority at the scene. The place is all yours until you tell us otherwise."

A patrolman approached Windy then and said, "I'm sorry, miss, this is a restricted area. You'll have to go back behind the yellow line."

Ash could understand the man's mistake. In her baggy overalls with a white tank top peeking out, cardigan, orange Adidas, and her hair held up with a pencil, Windy looked about sixteen. Like a cool sixteen-year-old.

Glancing at Ash now, rolling her eyes more like a frustrated sixteen-year-old, asking, "You were saying?" Windy flashed her badge, held up the Crime Scene Investigations vest she hadn't put on yet, and had the patrolman nearly wetting his pants trying to apologize. Before he'd gotten past the second "My orders said—" she cut him off, assured him she knew he was just doing his job, and ducked under the tape with a lack of rancor that told Ash this happened to her pretty often.

They were met at the foot of the stairs by a young criminalist Windy had been introduced to the previous week but hadn't worked with yet. He was medium height, lanky, his red hair was cut short but his sideburns were left long, with a red goatee and round, wire-rimmed glasses. Larry, that was his name. Larry had been sitting on the bottom stair but stood as they came up, his tense posture saying he was annoyed.

"We've got a hell of a problem in there, ma'am." Larry wiped his hands on his jeans and Windy made a mental note to take a sample of the dirt from the stairs to evaluate against particles found at the crime scene. Sometimes technicians destroyed more evidence than they found. "The victim's husband, Mr.—"

"Doctor," Ash corrected. "Doctor Waters."

"Yeah, well, whoever, he won't budge. I haven't been up there yet myself, got a uniform guarding the perimeter, but the patrol guys who got here first say he's refusing to leave the apartment. Wouldn't even move when the photographer went in to get the preliminary pics. And he's making a mess of the crime scene. Sitting right in the middle of it, if you can believe it."

He flushed from anger, and the way he was looking at her, Windy could tell Larry expected sympathy. She said, "I don't blame him for not wanting to leave. As soon as he walks out that door he has to admit it's real, that it's happened, that there is no going back, that his life, his home, will never be the same. And I suspect that is only the beginning of what he is dealing with."

He squinted at her, clearly having no idea what the hell she was talking about, then put his hands on his hips and said, "Be that as it may, ma'am, we can't do anything until he's relocated." Letting her know he did not like the way this was going.

"Of course. I'll talk to him."

Ash had watched their exchange but hadn't interfered, which Windy appreciated. Now he said to her, "I'll talk to Doctor Waters, if you want. That's not really your provenance." Speaking with the families of murder victims was one of the most difficult jobs a cop did. As head of the Violent Crimes Task Force, Ash did it a lot, but it never got easier. He would rather have been shot at than tell a mother her child was dead.

"That's okay," Windy said. "I'll do it. I'd rather. Fewer people in the crime scene."

Ash nodded. "If you need anything, send someone out. I've got two photographers shooting the crowd and I asked the news guys to film them, although it looks like they are more interested in you."

Windy followed his gaze, saw a television camera pointed in her direction, and had to resist the urge to make a stupid face.

She looked instead at Larry, trying hard not to feel dislike, only partially successful. He would be the technician who complained that a rape victim was uncooperative because she didn't want to take off her underwear in front of him. "You stay down here until Dr. Waters leaves. When he's gone, I'll do a quick walk-through of the apartment, then have you come in with a crime scene kit and camera. We will do the preliminary together, slowly, make a sketch. I've already put Ned Blight in charge of the rest of the team, and he'll bring them in when we're ready. Got it?"

Larry looked stunned. It was obvious he wasn't used to having his boss hanging around at the crime scene and he sure he didn't like it. "Yeah, I guess but wouldn't it make—" he started to answer, but he was talking to Windy's back.

Windy gave her name to the patrolwoman stationed outside the door of apartment five to write on the log, while she pulled on the blue sterile shoe covers.

"How many people have been through?" she asked.

"Two patrol officers and a photographer, ma'am," the woman told her, calling her "ma'am" even though they were probably the same age.

Three people since the 911 call. Damn. She could only hope the others hadn't done too much damage. "No medics?"

"It wasn't necessary, ma'am." Giving Windy her first hint of what she was going to see.

"Thank you, officer. Please stay here and keep track of anyone else entering or leaving."

"Yes, ma'am."

Windy ran through the names of the victims again. She always made herself learn them, because names made bodies more real, and that made her do a better job. Then she took a deep breath, knocked, got no answer, tried the knob, and found it unlocked.

The room she entered, the living room, was dark, blinds down, the only light coming from the open door of the kitchen behind it. The air was heavy with the smell of wet iron filings—the smell of blood—and beneath it, the scent of Lysol. The wallpaper had large paisleys printed on it and the wall-to-wall carpet looked like a medium beige. In front of her was a wooden coffee table, and beyond that, against the wall, a dark colored velour couch with four people on it. Three of them had no heads. The fourth, seated next to what had to be the body of his wife, was Maximillian Waters. He perched on the edge of the sofa, elbows on his thighs, his head resting in his palms. His shoulders were trembling.

For a split second all her years of experience deserted her and Windy wanted to turn and run away. She knew that what she was seeing was only the tip of the "much worse" iceberg.

The bodies of two little girls, Minette and Martine, sat next to each other, thighs touching, their heads on either side of them. They were holding hands. Their mother, Claudia, sat slightly apart from her girls, one arm extending toward them along the back of the couch. Her legs, crossed at the ankles, were covered in blood. There was no sign of her head.

Windy approached the couch, stopping about three feet away to study something on the carpet, and said, "Dr. Waters."

He didn't move at first but the trembling subsided. He took two deep breaths and looked up. He said, "Her wedding ring is gone."

Windy saw that his wife's hand was in his lap. She nodded, thinking to herself, My God, the woman's head is missing and he is focusing on her ring. Quickly replacing that with the thought that him being able to move his wife's hand meant rigor mortis had not set in yet so the bodies were relatively fresh.

"That seems to be one of the things this killer does. Take wedding bands."

"It was gold plated. Not even solid gold," he said, as if that made it more inexplicable. "And much too small for anyone but a child. She has very delicate fingers. Look." He held up the hand.

Windy moved next to him. "May I?" She gestured to the chair that was at right angles to the sofa he was sitting on. He nodded.

"Dr. Waters, my name is Chicago Thomas. I'm from the police criminalistics bureau. I can't pretend to know what you are going through, but I am immensely sorry for your loss."

He was not listening, caught in the bubble of his own grief. "I should never have taken that extra shift at the hospital."

"I don't think that would have made a difference."

He went on, not hearing her. "They are twins, you know, the girls. Every time I have to work late, they pack me a lunch box. They insist on making me a sandwich all by themselves. They are such good girls. Claudia and I, we wanted to do something really special for them for their seventh birthday in December so we thought we would take them to Disneyland. Combined Christmas and birthday present. So I've been taking overtime. On the weekends, you know, you make more money. That is why I was working. To go to Disneyland. For their birthdays. They are twins, you know. When I work late they make—made—oh God—" He stumbled over the tense and plunged headlong back into the well of pain. Windy knew how that felt. How sometimes just words could stab you.

He stopped talking and started shaking again. In the kitchen, a faucet dripped. After a while, Windy reached out a hand toward his shoulder.

"We have reason to think that your family was not chosen at random." It was not strictly true but some part of her was starting to believe it. "If you had been here last night, the killer would have waited until you went away another time."

The shaking continued.

"There was no way for you to stop this. But there is a way you can help us get whoever did this."

The shaking slowed. After another long pause Windy said, "I would like to bring my crime scene team in to collect evidence. The more information I can pick up from your house, the faster we can catch this killer."

Maximillian Waters did not look up, but she could tell he was listening now. His eyes had moved to her feet, where the orange tops of her shoes poked out of the protective covers.

She said gently, "We will be able to work more quickly if we are alone in the apartment."

He did not move.

"When my team is done, the police may have some questions for you. If you don't feel up to answering them, that is okay, just tell them."

"I'll answer," Maximillian Waters said. His eyes came to Windy now. "Claudia would have liked your shoes."

"Thank you."

He nodded once, stood and went to the front door. He paused there and turned abruptly back toward the couch.

One last look at his family. That was what he was taking, Windy knew, as time stood still and he stared at them. She would have done anything to spare him the haunting that image was going to give him forever.

"Good-bye," he said, to her or them, unclear. Then he pushed through the screen door and went outside.

Looking at the place he had vacated Windy was able to see that the velour couch was not actually dark colored. It was beige. But it was almost entirely saturated with blood.

CHAPTER 16

Larry was waiting impatiently outside the door of the apartment when Windy opened it a few minutes later. He came in, loping the crime scene kit, saying, "That took long—" but the words died. Changed to "Oh God."

"Don't," Windy cautioned as he was about to set the kit down on the carpet so he could cover his mouth as he retched. Larry stared at her, wiping his mouth on his shoulder, his already pale skin colorless now. Windy pointed to the middle of the floor. "I want you to do a dust lift for footprints around this whole area," she said, drawing a rectangle in the air above a piece of carpet with her finger. "And I want photographs and measurements of these." She pointed at two slight indentations in the wall-to-wall carpeting at the center of the area she'd indicated, indentations Larry had almost stepped on. When he did not move, Windy said, "Now."

"Right. Okay," Larry said, steadying himself, and got to work.

Focusing all your attention on work was the only way to stay sane with a scene like this, Windy knew, and she focused with pin-point precision. She had spotted the two shallow, round indentations in the wall-to-wall carpet when she had come in, and was pretty sure she knew what they matched, but Larry needed something to do, something to help him pull himself together. The electrostatic lift was useful for bringing patterns like tire treads or footprints to the surface even when there were none visible. The plastic sheet they used worked like a magnet to attract invisible particles of dirt and dust preserving the pattern it was deposited in. "Like dusting for fingerprints in reverse," one of the patrolmen she'd worked with in Virginia described it pretty accurately. Chances were that on a carpet like this one, it would bring up too much to be useful, but it was worth a try, and it was a technique that required more concentration than precision—perfect for helping an unnerved young criminalist regain his equilibrium after being faced with one of the most atrocious murder scenes Windy had ever seen.

"I'm going to do a walk-through while you do this," she told Larry, who didn't even look up as she clicked on the small cassette recorder she carried with her at crime scenes. She gave the time and date, and started walking the perimeter of the room, trying to visualize what had happened. Trying to put herself in the killer's shoes.

She checked the doors and windows. "My point of entry appears to be through front door, not forced. Living room is not primary crime scene—I moved the bodies there post mortem."

There were doors opening off the room on either side, one side going to a hallway and the kitchen, the other covered with amber beads leading to the master bedroom. Windy went to the bedroom first, following a trail of bloody footprints that led out of that room, but no blood spatter.

The shades were drawn and the bedside light was off, but the sheets on one side of the queen-size bed were creased, and *The Bloody Chamber* by Angela Carter lay open on the unrumpled side like an uncanny title for the scene, as if Mrs. Waters had been reading in bed and, interrupted, set it down to answer the door. Windy looked at the reading light and saw the shade was cracked, and there was a spot of something dark on it. There had been a struggle, the lamp had been knocked over.

Lifting the lamp, Windy saw that the space beneath it, like the rest of the bedside table, was covered with drops of blood, showing the lamp had been replaced after Mrs. Waters was killed, that the murderer had done some cleaning up. There was also a visibly clean place on the surface of the night table, roughly the shape of an octagon and, Windy was willing to bet, corresponding in shape and size with the clean place on Mrs. Johnson's dressing table.

Which meant the mark at the first murder was not accidental. The killer had brought something with him to both places. Something he liked to have close by when he killed the women.

"Damn," Windy said, frustrated by not being able to figure out what the object was. She turned away from the void and kept going.

There was an immense quantity of blood trailing over the rose-trellis bedspread and puddling by the edge of the bed, which showed Windy where Mrs. Waters had been killed. There was also faint blood spatter on the ceiling, and a wavy line of spray against the wall. Three sets of footprints, one leading to the puddle, and two leading away, all appeared to have been made with the same shoes. Opening the closet from the bottom corner so she wouldn't disturb fingerprints on the knob if there were any, Windy shined her flashlight over the shoes neatly arranged in rows, stopping on a pair of formal black wingtips that Windy would have bet Dr. Waters had worn to his wedding and not since. The front of the left toe had a dark spot on it, a smudge. The killer had worn Dr. Waters's best shoes to kill his wife.

Shining her flashlight on the wicker laundry basket, she spotted a blue button-down shirt, slightly frayed at the collar, on the top of the pile of clothes. It was saturated with blood.

This time the killer had not only put on the father's shoes, but also his shirt. Was this just sound practice, so he would not have to walk around covered in telltale blood? Or was it part of the evolving ritual of control? Of feeling at home.

Windy stood in one place, looking around, thinking out loud, talking into the recorder. "Either before or after I changed into Dr. Waters's clothes—change into him?—I put packing tape on Mrs.

Waters's mouth." The coroner's report from the Johnson family had
turned up traces of adhesive around the mouths of all three victims,
adhesive that corresponded with clear packing tape. Windy expected the same would be found here, and was fairly sure that the
bloody outline of a butcher knife that had shown up next to each of
the Johnsons was made when the killer set the weapon down to remove the tape from their mouths. Most killers used duct tape, so
the selection of packing tape was notable. Windy wondered if the
killer liked it because it was clear, less noticeable. Or maybe just because it was easier to manage.

"I suspect it is when I am trying to tape her mouth that the
struggle ensues which knocks over the reading lamp. It stays that
way until after I have finished with her. Then I lay the knife on the
bed, leaving a bloody mark on the bedspread, remove the packing
tape, put the table and lamp back where they should be." Like the
empty place on the table, the mark on the bedspread would have to
be measured and photographed, compared with the one from the
Johnsons', but Windy felt fairly confident it would match. There
was no question in her mind that the Waters family had died by
the same hand as the Johnsons.

Which raised more questions than it answered. The two-
bedroom, one-bath apartment the Waters family lived in could have
fit into the Johnsons' pantry. Economics were not the only thing
that separated the two families: they lived in different parts of Las
Vegas, were different ages, had come from different states originally, were different races, and had different numbers of children. They were both being supported by the fathers in the family,
but each man did different work, one a doctor, one a banker. There
was no apparent point of similarity, no overlap. Ash would have
a dozen men combing through the minutiae of the lives of both
families looking for anything—a travel agent, a bath product, a piano teacher, a wrong turn—that could link them. So far they were
linked only by a well administered knife cut to the throat.

Windy followed the footprints out of the master bedroom, down the hallway, and toward the second bedroom, the one occupied by the twins, finding what she expected, two dark puddles, two knife prints on top of their Barney comforters. Four trails of blood from the room out to the living room, as though he had carried a body in each arm and a head in each hand. Very efficient.

"I'm not getting any good tread prints, a few partials, but mostly just this mess," Larry's voice, not happy, broke into her thoughts. He was pointing to three sheets of plastic attached to cut-up file folders and Windy was relieved to see he had remembered to use smooth paper. She had once had a case destroyed in court because someone in the evidence room had used a pizza box to store electromagnetic lifts of tire treads and the fibers from the cardboard had obliterated the tracks.

The sheets Larry pointed at each showed something that looked like an asterisk, as if an object had been dragged repeatedly and from different angles toward the center. "Do you want me to keep going?" he asked, daring her to waste his time with more busy work.

"Show me exactly where these came from," Windy said. Larry aimed a finger at the places and looked up, surprised, when she said, "Oh boy."

"Does this mean something to you?" he asked but she was gone. When she came back he had eight asterisks lined up next to the places he'd found them, and was taking measurements of the two shallow divots she had pointed out. She was carrying a chair from the kitchen.

"What are these?"

"Footmarks." She placed the chair over one of them. Its other three feet sat exactly on three of the places Larry had just lifted the star-shaped rubbings from, and it was clear from the other indentation and marks that another identical chair had been placed next to it. The star-shaped tracks Larry had lifted showed where someone had tried to rub out the indentations in the carpeting, like with a toe.

Larry was a little impressed. "Okay, so he brought two kitchen chairs into the living room," he said. "But why? So he could sit there and look at th—" He stopped to clear his throat rather than finishing.

"No. He wasn't sitting here," Windy said, looking at the chairs. "If it had been only one chair, that might have been the explanation but with two, and the depth of the indentations—no. There is a large mirror in the master bedroom. I think he carried it out here and propped it on the chairs."

"Why?"

"So he could sit there—" Windy pointed to the gap between the twins and Mrs. Waters on the bloody couch, the gap framed by Mrs. Waters's extended arm. "—and look at himself." Trying the family on for size, Windy thought, her mind going to Goldilocks and the three bears: one family too big, the other too small. Would he stop when he hit just right?

CHAPTER 17

Larry had his face under control when the rest of the crime scene team came in two minutes later. Ned Blight, seeming more composed than the others, probably because he had more experience, gave Windy a grim but deferential salute and said, "I was thinking I'd start in the kitchen." Windy nodded, got the rest of the team started on bagging the victims' hands and printing the doors. She asked Larry to do his own walk-through, to see if he came up with a different interpretation of the crime than she had, and went back to staring at the kitchen chair.

Unlike Larry, what struck her most was not the fact that the killer had wanted to sit among his victims and admire his handiwork, see how it felt. It was that he'd wanted to keep that a secret. He had replaced the chairs and the mirror to their original locations, and the asterisk-shaped scuff marks showed he'd tried to even out the carpeting again afterward. If he had not missed two of the divots, they would not have known to look for his voyeuristic moment. Usually when a killer posed bodies he did it to exert control over the reaction of the people who found them. But this killer appeared to have another agenda—one he wanted kept secret.

Which, theoretically, made it that much more valuable for the investigation.

Theoretically. In reality Windy had no idea what it meant.

How and What, not Why, she reminded herself. That is your job. "Why" was what gave you bad dreams and woke you up at night with goose bumps, feeling inadequate, asking, *Why did I have to push, Why*—

Leave Why to someone else.

But the question was twisting into her stomach when Larry came up to make his own report on the sequence of events. Understanding how the crime happened, the order in which killings took place, would help the criminalistics team more efficiently collect and work with the evidence. Windy had an idea but she knew that no matter how hard she tried to be scientific, her take on the scene would be subjective, so she always assigned someone else to work it out on their own. Chances were that neither of their theories were exactly right, but each of them might reveal holes in the other's.

Larry started with, "I got it down cold," setting Windy on edge right off. She had asked Larry to do it to punish herself for not liking his mannerisms, not giving him the benefit of the doubt, but he was making it hard. He said, "Our guy does the same thing here he did at the Johnson house, putting on Dr. Waters's shoes—the wear pattern matches the ones I picked up in the living room and there were fibers from the carpet on the soles, so he was wearing them when he rubbed those marks out. Anyway, he slips on the good doctor's wingtips, then makes the little girls lie on their stomachs on the bed and kills them, then does the mom the same way in her room."

"Why lie on their stomachs?"

"Those huge puddles of blood? The only way you could get those is if he makes the vics lie on their stomachs, pulls it so their necks are at the edge of the bed, and slashes down."

"That doesn't explain the blood on the ceiling. Or the blood on the front of their thighs."

"That's from being dragged through the puddle."

"Wouldn't they have blood on their calves then too? And did you find any drag marks?"

"No." Larry, getting defensive now, his color rising. "Okay, what do you think happened?"

"I think he made them kneel at the edge of the bed and killed them there, the knife coming up from underneath, propelling some of the blood onto the ceiling, while most of it drained down their fronts and on their thighs."

"If you already knew what you wanted to hear, why did you ask me to do this?"

"It's not what I want to hear. It's what happened."

"Sure. Okay, if they were kneeling, why isn't there any blood on their feet? You know, like on the backs of their feet? Wouldn't the blood fly there." He picked up Minette's foot, showing how pristine it was.

Windy said, "They were wearing socks," and pointed to an indented line just above the ankle of all three victims.

"I didn't find any bloody socks. Where are they?"

"I don't know. I guess he must have taken them with him."

"That doesn't make any sense."

"No, not yet," Windy agreed.

"And why did he make them kneel? What is that about? He would have had more leverage with them on the bed."

"Maybe he was letting them pray."

"You seem to have an answer for everything. I guess you don't need me."

Windy reminded herself that she was supposed to be a professional. She'd had to do that too many times today. "That's not true. How do you know he killed the children first? He killed the mother first at the Johnsons'."

Larry's confidence was back in a flash. "Maybe so, but here at the Waterses there were two children in one room. Tactically, he'd want to subdue them first, before heading out for his real target, the mother. I've been reading a book by this profiler guy, Kit Wilson? He talks about how these guys work, getting more violent every time they kill, you know, more like moving toward killing their mothers. All these guys have a thing about their mothers. So maybe, leaving her alive a little longer it, like, increased his thrill."

Great, Windy thought. Larry could not have picked a better way to antagonize her. She wasn't crazy about profilers in general, they tended to screw up crime scenes, but she'd worked with Kit Wilson at the FBI and thought he was a nincompoop. She'd even told him that to his face. She couldn't say that to Larry, though, so she settled for, "Is there any evidence to support this idea? And how did he keep Mrs. Waters from interfering while he killed her children?"

"Locked her in her bedroom." Larry looking triumphant now. "The key is missing."

"Do you know where *your* bedroom door key is? Most people don't. It's the first key to get lost in a house, particularly an old house, with old hardware. But let's say it was there, and Mrs. Waters was locked in. Wouldn't she have tried to break out? If a killer was roaming her house, with her kids, wouldn't she be fighting like crazy? Did you see any marks on the door? Kick marks? Pry marks?"

"Nothing like that. Maybe he tied her up."

"Is there any sign of that? Any bruising on her wrists?"

"He could have used something soft like a T-shirt. Or he could have threatened her."

"He could have. But did he? Let's focus on what we know. We know Mrs. Waters fought with the killer in her room because the lamp was knocked over, but there is no evidence she was held captive in there. And then there's the blood trail from her bedroom into the living room."

"What do you mean? There is no blood trail from the master bedroom into the living room." Larry smarmy now, the kid with all the answers at school.

"Exactly," Windy agreed. "No blood trail because she wasn't bleeding any more when she was moved. She was killed first and bled out on her bed. The side of the couch the twins were on is the really bloody part. Their bodies were moved when they were fresher."

"Okay," Larry said, not so confident now, but not giving up, especially, Windy surmised, because Ned Blight had just joined them. "So maybe she was killed first. So what?" Then, getting an idea. "Hey, there's no evidence that the girls tried to break out of their room either? Right? If he locked them in there, how come they didn't kick the walls? And—" really warming up now, "—they don't have signs of having been tied up or anything."

"I know," Windy said quietly. "I can't figure that out." Getting Cate to stay in her room quietly was an almost superhuman feat; achieving that with two six-year-olds would have required—she did not want to think about what it might have required. "What do you make of the Lysol?"

"What?"

"In the air. I'm pretty sure that's what it is, I'll know for sure when I get the results back from the lab of the air sample. I had an officer ask Dr. Waters and he didn't spray any. I think the killer did it."

"Why would he do that?"

"My best guess would be that he has or thinks he has a bodily odor that he is uncomfortable with. See if you can come up with anything. I'll be in the twins' room trying to figure out how he kept them subdued."

She heard Larry mutter "This is bullshit," as she walked away, probably purposely saying it loud enough to get a rise out of her, but she didn't pursue it. He might think of it as personal, but deep down she knew it wasn't. She had given him a hard job and he had to be frustrated.

There was a corkboard hanging on the back of the closet door in the girls' room, covered with thumbtacked pieces of paper, a fancy-looking certificate proclaiming that Minette had read a book by herself, another one, with a scratch and sniff sticker on it, praising Martine's tooth brushing skills, a few drawings. She was standing in front of it when she heard someone come in, and turned to see Ned.

"I hate working cases with dead kids," he said.

She nodded. "Did you find anything in the kitchen?"

Ned didn't answer right away, sucking on something in his cheek. "Sorry," he explained. "It's tobacco. I don't chew any more but I always have a plug when there are corpses around. Keeps the taste out of my mouth."

Windy knew what he meant. Crime scenes had smells, but they went away when you took a shower. Or two. There was a taste, though, that got into your mouth and stayed with you.

"Anyway," Ned said, "I didn't believe it at first. Spent the past hour in there looking around, another one convincing myself. After that, I've got no choice. There's not a sign of blood anywhere in the kitchen. Not a drop. According to the father, there's an Elvis lunch pail missing, but he's not even sure of the last time he saw it, it could have been months ago, and that's it for suspicious circumstances. We found the bread and the strawberry jam in the cupboard but the only prints on them were Mrs. Waters's. No smudges like at the Johnsons'. No blood. Nothing. As I see it, there are two possibilities." Ned held up two fingers. "Either he cleaned up too good for us this time. Or he's started skipping meals."

The third option occurred to Windy ten minutes later.

CHAPTER 18

Ash had just come through the door to see if the bodies were ready for the medical examiner's people to take them away for autopsy when he heard a noise in front of him and saw Windy leaning over the part of the couch where the twins' bodies were. The noise was something between a gasp and a groan.

"What did you find?" Ash asked.

Windy swung around, startled, and very pale. She said, "There are crumbs on the back of Martine's nightgown."

Ash frowned, understanding only that this was somehow horrible, but not why.

Windy took two breaths. "There was no blood in the kitchen this time," she began, her voice almost steady, "so we thought, maybe, he had decided against a family breakfast. But then I had an idea." She moved toward the kitchen.

Ash followed her in, saw her opening the refrigerator. "What are you doing?"

"Checking the jam. The strawberry jam was in the cupboard with the bread. They both had Mrs. Waters's prints on them."

"Of course. I mean, she lived here."

"Fresh ones. On top. The twins made Dr. Waters his sandwiches when he worked late and then chose a lunch pail for him from the collection under the sink. He worked late today. Yesterday. Whenever." Windy shook her head with impatience as she lifted a bag of Nature's Best 100% Whole Wheat Bread from the cupboard and laid it on the counter.

"Mrs. Waters's prints," Ash was repeating as she unscrewed the top of the jam jar. "Do you think he used her hands, after he'd killed her, to—" he started to say, then stopped. *Next time it will be worse.* He said, "He had breakfast with them when they were still alive."

Windy nodded. "It was the strawberry jam in the cupboard that tipped me off. It should have been in the refrigerator. The Waters family, like most people, keep all their jam in the refrigerator. Its being in the cupboard could show whoever put it there was distracted." She stared at the loaf of bread. "But by keeping them alive, it ups the ante. He dominates even more by making his victim, making Mrs. Waters, *serve* him breakfast. Watch him eat it."

Ash took a deep breath and let it out, thinking. "Does that mean he knew them? I mean, how else would he get Mrs. Waters to do that without calling for help?"

"Yes and no. He had insurance. The girls." Ash looked puzzled so Windy explained, "I think he held Martine on his lap while he ate."

"Those crumbs." Ash spoke the word as if it were toxic. "Those crumbs on her back are from him holding her on his lap. That was how he controlled Mrs. Waters—'Do what I say or I'll hurt your daughter.' "

"Or some variation on that theme," Windy agreed, clearly hating it. "I bet he included that old favorite, 'If you follow orders you'll get out of this alive.' "

"Murder in the bedroom, breakfast in the kitchen. It's as if he's trying to create some kind of ideal domestic scene."

"But is it one he lived, or one he aspired to?"

"We'll have to ask him once we have him in custody." Ash looked around the immaculate kitchen. "So he has breakfast again, and again tries to erase all the traces. Maybe keeping them alive was just his way of becoming more efficient. Not escalating so much as trying to stay tidy."

"Maybe, but it doesn't seem like part of his script."

"Script?"

"Script is probably the wrong word. More like a set of rules he has for himself, the things he needs to do to feel fulfilled at the crime. Things beyond or not necessary to the killing. Some profilers call it a signature. He makes no effort at all to hide the killings, where he did them, how. But his rituals, he tries to get rid of the evidence."

"Rituals? Plural?"

"Breakfast and posing with the bodies. Yes," she said to Ash's surprised expression, "he did it here too. He moved the mirror from the Waterses' bedroom, propped it on some chairs opposite the living room couch, so he could sit there with the girls and Mrs. Waters and look at himself. Then he tried to conceal he had done it."

"Did he base the Waterses' postures on a photograph the way he did at the Johnsons'?" Ash asked, not sure he wanted the answer.

Windy's expression told him he didn't. She said, "Not exactly," and walked out of the kitchen to the twins' room where she pulled an eleven-by-seventeen-inch piece of white paper off the wall and handed it to him.

Ash took the paper, immediately wanting to hand it back. It was a crayon drawing of the Waters family on vacation. You could tell it was vacation because the two girls occupied the left corner, standing next to each other, holding hands, with their free arms looped around the heads of Mickey Mouse and Goofy. The characters had been painstakingly traced and colored inside the lines. Dr. Waters, more free-form, sat in the center of the drawing at a picnic bench, wearing a hat with mouse ears on it, waving. His wife sat next to him, her arm extended around his shoulders, her legs crossed. In the background a big flag proclaimed WELCOME TO DISNEYLAND, in carefully copied letters. The same hand but with more confidence had written BY MINETTE across the bottom. The poses were the same as those of the corpses, right down to the space left for dad.

"They were going to Disneyland over Christmas," Windy told Ash conversationally in a voice that only wobbled slightly. "For the twins' birthdays. They were going to be seven. He sat exactly where Dr. Waters sat."

Ash matched her tone. "Do you think he took the head because it didn't fit with his artistic vision? There isn't really a place for it in the drawing."

"Could be, or maybe he did something to it he didn't want us to know about. Although with this killer, I would not be surprised if he took it simply because he felt like it."

"That would have been hard to get out of here, though. Sort of a big risk for an impulse. It's one thing to get invited in, another to walk down the street carrying a bleeding head."

Windy remembered what Ned had told her about the kitchen, the one anomaly there. "Not necessarily. I think he took it out in an Elvis lunch pail. Just like Dr. Waters going off to work."

Their eyes met, and Ash said what she had been thinking. "He is escalating."

"Yes," Windy agreed. In the silence between them the other half of that message hung unspoken: *Unless we find him, the next time will be worse.*

CHAPTER 19

It was past four in the afternoon when Windy and Ash stepped out of the autopsy room and back into the bright sunlight.

"At least that went pretty fast," Ash said, sounding as weary as Windy felt.

"No surprises," Windy agreed.

"Thanks to you. Otherwise I think we all would have been staring gape-mouthed when we realized that the victims had eaten toast and jam only minutes before they were killed."

"I only knew he had breakfast when they were alive, not that he made them eat too. I think our killer is using food as a mechanism for control, an expression of power, the same way others use sexual violation. Someone with significant food issues."

"A killer with a weight problem. That'll narrow it down to most of America."

"At least the estimated time of death, eleven P.M. to three A.M., helps explain how no one saw him come or go."

"True," Ash said. "The street is probably pretty quiet then."

"Still, he's got to be the most innocuous looking man in the world. A woman alone with just her kids at night is not likely to open the door to a strange man."

"Unless he looks official."

"You're thinking someone with a badge? A cop?"

"I'm considering it. Or someone pretending to be one. It would be easy for a police or security officer to ask information about someone's schedule too."

"The truth is, for all we know at this point, it could be anyone." Feeling frustrated, Windy looked around the plaza in front of the medical examiner's building. This was her first time here, her first autopsy on the new job. She noticed that just down the street was a convenience store. A purple van painted with some kind of glitter paint so it gleamed in the sun was parked in front of the store, and she found herself smiling at the thought of how much Cate, whose favorite color was "sparkle" and who asked daily why they had to have such a boring red car, would have liked it.

Purple had been Minette Waters's favorite color, Windy knew, while green was Martine's. She had found these things noted carefully on a chart on the corkboard in their bedroom. She stopped smiling. Standing here on this beautiful evening, the kind of evening when those two little girls should have been out playing, it was impossible for her to forget that they ate their sandwiches on the same kind of bread Cate did, that they had the same kind of awkward writing, that they had been about a month older than Cate. That they could have been her friends. Her schoolmates. That it could have been her.

Except Cate didn't have a dad any more.

During the autopsy, the medical examiner had said that the cut on Claudia's throat was sloppier than the others, as though the killer had struck twice. She might have been alive for as much as twenty seconds, bleeding, before she lost consciousness. Twenty seconds knowing a madman was in your house with your children, that you could not protect them, that they might suffer too. The twenty longest seconds in the world.

"I bet those shoes could take you anywhere you want to go, but would you like a ride home?" Ash asked, cutting into her thoughts.

"I should go back to the office."

"There isn't anything for you to do there right now. The lab said they won't have any results for hours. Unless you were looking forward to staring at the wallpaper. Yours is nicer than mine."

Windy hesitated. Then she pictured Cate, being able to hug Cate even once and said, "A ride home would be great." Ash was right, she could go to the office later, if the lab found anything important. "Would you mind if I ran over to the convenience store first?"

"I'll pick you up there."

By the time Ash pulled up, Windy was standing by the curb waving her hands excitedly. She got into the car and said, "Surveillance cameras."

"What?"

She pointed at the corners of the building they were in front of. "All convenience stores have surveillance cameras. There's a store like this at the end of the Waterses' block. I was thinking—"

"They only have cameras inside, not outside," Ash interrupted. "We checked. But the pawn shop across the street has cameras that cover the front curb. I had Jonah pick up their tapes this afternoon."

"Sorry." Windy was blushing now. "I should let you do your job. I feel like an idiot."

"Nothing to apologize for." Not with the way she looked when she blushed, he thought, wondering in the next moment who had taken his brain and replaced it with that of a fourteen-year-old boy.

An even happier fourteen-year-old boy when she said, "This is a really cool car." She fastened her seat belt and then held out two small envelopes to him. "Let me make it up to you."

He glanced at them. "Pop Rocks?"

"The only way to get the taste of a crime scene out of your mouth." Her voice was muffled. Ash saw why when she smiled and her teeth were purple. "I gave you the cherry ones. Those are best but they only had one pack. The other one is grape."

"Thanks," Ash said, not convincingly.

"I swear they will help. Try them."

He poured some of the red crystals into his hand, and tasted them.

"They are better straight from the package. Just so you know. For next time."

"Sure," he said, still skeptical, but he dumped a few more into his mouth, straight.

"See?"

"Oh yeah. Much better."

"Come on. They're good."

They were. They were odd and refreshing and vaguely addictive and they made him smile despite himself, despite a monstrous investigation and a harrowing day.

He looked over at Windy in the seat next to his, watching for his reaction with great interest.

Yeah, right, it was the candy.

"Need more evidence," he said, ingesting the rest of the envelope into his mouth.

"Good thing I got you two packs."

The drive to her house took less time than he expected. Even more unexpected was her saying, "Do you want to come in?" and him saying, "Yes."

But Ash got his biggest surprise when the door of the house opened before they reached it and a blur shot toward Windy singing "Mommmmmmmmmmmmmmmmy!"

He should have guessed at the existence of a child, but he hadn't, and as he watched Windy hug the blur he was struck by the intense intimacy, by the strength of their bond. He felt awkward, in the way. But he did not want to leave.

"Did you catch any bad guys today, Mommy?" the tan little girl with her mother's gold hair and someone else's big blue eyes asked.

"Not today, honey."

"What about bad girls?"

"None of them either." Windy looked at Ash and explained, "We believe in equal opportunity criminals." She put the girl down and said, "Cate, this is Ash Laughton. He works with me. He is a detective."

"My name is Cate Thomas Kirkland and it is a pleasure to meet you, sir," Cate said with formality unexpected from someone with baggy overalls, a dinosaur T-shirt, and cat whiskers painted on her face.

"It's a pleasure to meet you too," Ash told her, equally formal.

Cate looked up at her mom. "Did I do it right?" When Windy nodded, Cate said, "Is he your friend?"

Ash smiled. "I hope so."

"Okay. That is good," Cate told him. "Because Mom doesn't have any friends besides me and Brandon and Bill. I have fifteen, but one of them is invisible. Bill says that means she doesn't count but Brandon says it's okay. She has a mouth on her, that's what Brandon says, that's why he calls her Princess Pert. Do you want to meet her? She's outside playing soccer."

"Soccer? Do you play?" Ash asked.

"I'm not very good," Cate confessed. "I can't kick right."

"I bet I can help you. I played soccer in college and sometimes I help my friend coach his teams. One of them is called the Lady Luck's. Have you heard of them?"

"The Lady Lucks," Cate whispered in a tone of awe.

"Who is that?" Windy asked.

"Oh brother, Mommy. They're only the best team in my league." Cate turned from her hideously uncool mom back to Ash. "You coach them?"

Cate was looking at him now with the kind of admiration he thought was reserved for pop stars. "Well, only now and then." When Cate's admiration did not dim, Ash stopped feeling in the way. "I've learned a lot watching Carter. I'd be happy to help you with your kick if you want."

"You don't have—" Windy started to say to Ash, interrupted by her cell phone ringing. It wouldn't have mattered anyway, she realized, watching Cate take his hand and drag him through the house to the backyard.

"Windy? What a relief," Bill's voice said when she answered. "Where have you been all day? Why haven't you returned my calls?"

"I'm so glad it's you." Windy followed Ash and Cate inside as she spoke, moving to the kitchen so she could see what they were doing and make sure Ash did not start to look too bored. She could spend endless hours fascinated by Cate, but she was partial. "I haven't been able to get near a phone before now. It's been crazy." She tried to change the subject. "How was your day?" She picked up a sponge and began cleaning invisible dirt from the fronts of the cabinets Brandon had painted two weeks before.

"Oh, it was great. I called my fiancée at her office and was told that she was at a crime scene. Then I called her cell phone and got no answer. For six hours."

Windy dropped the sponge. "I'm sorry. The killer I was working on this weekend? He struck again. He killed two little girls Cate's age. Two six-year-old twins. I had to go to the crime scene. I had to work on it." She realized she was babbling and stopped. "I'm really really sorry."

There was a long silence.

"Bill? Are you there?"

"I'm here." He sounded resigned. "So you were in the field. Did it go well?"

"I don't know. We won't have the lab results for a while."

Brandon came in, waved to her, frowned when he saw her face, and headed out to join Ash and Cate, who were laughing in the backyard. She couldn't blame him. She would have picked them over herself, too.

She turned away from the window as Bill said, "Do you know how worried I have been about you all day? When they told me you were in the field and then I couldn't get ahold of you? Do you know what I did? I called the damn hospitals."

"Oh, no." She put her hand over her eyes and leaned against the sink.

"What am I supposed to think? After the last time——"

"That was eight months ago, in a whole other state, and it was a fluke. I just went back to the crime scene for a minute, the man came out of nowhere. And in the end I was fine."

"You weren't fine when they found you. Remember? Your chest was sliced open and you'd lost so much blood that——"

"Oh brother," she said, not able to hold back her frustration now. Wanting to be outside. Wanting to be anywhere but here, talking about anything but this. Not wanting to remember. "Why do you have to keep bringing that up? I'm fine now. Completely recovered. I learned from it. I won't work a crime scene alone again. Ever. And nothing happened today. The place was swarming with cops. I was completely safe. Why can't you trust me to know what is safe and what isn't?"

"Why are you yelling at me for caring about you?"

It was an excellent question, and it stopped her cold. She searched the ceiling for the right words and said, finally, "Because I'm upset at myself for letting you down. Because I feel so bad for having made you worry. Because I'm furious at myself for breaking my promise to you. Because saying 'I'm sorry' doesn't seem adequate and I don't know what else to say. Take your pick."

She heard a low rumble, Bill laughing, and relaxed. He said, "I'll take one of each. And I accept your apology. I just want to take care of you and protect you, and when you disappear like that . . ." His voice got softer. "I just want to know where you are."

For an instant Windy wanted to ask him why he didn't strap a surveillance camera on her, but managed to stop herself before the words were out. He was doing this because he loved her, and her reaction was to recoil. At times like these she was amazed at her own incompetence to handle things other people thought were easy, like relationships. No matter how hard she tried, she seemed to do the wrong thing. Except with dead people. Probably because they did not expect anything of her.

But Bill did and he had every right to. She said, "I'm here and I'm safe and I've already told you far too much about my day. Now tell me about yours."

As she listened to Bill describing a meeting he'd had filling in the man who would be replacing him when he took his new position in Vegas, how well it had gone, she stared out the window at the backyard, where Ash was giving Cate some earnest-faced coaching while Brandon stood on the sidelines. She watched Cate kick and miss the goal, kick and miss again. Each time Windy felt her daughter's frustration and was proud of her undauntability.

Ash's encouragement didn't hurt, she knew. He demonstrated the kick and missed the goal. On purpose, Windy thought, and was sure when she saw Cate march over to him, hands on her hips. Cate saying, "You said to do it this way and you did it the other way," explaining to him what he did wrong. Ash nodding, taking her criticism seriously, saying, "Show me." Windy watched as Cate positioned the ball, headed toward it, kicked—and made a perfect goal. She did it twice more. Brandon and Ash high-fived each other front and back, and Windy couldn't stop herself from laughing.

"What was that?" Bill asked, interrupted.

"Sorry. Cate just kicked three perfect goals in a row. Outside in the yard."

"That's wonderful—" she thought Bill said but the rest was drowned out by Cate, riding on Ash's shoulders, reentering the kitchen triumphant.

"Did you see, Mommy?" she squealed.

"Yes, honey."

"Is that Bill? Can I tell him?" Ash dipped down so Cate could reach the phone, then winced as she shouted, "Bill, guess what! Oh, she told you. But did she tell you I scored a million zillion points? Yes a million zillion. What? You are right, in a real game it would only have been three points. But we were playing with different rules. And Ash says I am going to blow them out of the water at the game on Saturday. Ash? He's my friend. And Mom's friend from work. Okay, bye."

For a split second after Windy hung up the phone, Ash caught himself hoping that Bill was jealous as hell knowing he was there. Then he reminded himself that there was no reason for Bill to feel jealous. Bill belonged here. This was his family. His house. His life. His ideal domestic scene.

It was time to go.

Ash looked down and saw that Cate had slipped her hand into his. She said, "What are we having for dinner, Mom?"

"I thought we could have spaghetti and meatballs. But only if you shape the meatballs the way *you* like them, since I did them wrong the last time."

"You put smiles on them. That's gross."

"It turns out I'm sort of out of touch with what is gross," Windy confided to him.

"How about if Ash helps me?" Cate asked.

Windy was looking at him now. "What do you say? Would you join us for dinner? Cate is a perfectionist about her meatballs but I bet she could teach you."

The temptation to stay, to have dinner with this happy family, tugged on Ash like the centrifugal force on a roller coaster and made his stomach feel the same way. He could picture them eating spaghetti here in the kitchen with the yellow-and-white striped cabinets with purple jewel handles, the calendar on the refrigerator with sparkly pony stickers on the Saturdays and Tuesdays that Cate had games, could see them sitting at the light blue table and chairs with the placemats like big pink flowers, could picture it almost too clearly. But there was no place for him here. He made himself shake his head apologetically. Made himself say: "I can't stay. Sorry." It was true. He could not stay.

Cate let go of his hand and gazed at him, showing signs of disappointment no adult would allow herself. "You can't? For real?"

He reminded himself that he was opposed to family dinners on principal. Wouldn't even know how to act. "Unfortunately, I've got to be somewhere."

Cate's expression changed then, her eyes widening, head nodding. "Are you taming someone?"

"Taming?"

"We are reading *The Little Prince*," Windy explained. "To tame—"

"Means to establish ties," Cate quoted. "It is like making friends with someone. So that, when you see something that reminds you of them, like a golden wheat field reminding you that their hair is gold, or the sky reminding you of their eyes being blue, that makes you happy."

"I see."

"And the way you tame people," Cate went on, "is by coming to see them every day and sitting a little closer to them, so they can look forward to it. That is called observing proper rites."

"Observing proper rites," Ash repeated. "What happens next?"

"I don't know. That is as far as we've gotten. I could read it by myself but this way we can talk about it. Mommy promised we would read more last night but—"

"You fell asleep," Windy put in.

"I was just pretending," Cate protested, rolling her eyes at Windy's gullibility. Then she looked at Ash, putting her hands on her hips. "But if you are taming someone you should go. Mom says it's always important to be on time and extra important when you are taming someone. They prefer it."

"Yes," Ash agreed, "I think they do."

"I hope you can come back for dinner another time."

"We'll see."

"We can't promise such fancy literary conversation every time," Windy said, "but Cate's friends are always welcome."

"He was your friend first," Cate pointed out.

"So he was."

At the door, Ash bent for a hug from Cate and wished her luck in her game on Saturday, then said to Windy, "You did great work today."

"You too."

He sensed her hesitating. "What is it?"

"If you find anything on the tapes from the pawn shop—"

"Of course. You're my first call."

"What's a pawn shop?" Cate interjected.

Windy said, "It's a place where people sell things they don't want any more."

"Can I sell my toothbrush?"

"No."

"Can I sell—"

"Why don't we talk about this while we make the meatballs, honey? Ash needs to go." She was resting her hand on Cate's head, and he watched her look down, brushing the hair back with a gesture that was at once tender and fierce. Maternal. She said to him, "You'd better escape while you have the chance."

Having no idea how true that was. It took all his willpower to walk to the curb and get in his car. He let himself take one last glimpse of them standing in the open doorway of their house, waving good-bye. Windy barefoot now, smiling at him, then turning to Cate, who was making a face up at her. Windy sticking her fingers in her mouth and goggling out her eyes to make a face back. The two of them, mother and daughter, erupting into peals of laughter.

Go, he told himself. *Before you are truly lost.*

Still, he had to floor it to make himself leave.

CHAPTER 20

Sitting on his couch in his house staring at a white wall and feeling more out of place than he had at Windy's, Ash reached into his pocket to see what was poking him. He came out with his toothpick and the other package of Pop Rocks. He'd just poured the whole thing into his mouth, thinking that Windy was right, the cherry ones were better, when the phone rang.

"Ash Laughton."

"Are you okay?" Jonah's voice was unsure. "You sound weird."

Gulping Pop Rocks, Ash learned, didn't feel that great. "I'm fine. What's going on?"

"I was wondering if you'd had a chance to look at the tapes from the pawn shop."

"Not yet, why?"

"I just got a call from the guys doing the nighttime canvass in the Waterses' neighborhood. They got another sighting of a green car, like at the Johnson house? This time parked outside the Waterses' house. Two days before the killing."

"Is there any reason to think it was not just a random person parking his car there?"

"It sat there for more than an hour. And one of them thinks he'd seen it the week before. But that's not all."

"They got the license number? They can identify the car?"

"It's a hatchback was about all they could offer. They were a bit distracted, apparently. These two, Gregory and Ed, they are philosophers, spend their nights hanging out outside the pawn shop. When our man talked to them this evening he was interrupting a conversation about how America faked the moon landing."

"Ah. Do we have enough to put out an APB on the car? Can they describe it at all?"

"Foreign looking. But that doesn't matter. We don't need to. Because we have a leak."

Ash leaned forward on the couch. "What are you talking about?"

"I just got a call from channel three asking for confirmation that we are looking for a green car in the Home Wrecker decapitation murders."

"The Home Wrecker? They gave the killer a name?"

"Can't sell news without a catchy headline."

"What did you say?"

"No comment, but that's not going to stop them. They want to 'help' us by mentioning it on the air, to generate calls. It's all over the radio too."

"That'll be a huge help. To the murderer, in case he wasn't sure we were looking for him. This will put his mind at rest. He's probably making rental car plans right now. Damn." Ash stared at the wall for a moment, thinking. "Do you have any idea where they got the information?"

"No. Channel three made it sound like it came from the mayor's office, but I talked to them and they are denying it. More convincingly than usual. Gerald pointed out that having a named serial killer always reduces tourism by at least 3 percent."

"Well, it's nice to know the mayor's heart is in the right place. The Home Wrecker. Great name, too. I wonder how the killer likes it."

"You think we're dealing with a publicity hound?" Jonah asked.

"Given the way he stages the crime scenes, the kind of control he exerts there, it wouldn't surprise me if he didn't enjoy feeling in control of the media too. I only hope he doesn't perform for them."

"Are you still going to go over the pawn shop tapes? Now that the green car probably won't lead anywhere?"

"It beats whatever is on TV."

"Need help?"

"No, I've got it covered."

Ash had made it through three of the tapes from the pawn shop and eaten his way through four of the six leftover take-out containers in his refrigerator when he spotted something interesting. He rewound past it and watched it in slow motion.

He said, "Oh yes," aloud without realizing it, and knew his pulse rate had jumped. He didn't know which excited him more, the discovery or the thought of what he was going to get to spend the rest of the night doing.

He checked his wallet to make sure he had a wad of cash, then flipped open the yellow pages. He found what he wanted right away: Charlene's Massage Parlor and Internet Café, Open 24 Hours.

CHAPTER 21

When she'd stubbed out her cigarette in the overflowing ashtray on her coffee table and decided to go for a drive, Eve Sebastian had only planned to be gone for a little while. But once the car started it kept on going, like it was driving itself, until it ended up here. Four hours earlier, the car—not her—had eased to a stop across the street from the house she had been avoiding. The one house she didn't think she was ready to face yet. The next house on the list.

As evening turned to night she'd watched the shadows on the house grow longer and longer until they were darkness. The streetlights flickered on, the street got busier, people came home from work, a girl Rollerbladed behind a German shepherd, and she sat there. At one point the parking spaces in front and in back of her began filling up with SUVs and imported sedans driven by women about her age. They slid out of their cars, some in trim business suits and scarves, others in pants and pearls and sweater sets, but even in their different clothes, they all looked the same to her. Confident. Sure of themselves. Sure of their lives. They had thumbnail-sized diamonds on their engagement rings and wallets bursting with photos of smiling children. They waved at one another and hugged, right outside her window, and then marched smugly up the front stairs of the house next to the one she was watching, shiny shopping bags with cartoon animals and premade bows in one hand, foil covered plates in the other. She noticed that there were pink and blue balloons tied to the doorknob and it all clicked into place. A baby shower.

She lit another cigarette.

She had always thought that one day she would have a baby shower. More than one. She'd wanted a house filled with kids, a husband who came home and yelled, "Honey, it's me." Family dinners with everyone together. Occasional nights out on the town, just her and her husband, talking about how the children were doing in school, not really having much to say to one another, but comfortable, happy. She used to love to baby-sit when she was younger, first to play with the kids, then, when they were asleep, to explore the lives of grown-ups. She went through drawers and cabinets, stared forever at their family photos, the ones in frames, the ones in albums, the ones that were shoved in the back of the pen drawer, trying to guess what made some worthy of display and not others. Were the photos really there for strangers, or for the family to reaffirm that it belonged together? She would try to imagine what it was like when they were all gathered around the breakfast table in the morning, what they said, where everyone sat. Trying on the lives of all the families by herself, in the strange, quiet houses.

On the radio, the Hits from High School Hour started up on the eighties station and Madonna's voice came on singing "Like a Virgin," making Eve remember Victor Early. Victor, the reason she stopped baby-sitting, stopped playing "happy family." Victor with his wide chest covered in curly hair, the thick gold chain he wore around his neck, the diamond horse's head on his pointer finger.

Madonna had been playing on the tape deck in her bedroom that afternoon when the doorbell rang and she opened it to see a middle-aged friend of her father's. She had been not quite fifteen at the time, so it was twenty years ago, but she still remembered what he was wearing, a burgundy silk shirt unbuttoned to mid-chest, black pants.

He smiled at her and held out a hand. "Hi, I'm Victor. A friend of your father's? I saw you when you came with your mom to the casino to pick him up last week."

She hadn't known what to say. The experience had been mortifying. Her mother storming across the floor to the blackjack tables, then screaming at her father. "Where have you been? You have got to come home. I am so tired of being left alone like this."

Eve had stood off to the side, pretending not to be with them, chin up, looking around. Trying to seem like one of the models from a fashion magazine, the kind that could be standing in the middle of a Chinese fish market but look untouched in whatever white linen outfit they were modeling.

"My father's not home," she'd told Victor.

"I know. I just saw him at the tables. That's why I thought I'd stop by. Can I come in?"

She had shrugged and opened the door. As she led him into the living room she tugged her cutoffs down and let her hips go side to side. She'd known right away what he'd come to say, even though it took him ten minutes to get around to it. Knowing allowed her to have power. She sat down on the sofa and stretched her legs out, letting the strap of her tank top fall down. "What did you want, Victor?"

He looked at her in a way no one ever had, a way she'd longed for. Like she made him hungry. "Well, it's about your dad. He's having problems with money. A bunch of the guys and I offered to lend it to him, but you know how he is."

She did. She loved how proud her father was. She tried to sound mature. "Go on."

"Well, I was thinking, maybe you'd want to help out. How would you like to earn some money on the side?"

He started off saying a hundred dollars for a blow job, but she knew she could get more. In the end they settled on five hundred dollars for the works, ten times what she'd make baby-sitting in a week. They did it right in her room, on her twin mattress with the princess canopy. She liked Victor, liked his bald head and the grayish hair that curled on his back. The cologne he wore was the same as her father's. And it only took him five minutes to come.

"I'll call you," he said, still with admiration in his eyes afterward, and she believed him. Hoped so when she saw the look on her father's face as she handed him the cash.

"Where did you get this?" her father had asked, beaming. Not suspicious.

"I got a new job."

"For me? You did this for me? Oh baby, you are the best daughter in the world. My Eve is such a good girl."

She never forgot how tight he hugged her that night, how he kissed her on the top of her head before he left, looking at the money clutched in his hand and smiling. Never wondering how a baby-sitter could make fifteen hundred dollars a week. She knew he'd think about her the whole time he was gone.

In the car Eve lit a cigarette and Madonna promised to give all her love, because only love lasts.

Victor liked to listen to the Madonna song while they did it, turning it up loud, calling her his little virgin. She remembered one night when he told her to leave her school uniform on, especially her lace-trimmed anklets. Just looking at them could make him hard, he said. And then he'd said he loved her. Wished he could be with her, not his wife. She had let him do it without a condom on that night. It was only a little after seven, light outside, warm, and they had the window open. Victor with sweat sliding down his chest, his face ridged in profile, eyes closed, crushing her tiny breasts underneath him. He grunted into her, one two three, hard, like always, then, not like always, shouted out her name.

They hadn't heard the car pull into the driveway, her mother coming home from a lesson early, but they heard the footsteps and then the pounding on the door. Her mother screaming now, "What the hell is going on in there? Open this door, you little slut, before I break it down."

Victor dancing around, out of breath, trying to pull up his pants, pull on his undershirt, grab his silk button-down, throw his Italian loafers out the window, throw himself after them. Finally her mother banged so hard the door slammed open, just as Victor disappeared over the ledge. Thinking of him running down the street holding his pants up made her laugh, even as her mother stormed in, screaming at her, "You slut, you stupid bitch having boys in your room."

Boys. That made Eve laugh harder. Who needed boys? She had men who loved her.

Then her mother's hand went for that box. The special music box her father had given her. The one where she kept all her money.

She'd flown across the room and gotten her hand around her mother's wrist. "I hate you. Let go right now or I'll tell Daddy."

It had worked, her mother backing off, closing the door and locking it from the outside. She had waited all night with her school uniform on thinking Victor might come back, elbows resting on the windowsill, taking a drag of one of Victor's menthol cigarettes and blowing it out slowly. Bringing the lit tip to her forearm and holding it. She had to strain to hear the sound of her skin burning over the sound of Madonna's voice singing "Like a Virgin" from the tape player. Staring at herself in the mirror, flat chested, flat hair, wishing her daddy would come home, wishing Victor would come back for her in his big Cadillac with the burgundy velour seats. Finally picking up the jewelry box her father had given her for her seventh birthday, given it to her with the #1 DAUGHTER necklace inside. Her most prized possession. Throwing the box at the mirror, right at the center, watching it crack.

The next day she had found a yellow rose on the windowsill with a note on it that said, "I hope you feel better. Your friend, Harry."

She'd had to search her mind before realizing that Harry was the boy who lived next door to her, in the house on the corner. He must have heard her fighting with her mom, seen her upset. In fact, God knew what he had seen. She knew she should be embarrassed, but instead, gazing at the flower, thinking someone cared about her at all made her cry. She had peered out the window looking for him that day to say thank you, but she did not see him. When the flower dried out, she put it in the jewelry box with her money and her other prized possessions and forgot all about it. At least until four months earlier, at the opening party for her restaurant.

It had been a mad scene, and she had used an entire bottle of waterless antibacterial lotion, applying it after every time someone hugged her, just trying to stay clean. Unable to take it, she'd ducked outside and stood next to a tree, smoking a cigarette and looking into the restaurant, her restaurant, at all the people inside claiming to love her. She kept wishing Trish had come in from L.A. for it. Kept wishing for her dad.

"Ms. Sebastian?"

She looked up to see this man, gorgeous, standing next to her. He said, "I won't ask you to shake, it seems like you've had to do enough touching for one night," and she could have fallen in love with him there.

But it got better. He cleared his throat and said, "You probably don't remember me. I lived next door to you for a few years when you were growing up. On Cottonwood Avenue? Harry?"

"The boy who gave me a yellow rose." She stared at him, trying to match the pimply face of that fat boy to the stranger here.

"You do remember."

"I still have it. It was the first flower anyone ever gave me." And there hadn't been that many since then, she thought.

He smiled and looked more like the boy again, but still hand-some. Handsome and happy.

The next day her partners in the restaurant and the manager, Norton, demanded to know what had happened to her. She'd disap-peared in the middle of the party. Was she sick?

Yes, she said, not sorry about the lie. She wasn't about to tell them that she'd left with Harry. That they had gone to ride a roller coaster—a roller coaster!—because she'd said she needed to clear her head. And then he'd taken her home and left her at her door like a gentleman. She had hugged herself with joy that night as she fell asleep in her flannel nightgown, remembering the way he'd held her hand during the roller coaster ride. The way he had kissed her on the lips gently at the door and promised, "I'll call you tomorrow."

And he had. Called her and said, "I wasn't going to. I was going to make you wait, wonder how I felt about you, because I know that's supposed to be good for relationships. But I couldn't. I have to see you again tonight."

For three months it was like a fairy tale. They spoke every day, saw each other every night. She had been determined to do every-thing right this time, follow all the rules, be a good girl. She hadn't even slept with Harry until their one month anniversary. He knew that she'd had a difficult childhood, and he wanted to help her for-get that. He was an expert at dealing with bad memories, he told her. That was why he had dropped his stepfather's last name and re-placed it with his real father's. A name he was willing to share with her if she would do him the honor of becoming his bride.

He'd said it like that, old-fashioned, and she had thrown herself on him, trusting him in a way she'd never trusted anyone. Marriage, family, "Honey, it's me,"—all of it in her grasp.

"Just put whatever happened behind you and move on," he said. "Don't dwell on it. Don't go to the places that make you think of your father. Be with me, here."

She had tried so hard, but the pull of the past was too strong.

She had started forgetting to call Harry sometimes because she was sitting outside the houses, the ones that held all her memories. She had nothing else.

She could still see Harry's lips moving as he told her it was over. "This is taking over your life," he said that day in his office. "There isn't room for me. You have too many issues to work through."

She knew what he was really saying. He was saying that he couldn't love her. That no one could.

Eve wondered if Harry was listening to Hits from High School now, wherever he was. It was their favorite radio show, and he'd once dedicated a song to her on it, "Cheeseburger in Paradise," calling her his cheeseburger because she could be so silly.

She had her fingertips on the knife case when a knock on the window of her car made her jump. Looking over, she saw a woman in a sweater set standing there, smiling and motioning that she had something to say.

Eve pushed the button to lower the window, letting out a cloud of cigarette smoke that made the woman laugh. "On a bit of a health kick?"

"Yes."

"I just wanted to tell you that we're about to start opening the presents. So you might want to come inside and cheer the new mommy on."

Eve stared at the woman, uncomprehending.

"Aren't you a friend of Kelly's? Here for her baby shower?" the woman asked. She pointed at the house next to the one Eve had grown up in. "Kelly O'Connell."

"No. I'm waiting for my friend Harry to get home. He lives next door."

The woman put a hand up to her mouth. "Oh my. I'm so sorry. When I saw you sitting out here I just figured you were shy and—well, my mistake. You know, there's plenty of cake to go around inside if you want to join us."

"Thanks, but I am on a diet."

The woman smiled again and said, "Well, if you change your mind," and went back inside to rejoin the others.

The curtains were not closed all the way and Eve caught occasional glimpses of women leaning forward to laugh out loud, or of their lips making o's of appreciation for whatever gift Kelly was unwrapping. Some of them happily eating lemon squares and cookies with cherry jam in the middle, not worrying about the calories. She pictured how she must look to them, sitting all alone in a car filled with smoke, one of the sad single women they read about in magazine articles.

Part of her hated all of them with their perfect hair and wedding bands and husbands who reached for them in the middle of the night. But she knew it wasn't really hate, it was envy. She especially envied Kelly at the center of her adoring group of friends. They had everything and she had nothing. No one. It wasn't fair. Why did they get to be happy when she felt this way?

Madonna had stopped singing and the deejay of the Hits from High School Hour came on, Daisy Deluxe. She said she had an updated bulletin about the Home Wrecker killings, that the police were actively seeking a person or persons unknown in a green hatchback car.

Eve froze, her cigarette hanging in midair.

"And if you are listening, Home Wrecker," Daisy Deluxe said, "I want you to know I think you are a monster. I hope they get you soon, and when they do, I hope you rot."

"Home Wrecker," Eve whispered under her breath, feeling her hands shake. The woman had no idea what she was saying. Those were the most awful words Eve could imagine. She remembered the day she had first heard them, first been called them, the worst day of her life. The name had followed her to Los Angeles, like a self-fulfilling prophecy, and now, despite everything, had found her here.

She had driven to Harry's house by accident, but now she decided that she had to see him. *Needed* to see him. It was time to stop putting this off. She thought she would wait for him behind the house, surprise him, so she walked up the driveway and sat on the top step of the back door, half in the light, half in shadow. *Hi, Harry,* she would say. *I wanted to see you before I killed myself.*

And he'd say, *No, don't, you can't. Let me take care of you.* Because he had to. She knew he couldn't resist a damsel in distress.

And then she'd be inside. Then she would do it. She realized she was crying and wiped the tears from her face on her sleeve.

A quarter of an hour later he pulled in, looking handsome and tired. He hadn't seen her at first so she stood up and said, "Hi, Harry."

Before she could move on, everything changed. The look on his face was one she never could have imagined. Not surprise. So much better then surprise. Like he was happy to see her. Like she was good. He dropped his briefcase, all his papers, right there and ran to hug her. "Eve," he said, "I've been thinking about you all day. I tried calling you at work and at home. After our last conversation, I've just missed you so much. It's like I dreamed of you, and you showed up. Have you been crying?"

"Yes," she said, falling into his embrace. Wondering what she should do with the knife in her hand.

CHAPTER 22

Cate had finally agreed, with persuasion from Brandon, that meatballs did not have to be *perfectly* round to be edible, and after dinner, a bath, a promise from Windy that she could paint the walls of her bedroom with rainbows, and a few more pages of *The Little Prince*, had gone happily to bed, clutching Soccer Barbie.

When Windy came back downstairs from kissing both Cate and Barbie good night, Brandon had finished the dishes and was flipping through fabric swatches while he watched the Mexican soap opera he had taped that afternoon. A woman was sobbing on the screen, clutching at a man whose lips barely moved under his mustache as he said something with his eyes narrowed.

"Didn't we see the same scene last week?" Windy asked. Since her Spanish was virtually nonexistent, she could only follow the story lines through the images.

"LouLou and Diego have a very dramatic relationship," Brandon told her. "Fighting is their way of saying 'I love you.' They'll make up again after the commercial."

"But she is always crying. Or looking tense."

"She thrives on it." An advertisement came on and Brandon hit pause. "I don't want to sound like your mother, honey, but why don't you get yourself into your bed?" Doing his imitation of Mrs. Thomas's accent, a cross between Charo and the Godfather.

"Is that your sweet way of saying I look like shit?"

"*Más o menos.* More or less."

"Thanks. I thought I would go through that last box from the move, get it out of the way, and then go to sleep."

"Sure," Brandon said, keeping his face neutral, and restarted the video.

The box, plain brown cardboard, was sitting on the bottom shelf of the bookcase that stood next to Windy's desk in the living room. Going through the Waters family's photos and keepsakes that day had reminded her about it. She had meant to unpack it right after they moved in, but was always too busy or too tired. It mostly contained papers, things she needed to file, and a few old photos. She went over to it. Slid it off the shelf. Stared at it. Listened as Brandon sang along to a commercial in Spanish. And put the box back.

She was too tired tonight.

She sat down on the arm of the couch. Brandon paused the tape again—a different woman was on the screen crying now; didn't anyone have a good relationship?—and looked at her.

"What is it, honey?"

"I am really sorry to do this, but I think I need to ask you a favor. I might have to work some crazy hours the next few days. Would you mind—"

"Not at all," he interrupted. "Leave the Minx to me. I don't have anything going on and it would be a pleasure. We'll finally finish decorating her room. Who knows, we might start on yours. I'm thinking Moroccan kasbah."

"Sure, whatever you want," she said, not really paying attention. "I feel so bad. Abandoning Cate and you for work. It's just that—"

"It's just that it is your job, honey. That is what you do. Watching the Minx is what I do. And frankly, I *want* you out there doing it. Someone has to catch the bad guys."

Why did this make so much sense to everyone but Bill? Damn,

she had forgotten to call him back. She said, "Thanks" to Brandon then went into the kitchen and dialed Bill's home number. No answer. He'd said he'd be home and he always answered when he saw her number on the caller ID, even when he was sleeping. Unless he was angry at her.

She would have to make it up to him. Again.

She could not blame him for being mad, she knew. Not when she herself was still uncomfortable thinking about what had happened eight months earlier at that crime scene in Virginia. About the twenty seconds of consciousness she had spent lying in a pool of her own blood, not knowing what else the man was going to do to her, only knowing she would never see Cate again.

When her therapist asked about it, she shrugged and said, "It was a wake-up call." Two centimeters to the left or right and it would have been a death sentence, the knife hitting her heart or lungs, but it only got ribs, nothing vital. She was fine. There was no reason to dwell on it.

She had been on the job when it happened. Eight months earlier a man had walked into the police station to file a report, said he knew where a murder suspect was hiding. From what he said, the way he acted, the officers trusted him, followed up his lead, and arrested the man they found. The man they arrested kept protesting that he was innocent, but that mostly amused them, especially after the preliminary forensics work-up showed there were hairs on the victim—a twenty-two-year-old woman named Tawny Marks—that matched the man in custody's in color, texture, and length. That was pretty good, but what made it better was that he turned out to be the woman's estranged husband.

But even as she delivered the lab results on samples she herself had collected at the scene, something inside Windy said this man was not the killer. She knew better than to act on instinct—instinct lies, evidence never does—so she needed to return to the crime scene to look for more information.

Deep down she also knew she trusted her instincts less because she felt so personally about the case. She did not know Tawny Marks, the victim, but she had seen wide scars on her wrists, old ones, and asked Tawny's sister about them. Tawny had been through hell— her own demons, inside, the sister said. She had tried to commit suicide, slitting her wrists, when her marriage went bad. She had been the one to destroy it, Tawny knew—had an affair with a plumber. Her husband, the one in custody, had found out but had said he would take her back if she wanted. She had opted to leave. It was a low time for her, drinking, drugs, and she hadn't felt she deserved a man like her husband. But surviving the suicide attempt—it was a fluke, she overfilled the bathtub and flooded it into the neighbor's house downstairs so the super went up to her apartment—had shaken sense into her. Since then she had taken her life back, quit drinking. She was doing better. Great, even.

The sister's interview gave the cops plenty to work with on motive for the estranged husband—jealous spouses were great murder suspects—and gave Windy a need to find Tawny's real killer. Anyone who could piece their way back together after hitting bottom, who faced their demons, got her respect. And deserved justice.

She went back to the tiny apartment where the woman had been killed and started working the scene again, and while she was under the bed collecting a sample she heard a noise and felt a hand close around her ankle.

She froze. Froze as she was dragged out on her stomach. Froze as the hand flipped her over. Froze as she stared up at the man standing there, a man she recognized as the one who had pointed the cops to the estranged husband. A man who recognized her as the sheriff. It only took him a second to flip open his switchblade and stab for her heart.

That was when her twenty seconds of consciousness started, lying there, furious and terrified and unable to move, as the man grabbed the two hundred fifty dollars under the mattress he'd come for, kicked her once, and took off.

It came out later that the man who had attacked her was the real killer. Tawny's husband's hairs were found at the crime scene because she had invited him over, hoping for a reconciliation now that she was feeling better. The real killer was the plumber she'd originally run away from her marriage with. He'd found out that she was thinking of getting back together with her husband and lost it, shot her. And when the bitch fell down, dead, he explained at his allocution, damned if she didn't do it across the bed, and he'd been too afraid to move her to get the money out from under it, so he'd had to wait and come back later.

Windy learned the facts in the hospital when she regained consciousness, her chest a mass of bandages, her eyes searching only for Cate, thank God there she was in the corner, sitting on her grandmother's lap. In some ways, seeing her daughter again had been the happiest moment of her life.

In some ways it was the worst. Because survival brought with it terror, doubt, and recriminations. From her mother, her in-laws. Herself. What had she been thinking? Was this acting responsibly? What if something had happened to her, where would Cate be? Was this a good job for a woman?

The day before she was released from the hospital her mother-in-law had come to see her, Evan's mother. There was no one else there and she got right to the point. In her conservative cream colored suit, leaning against the table because she didn't want to touch the chair in the room, saying, "Evan's death has been hard for all of us. But you, Windy, you have to stop acting like your life doesn't matter. You have to stop taking risks like this. If you can't be safe and do this job, you should quit. I want my granddaughter to be raised by someone responsible."

Telling her how to raise her daughter when she'd hardly taken time out between Bridge and board meetings to raise her own son. Windy had felt a moment of indignation but it flared and died. Because Mrs. Kirkland was not all wrong. She had let down her defenses for an instant, stopped being watchful, made a bad call. It wouldn't happen again.

She would be responsible, think like a grown-up all the time, she decided. She and Bill had been going out for five months when she was stabbed, spending a lot of time together but not yet having what Cate called "slumber parties," and when he found out what had kept her from their dinner date that night, he was wonderful. He brought her home from the hospital, cooked for her, spoiled Cate rotten, canceled all his work trips so he could stay in town, was impeccably sweet and kind and understanding.

He pretty much moved in with them after that, it just felt natural, right. For the first time in a long time, Windy felt like everything was under control. It was a new kind of relationship for her, a new way to exist, no crazy oscillations between high points and low ones, just constant stability. A new start with Bill. A new job far from the Virginia farmhouse where she and Evan had spent their married life together. The confidence that she was making good, mature decisions, behaving responsibly.

"I don't want you just to layer denial on denial," her therapist had said. "I want to make sure you're dealing with Evan's death and your own trauma."

"Of course. I'm dealing great." She was. She didn't even cry or have nightmares.

She was taking precautions, being smart. She knew that from where she was standing right then in the kitchen of her house in Vegas, if she turned her head to the left she'd be able to see the mark on the cabinet she had made twenty-one feet from the back door. Twenty-one feet or less was distance from which the law said it was self-defense to shoot an intruder. Twenty-one feet was the Safe Distance. There was a similar mark twenty-one feet from every door in the house. Only she knew they were there. Only she knew about the gun she kept hidden between her mattress and boxspring.

She had been tempted to show them to Bill, prove to him that she was being responsible, but she knew he would want to talk about what had happened again. The more she got over it, the more he started to worry. It was only because he loved her more as time went on, he told her, and she believed it. Worrying was only his way of saying "I love you." How could she explain that every time he questioned her about where she had been, she felt like he was questioning her judgment, her ability. That his concern felt like doubt. That every "I have been so worried about you" and "Where were you, Windy?" transported her back to that room, back to the woman who made a mistake and could not be relied on.

She knew that her reaction was wrong and unfair, projecting her insecurities onto his words. He had a right to worry. She had been stupid, put her life in danger. And he had a real right to be frustrated with her now: she wasn't exactly living up to her end of the bargain, where she'd promised no more crime scenes, no more violence if she took the job as head of Vegas criminalistics, making them relocate. She was the one doing the wrong thing. She felt awful about it. Worse because she knew, no matter what she said, she wasn't going to stop.

She reached for the phone to dial him again, and stared at her hand, seeing that she'd bitten off all the nails while she was standing there, the first time in over a year. It doesn't mean that you are falling apart again, she told herself. Picked up the receiver, now punching in the number, determined to leave a message on the answering machine this time, half wanting to talk long enough that he would decide to pick up, half knowing that was only setting herself up for disappointment. In the end she said simply, "I'm sorry, Bill, and I love you," and hung up.

She checked the locks on all the doors and windows on the ground floor and went back into the living room. "Brandon, I'm going to bed."

"Good idea," he told her, adding: "Honey, I forget to say before, I can't believe you didn't tell me that your boss is be-still-my-heart-gorgeous. The man is a hunk. And not just cute either—he is *nice*. Confident in that quiet way. I really liked him. You can invite him over any time you want."

"I'm glad you approve."

An image of Ash out on a date flashed uninvited into her mind. She wondered what they had done. If they had fun.

She gnawed on her thumbnail as she checked the latch on the sliding glass door before getting into bed.

CHAPTER 23

Windy screeched past the DENTAL CENTER sign and into the criminalistics parking lot at ten minutes after eight. She was running late but she sat at the wheel of her car, making herself breathe, holding herself together.

Usually only the nights were hard, but pulling into the parking lot that morning she'd seen Dr. Waters coming out of the homicide building, immediately being swarmed by waiting reporters. As she watched, he put his hand up to shield his face from the camera lights, and she saw that his eyes were absolutely blank. Without hope. Without anything.

Windy wondered if this was what the killer wanted, to destroy a man, if he would get off seeing this. Wondered what "worse" would be if she didn't piece the evidence together fast enough to stop him.

She had made it out of her car but was still staring into space when a voice behind her said, "Hi there."

She turned and saw Ned Blight getting out of his SUV and lumbering toward her. "Don't tell the boss I'm late," he joked.

She tried out a smile. "I won't if you won't."

Ned looked past her, to the group around Dr. Waters, and ran a hand through his dark curly hair. "Makes my heart bleed."

Windy said, "How long have you been at this?"

"Criminalistics for the past five years, but I was in uniform with the department for twelve years before that."

"You must have seen a lot of awful things."

"Nothing like this." He looked at her. "Want to hear a weird coincidence, though? I wasn't quite sure, but I asked my wife about it last night and she remembered it the same way I did. My very first week on the job, twenty years ago, do you know where I was called to? The Sun-Crest apartments."

"The Waters' apartment building?"

"I don't know if it was the same apartment, that would be too much, but definitely the same building. Do you remember your first live case? The first crime scene you really worked, once you were out of training?"

Boy did she. As if it had happened that morning she could still see the body covered in the ice of the lake. Windy nodded.

"And this was a weird one. You know how those stay with you. It was these two women, a mother and daughter, screaming at each other. The original call had been domestic disturbance, a husband beating his wife we assumed, but we got there and the guy was just sitting on the couch while the two women fought, called each other liar, each one saying that the other was upsetting the man. I've got three girls of my own, but I'd never seen anything like this. Still haven't. I went home that night and told my wife about it, and she remembered it too. Sylvia, she believes in karma, has all these crystals from Arizona for channeling her energy, stuff like that and I always pooh pooh it, but being back in that building and seeing what happened, it did make me wonder. You know, if maybe things like that can happen, bad energy getting trapped in a place and haunting the people there." He got a sheepish look as if he just realized what he'd been saying. "I sound like an idiot. I think this case has got me all on edge."

"Everyone," Windy agreed. She ripped her eyes from Dr. Waters and started walking to the criminalistics building, determined to find something to help him, put some expression back into his face.

Her pager beeped. Looking down she saw *A/V Lab, ASAP. Ash.*

"What took you so long?" Ash asked when Windy burst into the audio-visual lab thirty seconds later. "Stop for doughnuts?"

His tone was excited. She said, "What did you find?"

"I want you to see it before I comment." He turned to a petite woman in her late twenties with purple spiked hair sitting at a computer. "This is Erica Ortiz, our computer guru. She rules this section. Erica Ortiz, Chicago Thomas."

The woman gave Windy a big smile, revealing a full set of braces. "Good to meet you. Welcome to our feature presentation."

She hit two buttons and a grainy movie appeared on her computer screen, a car parked at the curb in front of the pawn shop.

"Is that our green car?" Windy asked Ash.

"Just wait."

A shadow moved on the screen and then a man's profile appeared. He leaned into the car on the passenger side and appeared to speak to whoever was inside. He spent some time by the side of the car chatting, then gestured with his hand, pointing down the street. Like giving directions. After another exchange the car pulled away from the curb, out of the frame of the shot. The man waved and turned to go, giving the security cameras a front view.

Windy bent closer to the screen. "That man is in uniform. He's a cop."

Ash nodded. "Yep."

Windy's eyes came to Ash. "A cop talked to our suspect."

"A cop chased our suspect. Needed the parking place for the official vehicles."

"And he did not think to mention it to us? Or notice the APB on a green car?"

Jonah had joined them and he said, "Not immediately. I just got off the phone with the man, Officer Carp, and he said he didn't think to mention the green car because, and I'm quoting the good officer now, 'the operator of the vehicle was a female, and most known serial offenders are male.' "

Windy blinked. "A woman." Their killer a woman. How had she not thought of this? A woman would be able to get another woman to open the door to her at night.

"Not just a woman," Jonah went on. "By his report, a real hot number. Carp asked her out."

"You're kidding," Ash said. "Did he get her name or phone number?"

Jonah shook his head. "No, unfortunately the lady said she couldn't make it. She told him she was sort of involved with someone and very busy these days."

"Very busy?" Windy shuddered. "That is absolutely not what I wanted to hear. Did he at least get a license number?"

"Too busy trying to get her phone number."

"Don't worry," Ash put in. "Erica's been working on it. Show her."

Windy watched as the image on Erica's screen zoomed in on the rear of the car.

"You can get the plate this way?" Windy asked, leaning over the woman's shoulder.

"Not with our lousy software. But NASA and the Department of Defense have been developing a program to enhance photos at oblique angles. At first it didn't work, it still has bugs in it, but we made a few modifications and I think this is going to do it."

She hit a button and the screen filled with the white rectangular shape of a license plate. Slowly, darker lines began to appear, dots filling in to become words, until after two minutes the top read CALIFORNIA, and beneath it were the letters B-A-D-G-R-L.

"Bad Girl," Windy said aloud.

Ash turned to Jonah, who said, "I'm already on it," and disappeared out the door.

Windy marveled at the image. "Great work, Erica."

Erica shook her head and looked at Ash. "I only did the easy part. I'm not the one who hacked the NASA computer for the software and—"

"What?" Windy asked, staring hard at Ash.

"I could use some coffee, couldn't you?" Ash said, trying to push Windy out the door. "What about a Twinkie? I have Twinkies in my desk. We can wait in my office for Jonah."

"Were you here all night committing illegal acts?"

"Of course not. I wouldn't do anything illegal here. I did it somewhere else, somewhere they are used to ducking questions from government agencies. Besides, the encryption was so weak it was practically in the public domain."

Windy rolled her eyes. "Ah. That makes it better then. Don't you ever sleep?"

"Can you spell that word? I don't think I know it."

"I've never met anyone before who made my work ethic look healthy."

"I use it as a crutch to make up for the absence of other distractions in my life." He smiled to show he was just kidding.

Before she could say anything, Jonah bolted out of the homicide offices, holding a piece of paper in front of him, and bowed. "You are looking at the goose that laid the golden egg."

"What did you get?"

"Everything. The woman in the green car's name is Eve Sebastian. Formerly of Los Angeles, moved to Vegas five months ago. To open a restaurant. Feel free to call me your highness and worship at my feet."

"She's a chef?" Ash asked, incredulous.

"Oh yeah. And that's not the best part. Her specialty is breakfast."

CHAPTER 24

" 'Paradise' comes to paradise." Windy read aloud from the article by Storm Larke that Jonah had printed from the *Las Vegas Review Journal*. "*Celebrity chef Eve Sebastian's new restaurant, the Paradise Lost Café, opens today in the Mandalay Bay Hotel. Sebastian, one of* Gourmet Magazine's *Top Ten to Taste in 2003, has attracted an almost cultlike following among Hollywood's A-list for her home-style cooking, and a racy reputation for her wild partying, but I'm betting it will be the dining room of her new space that gets tongues wagging this time. The centerpieces of the over-the-top decor are five round beds, where you can enjoy an all-day breakfast-in-bed special menu. Having had a chance to meet Sebastian and taste her Angels-Don't-Know-a-Thing-About-It Cake, I can tell you that the only thing more mouth-watering than her cuisine is the woman herself. This gourmet will happily volunteer for breakfast duty any time.*"

"She's a chef who specializes in breakfast," Ash repeated. They were in Ash's office now, Ash behind his desk, Windy in a chair facing it.

"And *home-style* cooking," Windy said. She looked up and saw Jonah in the door frame. "Something else for us, your highness?"

Jonah shook his head. "You already got the good news. The bad news is that she's not at the restaurant today. I called Clive, our connection in Mandalay Bay Security while I was printing that out and asked him to go over there, low profile. He just reported back that Eve isn't around. I asked him to keep an eye out anyway."

"Let's take advantage of that and send Nick Lee and Bob Zorzi over to question the staff," Ash said. "Discreetly. I'm interested in anything they can learn, but tell them especially to try to get a home address for her. In case they can't, let's send someone over to records to check for recent home purchases. Oh, and tell them to find out what kind of knives she uses, if any are missing."

Jonah said, "Got it," and left.

"So," Windy said, "we have a name, a profession. The beginnings of a profile that fit what we know about our killer. We should be dancing or something. Why don't I feel more excited?"

"Because none of that is going to help us stop her if we can't figure out how she is choosing her victims."

"Oh, that's right. It's not enough to simply identify the killer. We've got to find her too. This looks so much easier on TV."

"On TV these families would have something in common. Schools, churches, jobs, restaurants, supermarkets, all dead ends. Aside from having the bad luck to get murdered, these two families have no overlap." Ash and Windy spent the next half hour reviewing any possible link they might have missed, coming up empty-handed.

"There has got to be something. Bike repair shops," Windy was saying, as Jonah knocked on the door.

"Nick Lee on line one for you."

Ash said, "Thanks," to Jonah, "Waterses had no bikes," to Windy, hit the speaker phone button and said, "Nick you're on."

"You have got to see this place, it's a trip. All the waiters and waitresses wearing big angel wings, you know, like in paradise. Anyway, we asked for Eve, were told she wasn't there, and a guy, the manager, comes over and says 'Finally. It took you long enough. We filed the complaint more than twenty-four hours ago.' "

Ash said, "What complaint?"

Nick's voice explained, "The missing persons complaint. He thought we were there to follow it up. For Eve Sebastian. It seems the head chef failed to show up for work on Tuesday."

Windy leaned back in her chair. "The day we found the Waterses' bodies. It isn't uncommon for killers to start acting strange when they go on sprees. Often at the beginning they just miss a few hours of work before a murder, but later they'll take off a whole day or week. To enjoy it more, the planning, the fantasy. It becomes part of a ritual. Ask them if she's missed any other days, or come in late, recently."

"I'll try. They're not that cooperative. Bob started talking to the assistant manager, who told him she thought Eve was dating a guy named Barry or Harry, something like that. Sent her flowers every week. But before Bob could get any more, the manager came over and started saying we were there under false pretenses and asked us to leave. I didn't know if I should tell him yet this is part of a murder investigation."

"No, let's keep that quiet. We don't need any more leaks to the press. Could he at least give you Eve's address?"

"He clammed up, started talking about Eve being a very private person. I could have pressured him but I figured it would be easier just to call a friend I have in Missing Persons and get it from him. The place was handled by a management company that rents furnished houses to executives just moving to town."

Ash took down the address, said, "Nice work. See if you can find anything else out about her boyfriend. That could be where she is staying."

"On it. And we asked about knives. All the chefs take their knives home with them every night. It's some chef thing. The assistant manager thought Eve used Japanese knives but she wasn't sure. I've got a connection at another restaurant if you want me to ask about professional brands."

"You have a lot of connections," Ash said.

"I have a lot of unmarried sisters with ardent admirers," Nick Lee explained. "Plus, every time I come through with something, Bob has to get rid of one of the Andrew Lloyd Webber tapes he makes us listen to in the car, so I have incentive."

Ash laughed, said, "Whatever it takes. Thanks, Nick," and hung up.

Windy looked at the address he'd written down for Eve, then at him. "How long will it take to get a warrant?"

"Forty-five minutes if we're lucky. Three hours if we aren't."

"I'll go get my team ready." She stopped at the door and turned back around. "Leaky faucets. Both the Waters house and the Johnson house had leaky faucets."

Ash shook his head. "They used different plumbers. We checked."

"No, I mean something else." She was remembering what Ned had said that morning in the parking lot, about the call he took as a rookie and evil being trapped in the walls, certain spaces being cursed. It had stayed with her, suggesting the idea of location as the link. She said now, "What if it's not the *families* that are her targets, the triggers for her rage? What if it's the *places*? The residences of both the Johnsons and Waterses are old. I haven't learned Vegas as well as I would like to yet, but one thing I have learned is that 90 percent of the residents live in new houses. The fact that both our crime scenes are older buildings could be significant. And the other day Hank Logan said that sometimes people go back to a place where something happened to them, to try to make sense of it." She caught Ash's expression and said, "You think I'm grasping at straws." Just what she needed, him to doubt her.

"Actually no," he said. "I'm feeling like an idiot for not thinking of it myself."

She went to the door. "I'll take Eve's house—"

"—And I'll start looking into former residences."

Ash watched her head back to criminalistics, thinking how much working with Windy reminded him of being on Army Ranger's operations with his friend Benton Arbor after college. The confidence of a partner you could count on, someone really smart who got what you were trying to do without you having to explain it. Someone you felt an instinctive bond with.

Only he'd never wondered what it would be like to make out with Benton in the break room.

"Ash," Jonah shouted from the open door of his office across the hall.

"What?"

"Stop humming."

"I'm not humming."

"Yes you are. You're humming 'You're the Inspiration' by Chicago. Loud. You've been doing it since last Friday and it's driving everyone insane."

"I am not humming."

"She's engaged."

"I really don't know what you are talking about."

CHAPTER 25

"Radio KRST, the station that puts the 'rest' in stressed," a sleepy-sounding voice said on the other end of the phone. "This is Charity, how can I direct your call?"

"Hello, ma'am, I'm calling from *Entertainment Weekly* magazine? My editor, Ed Sebastian, asked me to get in touch with someone at your station and I was wondering if you could help me."

"*Entertainment Weekly?*" The voice wasn't sleepy any more. "No way. I love that magazine. Are you doing a story about the station?"

"Sort of. We want to do a piece on the life of a female deejay, you know, in honor of Women's History Month? And the name of one of your deejays—here it is. She uses the name Daisy Deluxe? Has the Hits from High School show?—Anyway, her name came up."

"Daisy Graber. Sure. Daisy is great. How did they hear about her?"

"I don't know, ma'am, I just do the errands, make the calls, get the coffee, take the abuse. But someone must have said something pretty spectacular, because my boss came storming in and told me to get on it ASAP."

A grunt, then, "Bosses think everything has to be ASAP, don't they?"

"They sure do, Charity. When really ASPA is more like it—A Serious Pain in the Ass?"

Charity laughed. "Sounds like we have the same boss. So, you are looking for information about Daisy?"

"Anything you have? The boss, of course, would like it if you could Federal Express her direct to me at no additional charge, but I'd settle for a phone number or an address."

"What about both?"

"You are a goddess."

"To those who deserve it, anyway." There was a soft flicking sound, like a Rolodex being spun around, then Charity's voice saying, "Got it," and reading off the number and address. "Anyone asks, you learned it from 411 information."

"You bet. For that matter, it would probably be best if you didn't mention to anyone that we called. Whenever we start working on a lead like this, *People* magazine or *Us* tries to swoop in and steal our thunder, and the person who gets blamed for it is me, the peon. If you could keep this under wraps for a few days, help me keep my job, that would be great."

"You don't have to worry about me," Charity said. "I won't tell a soul and besides, I leave for vacation on Friday and I won't be back for a whole week."

"I'm jealous. Thanks so much for your help, Charity. You're great. And remember, if anyone asks, don't mention our story. My boss will kill me if he thinks it's been leaked."

"My lips are sealed."

CHAPTER 26

Eve Sebastian lived in a gated development called the Wetlands, just to the east of the Strip. It was a collection of two-story townhouses gathered around a series of pools, the whole thing inside a brick and wrought-iron fence with remote controlled gates at two entrances for the residents and a guard shack at the third for "All Others."

Windy peered through the gates at precisely manicured grass as the criminalistics van idled at the guard shack, waiting for admission. She was discovering that you could gauge how fancy any Las Vegas development was from the size of the body of water it was named after. She supposed the best one would be called something like The Oceans, and the worst maybe The Drinking Fountain. The Wetlands, she figured, was somewhere in between.

The guard finally raised the gate and they drove up to a white townhouse with red trim and fake shutters on the windows. Eve had rented the place furnished, generic gray carpeting, light gray walls, lemon yellow leather couch, dark wood coffee table in the living room, white duvet over gray sheets, gray flannel upholstered headboard, gray dresser in the master bedroom, gray towels in the bath. The dark wood night table had a fake white orchid on it, to give it tone, make it look like a boutique hotel. The air was cool and smelled of perfume and Lysol mixed together.

It was big for a single woman living alone, two stories, two bed-rooms, three baths, yet there was no sign of anyone but Eve living there. But there were plenty of traces of her. There were finger-prints everywhere, hair in the drains, blood on the toothbrush, brit-tle nail clippings in the wastebasket. Windy looked around the bathroom, then stopped abruptly and said aloud, "I think she's anorexic."

"You can tell that by looking in her garbage can?" Ned peered in himself.

"Not just that, although the brittle nail clippings are part of it. But look at what she has here." Windy gestured to the beige fake-marble counter of the master bathroom. There was a tube of Senso-dyne toothpaste for sensitive teeth and gums, athlete's foot powder, and two different kinds of under-eye cream, one promising to "Make You Look Younger Today," the other settling for helping to "End Your War Against Bags and Puffy Circles."

"All this tells me is that she should visit the dentist more often, wash her socks more frequently, and get more sleep. Hell, I use this toothpaste and you can see that I'm not anorexic." Ned patted his stomach.

"Maybe," Windy agreed. "But sensitive teeth, fungal infections, and puffy eyes due to dehydration are all symptoms of anorexia. And did you notice the extra blanket on the bed? Anorexics are always cold. It would explain the Lysol, because sometimes their bodies give off an odd odor, like those of people suffering from un-dernourishment. I'd bet we'll find calcium and magnesium vitamin supplements somewhere. And that all her clothes are size small."

Ned disappeared, came back a few moments later shaking his head. "Her clothes aren't size small."

"Maybe I'm wrong," Windy conceded.

"They're size extra small. Except for the ones that are size zero."

Windy had always thought that was an awful idea, in a world

where many women measured their self-worth based on size, to make clothes that were size nothing. What a thing to aspire to. She and Ash had concluded that the killer seemed to use food to control her victims and now it looked like she used it to control herself too. Windy felt an out of place pang of sympathy for the woman.

She walked around for over an hour saying, "Bag this, envelope for this, use the white powder to dust for prints on the thermostat, paper not plastic for the toothbrush. No! Don't lick the envelope flap closed, you could contaminate the sample, yes, take the washcloth too." The place was a DNA analyst's wet dream. And yet at the same time the whole apartment was sterile, not in the scientific sense, but in the figurative sense of impersonal. Unemotional. Cold.

The kitchen cabinets contained a can of chicken broth, calcium supplements, a sample pack of multivitamins, and a half-used package of Metamucil. The refrigerator held a container of milk and a two-thirds-empty jar of strawberry jam.

There were only a few clothes, almost all identical, black pants, black sweaters, black shirts, all in dry cleaning bags, all tiny. Three pairs of black shoes, size eight and a half. There was nothing white to match the thread on Mrs. Johnson's body. The only makeup was a dried out tube of brown mascara, a Blistex, and an untouched Berry Burgundy lip-gloss. Windy smelled perfume on the air but there was no sign of its bottle, no old bottles of nail polish or sample sizes of facial toner. She found a plain white Maidenform bra, no underwire, and pairs of white cotton underwear uncomfortably similar to the ones she had in her drawer at home, and wondered whether it said more about Eve or the man—Barry or Harry—who was her boyfriend. Not really the underwear she'd expect of a bad girl, though.

What kind would that be, Windy asked herself, hearing Bill saying that the expensive silk and lace lingerie she loved reminded him of a cheap brothel.

There were three books on the night table, and they gave Windy another unwelcome flash of sympathy for Eve as she bagged them. The top one was *The Rules: Time-tested Secrets for Capturing the Heart of Mr. Right*. The next one was *Sex Secrets of the Pros: What Every Good Girl Needs to Know to Keep Her Man Satisfied, by a Genuine Bad Girl*. And the bottom one was *A Little Princess*. That one was inscribed on the inside in a crooked scrawl: "To Eve, This is my Favorite book, Love, your Goddaughter Nikkie (Nicole)," with hearts for dots over the *i*'s. Eve Sebastian: lonely single woman, beloved godmother, brutal killer.

Quite a profile.

Of course, Windy told herself, you couldn't put too much stock in the books, reflecting on her own bedside table collection— *Living with Your Six-Year-Old Even If You Don't Think You Can,* a guide for preparing her tax return using some new computer software, and a well-thumbed copy of *Auntie Mame*.

The books and the items scattered over Eve's bathroom counter were as personal as the apartment got. There were no souvenirs from theme parks, no pads of paper with logos of places she had visited, no photos, no refrigerator magnets. No notes to, from, or about Harry. The only box of matches came from her restaurant, and the only magazine they found was *WHERE?*, the magazine that the tourist board put in hotel rooms. It lay on the coffee table like an existential question as Windy and her team kept looking for direct evidence linking Eve to the murders and found none.

The neighbors, the few they found, could barely confirm that Eve had lived there, much less when she had last been home, what hours she kept or if she had a boyfriend. The guard at the gate had no idea when she'd last been home, explaining that each resident had their own clicker and could come and go as they wanted. She hadn't put anyone on her visiting list in the last month, and renters couldn't put anyone on permanently.

Eve's townhouse was one in a row of ten that fronted the fourteenth tee, most of them rented by companies for their executives when they traveled to Vegas for conventions. Some of the town-houses even rented by the week. Everyone minded their own business when they were there, and it was only the most astute who could come up with a description of Eve as complete as "that skinny woman who lives up there."

Windy was lying on her stomach on the couch, doing a tape lift on the area of carpeting immediately in front of it, when she felt someone tap her on the shoulder.

"Ma'am?"

It was the same young female patrol officer who had been in front of the Waters house. Officer Franca, her name tag said. Windy remembered Ash had sent her and two others to canvass the neighbors. Now the woman said, "You asked us to tell you if we found anyone who knew anything, ma'am. There is a lady, three doors down, who claims she spoke to Eve often."

Windy sat up. "Please stop calling me ma'am. It makes me feel like I need a better wrinkle cream. Call me Windy. And what do you mean by claims?"

"I don't know, um, Windy. I guess I'm not sure she is reliable."

Windy followed Officer Franca to an open door, where a woman in her sixties with a tinted blond bob and gold shoes was standing in a gold workout suit, the kind no one ever worked out in. She looked up at Windy and the lenses of her glasses caught the light.

"This is Mrs. Dutton," the officer said.

"Chicago Thomas, Metro Criminalistics," Windy said. "I'm told you are friendly with Eve Sebastian."

The woman lifted her eyebrows meaningfully behind the square frames of her glasses. "I would not say we were friendly. A bit too aloof, that one, for friends."

"Did you ever see her with anyone?"

"See and hear. They were hollering at each other."

"Who was she with?"

"A man, of course. He was tall. Had a ponytail, you know. One of those artsy-fartsy Hollywood types. Wearing a cap backwards, and a leather jacket, a real hot shot."

"I see. Could you see the color of his hair? Or his jacket?"

"Yellow."

"Which one?"

"Both. All of him. The lights outside? They turn everything yellow. They call these safety lights. Whose safety, I want to know? It would only take one burglar with hepatitis to blend in with the background and rob the entire street. And I saw on the Discovery Channel that there are more cases of hepatitis in America now than ever before."

The woman looked at Windy like she expected a response so Windy said, "Oh," as noncommittally as she could. "Do you remember when this was? That you saw the man?"

"Last week, or two weeks ago. I'm not sure."

"What about the time?"

"It was late. I was watching the television, *CSI*? Wonderful show. Have you seen it?"

Had she ever. Windy dreamed of equipment like the stuff they showed. It came on Thursday nights. She said, "If you remember which episode, we can probably learn when it was. Did you hear the man's name?"

"No. Just 'leave me alone' and 'I told you I didn't want to see you again.' "

"He said that?"

"No, she did."

"Had you ever seen the man before, Mrs. Dutton? Here?"

"One other time. About a month earlier. I asked her if he was her boyfriend and she said no. But she did have one. At least, she *said* so. I offered to set her up with my grandson, Ernie, who is a fine boy. He drives for UPS. You should see how cute he is in that outfit. But she always shook her head, no, she had a boyfriend.

Could not have been much of one if I never saw him." She eyed Windy again and said, "Are you related to her?"

"Me? No. Why?"

"You look like her is all, only fatter. And with different colored eyes." The woman's eyes moved from Windy's face to her left hand and back up. Windy didn't understand the meaning of the gesture until the woman said, "You're single. Would you like to meet my grandson?"

Windy felt herself take a step backwards. "Thank you, ma'am, but actually I am engaged."

Mrs. Dutton shook her head with disapproval. "Why aren't you wearing a ring? My grandson, Ernie, would give you a ring. Like I told Eve, a ring isn't just a present. It is a sign a man respects you. Even those girls on that *Bachelor* show know it."

"Thank you for your help, Mrs. Dutton," Windy said, moving away, fast. "If you think of anything else, please be in touch." And then, to Officer Franca, "Maybe I don't need to talk to the neighbors." Wondering how long it would take for the exchange about Ernie Dutton and the rings to get around the squad room.

She forgot all about it and Mrs. Dutton, as she worked the rest of the room with her team. They took samples of all the materials in the rooms and of Eve's clothes to use as standards, a basis of comparison, if the lab was able to find any trace evidence on the victims. If Eve was the murderer, she likely had a murder kit with packing tape and the knife in it that she kept with her. That meant there could be virtually no trace of the killings at her house. But there had to be *something* and Windy was determined to find it.

At that point she turned the magazine over so it would stop asking her *WHERE?* The back side was an advertisement for a jeweler, a picture of a man and a woman in close profile, telling them to "Make it Tonight, Make it a Diamond, and Make it Forever." Make it Pepto-Bismol, Windy thought, lying on her stomach on the couch and checking beneath it.

The beam of her flashlight showed her a few dust balls, a broken nail, another hair. Then something glinted in the back against the wall, and her heart leaped. Using a set of sterile tongs, she brought the object toward her, gave a low whistle and said, "Aren't you a sight for sore eyes," as she admired the roll of clear packing tape she found.

A roll which Gianni Basso, the head forensics technician, called two hours later to say was a possible match to the tape used by the killer, but nothing concrete.

"It is statistically probable that the adhesive on this tape you found and the adhesive we got from the victims' faces is the same. But this is also one of the three most common brands of packing tape in the country, the second most common here in Vegas."

"Were there any prints on it?"

"Nothing we've been able to raise yet."

"So this object, the only piece of evidence I've been able to come up with, might not have any connection to the crimes at all? Don't you have any good news for me?"

"We're still working on it."

Windy hung up and sank back into the couch, the full weight of the letdown hitting her like a punch. She'd thought she had found something. It had felt right.

She sat forward and dialed Gianni again. She didn't even let him answer, just said, "Try treating the tape with acetic acid and then fuming them with super glue."

"Acetic acid? Why?"

"I think there might be prints with less oil secretion that will be harder to pull up."

"What kind of prints are those?"

"Just do it."

She paced Eve's living room until her phone rang, Gianni's voice saying, "Lady, I want to buy you a drink."

"You found something? Prints from one of the twin girls?"

There was a pause and then he said, "You know, you could give a person a heart attack the way you read minds. Yes, Minette Waters's prints are all over the roll. There are two especially good ones, an index finger on the outside and the pointer finger of the other hand on the adhesive part, right where it was cut."

Windy moved her hands around an imaginary roll of tape. "As though the child had been holding the roll when the last piece was removed?"

"Exactly." He coughed, then said, "Can I ask you something? How did you know to use acetic acid? And even that the girl's prints would be on the tape?"

"Children younger than seven usually don't secrete the sweat and oils that adults do so their prints are harder to detect and less stable, but the acid brings them up. As for knowing the prints would be there, that was just a lucky hunch." It was the only thing she could think of that would have kept the girls quiet. She imagined the scene, Eve knowing how to talk to little girls because she had a god-daughter, saying: Want to play a fun game? Want to be my special helper? Just hold this while I tape your sister's mouth shut, and then yours. Could imagine Cate's reaction to such an offer, wondering what it would be like, if the tape would taste yummy, willing to try anything once.

It made her want to be ill.

Gianni was going on. "If that was a lucky hunch, it must be your lucky day. When we shined the black light, we found a tiny fiber stuck in the edge of the tape adhesive. Possibly from the lining of a purse or jacket pocket."

"Is it white?"

"Not only is it white, Ms. Thomas, it matches the fiber found on Mrs. Johnson's body. Your killer's partial to a silk-polyester blend that is not all that common."

Until now some part of her had not wanted to believe that she was standing in the home of a killer. The home of a woman she could feel for. But now there was no denying it.

Either Eve Sebastian was the Home Wrecker, or the Home Wrecker just happened to have come to Eve's house after the Waters murders, happened to accidentally drop a roll of packing tape linked forensically to the Waters house under her couch, and then managed to take off, miraculously depositing no prints, no shoe marks, no other evidence, but not disturbing the signs that Eve lived there. Which was pretty much impossible.

"Sounds like a smoking gun to me," Windy said to Gianni, then hung up and dialed Ash. She was sitting on the edge of the couch, excited. "Congratulations, Detective Laughton. I'd say we've found our killer."

"I can go one better," Ash said. "We've also found our motive. The Sebastian family lived in the Johnson house from December 1984 to August 1985 and the Waters apartment November 1985 to November 1987. You were right. She's killing where she grew up."

"Those dates you said. There's a three-month gap. That means we're looking for another residence."

"At least one."

CHAPTER 27

Three hours later Jonah walked into Ash's office and said, "I feel like punching something. I'm getting nowhere with these leasing companies. How about you?"

"Oh yeah," Ash said. "I learned in two years it will be easy to search deeds on houses bought and sold in the 1980s. If you want to see them today, though, you've got to go to Arizona where they're being put into the database. Part of the mayor's efficiency program."

"At least now I know who I want to punch," Jonah said, and walked heavily out the door.

Ash started dialing the next number on his list of utility companies, hung up halfway through, and dialed a different number from memory. She answered on the second ring.

"Windy? It's Ash. How is it going?"

"That depends on which you think is worse, dismal or horrible."

Ash found himself chuckling. "I'll take dismal. Anything in particular?"

"No. Nothing. That's just it. I wish we were finding more evidence here."

"The tape is great. It's a strong piece."

"I'm not thinking about court. I guess I'm having trouble reconciling this woman who lives in a gated community, locked away, reading self-help books about how to get married, with a license plate that screams 'bad girl' and, even more, with those horrible murders. It's like part of her, the part that is trying to learn how to meet Mr. Right and please him in bed, craves a traditional life and a family, while another part of her loathes those things enough to brutally murder. Home maker and home wrecker all in one."

"Having conflicting views on commitment only makes Eve normal. If that were her only problem, I doubt she'd be killing. I wish we knew what had actually happened in her family growing up."

On the other side of the phone Ash heard a bang. "Are you okay?"

"Hold on." Her voice was far away, and then she came back. "Sorry, I got so excited I fell off Eve's couch."

At that moment, Ash knew that what he felt for Windy Thomas was more than a crush. "Excited about what?"

"You know Ned Blight, on my staff? He took a call at the Sun-Crest seventeen years ago, when he was walking a beat. A domestic violence call against the father but when he got there, the mother and daughter were fighting with one another, the father sitting peacefully on the couch between them. That would be about the time Eve lived there, if she did."

"You're thinking it was Eve's family. That would be quite a coincidence."

"Not necessarily. We know she lived there and we know she must have experienced some kind of abuse or trauma within her family, her houses, to get her to act out the way she is now. First stalking the houses. Then killing the mothers and children, leaving the father alive. We have no idea what the family dynamic was that turned her into a killer, but what if Ned's call really was to her family? The two women rivals for the man's attention or affection? That sounds like someone looking for attention from a father figure. It could be her. And it might tell us something about what happened between those walls."

"I'll look into it. Although by the time we get case notes from a

case in the eighties out of storage, she could have slaughtered everyone in Vegas. What we need to find is a friend of this woman's.
Someone who can tell us where she lived, what she is like. I sent officers to the restaurant, both plainclothes and in uniform and none
of them can get anything. And no more information about the man
she's dating."

"She has a goddaughter named Nicole, so she must have friends
somewhere. Maybe in L.A."

"I've got a call in to my counterpart in the LAPD, but they have
a huge cold case homicide going on and he hasn't gotten back to
me. I'm thinking of flying down there myself tomorrow."

"Isn't the Waterses' memorial service tomorrow?"

"Yes, in the morning. I propose to go to L.A. in the afternoon.
Hey, speaking of proposals, I hear you got a nice one today. What is
his name? Ernie?"

"Very subtle. That news only took three hours to get all the way
from here to you."

"There are perks to being the boss. Seriously, thanks for taking the time to talk to the neighbors. That's outside the scope of
criminalistics."

"But not of the task force. And I feel—I feel like I need to get to
know Eve better."

"Are you done at her house?"

"I think I'll send my team home but stay a little longer. Do a final walk-through."

"Keep an officer outside the door. Just in case Eve decides to
come home."

"Yes, sir," Windy said.

Ash realized what an asshole he must sound like, trying to protect her. "It is standard procedure."

"I know. I was planning to. What are you going to do?"

"Damned if I know. I've got about three dozen patrols out looking for Eve Sebastian or a green car with the license plate BAD GRL,

and ten people looking through records to come up with some creative way to figure out where else she's lived."

"Whatever you do," Windy said, "keep an officer outside your door."

"Thanks. Give my best to Ernie."

"That was low," Windy said, but Ash had already hung up.

CHAPTER 28

Windy sent the rest of her team away and sat on the couch, taking in the space. She felt like she was in the eye of the storm. Outside there was a massive manhunt—woman hunt—going on. But in here, in Eve's apartment, it was completely peaceful.

What Eve was doing seemed like more than just putting her past behind her, making a fresh start. The place felt to Windy like the home of a woman running away from something. Although Eve had been there five months, everything about the townhouse felt temporary—the milk in the refrigerator was a half pint, the plates were paper, even the moisturizer, shampoo, and conditioner were only travel size. As if Eve were afraid to make too long a commitment to anything. Afraid to let herself believe she was staying.

Eve was a contradiction, her books suggesting she was attracted to permanence even as she seemed to avoid it. But sometimes, Windy thought, What is missing says more than what is present. Sometimes what you avoid is as telling as what you go after.

The only thing that suggested any kind of commitment was the carton of Marlboro cigarettes on the floor of Eve's closet. Apparently she had been comfortable with her long-term relationship with those. There was an open pack on the coffee table in front of Windy and she slid one out of the pack now and looked at it.

She had never been a smoker. She had only tried once, on a

rainy day in Paris, during her junior year abroad, when a thunderstorm came out of nowhere and she found herself taking shelter in a doorway next to a sopping wet man who, when he turned his eyes on her, made her weak in the knees. Her bag bumped him and she said, *"Pardonnez-moi, monsieur"* and he said, *"Non, mademoiselle, pardonnez-moi,"* and offered her a cigarette and she accepted, because it seemed French, to stand in a doorway with a handsome stranger in a downpour, smoking.

Only she had started to choke, and then discovered the stranger was American, spending his junior year in Paris, just like her. And he had said, I don't really smoke and she had said me either and then he said I don't really mind the rain and again she'd said me either and he had suggested, since they were so compatible, that they have a picnic in the Palais Royale and she'd accepted and it was only when he opened the bottle of champagne he'd bought from a café under the arcade, both of them soaking wet now, that he introduced himself.

Evan Kirkland. Evan Monroe Kirkland III, he corrected, telling her about his dad and his grandfather, Evan Monroe numbers one and two, and how his relatives all thought he was crazy but that was okay with him. Staring at her, disbelieving, when she swore, scout's honor, that her middle name really was "America."

She could still see him as he was on that day, a handsome, carefree boy, gray-green thunder clouds behind him, sitting on a bench in the Palais Royale gardens eating chocolate truffles out of a brown box with FAUCHON stamped in gold on the top, and toasting her with a bottle of pink champagne.

Him asking, "What do you want to do most in your life?"

And her, caught off guard, saying, "What do I want to *do* most? I don't know. Be happy, I guess. What about you?"

The answer for him was easy. "Everything."

There were no cloudbursts like that in Las Vegas. No chance

meetings. No one to catch you by surprise. No Fauchon truffles. All good reasons to move there.

Sometimes what you avoid is as telling as what you go after.

Windy looked for an ashtray, couldn't find one, and crushed the unlit cigarette vehemently in her hand.

Yes, Eve Sebastian was running from something. But tonight she was too tired to figure out what.

Carrying the crumpled cigarette into the kitchen, she put it down the garbage disposal. She reached to flip the disposal on by force of habit, but stopped herself. Never use a sink, flush a toilet, wash a drain at a crime scene without emptying it first. She couldn't remember checking the In-Sink-Erator so she did it now, sticking her fingers in, making a face, coming out with a handful of moist cigarette. And two slightly beat-up bands of metal. Two rings, one of them platinum, the other one showing spots of dull metal through the yellow gold. Gold plated. And quite small.

Just Mrs. Waters's size.

Windy's heart began to pound. She knew what she had but she made herself check the engraving in each ring just to be sure, seeing the Johnsons' initials in the platinum band, the words "For My Beloved Claudia" in the gold-plated one.

Had Eve put the rings down the disposal simply to hide them? Or was she making a statement about marriage and relationships?

And, more important, were there any others in there?

Windy reached in again, her stomach flip-flopping as she felt in all the corners, finally bringing her hand out wet but empty. There were only the two rings. The Home Wrecker had only killed twice.

She could have done without the voice in her head that said: *So far.*

CHAPTER 29

Eve spent the day doing everything she could to erase the words "Home Wrecker" from her mind but, like a torturer, it kept circling back. Making her relive that day, seventeen years earlier, when she had heard them for the first time.

After her mother had walked in on her and Victor in her prissy bedroom, they had started meeting at a dive on the Strip, the Yucca Motel. And he started introducing her to his friends. That was okay with her, they all had money. She'd do anything that could make her daddy smile at her.

She told her parents she had a regular baby-sitting job, five days a week after school, so they never asked where she was. Never suspected she had a regular room at the Yucca, knew all the guys who worked the front desk by name. The place seemed cozy to her, a home away from home. She was just getting used to it when one of Victor's "friends" turned out to be an undercover cop. It had never occurred to Eve, not really, that what she was doing was illegal. It was just easy money.

When the two policemen brought her into the station, the first person she saw was Victor Early. He was standing with a stout woman, his wife. Crying. Begging for her forgiveness. As Eve was led past them, a police officer on either side of her, the woman's eyes held hers, boring into her. She said, "You filthy home wrecker, you ought to be ashamed of yourself." It was the first time anyone ever called her that. Her cheeks felt like they were on fire.

They led her to a holding cell and she had begged the police not to call her parents. Yes, she was only seventeen but please, she would find a way to make bail. She would do anything. Please. The same cop who had trapped her just smiled and shook his head. Sorry, little lady. Got to call your parents. It's the law.

Had the law been on his mind when he had fucked her before arresting her? He'd still had his shirt off when he snapped the cuffs on her wrists.

Her mother was the one who came to the station to get her. It was the only time in Eve's life she'd ever been glad to see her and the car ride home was the longest the two of them had spent alone together in years. Neither of them spoke until they were at the front door of their apartment at the Sun-Crest. Then Eve said, "Please don't tell Daddy."

And her mother said, "Go to your goddamned room."

An hour later her father came in. He looked older than she remembered from that morning. His face was carved with disgust.

His shoulders slumped, his hands hung at his sides. He said, "How could you?"

"I just wanted you to be happy."

Now his hands came up. "By whoring yourself? You thought that would make me happy?"

"No, but the money—"

He reached into his pocket, opened his wallet, and threw all the money inside at her. "I didn't need money like this. This money is filthy. Disgusting. Take your filthy money and leave."

"It wasn't like that. I didn't mind doing it," she said, to reassure him.

Horror covered the disgust on his face. "You liked it? You liked being a whore? What happened to my good little girl? My precious Eve?"

"She's still right here, Daddy." She reached for him and he recoiled.

"Don't ever call me that again. I am not your father. You are nothing to me. You have no family now."

Ten minutes later her mother entered without knocking. "There is a bus to Los Angeles leaving in an hour. I will drive you to the station. Your aunt will pick you up. Pack up anything you want because you are never coming back."

"Can I say good-bye to Daddy?"

"I think you've hurt him enough already, don't you?"

She had started screaming then, tried to attack her mother, and the police were called. They came and asked her father what was wrong and he couldn't say anything, just shook his head from side to side. She wanted to go to him so badly, apologize, say anything that would make it okay. But her mother wouldn't let her.

On the bus ride to Los Angeles all she could think about was how happy her mother must be to have her father all to herself now. She tried phoning a few times but her mother always answered, so she hung up.

In the end, the police never even pressed charges, and she had no record. But they had ruined her life. And branded her with those words, "home wrecker." When her father was killed by a heart attack a few months later, she knew what it meant. It meant he died of a broken heart. The heart she'd broken.

She never got to say good-bye.

Sitting in Harry's kitchen now, she saw the sweep of his headlights coming up the driveway, and ran to the door to meet him. It was late, after eleven, and she had been worried that he wasn't coming back, but was determined not to show it. When he came in, he smelled like bubble gum, like he had been with someone else. She smiled at him brightly.

"Harry. How was your day?"

He kissed the top of her head, familiar, sweet, and said, "Long. I had hoped to be home hours ago. How was yours?"

"I talked to Nadene and found out when she was coming back, but other than that, uneventful."

"You look great wearing my shirt." He looked at her more closely. "What did you do to your wrist? And why are your hands so dirty?"

"Nothing. I don't know what you are talking about."

"Eve."

"I—It's a paper cut. I went out for a sketch pad and I've just been doing some drawings."

"You left the house?"

She shrugged. "I was bored and I wanted to draw. I borrowed your other car to do some errands. You don't mind, do you? I got it washed as a thank-you."

"I think we need to talk." He took her hand and led her to the table, turning on the television on the counter. "You should not have gone out," he told her as he flipped channels.

"What are you talking about? Why did you put the TV on?"

"Because I wanted to show you this."

He had turned it to the news. On the screen a blond woman ducked under some crime scene tape and ran up the stairs of the Sun-Crest apartments. Across the bottom of the picture it said CHICAGO THOMAS, METRO CRIMINALISTICS. As Eve watched she realized that this was the woman she had seen coming out of the Johnson house, the one she had followed home. And now she was at the Waterses'. As though the woman were following *her*. She looked up at Harry, uncomprehending.

"You are in serious trouble, Eve."

"What do you mean?"

He pointed at the screen. "All those people are looking for you."

"For me? Why?"

"They think you had something to do with the Home Wrecker case. Those murders. The ones in the houses you used to live in."

"How do you know that? That I used to live there."

"You drove me by them, remember?"

She didn't, but it was possible.

"I'm afraid that's not all," Harry said. "I used your gate opener to go to your house today, like you asked me to? There were police all over it. I couldn't go in."

"Police? At my house?" All of a sudden she couldn't think straight. The police, looking at her things. The police calling her the Home Wrecker. "Harry, you can't let them get me." She had to make sure she could count on Harry. She could not get caught by the police, not now. She had to make him want to help her.

She grabbed his hand. "Harry, I need you."

"Calm down."

"No, you don't understand. You can't trust them."

"Of course you can."

"No. They don't care about the truth, they just care about their own cases. I hate them."

He brought her hand to his lips. "Okay, we won't go to the cops. But can you think of anyone who could be behind this? Anyone who would want to frame you for murder?"

"No." She started to tremble, her mind shouting *Home Wrecker Home Wrecker*. "I can't believe this is happening to me. I can't believe it."

"Shhh," he said, wrapping his arms around her. "I have an idea. You're a mess. Why don't I run a bath for you? A long bath. It will calm you down."

"I don't want to be alone. If I'm alone I might hurt myself."

"I'll be right here. I'll even wash under your nails and your hair for you."

"Harry, you do love me, don't you?"

"I do." He smiled at her so nicely. Sincerely. Like he meant it.

She knew it was a lie but she held onto it anyway. What was a few more hours? Maybe even one more night? She could give him one more night.

"Okay."

She heard him chuckle over her head. "Those are great sketches. How did you come up with the faces? I especially like the twin girls."

"They're just people I've seen on the street. People who interested me. Drawing helps me get my mind off—other things."

"Do they have names?"

She pointed to each as she said the names. "Claudia, Minette, Martine, Carol, Ellie, Norman, and Doug Junior."

"What about this one? It only has half a face."

"That's Kelly. I'm not quite done with her yet."

CHAPTER **30**

Windy got a ride from one of the officers stationed at Eve's back to criminalistics. After four tries she finally entered the pass code for the evidence room correctly and put the rings in one of the beige lockers with orange keys that looked like they should be in a train station, except you didn't have to pay a quarter. She recorded them on the Evidence Status Board and scanned the rest of the items listed there, then went to flip through the Major Incident log book, a weak attempt, she knew, to stay on top of the cases the rest of her staff was working. In her office she made a few notes for the report she'd write the next day, ignored the tall stack of messages and mail that had come in, tossed the "engagement ring" made out of a paper clip and a Good 'n' Plenty that someone had left on her desk with the note "Love Ernie" into the trash, and headed for the parking lot.

There were a lot of people around for the late hour, Windy thought as she dug around her purse, looking for her car keys. She could feel the round keychain of her office keys, but not the unicorn keychain Cate had chosen that she kept her car and house keys on. Walking to the car, she went over all the places she could have left them that day, thinking it might be easier just to call a cab and give up, when she spotted them. They were in the door on the driver's side, where she must have left them that morning when she locked it, even more distracted than she'd thought. Some detective—can't even keep track of her car keys, she told herself.

Telling herself that no, she was not going to fingerprint them. There was no reason to get paranoid. She had just left her keys there. Or dropped them.

Everything at home would be fine.

The traffic on the road at one in the morning was minimal and she floored it. When she pulled into the driveway, the house was completely dark. Her hands were shaking so much that she had trouble with the locks. The front door was double-locked and the alarm set exactly the way she'd instructed Brandon to do it. She ran upstairs, her heart pounding. Both Brandon and Cate were sleeping peacefully. See, she told herself, everything was fine. She needed to stop overreacting like that. It wasn't responsible. It wasn't stable. She was not falling apart.

She checked to make sure all the doors and windows were locked, read the message Brandon had left saying her mother called again wanting to talk about where they would have dinner after her wedding, reset the alarm, stripped off her work clothes, put on her Supergirl pajamas, checked the doors and windows again, and finally, finally tiptoed down the hall to kiss Cate good night.

It is not only the things we are afraid of that we circle around, leave for last, she thought. Sometimes it is those we most look forward to and hold most dear.

When she woke up the next morning, she was curled around Cate, hugging her tight.

CHAPTER **31**

"We've got a four-twenty in the desert," Ned told the group sitting around the fake wood table in the briefing room. "Not another Home Wrecker, this one is just your standard issue Jane Doe dead body. Corner of Rainbow and Warm Springs."

Windy was only supposed to be sitting in on his briefing of the A-Team but she raised her hand and said, "I'll take it." When everyone looked at her, she started making excuses. "I haven't had a crime scene in the desert yet. I can use the practice."

"Really?" Ned asked.

Really. Not admitting that she would jump at any excuse not to attend the Waters memorial service. Death she could handle but grief still knocked the wind out of her.

Driving there, Windy felt like she was playing hooky, doing something really illicit. She was being bad, irresponsible in numerous ways. Bill would kill her if he knew she was working a crime scene, much less that she'd volunteered for it. And skipping the Waters memorial service was wrong. She turned up the radio and sang along.

Windy knew criminalists who avoided looking at family photos at their crime scenes, saying that it interfered with their ability to be scientific and objective. For her, after years of seeing death daily, the opposite was true: looking at the photos helped her do a better job by reminding her that the victims were individuals with lives, not just case numbers.

And yet, getting out of the car with only the desert and the crime scene and an unknown dead woman in front of her, she could appreciate the other opinion. When you didn't know anything about the victim you could get lost in the crime scene in a way that was almost meditative. Most people would say she was demented and they would be right. She suspected that Ash would understand.

The victim, female between thirty-two and thirty-eight, Caucasian, cropped brown hair, had been hit with a heavy object on the head from behind but there was no puddle of blood, so the dump site was not the site of the murder. This was a secondary crime scene. Someone had transported her here, dragging her body from a car parked on the shoulder of the road, leaving three partial tire track impressions but no footprints.

She had been there for half an hour when a shadow fell across the ground in front of her. Looking up, she saw a Nevada Highway Patrol officer, hands on his hips, sun glinting off his aviator glasses, the toe of one of his shiny black boots grazing one of her tire marks.

"Anything for us?" He shifted his weight dangerously.

Windy squinted at the man. "Not yet. But you might get some people talking to mechanics, asking for the names of customers with Camaro IROC Z's in a light color, white or with white accents. My guess would be a 1985 in yellow beige, but it could be anything from '85 to '89."

"Right." The officer laughed, like he was getting into the spirit of her joke. She could practically see him thinking that next she'd be telling him what he ate for breakfast. "T-top or just regular two-door model?"

"They did not make a T-top. And there will be an air freshener hanging from the rearview mirror. One of those little trees? Yellow. Sorry I can't be more specific."

The officer started to laugh again, then seemed to realize she wasn't kidding. "You're serious. Aren't you?"

"Of course. This is a crime scene."

"You can tell all that? About the car and the air freshener? You know all that from two tire treads?"

"Three," Windy said. "These are special tires. Original Goodyear Eagle VR50 Gatorbacks. The same treads as they put on Corvettes, but the axle length has IROC written all over it. These tires are beauties. Someone has been storing them or collecting them."

"And the air freshener? Where do you see that?"

"I smelled it, on the woman's clothes. Fresh Lemon Burst is the flavor. The color of the car I got from paint scratches on the victim's metal watch band. It must have scraped the side of the car when she was dragged out. Many people like to match their air fresheners to their cars, so the yellow could be a hint. I'd say the car is clean too."

"Yeah, of course," the officer said soberly. "I bet you find cleaning fluid, soap bubbles and stuff in the tire treads. And those yellow air fresheners, you buy those at the car wash. That makes sense."

Windy gave him a smile, A for effort. "Soap would be gone in about ten seconds on the street. It's designed to wash away. I was actually thinking that the woman must have bled from this head wound all over the car and whoever did this would have wanted to get it cleaned off."

"Oh."

Clearly disappointed, the officer started to head to his car to and call the ID in, but stopped when she said, "Beef jerky."

He turned slowly and looked at her.

"You had Beef jerky for breakfast. Teriyaki flavor." She let him walk away, fast, his expression almost scared now, not mentioning to him the wrapper was sticking out of his back pocket. It was a cheap trick but he had stepped on her crime scene.

Windy could tell them a lot about the car that had left the body there, but not much about the body itself, especially about the cause of death. The injury to the head was a bleeder, but it did not look fatal. Broken capillaries in the eyes could mean asphyxiation, but there were no ligature marks, no bruising to the neck to suggest strangling. What were present were insects, more than Windy would have expected for a body that had only been dead a few hours and lying outside even fewer.

"Your Jane Doe was dead approximately twelve hours when she was found out there," Dr. Bob, the medical examiner, told Windy at eleven that same morning in the autopsy room. Dr. Bob tucked a stray red hair behind her ear as she hunched over the dead woman's face, using a light and a magnifier. "And I think I've just figured out where all your insects came from. I can't be positive until I cut her open, but I'm 90 percent convinced this woman died from eating dirt."

"Dirt?"

"Fertilizer, to be more exact. A rich blend, probably for flowers, with a fair bit of organic material in it. That's what brought out the bugs."

"I've never heard of anything like that before."

"Me either. Reminds me of being on the school yard, 'Eat dirt or die'. Only this woman didn't have a choice."

"How do you get someone to eat enough dirt to kill them?"

Dr. Bob slipped off her mask and shrugged. "It wouldn't take much. The stuff isn't that easy to swallow. But from the bruising on the inside cheek, it looks to me like there was something stuck in the mouth. Maybe a funnel? Like stuffing a foie gras duck. I'll know more when I get a closer look. I'll do a dental impression too so we can send it out, maybe get an ID, and notify her emergency contact. Although I'd say for her the emergency—hey, are you all right?"

Windy was pulling off her latex gloves and moving toward the door, fast. "Yes, I'm fine. I just thought of something I've got to do."

She said, "Send me the results as soon as you have them thanks bye," over her shoulder and disappeared.

"—the emergency is over," the medical examiner finished her joke, thinking that she'd have to work on the punch line a little more if it was going to send people running out the door.

CHAPTER 32

"Am I interrupting your breakfast?" Windy asked.

Ash looked up from the package of Lifesavers he was crunching his way through to see her standing in the doorway of his office, her hair half out of its ponytail, two dirt spots on her knees, and realized he'd been waiting all day for this.

"Lunch. Care to join me? I have a fresh pack of Big Red."

"I wouldn't want to deplete your stores. Sorry I missed the memorial service. How was it? Do you think you got anything?"

"Not much. Dr. Waters standing there in a brand new suit, and the pair of Nikes he'd been wearing the day he found his family dead. Not crying, not moving, nothing. Had to have been over a thousand people there." Ash shook his head. "And then, just as it ends, my phone rang with an SOS from the mayor's office about a friend of his who needs help."

Windy leaned against the doorjamb. "Is that the vehicular manslaughter I saw listed in the log book?"

"Exactly. At least it's a change from senseless serial murder. Wife runs over her husband in her Mercedes three times, leaves the car parked on his body, gets caught a mile from the scene of the crime ordering a hamburger. What do you think she says?"

"Can I get that to go?"

"Good one. No, she says, yes she ran over her husband and left her car there, that it was a lapse of judgment."

"Lapse of judgment. That's one way to put it. Homicide is another."

"Oh, she's not talking about running over her husband. She's talking about leaving the car. She says, 'I should have driven away. I would have been done with my burger by the time you got here.' "

"Crazy."

"Or pretending. I can't believe I had to miss my flight to L.A. for that. Apparently she's a heavy contributor to Gerald's campaign. Which ought to help her insanity plea, if she chooses to make one." Shaking his head again. "Okay, your turn. I hear the highway patrol is thinking of making you an honorary member."

Windy rolled her eyes. "It was kind of exciting, really. My first ever case of suffocation-by-fertilizer."

"You got Dr. Bob for the autopsy, right? Did she make any jokes? Something like that ought to have been perfect for her. She's just doing pathology to pay the bills—her real dream is to do stand-up somewhere on the Strip."

"How would you advertise that, the laughing pathologist? I think she might have tried, but she accidentally gave me an idea. That's why I came down here. She started talking about checking the dental records to get an ID and it made me think, what about checking Eve's medical or dental insurance to see if she had an emergency contact number? Maybe it can give us a starting point."

"We'll have to get a warrant, but that shouldn't be too hard."

"Or maybe you could ask Nick Lee. He must have a friend somewhere that can help with this."

"He'll be flattered."

Windy had just changed from the clothes she had worn to work the crime scene, back into the suit she'd planned to wear to the Waters memorial service when her phone rang.

"I got Eve's emergency contact. Patricia Madden, Trish to her friends," Ash's voice said. "Lives in a rented house in Hollywood with her two children, ages four and seven and a husband, Dusty, who is an actor. She works in an art gallery in Beverly Hills to support the family while Dusty goes on auditions. Trish is also the beneficiary of Eve's life insurance. On the off chance that Eve is hiding there, I pulled some strings and got the LAPD to put someone outside the house. Trish doesn't start work until two on Thursdays."

"When are you leaving for L.A.?"

"It's twelve now, so I was planning on the one-twenty flight." He paused. "I actually booked two seats, on the off chance that—"

"Yes," Windy said. "Yes, I want to come."

"We can take the six thirty flight back which should have you home by seven thirty. Would that work for you with Cate? Can Brandon stay with her?"

"I'll check but I'm sure it will be fine," Windy said, and he heard her laugh. "Thank you for thinking of Cate. That was really—thoughtful."

"Of course. Can you be in the parking lot in ten minutes?"

"Five, if necessary."

"Great. See you then."

Why the hell was he grinning, Ash asked himself as he hung up. Just because they were going to be somewhere other than the office, it was not a date.

She is engaged to another man, he reminded himself.

That was okay. They were friends.

"Don't be a fool," Ash remembered his mother saying to Winston Ogilvy, her fifth husband, as she waited for the chauffeur to load their luggage into the car and drive them away. "Men are good for two things, and neither of them are friendship."

Just one of the many things his mother had been wrong about, he hoped.

CHAPTER 33

The air at LAX felt humid compared to the dry air of Las Vegas, with a light layer of marine fog making the sky a hazy blue. Standing in the Hertz parking lot, Windy looked from Ash to their car, then back again. "You rented this on purpose?"

"Just because we're in the middle of a murder investigation is no reason we can't drive a cool car."

Ash said it straight out, his toothpick not tipping up to show he was joking, this man who in Las Vegas drove the sexiest sports car she had ever seen. She said, "And that would be a minivan?"

"Oh yeah. Have you ever driven one? You get a super view of the road because you're up high, and it feels like you're riding in a couch. Why?"

"I don't know. It just doesn't go with your image."

"My *image*?"

Windy shrugged uncomfortably. "You know, millionaire cop, living a life of dashing glamour."

"I lead a life of dashing glamour? I must have missed that memo." The toothpick tipped up, slightly. "To be honest, I've never thought about having an image, but if I do, I certainly hope it includes a car that can do this." He pushed a button, and the side doors of the van on both sides slid open. "That is glamour. Not to mention the cup holders. Look at these things," he said as they swung into the seats.

"They're practically Jacuzzis. The best part is we look just like normal people. No one will ever suspect we're cops."

"Thank goodness," Windy said, but she had to admit the cup holders—all twelve of them—were impressive, and they did get a panoramic view of the Los Angeles traffic her Volvo could never have duplicated.

At three-fifteen they turned onto World Famous Rodeo Drive, Beverly Hills, the tony address of the gallery where Trish worked. There was a tour bus with lettering in Japanese disgorging a stream of young women at the corner but the street was relatively uncrowded and appallingly clean. "Only fake things are ever this clean," Ash observed. "Real life is messy."

"But for some people this is their real life."

"True, like my mother. Her houses are always this clean. And she is bored out of her mind. You know, they give tickets for jaywalking in Beverly Hills. Jaywalking. That's how bored the cops are." Ash scanned the curb in front of them as he talked, saying now, "Gosh, I wonder if this is our guy," and pulling the minivan up next to an unmarked navy blue Crown Victoria. Windy wondered if anyone ever *didn't* know that was a police car. Still, sticking to the fiction, the very young officer inside pretended to be furiously consulting a map until Windy reached out her window and tapped on his.

"Hi, I'm Windy Thomas from Vegas," she told him.

He looked at the minivan, then back at her, and gave a dim smile, humoring a tourist. "I'm sorry, ma'am, I don't know where any of the stars' homes are."

Ma'am again. Definitely time for new moisturizer. Windy shook her head and held out her badge. "From Las Vegas Metro Police."

"Oh." The Beverly Hills cop's eyes did another quick tour of the minivan. "I didn't, um, recognize you."

"Incognito," Ash said, cool guy leaning back against his couch seat with his sunglasses on, and Windy had to swallow a laugh.

The young officer nodded. "You're the one we're watching that woman for. Patricia Madden. She's in there." He pointed to a dark granite façade engraved with the words HAYWORTH GALLERIES in gold. "She went in at two o'clock and hasn't been out yet. Proprietor of the coffee cart says she usually takes a break about three thirty, before the afternoon crowd comes in. I've got a log if you want to see it." He flashed Windy a piece of paper in a way usually reserved for pornographic snapshots.

"Thanks, I'll take it when I come out." To Ash: "Have fun in your cool car."

"Driving the streets of Beverly Hills? You bet. I'll pick you up here when I'm done with Bubba O'Leary. He only lives a mile away so it shouldn't be more than forty minutes."

"I'll be right here," Windy said, pointing to a square of sidewalk, used to giving nearly compass-precision coordinates to Bill.

"Even a foot or two in either direction would be okay. I'm pretty sure I'll be able to spot you again." Not saying that in her navy blue three-piece pantsuit and French-cuffed white shirt, there was no one even on world famous Rodeo Drive that held a candle to her.

Windy rang the brass bell alongside the door of the Hayworth Galleries and waited to be buzzed in. An enormous bald man wearing black pants, a blue-and-white striped shirt, a red scarf knotted on the side, and earrings in both his ears crossed the floor toward her. He made Windy think of Yul Brynner on steroids playing a pirate.

"Yez?" he asked, his accent more Italian than pirate. "I can help you?"

"I'm looking for Patricia Madden."

"Patrice is in the back. If you stand, I will go."

Windy stood, he went. Her eyes caught on a painting that gave her a feeling of déjà-vu. She was trying to think of where she'd seen it and had just realized that it looked like part of a dream she'd had the night before, when she smelled Jo Malone lime and basil perfume and heard a woman come up behind her.

"I'm Patricia Madden," the woman introduced herself. Windy knew she was thirty-five but she didn't look it. She was about six feet tall with short cropped blond hair, a face that was austerely beautiful, and the bearing of a member of the British aristocracy. She was wearing a black fitted sweater with an asymmetrical neckline and black trousers that had been expertly tailored. The kind of woman that made Windy feel short, dumpy, and uncultured.

She eyed Windy up and down, not hiding it, then said, "What can I help you with, ma'am?"

The "ma'am" did it. Windy eyed her back, flipped out her badge and said, "I was wondering if we could talk somewhere."

Trish studied the badge and raised an eyebrow. "Las Vegas police. What do you—is this about Eve?"

"Yes."

Trish handed her back the badge with a shrug. "I haven't talked to her in nearly four months, so I don't have anything to tell you."

"Please," Windy said. "This is very important. She may be in a lot of trouble."

Trish crossed her arms. "Undoubtedly. Eve *is* trouble." She seemed to soften for a moment, but said, "Besides, I can't just take off to talk. I'm at work."

"You are due for a break. You always take a break about this time."

"How—" And right away Trish's tone changed, going from haughty to wry. "Oh, *you're* the reason Pimple Face trailed me here in that patrol car, asking questions. And here I thought I had a celebrity stalker. Damn. You should tell him, from me, that he should watch a few more episodes of *Cops*. That look at you–look away move he's got going on is not as subtle as he wants it to be."

"I'll pass that on," Windy said, her eyes drawn back to the painting she had been staring at before Trish came in.

Trish looked from Windy to the painting. "I see you like our Jorge Delgado. The man is a genius. What do you see in it?"

It was an innocent enough question but Windy felt like it was some kind of test.

She said, "Red wine spilled on a white tablecloth at a party." At least that was what it was in the dream it resembled. Her spilling the wine at her wedding dinner, everyone going crazy, the tablecloth being pulled off, her mother shrieking.

"Very interesting, Officer Thomas. Most people see it as blood. The piece is called 'The Last Supper.' It's one of our most profound artworks. You can almost hear the sound of the Apostles pushing their seats away from the table, can't you?"

Trish's tone was pure reverence and Windy matched it when she said, "Oh yes, absolutely." Paused, then added, "Although blood would have clotted in a different shape. Settled on top of the fabric more."

She felt Trish looking at her out of the corner of her eye, then heard her laugh. "Okay, you'll do." Trish smiled, showing a slight gap between her teeth that turned her from beautiful into stunning.

"Does that mean I passed?"

"It means you have a sense of humor and don't take yourself too seriously. You didn't fall for my ice princess routine, but you're not a paying client and I don't waste my free time on people who are a pain in the ass. Plus you'll need a sense of humor to understand Eve." She turned to the pirate. "Davido, can you watch the front? I'll be back in half an hour."

"But Patrice," the large man said, nervously reaching fingertips to the knot of his scarf. "You know I am so bad with the cash register."

"Davido, no one is going to come in and buy a hundred-thousand-dollar painting for cash in less than half an hour."

"It happened one time."

"Not before six P.M. You know the drug money sleeps until at least then. But if something happens and you need me, just stand in the door, put your lips together, and blow. I'll be at Carl's having coffee."

They left Davido looking enormous and confused in the doorway, pushing his lips in and out, and started down the street to Piazza Rodeo, where a few chairs and tables were set up around a coffee cart. Windy was surprised to discover that all the tables jiggled a little; not everything in Beverly Hills as perfect as it looked from afar.

When they were settled at the table that wobbled the least, Trish lit a cigarette, exhaled, and said, "Okay, what has Eve done now?"

CHAPTER 34

"I know I should stop this, stop calling you and spending all this money, but we just moved here and I have friends but not real friends, real friends I can talk to like this. It's like, ever since I found out I was pregnant, I've been wondering, filled with these doubts."

Jennifer looked down at the paper in front of her, then at the clock. Eight minutes so far. She needed to keep the woman—KELLY O'CONNELL was the name written on the paper—in conversation for at least another twelve minutes if she wasn't going to throw off this month's average. Only by keeping her average above twenty minutes would she continue to get calls assigned to her from Baroness Ruby's Psychic Hotline, and she could really use the money.

There was one guaranteed way to keep them on the phone. She made her voice go trancelike and said, "I see a cloud of dark suspicion and betrayal around you, Kelly."

"Oh god."

The woman sounded so anguished that Jennifer felt bad. "It's around you, but it's moving behind you. I see trouble in your past."

The woman's voice was muffled now, like she was speaking from between her hands. "It's true," Kelly sobbed. "In the past, I am almost sure of it, Kurt had an affair. With this woman at the casino he was helping manage in Mississippi. It's so easy for them, all those vacant rooms. But then he got transferred here, to work with the high rollers, and he swears he's been faithful for the last year. I don't know what I will do if it's a lie."

Planting doubts about Kurt's fidelity would definitely prolong the call another nine minutes, but Jennifer just didn't have the heart for it. She tried a different tack. "You're worried that the baby will change him. I see concern inside of you. Concern making you nauseous."

"Yes," Kelly said, sounding better. Jennifer pictured her sitting up. "That's right, I am nauseous all the time. It must be concern."

"You're worried he won't find you attractive when you're more pregnant," Jennifer said, calling on her memory of a *Jerry Springer* episode she'd seen that summer, "Men who stray while their wives wait for bebe" or something like that. "And then when the baby comes, and you're so busy, you're worried he'll feel neglected."

"Oh god, you can see everything. He was so loving at the beginning of our relationship, and he always said he wanted kids but now—" Kelly took a breath. "And with all his traveling for work, he's never around. Like this trip, all the way to Asia, he has been gone for over a week. And when he is here I feel ill and—" Kelly broke off. "That is my side doorbell. Do you think I should answer it?"

Sure, lady, just as long as you don't hang up the phone for another seven minutes, Jennifer thought. Said, "Why don't you see who it is and I'll hold on. When you get back, I'll do an angel reading."

"Oh, that would be so great. I've never had an angel reading. You're sure you don't mind holding on?"

"Not at all," Jennifer said, barely resisting the urge to say "Take your time."

Keeping one eye on the clock, Jennifer hit the speaker phone button and picked up her highlighter, going back to her psych lecture notes. You could learn more about people's minds being a telephone psychic than in three years of being a psychology major, she thought, but only one of them landed you a diploma.

On the other end of the phone Jennifer heard a sound like a woman's laugh, and thought, Good, you tell jokes with your afternoon visitor and I'll keep studying for my midterm. Then there was something that sounded like—humming maybe?—and then all of a sudden, a loud, piercing scream.

Jennifer jolted upright out of her notes, and grabbed the phone. "Hello? Kelly? Are you there?" Nothing. "Kelly? Are you all right? Mrs. O'Connell? Can—"

The line went dead and her timer shut off at eighteen minutes, three seconds. Damn. That wasn't going to help her average, or her bank balance. What about Kelly, a voice in her mind asked her. Had that really been a scream? Should she tell someone?

The phone rang and she snatched it up, hoping it was Kelly calling back. She answered saying, "Hello," instead of the standard "Welcome to Baroness Ruby's parlor, Genevieve speaking."

"Is this Baroness Ruby's Psychic hotline?" a timid voice asked. Not Kelly's. "I have a problem and I really need help. My name is Fiona and I think my boyfriend might be cheating on me."

Kelly would be fine, Jennifer told herself, pushing her psych notes aside and saying, "I see a cloud of dark suspicion and betrayal hovering around you, Fiona," and watching the timer start to tick. She'd try to make this one go to forty. That ought to blow her average out of the water.

Then she thought about the scream again and said, "Actually, Fiona, I'm wrong. What I see around you is an aura so bright, so pure, that I mistook it. It's nearly invisible. You have dark hair, right?"

"No, I have—"

"That's what I was seeing. And if you hang up now, you'll

get this call for free. Part of your good luck. Bye." Jennifer clicked
the flash button on the phone and dialed 911. She would probably
lose her job over this—not just the averages, they weren't supposed to give out client information. The cops had better take her
seriously.

"I'd like to report a crime," Jennifer told the operator. "I don't
know the address, but I was talking to a woman at 702-555-7561
and she cut out on me in the middle and then I heard a scream."

"Your name, ma'am?"

"That doesn't matter. Her name is Kelly O'Connell. You should
send some officers to her house right now."

"How do you know Mrs. O'Connell, ma'am?"

"I'm a psychic. She called me."

"Oh, you're psychic."

"That doesn't matter. Just go. Send them. The woman is in
trouble."

In the 911 emergency call center, Wanda List punched the disconnect button on her phone and shook her head.

"Another fruitcake?" Desiree Bolton asked from the seat next
to hers.

"I don't know. She gave me a phone number where she says a
crime is being committed but no address. Says she's psychic."

"You could run it through the directory, have dispatch send a
car over if they've got anyone in the neighborhood."

"Melvin said it'd be my job if I sent them on another wild goose
chase. Says I'm too soft, believe anything. You know how the mayor
and the sheriff are crawling all over him about the budget."

"Melvin's got no right to say that. It'd be your job if you missed
an important call. Yours and Melvin's."

"You're right," Wanda agreed. "I'd better let someone know."

"But do it low priority," Desiree advised, picking up another
call. "That way Melvin can't get too mad."

CHAPTER **35**

Windy looked around the fake flagstone piazza, noticing how different the quality of light was in L.A. from in the desert. In Vegas things seemed to have sharp angles. Here it was more subdued, the afternoon shadows almost lazy. A young man in a gray uniform was diligently cleaning one of the Cartier windows, this one containing a pair of earrings and three watches worth more than the man would make in ten years at his job. What kept him from one day reaching around and taking them, Windy wondered. Was there something good inside people or was it just the alarm system? She moved her eyes back to Trish.

Trish was saying, "What do you mean, Eve is missing?"

Eve. The one who gave in to the snake's temptation and left us all with a legacy of sin and death. But who could really blame the woman for being curious? Wasn't forbidding something the best way to guarantee people wanted it? Just ask any six-year-old.

Cool it, Windy told herself, *stop stalling.* She said to Trish, "Eve is gone. Disappeared. We think it might have something to do with her childhood in Vegas, so we are trying to learn as much about that as we can. For starters, the addresses of the houses where she grew up."

"I'm afraid I can't help you much with that. I met Eve at Sunday school—or rather ditching Sunday school. We both snuck out for a smoke and found each other. We'd draw caricatures of all the people inside, make fun of them. And we saw a ton of one another, but not at her house. Her mother didn't like visitors so we mostly hung out at my place."

Windy took a minicassette recorder out of her pocket. "Do you mind if I tape this?" Trish looked curious, mildly amused, but shook her head. Windy said, "So you never saw Eve at home?"

"A few times I went to this big place they had, practically a mansion. Looked like Versailles and it was big enough that her mom wouldn't even know if the French army was stationed there. But after that they moved to an apartment uptown, in North Las Vegas, and Eve didn't want anyone going there, said she was embarrassed and besides there wasn't room. The building had a funny name, something like the Sun Block. Sun Shield."

"The Sun-Crest?"

"Yes."

Versailles had to be the Johnsons' house, and the Sun-Crest was the Waterses' apartment, the two they already knew about. Windy said, "Her family lived somewhere else between the big house and the Sun-Crest."

"They moved around all the time for a while."

Windy's stomach tied itself into a knot. "This was three months, including the summer of 1985. Do you have any idea where that was?"

"Nineteen eighty-five. That was the summer my mom shipped me off to Nebraska to become wholesome with my cousins. Didn't realize, apparently, how strapping corn-fed farm boys could be." Trish smiled to herself at the memory. "Let me think, though. I'm pretty sure Eve wrote to me—that's right. They were living in a mobile home park, at least for the summer. Eve complained that it was foul, but I don't think she ever said where it was. Someplace in the desert. And they had some neighbor who liked to spy on Eve when she was naked in the bathroom. She drew pictures of him and sent them to me."

"Do you know which mobile home park they were living in?"

"I'm afraid I don't."

"What about where she lived before the Versailles place? Did you ever see her there?"

"No. That was where she was living when we met—I think it's where she grew up—but she moved to the big fancy house pretty soon after."

"You said you got to know each other during Sunday school. Could they have been living near the church that sponsored it?"

"I doubt it. It wasn't like a local church you go to because it's in the neighborhood. It was Father Elmore's Spiritual Mission Church. People drove from thirty, fifty miles away to see Father Elmore. I'm sure it had nothing to do with him looking like a suburban Cary Grant. Anyway, the ministry was out in the desert, no one lived near there. By now I'm sure there's a mini-mall on the spot and a thousand houses, but at the time it was pretty remote."

Back to square one. "Okay, what about after the apartment in North Las Vegas? Do you know where they moved then?"

Trish put out her cigarette in the plastic lid of her coffee cup. "Not the family, but I can tell you about Eve. She somehow convinced her parents to let her move to L.A. and live with her aunt. Man, was I jealous."

Ash had already talked to the cops in L.A. and they knew there hadn't been any killings like the Home Wrecker's anywhere in California, and Eve's aunt had succumbed to cancer four years earlier, so that was a dead end.

Windy decided to go in another direction. "How did her parents get along?"

"Not great. They fought all the time." Trish stirred her café latte for a moment then gave Windy a straight look. "Why do you care about her parents' relationship? This isn't really about Eve being missing, is it?"

"Yes and no. Eve really is missing. But we think there may be something else going on as well."

"Something you're not going to tell me."

Windy nodded. She said, "Any insight you can give me into Eve would be a huge help, especially into her childhood. Why did the family move around so much?"

"You don't know? Her father, Eddie? Slippery Sebastian they called him because his fingers were so slippery money just fell out of them. He was a gambler."

"A professional gambler?"

"A professional loser. A gambling addict would be more apt. Almost a textbook study. The way I've pieced it together, around Eve's ninth birthday he started playing blackjack several nights a week, maybe more. Eve's mother nagged him for being out so often, and Eve and her father formed this bond against her. He told Eve she was his special helper, his good luck charm. She used to wait up for him at night to hear how he had done. That was how she first learned to cook, making him breakfast late at night when he came home from the casino so he could turn around and go to work."

"He worked?"

"He ran a shoe factory with his brother."

"A shoe factory? You're sure?"

"Yes. But he lost that gambling. Anyway, after a while he stopped coming home for breakfast or came home irritable and even though Eve knew it was because he had lost a lot of money, she blamed herself, thinking that she was no longer his lucky charm." Trish took a sip of coffee and went on. "Then, when we were about fifteen, out of the blue Eddie wins the lottery. Not just a small jackpot, either, several million dollars. So, just like magic—which both Eve and her father believe in—everything was great again, and they moved into that big Versailles place."

Windy frowned. "Why do I feel like this is one of those *VH1 Behind the Music* documentaries where everything was going great until the addiction brought it all crashing to the ground?"

"Ah, you've heard this story before. Yes, snapshot of the Sebastians, rich as can be again, big house in the background, everyone smiling and happy. Then cut to less than a year later, all sepia tones now, and they're living in a trailer park." Trish looked into her coffee cup and shook her head.

"A real Hollywood tale," Windy said, maybe a little too flip, because Trish's eyes shot up and bored into her.

Windy frowned. "Is something wrong?"

"No. I'm sorry." Trish was shaking her head now, settling back against her chair. "It's just sort of eerie. You look a lot like Eve, some of your expressions especially and the tone of your voice when you are being sarcastic, but then your face changes and you're not her at all." She twisted her red stirring stick around her index finger, then let it unravel. "I guess I miss her. This time of year makes me think of her."

"The fall?"

"Well, Halloween mainly. She loved Halloween, would start getting excited about it at the beginning of October. She loved carving pumpkins, dressing up, all that stuff. She was kind of immature that way. I think it was like an escape from her real life, getting to pretend she was someone she wasn't. One year she dressed up as a nun."

"What was she escaping from?"

"God, who knows. Herself. Her mother. She hated her mother."

"Why?"

"She would say because the woman was mean to her father, hated his gambling and so would nag him, which just made him stay

out more. But really I think it was because they were both competing for his attention. I also think that's why she became anorexic."

"What do you mean?"

"When she was about sixteen, her father started to lose again
and he shut her out entirely, no more late-night breakfasts or secret
messages. See, he started treating her the way he treated her mom,
a woman Eve had always hated. So she became determined not to
be anything like her mom."

"Her mom was heavy, so Eve was determined to be thin,"
Windy said, mentally put a check next to the line item "Substitutes
food for sex as means of control" on the killer's profile.

"Exactly. When we were younger I thought Eve always went for
drugs over alcohol just because she liked them better, never really
paying attention when she muttered about 'empty calories.' For two
months all she would eat were dog biscuits. She wouldn't eat bread
long before no-carb diets became fashionable and she used to give
blow jobs because she read in *Cosmo* they were a good source of
low-calorie protein."

That was one of the saddest things Windy could imagine. "It
seems so unlikely, a chef being anorexic."

"Oh, that's Eve, full of contradictions. Like, you'd expect her to
drive some sporty car, with her bad girl license plate, right? But no,
she goes Soccer Mom and chooses the car with the highest safety
rating she could find. Or her apartment when she lived in L.A. She
decided where she wanted to live based on where they had the best
armed patrol system. And she still put extra locks on the door."

"In Vegas she lives in a gated development."

"Figures. She probably did a lot of research to find which one
was the safest. But at the same time she is overprotecting her body,
she puts herself in positions that set herself up to be hurt emotionally. Eve's worst enemy has always been herself. One time she was
staying at my house and she passed out so I put her on the bed, un-
dressed her. She was always wearing long sleeves, always cold she

said. Anyway, I took off her sweater and I saw her arms. They were covered with cigarette burn marks." She looked straight at Windy. "When I asked her about it, she eventually admitted she had done it to herself."

"Why?"

"She said she was curious what it would be like. But I think it was a way to punish herself, because her bastard father didn't love her." Now Trish shook her head. "She wouldn't let me help her with it, refused to talk about it. Being friends with Eve is not easy."

"You obviously care about her if you made her Nicole's godmother."

"How did you know about that?"

"I saw the copy of *A Little Princess* Nicole gave her at her apartment. She keeps it on her night stand."

Trish looked away, fumbled for a cigarette, and took a long drag. She shook her head. "Nikkie and Devon, my youngest, they both keep asking when we're going to get to visit Aunt Eve. She's really great with kids. She used to baby-sit all the time when we were growing up. Kids adore her."

Windy thought of the six-year-old Waters twins, Minette and Martine, and needed to change the topic. "Did she ever talk to you about anyone she was seeing in Vegas? Or even just any friends? Anyone named Harry or Barry? Or anyone from her past?"

"No. She never really talked about the men she was seeing with me. She was really private about that. And our fight happened the day before her restaurant opened. She'd only been there a month. Not that that isn't long enough for her to have fucked a dozen guys."

Hearing the anger in Trish's voice, Windy asked, "Is that what you fought about?"

"More or less. Here in L.A. she was like the unstoppable sex machine, the Bad Girl. Another leftover from craving her daddy's attention if you ask me. She'd sleep with anyone if it would help her career, which is a pity because Eve is a damn good chef. Moving up the ranks the way she did, she's managed to convince herself it was only because she was a good lay. Anyway, she swore when she got to Vegas she was going to settle down, find a real relationship with a man who wasn't already in a relationship with someone else. It was like she thought that she could trade in her bad-girl persona for a new improved Good Girl model and like that—" Trish snapped her fingers, "—find herself in a long term relationship. All she had to do was deal with her 'intimacy issues.' "

And her license plate, Windy thought. Said, "You don't sound like you believe in 'intimacy issues.' "

"Eve has always loved self-help books, easy answers. Branding her inability to get into a relationship an intimacy issue was like that, a way to pretend she'd dealt with it. She definitely has a problem letting people get close to her, but that is a symptom of something larger, not the cause. You can't be close to someone unless you let yourself get vulnerable, and Eve's not willing." She looked intently at Windy. "It really is uncanny how much you remind me of her." Trish sighed and stood up. "I should probably go back and save Davido. This is about the time when tourists start to emerge from the Beverly Wilshire with a hundred grand burning a hole in their pocket, just waiting for me to turn it into a commission, and then new sneakers for my kids."

"Do you like selling art?"

Trish's voice became patrician. "Not selling, assisting our esteemed clients acquire quality artworks. Last week a gentleman bought a five-hundred-thousand-dollar painting without even removing his sunglasses. It is an honor to be part of a transaction like that." She smiled, tossed the cup toward the garbage can, and missed. "Does that answer your question?"

"Oh yes."

"Have I helped you?"

"Yes, very much," Windy said, not sure if it was true. "You mentioned that Eve wrote you letters that one summer. Is there any chance you still have them? Or anything with her writing on it?" she asked, thinking of return addresses and handwriting samples.

"Sorry, no. I'm not sentimental that way."

"Just a shot. If you think of anything else, will you call me?" She handed Trish her card. "Or if you hear from Eve."

"She's not in trouble, is she? I mean if I hear from her and then call you, she's not going to go to jail."

Windy's cell phone rang then but she ignored it, standing up to hold Trish's eyes. "I'm not going to lie to you. She probably won't go to jail. She'll probably wind up in a hospital. She needs help. You know it as well as I do."

Trish stared at Windy's card, went to slip it into her pocket, then said, "Wait." She pulled a wallet out of her pocket, old and worn, a contrast with the rest of her expensive outfit, another layer to the woman. She extracted a school photo of a teenage girl taken at least fifteen years earlier, judging from her feathered hair.

"This was Eve our senior year of high school," Trish explained. She looked at it for a long moment, then held it toward Windy. "It has her writing on the back."

Windy turned it over. *Don't let the bastards get you down—unless they have a NICE car!,* it said in big, loopy writing and then below it, in all capitals, *BGNSA.*

"What does this mean, B-G-N-S-A?" Windy looked up to ask, and discovered that Trish had already started walking away.

She stopped and faced Windy, hugging herself. "B-G-N-S-A. Bad Girls Never Sleep Alone. It's Eve's motto. Something she is proud of."

Their eyes met. "Thank you."

Trish nodded, saying, "I want to help. Help Eve. She—she is not a bad person. Whatever she has done, she's not a bad person."

Windy was glad that the woman turned around again and started striding back to the gallery then, because she knew she couldn't give Trish any comfort. Settling back into the uncomfortable metal chair, Windy pulled out her cell phone, checked the caller ID and found another UNKNOWN NUMBER, another call with no message. She sat and stared at the photo thinking that Eve was much prettier then she was, thinking about red wine on a white tablecloth and what it really meant to be a bad girl.

Then caught herself, as she waited for Ash to pull up, wondering if a minivan would count as a NICE car.

CHAPTER 36

Officers Steve Birch and Paul Kenny were just debating whether it would be Baja Fresh for break time or maybe get some burgers, when the call came over from dispatch, asking any unit in the area of 2204 Cottonwood to do a check of the property, possible woman in need of assistance.

"Always at break time, huh?" Paul said, pulling a U-turn and hitting the flashers. They logged their arrival at 4:18 P.M., no suspicious vehicles in the vicinity, and approached the house. They passed the mailbox with THE O'CONNELLS painted in script on the side, Steve telling Paul he and his wife had gotten one like it for their wedding.

They rang the doorbell and as they waited, Steve fingered the blue and pink ribbons tied around the door handle, one of them dangling a half inflated balloon. "Looks like someone had a baby shower."

"Nice work, Sherlock," Paul said. "Just a matter of time before your promotion to detective comes through."

"When Marcy had a baby shower, the place smelled like those scented candles for weeks afterwards. Maybe that's why the person was screaming. They could make you loony."

They rang again, got no answer, knocked. No answer. Paul went left, Steve went right, they walked the perimeter of the house, looking for lights on inside, a window broken, anything suspicious. They couldn't bust in on a simple suspicion call.

When they met up at the front of the house they heard a woman's voice through the door. "Hello?"

"Hello, ma'am?" Paul said, standing in front of the peephole so she could see him, not be afraid. "We got a report of a strange noise over here and wanted to make sure you were okay."

"Officer, I'm——" They heard a choking noise, then "——fine."

"Are you sure, ma'am? Could you open the door?"

"No!" Choking again. "I'm pregnant. Please, I'm pregnant. I have to——" Another choking sound.

"I remember this from when Marcy was pregnant too," Steve whispered. "Morning sickness. Poor woman. I bet she's embarrassed to open the door. Us being here is probably making it worse."

Paul nodded, then said to the door, "That's okay, ma'am. We just wanted to make sure there were no problems."

They heard a muffled "Thank you," and then the sound of steps moving away fast.

"Someone must have heard her getting sick and called it in," Steve said as they got back into their cruiser. "Poor lady, she must feel like crap puking her guts up all day."

"Probably. So, burgers or burritos?"

They made their all clear report at 4:30 and were on their second In-N-Out Burger Special by 4:42.

Eve had watched the two officers walk around the house from behind a curtain. They had been so close. She'd thought this was it, they had found her.

But then they left.

She looked down at her hands. Made herself take a deep breath, focus. She had to finish before Harry came home that night. She'd better get back to Kelly.

CHAPTER 37

Windy climbed into the minivan when Ash pulled up and said, right off, "Her father was a gambling addict for whom she used to cook late-night breakfasts when he returned from the casino. Oh, and he owned a shoe factory. That's my best shot. What did you get?"

"Her nickname here in Los Angeles is the Home Wrecker."

Windy stared at him for a moment, then sank back into the seat and put her hands up, surrendering. "Okay, you win. That's better. Tell me everything."

Ash was still trying to piece together the interview he'd had. Or rather, two interviews. Bubba O'Leary, the man who had been Eve's mentor and most notable lover, lived in an art deco house on Beverly Glen, hunched up against the property line in all four directions to make the most of its expensive Beverly Hills real estate. Bubba himself, in a calf-length gray silk robe and gym socks, opened the door. He was stout but looked to be all muscle, like a hearty underworld hatchet man. He said, "You're supposed to be the masseuse."

"Sorry." Ash held out his badge.

"Las Vegas police department. I haven't been to Vegas in ages."

He had a pointy goatee and long sideburns. His hair was thinning on top but he had a ponytail in back, and Ash could just picture him in a cap, turned backwards, sunglasses on even at night, a white guy in his mid-forties trying to look down with it, whatever "it" was this week. Taking a chance he said, "That's not what I hear. I hear you were there two weeks ago."

Two ideas clearly warred in the man's head, slam the door and deny everything, or open it wide and pretend to be Nice-Guy-with-Nothing-to-Hide. The fact that he even hesitated told Ash that both would be an act, but he was glad when the door opened. Easier than having to jam your foot in it, and more legal.

"Why don't we talk in the living room? Close the door," Bubba said and loped off toward the back of the house.

Ash followed him into a living room that looked like it had been stolen from the *Titanic*, or more likely *Titanic* the movie.

"Sit," Bubba ordered, pointing to a curved chair in dark blue leather and wood that belonged on the Lido deck. Ash sat on the sofa.

"Do you want a drink?" Bubba made for a wood panel that turned into a pop-out bar, complete with brass rails to keep the glasses from sliding off in a storm.

"No thanks."

The man took out a glass anyway, reached for a bottle of scotch, poured himself four fingers, and tossed it off. His eyes were a little shinier when he faced Ash again. "What do you have that toothpick in your mouth for?" he demanded.

"Bad gums." Ash crossed a leg over his knee, leaning back comfortable, like he had all the time in the world.

He could have told Bubba the drink was a mistake. It was almost too easy to make him lose his cool, not three seconds passing before Bubba blurted, "Okay, so I was in Vegas two weeks ago. So what?"

"What were you doing there?"

"Visiting a friend."

"A friend named Eve Sebastian. From what I hear, you weren't very friendly."

Bubba poured himself another drink, swallowed half of it, and brought the other half to a chair near Ash, compressing himself into it. "Not for lack of trying." He gave a hard grin.

"Why did she object?"

"Hell, why does Eve do anything? Move to Vegas for example. She was miserable there, miserable without me, and yet she refused to let me help her."

"Help her how."

"Relieve her stress." With his pointy beard and glittering eyes he was really starting to look like a satyr in a bad eighteenth-century painting.

"When was the last time you spoke to Eve?"

"Then. Two weeks ago."

"You haven't called her?"

"No, I haven't called her," Bubba said in a mincing voice. "I've got my pride, you know."

"Did she break things off with you because she was seeing someone else?"

"That's never stopped her before."

"So she was seeing someone else?"

"No. I have no idea. We didn't exactly talk about other men."

"Did the name Barry or Harry come up?"

"Are you listening? When Eve and I were together, we didn't discuss that kind of thing."

"I don't think they discussed much at all," a woman's voice said from the door behind them. Ash swiveled his neck and saw her, tall, naturally redheaded, stunning in a burgundy satin robe edged with cream lace, a large *L* embroidered in cream over one breast. She was the kind of woman that had set Ash's blood on fire as recently as two weeks ago. Now he watched with detached admiration as she gave him a slow smile and floated into the room. She held onto his eyes but addressed her husband, saying, "Bubba, darling, did you tell the handsome police officer about your love affair yet? I hope I haven't missed that part."

"Lonnie, stay out of this," Bubba growled, but he seemed more jealous than mad.

Lonnie slid onto the couch next to Ash. "Why are you holding back, my love? It's so interesting." She crossed her legs, giving Ash plenty of smooth thigh and the faintest glimpse of what lay beyond. "You see, Mr. Policeman—"

"Ash Laughton."

"Ash," she said and the word sounded almost pornographic. "You see, Ash, Bubba and Eve were having a thing. The bad boy chef and the mother of sin. Perfect, isn't it? But they—"

"I told you to shut up."

Lonnie looked at her husband. "If you don't want to hear about it, you are free to leave, darling. I think it's adorable." She was smiling but her voice had a cool edge in it that sounded to Ash like a command.

It must have sounded that way to Bubba too because he heaved himself out of the chair and trudged out of the room.

Ash expected Lonnie to move closer to him but she didn't. She stayed where she was and used her eyes, looking him over slowly, with heat. She said, "Bubba is a fool to leave me alone with you. Tell me, what has the little home wrecker done now?"

"You call her the home wrecker?"

"Home wrecker, bitch, slut. They're interchangeable." She shrugged and her robe came open at the neck just enough to expose the edge of a nipple. "So what is it this time? Has she stolen someone else's husband?"

"Not exactly," Ash said.

"Are you involved with her? Because maybe then you can tell me what she does. Is it some special way she sucks your dick? I'm a very fast learner. I bet it wouldn't take more than a single lesson for me to get the basics. Of course, there would have to be practice after that."

"I've never met her."

"Your loss, apparently. Men seem to fall at her feet." She began to trace the outline of Ash's hand with a fingertip. "Bubba won't be back for at least twenty minutes," she told Ash.

"Thank you for the offer, but I can't stand a ticking clock. Are you certain your husband had an interlude with Eve?"

"Interlude. I like that. All of Los Angeles knows about it. But he doesn't call it an interlude. He calls it a love affair. Says he was in love with her. He wanted to leave me, divorce me, and marry her. I built his damn restaurant and he was going to leave me for some fry cook slut."

"But you two are still married?"

"Yes. You know why? Because she didn't want him." Lonnie leaned back, tipping her head into the couch, and gave herself a private smile. "She came here and told me herself. Said they had been involved, but he still loved me, and I should do everything I could to keep him. Smug little bitch."

"And you did. I mean, he still lives here."

She tilted her head so her eyes got his. "Of course. I love my husband." As if she had not just been propositioning him.

Ash was almost at the front door, letting himself out, when a heavy hand grabbed his shoulder. Bubba, red-faced, stood there, scanning Ash.

"Did you have a quick one with my wife?" he demanded.

"No."

"Why not? She's gorgeous. She's a babe. Have you met Eve?"

Ash felt a strong urge to punch Bubba, knock some sense into him, tell him to stop being an asshole and treat his wife better because she deserved more than he was giving her. He contented himself with shaking his head.

"Eve's got nothing on my wife. I was an idiot to have a fling with her. She was just there, an okay piece of ass. A little on the bony side. Is she in big trouble?"

"Possibly."

"Good," Bubba said.

"And that," Ash concluded to Windy in the minivan, having edited out only a few parts, "is the difference between a woman scorned and a man. Men are complete babies when it comes to emotions."

There was a tense pause and then Ash said, "Why don't you and Cate and Bill come over for brunch or something one weekend when Bill is in town? I'd love to meet him." He thought it came out sounding very much like he meant it.

Windy pictured Bill and Ash next to each other—Bill in his polished loafers, perfectly creased khakis, ironed shirt with his monogram on it, cufflinks, the shirt unbuttoned on top because it's a weekend; Ash in a pair of jeans with the pocket faded in a line where his wallet went, a T-shirt, maybe a sweater, broken-in tennis shoes. "Yes, that would be great," she said, glad she wasn't answering on a polygraph.

Neither of them got much farther in their thoughts because both their cell phones rang simultaneously, Jonah on one, Ned on the other, to tell them the Home Wrecker had murdered again.

CHAPTER 38

The van that drove them from the Vegas airport to the crime scene hadn't even pulled up in front of the house before Windy said, "This is wrong."

Jonah looked in the rearview mirror at Windy in the backseat, holding the map on her lap. "Did I take a wrong turn?"

"No, I mean this isn't Eve. The Home Wrecker. Whoever. She's not the one who did this murder."

Ash turned all the way around in his seat, staring at Windy. "How do you know?"

"The trees. And the entrances. I should have known when I saw the address, 23066. Old houses don't have five-number addresses, you usually get them in fancy new tracts. But mostly I can tell from the scale of the doors and the foliage." Windy was learning that you could date the age of the developments around Las Vegas based on the relative sizes of the doors to the trees. New houses had big doors and small trees. The tress lining this street were saplings, the doors worthy of cathedrals. "This area was probably built in the last three years, not more than the last five," she explained. "It's not old enough for Eve."

"What if she lived out here and the house she lived in was torn down and replaced with this development."

"Maybe," Windy conceded, "but I'm not sure that would be enough of a trigger for her."

"Damn." Jonah slammed on the brakes. "Look at this place." The area around 23066 Hartwell was swarmed with press vans, their satellite antennas coiled with red and blue cables spiking high into the air like bug-eyed Cyclopses. "They must have heard the dispatch from the 911 call," he said. "The mailman called it in, saw bloody footprints leading from the front door when he went to deliver the mail, then found the door unlocked and—"

Windy gripped the front seat, leaning forward. "Blood from the doorway?"

"Yep."

"This isn't Eve," Windy repeated, but she knew she was going about this wrong. Evidence, not hunches.

Ten minutes inside was enough to back her hunches. The woman who lived in the house, Martha Carson, a pretty brunette twenty-two-year-old dental receptionist, had been beheaded like the other Home Wrecker victims. Her above average face lay smashed into the carpet, her hair matted with blood from a hard blow to the scalp that looked to Windy like it had been made with the butt of a pistol. There were pieces of her hair all over the floor of the carpeted entry hall that still had their roots on them, showing they had been wrenched out of her head in a struggle. Her nude corpse was lying a few feet away pressed against the wall, hands and feet tied behind her, the spray of blood at that point showing the head had been cut right there. The knife work was crude, more sawing than slicing. The other rooms of the house had been ransacked, the mattresses cut open and sofa cushions unstuffed, but there was no sign of posing, no sign of breakfast and, Windy thought most telling of all, no sign of Lysol. Even if the other parts of the killer's MO changed, the Lysol was something she thought they could count on because it was masking something that embarrassed the killer.

Larry stood up from his examination of Martha's head, rubbed a hand over his red goatee, and whistled low through his teeth. "Wow, Kit Wilson really called it."

Windy faced him. "What are you talking about?"

"He said on TV the other night that the Home Wrecker used a gun to gain entry, knocked his victims out. That looks like exactly what happened."

"He said that? Where?"

"On one of those news shows. They did a reconstruction of what happened—he reads it different than we do, you know—and then he profiled the killer. He talked about a gun, violence, restraints, got it all, everything you see here."

Windy felt her spine going tight, thinking of the words she would use when she fired Larry, knowing he was just doing what she did—jumping to conclusions—only doing it wrong, when he shrugged and said, "Yeah, Kit, he really set it all out. That must be where our copycat got the idea. No way this is the work of the Home Wrecker." He looked up at her and Windy could see him struggling with his face, finally breaking into a smile and going pink at once. "Fooled you, didn't I, boss? You thought I was going to say he got it all right and you were wrong and this was our guy."

"No," Windy insisted weakly.

"Don't lie to me, boss. I'm learning," he paused, adding, "to read you anyway. Crime scenes, I could use a few more years before I take over your job. I think you still have a thing or two to teach me."

"I'll be waiting," Windy said, giving him a little smile.

She went out through the massive double doors to find Ash, tell him the great news about Kit Wilson, saying at the end as she pulled off her protective slippers, "This is not Eve's work. I would gladly bet my job on it."

Ash, grim, nodding, said, "You won't have to. We just got the bio on the victim. Martha Carson, girlfriend of Norman Dicks, known as 'Lice' on the street, because he's always got so much white powder in his hair he looks buggy. He's an international businessman who travels often to meetings, almost always in places like Thailand, Mexico, Canada, and Florida."

"A drug courier," Windy said. She put a hand on the crime scene van for balance as she climbed back into the pumps she'd taken off to go into the crime scene. She was still wearing her suit, was beginning to feel like she'd be wearing it all her life.

"Yes. And apparently one who recently decided to demand a larger share of the action for himself from his bosses."

"So someone wanted to teach him a lesson. This was a drug hit."

"Looks like it. We're handing it over to narcotics, unless you think we should hold on to it."

"I can't think of any reason." She looked past him, into the dusk. "This is awful to admit, but I'd half hoped we had another Home Wrecker killing."

"I understand. More clues. More chances to stop Eve."

"That, and a reprieve."

"What do you mean?"

"She seems to like order, patterns. We found the Johnsons' bodies on Friday and the Waterses' on Tuesday. That means we should expect to find bodies every five days."

"Five days? From Tuesday, that would be—"

"Saturday," Windy finished for him. "The day after tomorrow. Of course, she could be accelerating."

CHAPTER **39**

It was almost eight thirty when Windy got home. She sat in her car in the driveway for a moment, looking at her house in the glow of the streetlights. The bushes in front needed to be trimmed, or even replaced with cactus, something a little more indigenous to the desert. And maybe they should repaint the door. But it looked peaceful. She liked her house. They had only been here a month and a half, but it already felt like home. She liked knowing that Cate and Brandon were inside waiting for her. That there was sanity in there, a place to lock out all the crap she had seen that day. Everything in the world that mattered to her was right here.

Or almost. Bill had called her while she was at the grocery store and after the preliminaries—where are you, how are you, reversed from their old order now, that hint of suspicion always there—he'd gone on, sounding hyper, about a house he'd seen on the internet that would be perfect for them. He ticked off the merits, new construction, in a gated community in Summerlin, sounding like a living advertisement. Four bedrooms, for when they had another little one running around, a pool, on a golf course. The schools in the area were great, better than the one Cate was going to now. It was expensive, but it would appreciate, he assured her, and there was a nice group of people, lots of families, moving in. He'd made an appointment for them to drive by it this weekend. Get rid of that small place she was living in, move into a place that would be a real, solid, family house. She'd only planned to stay in that shabby house temporarily anyway, right?

Windy's eyes moved from the front of her house to the closed garage door, which definitely needed to be painted, but still did not make the place shabby. She liked it, didn't want to move to some generic house with great big doors and tiny trees, with rooms described as "perfect for entertaining" but lousy for living in, and a backyard so landscaped that looked like it was in Ohio rather than Nevada.

Why was she getting defensive, she asked herself. It had happened on the phone with Bill, too, until she'd had to promise to call him later and hung up. She had no real attachment to this house. They could use more space. And Cate would love having a pool. She could even picture it, picture sitting on the edge of the pool in a big hat while Cate did somersaults in the water and Bill stood at an outdoor grill with a cigar in his mouth, the perfect family. Picture them having unknown friends over for dinner in their formal dining room, Bill opening the wine, her bringing out a perfectly cooked prime rib, with individual spinach soufflés on the side, the mahogany table glimmering with china and silver and crystal, the perfect hosts, the perfect couple.

Of course, first she'd have to learn to make soufflé. But a formal dining room was a good place to start. She had never had one but it seemed like the kind of thing mature, settled people had. She wondered if she would ever not feel as though she were living her life on a stage set.

Playing pretend.

Her pulse picked up. She dialed Ash's cell phone number from memory and waited impatiently through four rings. When he answered there was low music playing in the background and she realized he was probably with someone. She would have hung up if he hadn't said, "Windy? Is that you?"

Damn caller ID. "Yes. I'm sorry to call like this after work."

"No problem. What is it?"

Windy wondered how the woman he was with felt to hear him say it was no problem to be interrupted with work. Probably about how Bill felt when she did it. "You know what? It can wait until tomorrow."

The music got quieter—was it a polka?—like he was shielding his phone. "No. Really, I'm not doing anything crucial. Did you think of something?"

Windy pictured him having dinner, candles, a fancy restaurant. Or were they at his house, wanting to be more alone. Could Ash cook? Maybe they were just having pizza, but it was romantic because of the ambiance, the way he looked at his date. Even with a polka playing in the background.

"It's the white thread," she admitted. "We've been thinking that it came from the lining of a bag or pocket. But what if it came from something like a wedding dress."

"A wedding dress."

Why had she called? "Maybe Eve was dressing up, pretending to be what she wasn't, what she's been aspiring to, you know, the good girl—forget it. I was just thinking maybe no one mentioned it because first of all, you wouldn't associate murder with a bride and then here in Vegas there are so many women in wedding dresses walking around, you stop noticing after a while."

"Vegas camouflage," Ash said. "I like that, Windy. I like it a lot. It meshes well with Bad Girl and her taking the wedding bands."

"I'm sure it's wrong."

"I'm not so sure," he said, sounding like he meant it.

In the background Windy heard someone speak to him, and she said, "I should let you go. It sounds like you're in demand."

"Yes. Things are sort of heating up. Thanks for the idea."

Windy stared at the phone in her hand, aware of a feeling of disappointment she couldn't, or did not want to, explain.

———

Ash flipped his phone closed and walked back across the sea of card tables topped by dominoes in the rec room of the Ashley DeLordes Senior Center, where he volunteered Thursday nights.

A man with white hair that looked electrified said to him, "You done? We got important things to take care of over here. You're only here once a week, you got to make your time with us count, boy. Now sit back down."

Ash did as he was told. "Sorry, Arnold. What did I miss?"

"You missed losing to Josell."

A sweet-looking woman with coal black hair and sparkling eyes winked at him and said, "Damn right you did, now pay up. That's a quarter for each of us, hot stuff."

Ash looked aghast. "It was a dime a week ago."

"That damn inflation. You got to pay to play."

As Ash reached into his pocket for the quarters, Arnold said, "So, who's the new girlfriend?"

"Woman friend, Arnold," Josell corrected. "Where the hell have you been? This is the twenty-first century. We women are liberated."

"Your mouth is anyway," Arnold said, then to Ash, "So who is she?"

"Just a woman I work with."

Joselle's eyes pinned him. "You've got a crush on her. This woman you work with."

"She's engaged. Not available."

"She's a fool," Joselle said. "You're one damn hot potato. You can tell her I said so."

Ash pictured saying to Windy, "This eighty-eight-year-old woman I play dominoes with thinks I'm a damn hot potato." And realized he would do it, if he thought it would work. "I'll pass it along."

CHAPTER **40**

Harry knew there was something wrong with Eve the moment he walked in the door. She was sitting on the bottom step, wearing nothing but one of his old sweatshirts with the cuffs rolled up. And she was holding a framed photograph.

He knew what it was. He had no idea how she'd found it, but Eve was industrious that way. He also knew that her having it meant things between them were going to come to a head. He had sensed her becoming more and more unstable, knew what that meant, but he hadn't expected this moment to come so soon.

He put all the compassion he could into his voice. "Eve. What are you doing here. Dressed like—well, not really dressed?"

She held the photograph out toward him. It was a picture of him in a tuxedo and a woman in a white dress. A photo from his wedding to Amanda. "What is this?"

He moved toward her. "Let me explain."

"Tell me what this is!" she yelled. "Are you married?"

"It's a long story."

Her voice quivered and she said, "She's so fat."

He had to smile. Amanda couldn't have weighed more than 105 pounds on their wedding day. "She looks just like you."

"What?"

"That's why I married her."

She started to tremble. "Then you are married. You've been ly-ing to me all the time. You are married."

She threw the photo on the ground, hard, and the glass shattered.

He sighed. "Let me clean up this mess and I'll explain the whole thing to you." He went into the kitchen for the dust pan and broom but paused on the threshold. "Don't touch that glass, okay? You might get hurt. Let me clean it up."

When he came back she was crouched over the broken pieces, holding a large shard in one hand and a photo in the other.

Not the wedding photo. The photo that he kept hidden under-neath it. She looked from it, to him and gaped.

"I told you not to touch that."

She stared at him as if she was seeing him for the first time. As, in fact, she was. Her eyes seemed to glaze over, like she couldn't be-lieve it. "You," she said. "You are the Home Wrecker."

"Yes and no. I'm the one doing the killings. But you're the one who is going to take the blame for them."

Eve surprised him then. She rushed at him with the shard of glass she was holding, aimed for his head, and ran for the door.

CHAPTER 41

Eve didn't know where she was going, couldn't even think, she just knew she had to run. She skidded down the driveway, cursing herself for being barefoot, for being half-naked, for being so gullible, for believing—

She'd hit Harry hard enough that he had gone down on his bad knee, which would give her a little time, precious seconds. Where could she go, where could she *go*?

Kelly O'Connell. Next door. Kelly's perfect house would be safe. The lights were on downstairs so Kelly was awake. Kelly would save her. Slipping on the grass in front of Kelly's house, she grabbed onto the mailbox for support, got up, kept running. No Harry yet. She bolted up the stairs and pounded on the door.

"Kelly!" she yelled, making her shaking fingers press the doorbell. "Kelly, open the door!"

Finally she heard heavy footsteps. She checked behind her, no Harry, then started to cry with relief as the bolts on the door opened. Home free. "Kelly, thank god you heard me. You've got to help me."

Eve looked over her shoulder one last time, saying, "Kelly, thank you," as she felt herself being pulled inside.

"Kelly, there's a crazy man—" She stopped and stared.

Harry was standing in front of her. He was the one who had opened the door. He was holding her by the shoulders, hard.

"Where did you think you would go without any clothes on, Eve?" he said, wiping blood off his forehead. "I might remind you that you are wanted for murder. You might even be the most wanted woman in America right now. Which, I'm sure, is something you can appreciate."

"No!" Eve screamed. She tried to pull away from him but his grip on her arm was astonishing. "Let me go!"

"Oh no. You and I have so much to talk about."

"Help! Kelly, help me!" Eve screamed, clawing at his face. She had to get away. Where was Kelly? Where the hell—

He was laughing at her. A low chuckle, above her head. And then she knew. At that moment Eve felt the fear leaving her body, replaced now with an eerie calmness she recognized as rage. "Where is Kelly?"

"We'll get to that. Come, sit down. This sofa is exactly where my mother had her sofa when we lived in this house." He dragged her to the sofa and shoved her into it.

"You killed Kelly. You killed her too."

"Not yet," Harry said.

She tried to get up but he pushed her back down, hard. "Where is she? I want to see her."

"It's funny, Eve," he said, standing over her. "For the longest time catering to your desires was all I thought about. But now it isn't really part of my plan."

She made herself stay on the couch. At least there he wasn't touching her. She looked around, searching for something to use as a weapon. There was a potted fern next to her, but it looked fake, the pot plastic. There had to be something. Keep him talking. "What is your plan? To kill people and frame me?"

"To put the responsibility for their deaths where it belongs, yes."

The house was so damn tidy there was nothing lying around. "How am I responsible for their deaths?"

"Because you couldn't stop looking. I told you to stop looking. I warned you what would happen. Don't go there, I told you that. It won't help you. It will just bring the memory of your father to the surface, make you upset. But you didn't listen, did you? You disobeyed me."

Maybe she needed to get closer to him. Up close she could use some of the self-defense moves she had learned in Los Angeles. But she would have to catch him by surprise. She got up and threw herself on him, clutching the lapels of his jacket. "Tell me, then. Tell me what to do. I don't care what happens to me. I'll take full credit. As long as you stop."

"But I don't want to stop."

She kneed him in the groin as hard as she could.

He didn't even flinch. He grabbed her arm, twisted it behind her, and pressed her into the couch, his knee in the small of her back. "You'll have to try much harder than that if you want to hurt me, Eve."

She struggled to turn her face out of the cushions, to breathe. "What kind of a monster are you?"

He bent her arm up, making her moan with pain. She heard him laugh and then say, "I'm one you made. Not alone, of course, there were others who helped. But you were the star. They taught me, but you ignored me. I followed you around from house to house when you moved, followed you after school to that cheap motel, hung around, waiting for you to notice me. For three years I waited. But you didn't. And then one day you left without saying good-bye. You made me, Eve. All I ever wanted was your attention."

"You've got it now. You can stop," she said, her cheek smashed into the couch.

"I'm afraid your attention isn't what I am after anymore. I've found something considerably better."

"What?"

"Not what. Who. She looks like you, only she is smarter. She doesn't want to be wooed with flowers. She likes crime scenes."

"That policewoman? The one from the television."

"Ah, you remember. Yes. I see it as an upgrade."

"No." She jerked to shake him off of her and he retaliated by twisting her wrist until she cried out. "Stop it. *Please.*"

He leaned over her to whisper in her ear. "This is only the beginning."

She felt his erection press against her side and felt it get harder when she flinched. He was getting off on this. The realization cleared her head, showed his weakness. He needed her. "You can't hurt me too much. You've got to be careful, don't you? If I die, you won't have anyone to blame."

He laughed, a horrible sound, right in her ear. "No. I only need to make sure no one knows you are dead. Those are not the same thing. I can keep your presence alive as long as I need to. It's all right here." She felt his fingers on her head. "Such beautiful hair."

Her hair. She remembered the night before, when he'd run a bath for her. He had shampooed her hair, combing it out gently, the way she loved. Carefully cleaning out the comb, the drain, afterward. Collecting her hair. Samples. She twisted her neck away from him.

He laughed again. "I got a few things from your apartment, too, of course."

"You said you couldn't go there. That the police were there."

"They were. After I was. Gave me a chance to leave them some surprises. I have to say, your paranoia made it so easy for me. Refusing to get a liquor license because you didn't want your records, your prints on file. Refusing to get a Nevada driver's license. No credit cards. Taking over your life is almost embarrassingly simple. Then with you 'working through your issues' sitting outside all those houses."

"I was trying to understand."

"I know, dear. I know. It's just a pity that sitting there reawakened all those horrible feelings of inadequacy and rejection in you, isn't it? Too bad you couldn't stay in the car but instead went in there and killed those innocent people, slashing their heads off in order to make yourself feel better. Brutally punish them for what happened to you, destroy their families the way your family was destroyed."

"You are talking about yourself, not me." She did not know what had gone on in his family, his house, when he was growing up, but now she remembered one time, when the window had been open, and she had heard his stepfather yelling and his mother crying about what a bad son she had. "You are the one who has done all of this. You are the one who hurt all those people."

"Not according to the evidence. None of this is my fault. I've never done anything wrong, I was just always the one who got blamed. But not any more."

"Why are you doing this?"

"Because I am merciful."

"You've got to be kidding." She tried to turn around, look at him, but he jammed his knee into her lower back until her face contorted in pain.

"That's better. I am not kidding. I am very merciful. I *could* keep you alive and let you live with the pain of knowing all those people died because of you." His voice changed, became mocking. "Come off it, Eve, you've been planning to kill yourself for three weeks. Since I broke up with you."

"How did you know?"

"That was part of the plan, wasn't it? Shred your confidence, get under your skin. Make you feel small. Vile. And you weren't exactly subtle, the way you walk around with your knives nearby all the time. I'm not doing anything you haven't thought of doing yourself. Only I'm doing it with panache."

Everything he said was true. She had been planning to kill herself. Had been revisiting all the houses, all the bad memories from growing up to work up enough courage, to do it. She had been in a cocoon of hopelessness and self-hatred; despising herself for not being strong enough to end her life. She'd been so close that night. Had taken off all her clothes except the sweatshirt. She wanted to die in that house, the house where it had all started, but she knew how Harry hated messiness so she had gone into the garage to find a plastic garbage bag to put under herself so there would not be too much blood on the floor. That was when she'd seen the photograph of Harry at his wedding.

Maybe it happened then, realizing he'd lied to her, that he wasn't who he had claimed to be. Who or what. Or maybe when she fled from him. But she realized that she no longer wanted to kill herself. Everything that had felt overwhelming now seemed small, manageable. She wanted to stay alive. She did not want to die this way.

But she wasn't going to let Harry know that. It was the only secret she had, the only thing that could possibly give her power.

He shoved her onto the floor, wrenching her shoulder, and brought the fingers of his other hand to her throat. Tightening them hard, he dragged her away from the couch.

The backs of her bare thighs burned against the carpet as she struggled for breath, reaching up now to claw his hand off her throat, twisting to get a purchase on the fingers. He laughed at her, standing just outside her range of vision, laughed at her writhing. Totally unmoved, totally unmovable. Impervious to pain.

"Are you done yet? I could strangle you with two fingers before you could get me to let go, so you might as well stop."

She ignored him and kept trying, pleading, "Why are you doing this?"

"Because it turns me on. And the more you fight, the more I like it."

Her body went limp.

"That's better." A roll of packing tape hit the floor next to her. "Tape your ankles together," he said.

"No."

"Do it or I'll kill you."

"I don't care."

He bent down close to her. "Do it or I kill Kelly."

Her heart started to pound. She turned to try to see him. "She's still alive? Let me see her."

"You have ten seconds to tape your ankles together or I kill her."

"How do I know you're telling the truth?"

"You don't. All you know is that her life is in your hands. You have eight seconds."

Fingers trembling, thinking please let Kelly be alive, Eve taped her ankles together. Please, she thought, please let me save one person.

"Tape your hands in front of you."

"How?"

"Use your mouth. That's the beauty of packing tape rather than duct tape, so much easier to rip. You have fifteen seconds."

She did it.

"Now beg for your life."

"I don't care about my life."

"Make it sound like you care. Make it good. Or I'll kill you slowly. And Kelly slower." He jerked her up by the neck so she was on her knees and stood behind her, his legs planted on either side of her. The hand that wasn't around her neck was in his pocket. Probably touching himself, she thought, then had to stop thinking it, the idea making her ill.

She said, "Please. Please, Harry, don't kill me."

"That was hardly convincing. You'll have to do much better than that."

Eve ransacked her mind, trying to guess the magic formula. What would a narcissistic psychopath want to hear. His own words. She said, "This is my fault. I am responsible for all these killings. All these families died because of me. Whatever happened to you growing up, it was not your fault. Please make it stop now." She paused, unable to keep from saying it. "Please don't kill me."

Above her she heard something click. "That's pretty good. It'll work." Then a hand reached around and slapped a piece of packing tape over her mouth.

"Kelly," she shouted through the tape. "Show me Kelly."

He said, "Okay," and when he started dragging her toward the back of the house by her neck of the sweatshirt she didn't feel the rug burns, she was just so relieved that Kelly was actually alive. Maybe one of them could survive. Maybe one of them could catch him.

He stopped abruptly, banging her body into the door frame. "Actually, I don't think so."

Eve realized he'd never intended to show her. He had just pretended. Manipulated her, to get her hopes up, so he could humiliate her. So she could humiliate herself.

She wanted to be brave but she couldn't. Hating herself, she started to cry, the tears pouring down her cheeks, over the packing tape. She pictured Kelly the way she had last seen her, the way she had sketched her, smiling shyly, and wanted to say I'm sorry. *I'm so sorry.* She closed her eyes and when she opened them his face was inches from hers, his tongue snaking out to lick a tear.

"Salty. They all taste salty," he told her. Then he bashed her head, hard, against the wall. He did it again and again. Reaching her bound hands for the door frame she grasped it as tightly as she could, as though holding on to it would help her hold on to consciousness. Her body got heavy, her head clouded as he kept bouncing it against the wall. *Bang! Bang!* Heavier and more clouded, until finally she couldn't fight anymore. She felt her fingers slip off and her body hit the floor. *Bang!* And everything went dark.

At some point she woke up and thought she was in a car, driving around, not sure if it was real or a hallucination. She felt indentations under her, maybe a spare tire, and smelled oil. Her head ached and something was oozing down the side of her neck and there were tears on her face. Those, she knew, were real.

And they were not for her. They were for Kelly. For all the families she had watched and envied. For all the families she had unwittingly brought to their death. And for the policewoman whose attention Harry now sought.

Eve had never felt so hateful in her life, or wanted to live so desperately. She had imagined death as a deliverance, a release, and now it was a curse. There was so much that she had not done, had not enjoyed, hadn't learned. So many people she had not helped. In the back of the car she waged a war against death, praying for forgiveness, for the chance to try again. She willed herself to live with every ounce of strength she had. Even as she struggled for life, she felt it slipping away. *No,* she tried to shout. *Not yet. Please!*

And then the blackness took over.

CHAPTER 42

The call came through to Jonah's desk at nine thirty Friday morning, as he was finishing his second cup of green tea.

He could barely hear the officer on the other end, like the man was whispering. "I think we got her," he said.

"What?"

"Her. I think we have her here. Eve Sebastian."

Jonah heard that. He got out a pad of paper. "What are you talking about?"

"Woman was brought in for soliciting. Beat up bad. Wouldn't talk. But we went through her purse and her ID says Eve Sebastian. That's the name of the woman you're looking at for the Home Wrecker, right?"

"Hold her," Jonah said. "We're on our way."

Ash beat his own best record to Central Booking by three minutes. He and Jonah bolted up the stairs, were pointed to an interrogation room, and stared through the one-way glass for a moment before Ash went in.

The woman in the room didn't look like a serial killer. She didn't look like any of Eve's press photos either, but it would have been hard to tell, with her black eye and puffed lip. She was small and bony, with long greasy hair matted to one side of her face. She was clutching a short trench coat around her body, and wore red patent leather stiletto heels that were caked with dirt. She looked up at Ash with a dazed, sort of sad expression when he came through the door.

"Finally," she said. She had a low throaty voice, like she'd been smoking cigarettes for about a century. "I want to go to sleep."

"Maybe in a little while. Your name is Eve Sebastian?"

"That's what the ID says, isn't it? I'm so tired. Can we do this later?"

Ash said, "What happened to your face?"

"Fell down some stairs."

"Where?"

"Where there were some." She looked at him now. "Why do you have that toothpick in your mouth? You afraid of being kissed?" Then she started to giggle.

There was something wrong with her. Could have been drugs, but Ash wondered if instead she was in shock. "How did you get here?"

"In one of those light-bright cars you officers are so proud of. Whoo-whoo lights on the top. Fancy. You know why porcupines have quills? Protection. They're so soft on the outside, got to keep people away." Ash opened his mouth and she put up her hand, frowning. "I'm not done talking."

"Let's talk about where you live."

"When I was little, I had a pet porcupine. His name was Scamp. With that toothpick, you remind me of him."

Ash saw that she was wearing a gold chain with a charm on it that said #1 DAUGHTER. "Where did you get your necklace?"

She fingered it absently. "From my daddy."

"Where is he? Where did you grow up?"

"Here 'n' there." Her head lolled to the side and she half slipped off the chair. She reached down to steady herself, then crossed one stiletto heel over the other. "Sorry about that, Scamp. Where were we?"

"I need you to tell me where you got the ID you are carrying. The one you had the officers book you under."

"It's mine."

"We both know that's not true."

She sighed, one eye coming open. "I found it."

"Where?"

"I'm not telling. Not even you, Scamp."

Ash leaned forward. His voice was low but there was something menacing in it. "Where did you find it?"

Both eyes opened now. "Dumpster. Back behind that motel, the one with the cactus on the sign looks like a big dick. Oops, shouldn't say 'dick' in front of the detective, should I?" She started to giggle again.

Ash frowned. "The Yucca Motel. When?"

"Before I got here, obviously."

"Try answering accurately this time. If you don't, I can see to it that you see prison. And I bet you don't want that. An attractive woman like you. So, how long before? Yesterday?"

"That's low, Scamp. Not yesterday. More like this morning. Early. Right when the sun was coming up. I saw a car pull up and dump this bag of stuff. I happened to be unoccupied at the moment so I went for a look-see. You're not going to take the ID from me, are you? I had to fight for it."

"What color car?"

"Funny looking. Dark."

"Black?"

"No." She squinted at the force of memory. "Green. Car was green. Hey, where you going?"

Ash was at the door of the interrogation room. "I'll get someone to take you to a private cell."

"You're a good guy. For a dick. Bye, Scamp. Come see me you need any kissing lessons."

Jonah was trying hard not to laugh as Ash came out. "My advice, if you like your job, is never to say anything about that," Ash told him as they sprinted to the parking lot.

"You bet. Gone from my mind." Jonah was still smiling, though. "Tell me one thing. How did you know she wasn't the one?"

"You remember how she fell off her chair? Crossed her legs? Well, she wasn't wearing anything under that trench coat."

"So? You get an eyeful."

"You could say. Of something. That wasn't a woman."

Now Jonah did laugh. "Shit, that's good."

"Would have been better if it was the Home Wrecker. Call Criminalistics and have them pick up that Dumpster and bring it in."

"All right, Scamp."

CHAPTER 43

Black Dog Demolition was in a converted airplane hangar in North Las Vegas. The advertisement boasted that with their advanced equipment they could crush anything flatter than anyone else in Nevada, and Harry intended to put them to the test. He worked hard not to kick the old black Labrador drooling next to his leg as he listened to Dwight, the owner, bullshit over the price.

"Car like that, it's going to take a lot to crush it."

"I'll pay."

"I'm just saying, you could make a lot of money selling it for parts."

"Look, I told you. I want to make sure the car is demolished."

"You sure?"

"Yes, Dwight. Bad memories. It was my ex's car. If I see it driving around, any part of it, I'll know. It's got to be pulverized. Now let's do it."

"Right now? I got a dozen cars ahead of yours."

Harry took a step forward, accidentally knocking into the dog, making it grunt and lumber away. Good. Dwight's eyes went from the animal to the crisp hundred dollar bill Harry was holding out. Harry said, "Right now. I want to watch. To make sure."

He wished he had been able to leave Eve conscious for this so she could feel the car closing in on her. She had such a dislike of compressed spaces and it didn't get much more compressed than this. He gave a little wave and said, "Good-bye, Eve."

Dwight paused putting in his earplugs. "What?"

"Nothing. Just crush the car."

Dwight smashed out the windows with a mallet like a man who loves his work, then stepped to the controls of the hydraulic press. As the steel plate came down on the roof, the car made a low moaning sound. He rotated the car and crushed it again, turned and crushed again.

Harry watched, rapt, as the machines mashed the car smaller and smaller. Finally Dwight hit the stop button and it went quiet. In front of him was a compact rectangle.

"Beautiful," Harry said.

Dwight joined him then. "Almost like they're alive when they groan like that, isn't it."

"Almost."

"She was a tough one. Saabs are solid. Ought to weigh about two thousand pounds," Dwight said, sounding like a doctor delivering a baby.

"Give or take ninety-eight."

"Yeah," Dwight looked at him. "Sure." He peered forward, then said, "Hey, there's something dripping out of your car."

"Must just be coolant or oil."

"No way. I always drain those out. No, that's got to be something you left in the car."

"Fine."

"It's just that—if it's hard to clean up, I'll have to charge you extra."

"Very well. Why don't we go check."

Dwight walked around the car then stopped and pointed to a trail of red drips. "I found the source of the leak."

"Yes?"

"Seems to be coming from the back of the car. Hope you didn't leave anything in the trunk." He chuckled to himself like he'd made a good joke.

Harry chuckled with him. "Nothing I want to see again."

"Well, I'll go get the bill ready."

"I'll be right here."

As Dwight loped off, Harry's phone rang. He glanced at the caller ID, smiled, and answered it. "Hello, Windy. What a nice surprise."

"Hi there. I'm sorry I didn't call earlier. Are you busy?"

He looked at the mangled hunk of metal in front of him and smiled wider. "Actually, I'm just saying good-bye to an old crush. Let me call you back."

Harry hung up the phone and adjusted his pants to cover his erection. He could not believe how well everything was coming together.

CHAPTER 44

Ash went to work chasing after sightings of their green car and getting a schedule of the Dumpster's days to be emptied, while Windy and Larry moved it into the criminalistics garage and started on its contents.

The garage had two bays that cars could be pulled into, but it was also one of the main storage areas for the department, the walls lined with cabinets of chemicals and equipment for fuming fingerprints. It was divided down the middle by a long metal work table. The Dumpster was in the center of the larger bay.

"The woman said she found the ID this morning, right on top. That means we only have to look at the stuff on top, right?" Larry said.

"In a perfect world. Have you ever made chocolate chip cookies from scratch?" Windy realized it was a stupid question after she'd asked it, right up there with the way sports analogies were lost on her. Given Larry's age and the fact he was single, she should have tried something about Tomb Raider.

But to her surprise Larry nodded. "All the time. I have a great recipe if you want it. Total improvement on the standard Toll House. Why?"

Larry baked? There were a dozen questions she wanted to ask about that but decided to save them. "You know how you fold the chocolate chips into the dough? Stirring from the bottom onto the top? That's how most Dumpster divers do their work too. Even if our guy only skimmed the surface, chances are other people have messed around in here since then."

"Churning it up." Larry snapped his gloves efficiently. "Well, let's get to work."

He spread plastic sheeting on the ground while Windy wheeled a ladder over to the side of the Dumpster. It was half full and she wanted to be careful as she reached in not to disturb any prints that they might pick up later from the outside.

She removed the items and handed them to Larry, who laid them out on the plastic sheet. They decided to keep them in the order of their removal rather than grouping by type, in case they hadn't been mixed up. After an hour they had everything out. They stood back to survey their haul.

Windy felt like an archeologist, plumbing the depths of a lost society. A society, apparently, with a penchant for junk food. There were six pizza boxes, a dozen candy bar wrappers, an empty Ding Dongs box, three hamburger wrappers from different chains, a piece of a sugar doughnut, fifty-two empty blister packs of Sudafed, ten empty nail polish remover bottles, a T-shirt with blood on it, eighteen pieces of paper of various sizes, some with writing on them, some without, the current issue of *Sophisticated Bride* magazine, an unkempt blond wig, and nine used condoms. On the very bottom they hit pay dirt: two California license plates saying BAD GRL.

Larry got excited when he saw that. "At least we know we're in the right place."

Windy nodded. "There must be evidence of a dozen crimes here. It's too bad we can't use this to close up the meth lab that is operating in the motel."

"Meth lab?" Larry asked. "What are you talking about?"

"Those fifty-two Sudafed packages and the ten nail polish remover bottles," Windy explained. "Someone's been converting the pseudoephedrine from the pills into methamphetamine. That many pills could make about two ounces. With a street value of at least fifteen hundred dollars."

"And I thought your former gig was as a small town sheriff," Larry said, clearly impressed.

"Small towns aren't what they once were." Windy's eyes went back to their selection. "But at least it means we can eliminate some of this stuff. Why don't you run the bloody T-shirt over to the lab and have them type it, while I start on *Sophisticated Bride*."

"You think our killer is planning a wedding?"

"It's just a hunch."

Larry started packing the shirt up quickly. "I know about your hunches. Don't discover anything cool until I get back."

Windy spread a piece of brown paper over the table in the middle of the garage and shook the magazine over it to collect the trace particles of dirt and fiber that fell out. She sent them to the lab with a plea that they get moved to the front of the line, then started working on the magazine itself.

A piece of paper had been inserted toward the middle of the magazine and Windy flipped to the place, glad she was wearing a surgical mask because it cut down on the power of the Nuit Speciál Parfum sample that assailed her. She removed the three-by-two rectangle of white card stock that had marked the place, and studied the pages. One side was an advertisement for plus-sized gowns; the other an article about "How to Tame Your Inner Mother-in-Law." Windy grimaced. An outer mother-in-law was plenty. She could even admit that it had been a bit of a relief when Bill told her both his parents were dead.

Windy grimaced again, berating herself for thinking that.

Plus-sized gowns and mothers-in-law. If this was Eve's magazine, what did that tell them? Even at her most delusional about her weight, Eve could not think she needed an extra-large gown. So was she worried about her future mother-in-law?

Windy decided to set the magazine aside and delay checking it for prints until she found out if Lisa in Trace could link it in any way to Eve. Tiptoeing between the pizza boxes and candy wrappers, more things she doubted Eve had touched, she began examining the eighteen pieces of paper. Three of those she set aside as having contained food. Four others were tissue paper held together with a sticker from a fancy store, not what she would expect to find behind the Yucca Motel. She would come back to those. Five were the kind of flyers people shoved under windshield wipers, three advertising a new after-hours club and two for a free psychic reading. The remaining six had writing on them.

Windy was flattening the fourth one out when her heart rate jumped. A shopping list ripped from a pad of lined paper, the kind she kept next to her phone.

Diet Coke
Celery
Ex-Lax
Black mascara
Crest White Strips
Skim strawberry milk
Corkscrew
Packing tape
Choke chain
Lysol

It was the last item that caught Windy's eye first, the Lysol, but the others filled in the picture for her. The picture of a weight-conscious killer replenishing her stores.

Larry came in while she was still staring at the list. "Get anything off the magazine?"

"No, I think that was a bust. But I found something better. Or worse. Depending on how you look at it."

Larry glanced at the list and frowned. "You think this is Eve's? The Diet Coke, celery, packing tape, all that I get. But what would she do with a choke chain?"

"I'm pretty sure you don't want me to answer that. The possibilities are endless."

"Okay, now I have the creeps."

"I could be wrong. The mascara at her house was brown. If she really does look like me, black mascara would be the wrong color for her. This might not be her shopping list."

"Unless she dyed her hair," Larry pointed out helpfully. "Which she probably did, since she's on the run. I mean, I would."

"Good point." Windy stared at the list, different combinations of the items jumping out at her, celery and strawberry milk, mascara and Crest White Strips. Each of those made sense, a weight-conscious woman, concerned about her appearance. The corkscrew might suggest a touch of romance. But add the choke chain and packing tape and you got a serial killer.

"I'll get the ninhydrin ready to fume for prints," Larry said, opening one of the large steel cabinets that lined the back wall of the garage. He started pulling out chemicals, talking the whole time, because he was excited, Windy knew. Saying now, "You know, I tried those Crest White Strips. Couldn't stand them—they made my teeth really sensitive. I was bummed because they're expensive, right? But now I'm glad. The fewer things I have in common with a serial killer the better. Still, it's a weird list for a chef."

"We don't know it's her list *yet*," Windy said.

Larry said, "Come on, strawberry skim milk? Totally a serial killer."

"Let's see if we can find some prints to back up that *scientific* assessment."

They sprayed the paper with ninhydrin and used the heat and steam from an iron in the chemical hood to speed up the process of developing prints. They worked on the other objects from the

Dumpster while they waited, Larry checking on the paper with the obsessiveness of a new father. They had just tagged the last of the items, finding no other evidence of Eve, when he said, "Uh-oh. This is covered with prints."

The paper had been touched by dozens of people, probably while they were sorting through the Dumpster, and it was a sea of whorls, y-lines and bifurcated flurries. Checking all of them would take days.

Like a magician picking the ace of hearts out of a deck, Windy looked at the paper and pointed to a print on the left-hand corner. "It's this one."

Larry walked off with a puzzled expression on his face. He was back two minutes later, beaming. "You are right. It's hers. And I figured out how you did that."

"Great." The shopping list was Eve's. That meant—

"Don't you want to know?" Larry asked.

Windy glanced at him, said, "I already know," and went back to the list.

"It's because the corners are where you hold to rip or turn a page on a pad," Larry said, not able to contain himself. "That's how you knew to look there."

"Maybe." Windy's eyes kept flipping from "Ex-Lax" to "Choke chain." There was something unutterably sad about the convergence of those two items, she thought, then shook her head at herself. She refused to feel another flash of sympathy for a serial killer.

Putting the list aside she looked at Larry and said, "Actually, it was just a lucky guess."

CHAPTER 45

The old man was skinny as a rail and only about five feet tall, wearing rectangular tinted glasses, his hair brushed back in a pompadour. He sported a black suit, white dress shirt, and bolo tie that said I LOVE JESUS. He stood behind the beige Formica counter of the Yucca Motel reception area, in front of a handwritten sign proclaiming: "RATES: $29/hour, $150/week. Adult channels inclu. No Exceptions. No Excuses. SAVE YOUR SOUL. Cash Only," and a framed picture of Sammy Davis, Jr.

Oscar White was the head desk clerk of the Yucca Motel. "Also the only one, but I don't like to tell people that, makes them take me less seriously," he confided to Ash, leaning across the counter and whispering it.

Ash had returned to the Yucca Motel after lunch, walked around the place, trying to figure out if Eve had used the Dumpster behind it on purpose, or if it was just convenient. The fact that the Dumpster was in an alley behind the motel suggested convenience, but it was in a line of other Dumpsters, all backing up to motels, and many of them closer to the major side streets. What argued the most strongly against coincidence for Ash was the fact that the Yucca Motel had been in continuous operation since 1973. That made it older than many of the others, part of the Vegas landscape when Eve was growing up.

But establishing a connection between her and the place was going to be impossible.

Oscar spread his large, bony hands wide. "The good Lord knows that I would love to help you, detective, but there's not a thing I can tell you. There are no records past the last few months and I've only been working here two years. I can promise you that I've never seen that woman here." Pointing to the photo of Eve they had managed to find for circulation. He patted the worn-looking Bible at his elbow. "I'll swear to it on my book if you want."

"That won't be necessary. Would it be possible for someone to come into the motel without you seeing them?"

"You mean, if they already had their key? Yes, I suppose. But unless they stayed in their room all the time, I'm bound to see them at some point. I would have remembered that girl. She looks lost. I bet her family can't wait to have her back."

Ash nodded. "Thanks for the help."

He touched the Bible and said, "I do my best."

Ash listened to the office door tinkle shut behind him, looking around the parking lot of the motel. Three long beige buildings flanked the a parking lot in a classic U shape, with a driveway at the mouth of the U that opened onto the Strip. The alley ran behind the middle building.

Ash crossed the half-empty parking lot and headed there, noticing the way curtains flicked in windows as he went by but pretending not to. Even without a police car or uniform, he knew he stood out to those people as a cop. One of the liabilities of having to wear a suit and carry a gun, particularly at the same time.

He slid through the slash in the chain-link fence that was supposed to separate the motel from the alley. It was a warm, dry day and the alley had a sort of abandoned lazy feeling, like you saw in movies about the Wild West, everything tinted slightly brown. Ash walked around the empty space where the Dumpster had been, kicking over cigarette butts and bottle caps, thinking about the case.

It felt like it was in a state of suspended animation. He had two officers looking for Ned Blight's old case file on the domestic disturbance at the Sun-Crest, and a detective at the hall of records, combing through whatever files they had there. That morning he'd thought he had figured out a way to get all of Eve's old addresses easily by checking her school records, but it only took forty minutes for Nick Lee's connection in the board of education to squash that. Yes, the records existed. Yes, they could see them. But the only address listed for Eve Sebastian on any of them was her father's shoe factory, now defunct.

It wasn't just chasing down Eve's past that was hard. Where most people today left some kind of electronic trail, Eve was invisible. She had no credit cards, didn't use her ATM card, no computer, and no cell phone in her name. No way to trace where she'd been, what she'd been doing, or who she knew. The woman could have been Amish, Ash thought. Except that she drove a car.

That was the only thing his officers had been able to confirm, that a green "funky ass looking car," more officially identified from photographs as a Saab, had pulled up to the Dumpster for between twenty seconds and two minutes, during which an arm had come out of the driver's side window and begun tossing things in. Apart from one man who suggested to the cops that it could have been Elvis, no one really got a glimpse of the tosser, everyone too interested in what they might find when the car left.

Which meant they might have grabbed first, and gone through their loot later, dropping anything that didn't look interesting on the ground around the Dumpster. That had been Ash's thought, anyway. Turning around one last time before giving up, his eye caught on something pressed into the links of the fence. He bent down to get a better look, reached into his pocket for a rubber glove, and carefully extracted a wadded-up sheet of lined paper. Unfolding it Ash discovered a piece of chewed gum stuck to the bottom half, and the words "Nadene, Tues.1230" written on the top.

It could have been nothing. The chances were it was someone else's trash. But something in Ash's gut said otherwise, and it wasn't just the Twinkies he'd had for breakfast that morning.

CHAPTER 46

It was after four in the afternoon when Windy came into Ash's office and dropped into the chair opposite his.

He looked up, trying to read her face. "You didn't find any useable prints on the paper I found," he said, breaking the news to himself that there was no discernible link between it and Eve.

She shook her head solemnly. "Not yet."

"Oh well. It was worth a try."

"Yes. Because it turns out we didn't need prints. We have something better."

Ash sat forward, his eyes wide. "You found a connection to Eve?"

Windy, unable to contain herself, grinned. "A good one. You'll like this."

"That was mean. You should play poker, that deadpan expression you have."

"You're not bad yourself. Look at this." She pushed a photograph across Ash's desk toward him. It showed the piece of paper he'd found, but now a bunch of marks were lightly visible all across it.

"Is that writing?" he asked.

Windy nodded. "Using low angle lighting we were able to raise the impression of writing from the preceding page on the pad."

"But what does it say? How do you know it links to Eve?"

"Because we just happen to have that page." She handed him another photograph, this time of the shopping list. "The tear marks from the top of the pages match."

"Well, at least she's eating her vegetables," he said, scanning the shopping list, then added, "I'll get someone out talking to adult stores about choke chain purchases."

"Oh. I'd only thought of pet stores."

"You just haven't lived in Vegas long enough."

"I can hardly wait to feel like a native. Apart from that, the shopping list seems straightforward. But what do you think this note you found means? 'Nadene Tues. one-two-three-zero'?"

"My first thought was an appointment, twelve thirty, but most people indicate time with a colon between the hour and minutes."

"Have you come across the name Nadene in any of your searches?"

"We've barely come across the name Eve Sebastian in our searches," Ash said, and gave her the highlights of Eve's virtual invisibility. He was just saying, "She almost could not have planned it better if she had tried," when his phone rang and Jonah's voice on the intercom said, "It's for Windy. It's Lisa, from Trace."

Ash put it on the speaker phone and they had Lisa's voice saying, "I found two black carpet fibers in with the dust you sent over from the bridal magazine."

Windy frowned. "Black fibers? Eve had a lot of black clothes but no black carpet in her house. Are you sure they're carpet?"

"Positive," Lisa said. "And not just carpet. Tri-lobal. That means auto-grade. Lucky for you, I just happened to do my graduate work on auto carpeting."

"You can ID it?"

"It's not all that common. In fact it's only used by Scandinavian car manufacturers. This particular type has been discontinued. If I had to guess, I'd say your magazine spent some time riding around in the trunk of a 1996 Saab."

Windy felt a chill, thanked her, and hung up.

Ash said, "So the bridal magazine in the Dumpster was Eve's. Looks like your hunch about the white material we're finding at the crime scene coming from a wedding dress might be right."

"Might be." Windy sighed. "It's another piece of the puzzle anyway. I just wish one of them would tell us where to find her now, not where we could have found her in 1984. Speaking of puzzling—" She reached into her bag and pulled out a large brown envelope. "Did you get one of these? Or did you send this to me? I can't find a log of it, and Vera at the front desk doesn't remember seeing it. It just ended up in my mailbox." She pushed the envelope across his desk toward him.

Ash opened it and slid out the eight-by-ten photograph. It showed a kitchen with dark wood paneled walls and a table in the middle, like a million other kitchens in America. There were breakfast dishes and a milk carton on the table, two wood chairs next to it, and a high-chair pulled up to one side. What made it different from other kitchens was the body of a woman lying on the floor perpendicular to the table, her legs pointing into the lens of the camera. It had been taken with a flash so part of it was brightly lit, the other half in shadow, and there was a glare bouncing off the window over the kitchen sink.

"I haven't seen this before. What do you think it is?"

"It looks like a crime scene photo," Windy said.

"How do you know it's a crime scene? Maybe she just slipped and fell."

Windy leaned close to the desk. "Look at these." Her finger hovered over four small ovals leading from the woman toward the edge of the frame. "Those are footprints. And I think there is something over here—" pointing to the shadowy corner of the photo now, "—an object."

"And you have no idea where it came from?"

"No. I imagine it ended up in my box by mistake. I wanted to check with you first in case it was something you recognized."

"Not one of mine." He handed it back to her. "Do you want to have Erica see if she can clarify any of the images using the computer? Maybe help figure out where it is, who it should go to?"

"I think the mayor would explode if he thought we were using valuable lab time on a crime we don't even know was committed here. No, I think I'll just hold on to it."

"I really like the idea of Gerald exploding. Are you sure?"

Windy smiled and said, "Tempting," but Ash could see from the little indentation between her eyebrows that something was bothering her.

"What?"

"It's the fact that she threw away her license plate."

"She could just be trying to make herself harder to spot. The license plate is the most obvious part of the car."

"Maybe. But what if it means she's stripping off her bad girl image?"

"Do you think that could mean she's changing her MO? Changing how she picks her victims?"

"And what she does to them."

Ash's jaw tightened. "We might be in for a nasty shock at the next crime scene."

Windy's eyes went to the words "choke chain" on the shopping list. "Yes, that's what I'm afraid of."

Ash looked at his watch then and Windy said, "I'm sorry, I forgot it was Friday night. You don't need to be listening to my prognostications of gloom. You probably have somewhere to go."

"No," he said, "but you do."

"I do?"

"Home for dinner. I hope you're having something good, in honor of Cate's big game tomorrow."

The smile she gave him was intoxicating, and erased the crease between her brows. "You remembered Cate's game."

He shrugged, playing it down. "My friend Carter coaches a team so I get all the updates. Tell her good luck for me. Oh and L-S-K."

"L-S-K? What does that mean?"

"Secret soccer lingo. She'll know. Now go home."

"I'll have my phone on if you need me."

"No."

"Tomorrow is Saturday. If Eve—"

"If something happens this weekend, we will find you."

CHAPTER 47

Harry poured himself a glass of seltzer and sat down in front of the television. It had been a hard choice, which house to watch in, his or the O'Connells'. They both held so many memories. He had grown up in the O'Connell house, but had spent all his time staring at the house that was now his. The house where Eve had grown up.

In the end he decided to stay in his current house. He didn't want to leave too much evidence to distract Windy at the other place and he wanted to stay close in case his project in the back room needed attention. But he had put the television on at the O'Connells' so it would seem like someone was home, in case more of those annoying cops came by, and as he looked over now he could see it flickering behind the closed curtains.

He remembered his mama best in the flickering light of the television in that very room. She'd look down at him sitting on the floor at the foot of her lounger, and rub her fingers through his hair, picking up her drink in the other hand. Television turned her hair and the drink the same bluish color, so she looked like she could be on the screen.

"What are you looking at, baby?" she'd ask when he stared at her instead of the program.

"My beautiful mama."

She loved it when he said that. Sometimes she'd pick him up, let him sit in her lap. He loved the way she smelled like cigarettes and strawberry lotion all together.

They watched the soaps together and all the cartoon movies about princesses. At dinner they would talk about them, or she'd tell him about her day at the doctor's office, helping people check in and out. She had an important job.

She made him good stuff to eat, grilled cheese with tomato soup, Hamburger Helper. They ate together at the table in the kitchen and she smiled at his excellent table manners. "You're the man of the house, Harry," she told him. "You're my little man." He had to be the man of the house because his father had died. It was a big responsibility, making sure his mama was all right, but it was his, and he loved it.

One day when Harry was seven, a man named Charles Williams came over for dinner. Mama made Harry's favorite casserole, tuna with those green noodles and corn flakes crumbled on top, and he got to drink Coke with dinner. But his place was moved. Charles got to sit in the chair opposite his mama. "I want you to be closer to me," she told him, but her eyes were on Charles. "Tell Charles about those models you like to make."

He told the man about the airplanes he had built, moving on now to a ship in a bottle. "It's an illusion, see. Because how could a ship get into a bottle?"

"Harry has been working so hard on it," his mama said, stroking his hair.

"I am sure," Charles had said. "But it sounds like it requires a great deal of time. Wouldn't you rather be learning something useful, like the piano?"

"What a wonderful idea, Charles," his mama said.

Charles touched the corner of his napkin to his lips underneath the mustache after every bite. When they were done he said, "Thank you, Marissa, that was delicious." But not meaning it.

"Are you sure?"

"Next time perhaps we could do with a bit less cream of mushroom soup mix and something more, well, home cooked. But otherwise fine."

When his mother stood to clear the plates, Charles made a clicking noise with his tongue. "Let the boy do that, Marissa. Why don't we go into the living room."

He could hear them in there, his mother giggling, then smacking sounds, while he did the dishes. When he came in later, his mother's blouse was half off and Charles had a strange look in his eye.

"It has been nice meeting you, Harold," he said. "Good night."

"But my bedtime isn't for an hour. I get to watch television."

"Not tonight." As he went upstairs, Harry heard Charles saying, "You are too lenient with that boy. You need to discipline him."

His mother and Charles got married in a quiet ceremony he wasn't invited to, and he was sent to stay with his father's sister while they were on their honeymoon. It was paradise. He was the best boy he knew how to be, hoping his aunt would want him all the time. But she just smiled and said, "Come back and visit again some time," and dropped him off at the end of the week.

It had still looked like the same house, but it was different inside. He could sense it right away. When Charles wasn't home things were like before, but when he was, his mother treated him differently, like he was something to be careful of.

"Don't coddle the boy," Charles said once when his mother gave him a hug.

Charles took away his models, bought a piano and gave him piano lessons. "Isn't that wonderful of Charles?" his mama asked, and he said yes, because he knew it would make her happy. He was to practice when Charles was at work, and then every Sunday show what he had learned.

The first Sunday he was so nervous he lost his place. Charles stood behind him, staring at the music. "You haven't been practicing, Harold," he said.

"I have. I practice all the time."

"It's true, Charles," his mother said, coming to his rescue. His wonderful mother. "Every day after——"

Charles slapped her across the mouth. "I've told you to stop babying him." His mother shrunk, weeping, into the couch and when Harry tried to go to her, Charles stopped him.

"You hurt your mother when you don't practice. Can't you see that?"

Harry ran down into the old bomb shelter he called his workshop and wouldn't come up, pretending he still had his models to play with down there, picturing them in his head and making up stories.

He did his best to stay hidden when Charles was home, but sometimes he miscalculated. Once, when it had been quiet upstairs for over an hour, he came up to go to the bathroom and found Charles with this mother in the living room, his mother's lipstick smeared, Charles's pants undone.

"What do you do down there all the time," Charles asked, leaning back in the couch to show he was Mother's favorite. Not even zipping up his pants.

"Jack off," Harry said.

His mama looked horrified. "Harry! That language."

"That was very disrespectful to your mother, Harold. How do you think that made her feel?"

"I don't care."

"Really." Charles took Mama's hand and pushed the index finger backwards until she screamed in pain.

"Stop it!" Harry shouted.

There was a snap, and Charles let go. "That is what you did. Now apologize to your mother for hurting her."

"I'm sorry, Mama. I'm sorry," he said, on his knees.

He begged to go to the hospital with them but they wouldn't let him. "Stay here and think about what you've done," Charles said. Harry sat in the corner and cried and dreamed of all the presents he wanted to buy for his mama to apologize. She came back with a big bandage on her finger and wouldn't look at him.

She had a cast on her arm the time he forgot to take out the garbage, and a black eye for a week when he ate all the cashews out of the mixed nuts. They had to buy special ointment for her palms after the time that Harry heard Charles come home and ran and hid downstairs, leaving a pot of water to boil over on the stove. The house smelled funny for a long time after that.

Charles started traveling more but even still his mama wouldn't look at him. She left his dinner on the table and went into the other room with her drink to watch television. She made it clear somehow that he wasn't allowed there.

And then one day something magical happened. His mother got pregnant. She was so happy she kissed him and hugged him. Even Charles was happy. He let Harry help paint the nursery and did not do anything to Mama when he spilled some paint, because of her delicate condition.

Harry was ten when she gave birth to his little sister, Misty. She was so tiny and perfect. Beautiful. She made the house so happy. She was a miracle to him.

He loved to hold her and change her. He loved to watch her. One night when he couldn't sleep he went into her room and just looked at her, opening and closing her little fists as she dreamed. He had been there half an hour when she woke up, hungry, and started to cry. He picked her up and held her against him, rocking her, to quiet her and it worked. But just when she'd fallen asleep the light in the nursery came on and Charles's voice said, "What the hell are you doing with my daughter?"

He was so startled he almost dropped her. Almost. He caught her. But she started to wail and Charles pushed him aside and grabbed her out of his arms.

"Go to your room—no, go to that other room you like so much. You'll sleep there from now on."

The next morning at breakfast his mother's face was puffy and there was dried blood under her nose. She did not look at him as she put toast in front of him and said, "Harold, your stepfather and I would appreciate it if you would stay away from your sister. It's not right, you being in her room at night alone."

She talked like a robot, like a mimic of Charles. His words, his inflection. Only the voice was different.

"I would never harm her, Mama."

When she looked at him now it was with her own eyes. Her own voice saying, "Harry, why can't you be good? What did I do wrong that you can't be good? Why do you insist on hurting me this way all the time?"

He had hoped she was saying that because Charles was in the room. Playing a game. But Charles was already at work. This was his true mama now.

When he got home from school that day, a mattress had been thrown down the stairs into his workshop and there were fittings for a padlock.

He spent more and more time down there. Once when he'd forgotten to replace a roll of toilet paper he heard a thud above him and his mother sobbing. Then Charles's voice, right over the pad-locked door, saying, "Beg for his forgiveness, Marissa. Crawl to me on your hands and knees and beg for it."

He heard his mother say, "I'm sorry. I'm sorry I have such a wretched son. I'm sorry for the burden to you. You have been more than kind to him, and more than kind to me. I am sorry for his vile-ness. He is a monster."

Harry stole a pot from upstairs so he would not have to use their bathroom and after that, they seemed to forget about him. The padlock was undone in the morning so he could go to school, and relocked at night, but he didn't see them. It was okay with him, he didn't mind being alone, except that no one thought to give him any food. Once he made a sandwich in the kitchen, cleaned up spotlessly he thought. But not well enough. That night Charles banged open the door to his workshop and said, "Harold, your mother wants you."

His mother was in the kitchen, pressed in a corner of the counter, sobbing. She looked smaller than he remembered.

"Did you sneak up here and steal our food?" Charles asked.

"I didn't sneak."

Charles grabbed his mother's hand and dragged her to the sink. "You insolent bastard, answer the question." As Harry watched, Charles jammed her fingers in the garbage disposal, holding them there with one hand. His other hand hovered at the switch.

"Answer me. Did. You. Sneak. Up. Here. And. Steal. Food."

"Yes," he whispered. "I did. I was wrong to do it."

Charles's hand stayed at the garbage disposal switch for another ten seconds. Then he moved away, releasing Mama's arm. Sobbing, she clung to Charles, her lips moving, eyes staring at Harry like he was something she did not recognize, something she feared. Something she loathed.

Charles touched his mustache with one of his long fingers. "You are not to do that again. You have got to stop hurting your mother this way. Go back to your room."

Not knowing what else to do, he started stealing outside the house. Food. Money. Anything he could turn into something edible. He got caught sneaking the powdered creamer out of the teacher's lounge. His favorite teacher, Miss Kincade, was the one who caught him.

"Harry, what are you doing?"

"I'm so hungry," he said. Afraid to say anything else. "Please don't tell my mama."

But when it happened again, this time with another student's lunch, she'd had to. She had called his mother and told her this kind of acting out behavior was the sign of a problem at home. That Harry should get some help.

His mother was in the hospital for almost a week with her concussion, but Harry didn't really notice. After that they started dropping food into his workshop every few days. And by then he had discovered the girl next door. Eve. Since then it had been one Eve after another.

He settled into the couch and pushed PLAY on the VCR. Fast-forwarding through the introduction, the commercials, until he hit the part he wanted. He watched it, rewound, and watched it again, hitting pause in the middle.

He raised his glass to the television and said, "To us, Windy." He took a sip. "See you tomorrow." He hoped she liked the present he'd sent her.

CHAPTER 48

On the way home from the office that Friday night, Windy did one thing she was proud of and one thing she was not. She turned off her cell phone, opened the windows to the warm night air, and sang "Ninety-nine Red Balloons" along with the radio at the top of her lungs. That was the good thing.

The bad thing was buying a copy of the current issue of *Sophisticated Bride* at the supermarket when she went to pick up Cate's all time favorite food, chicken fingers. She supposed she should be more embarrassed about feeding her daughter chicken fingers than buying a wedding magazine, but as she went to get in line she could not shake the feeling that everyone was staring at her. She added a head of lettuce to her cart. At least that canceled out the chicken fingers. And it covered up the magazine.

Why did she care if people thought she was getting married? Hell, she *was* getting married, she reminded herself. She was a bride. She probably should have been reading *Sophisticated Bride* for months.

But that wasn't why she was buying it, and she knew that. She was buying it because she could not leave work alone. Because she was obsessed with the case and she was letting it spill over into her normal life. And because she could not stop thinking about Eve.

When Windy got home, she found a long message from Bill on

her voice mail saying he wasn't going to make it into town the next day in time for Cate's game but he'd see her that night, and an enormous bouquet of white lilies from him on her desk, "So I can be present even when I'm absent," the card said.

"Someone's planning on getting laid this weekend," Brandon whispered, then disappeared into the kitchen to start dinner before she could glare at him.

At dinner they discussed the merits of leaving the flowers on Windy's desk, or moving them into Cate's room, Cate lobbying for the latter, all others against. The voting broke down on the issue of changing the name of chicken fingers to chicken toes since, as Windy pointed out, chickens had toes not fingers. Cate opposed the name change on the ground that chicken toes sounded "totally gross." Brandon abstained, saying no matter what you called them, they were "totally gross," so it didn't make a difference. Windy had to kick him under the table to keep him from explaining what he meant; she was still recovering from what happened after he told Cate what was in hot dogs.

Cate was so excited about her game the next day and the slumber party she was attending afterwards—her first one ever—that she got out of bed five times to remind Windy to pack this or bring that. But even in her excitement, and under threat of the longest tickling of her life, she would not reveal what Ash's message to her, "L-S-K," meant. "It's a special secret between just me and Ash," she told Windy.

When Cate was finally asleep, Windy sat down at her desk with the *Sophisticated Bride* and started to read it. She wanted to go straight to the article that Eve had marked, but she forced herself to begin at the beginning, thinking maybe there was something earlier on that had triggered Eve to mark that piece later. By the time she reached "Taming Your Inner Mother-in-Law," she knew a lot more about "The Perfect Bridesmaid Gift for Under $200," "Banishing

That Bulge Before Your Big Day," and "Elegant Floral Designs That Never Go out of Style," but nothing more about Eve.

She hadn't even realized floral designs had styles.

She no longer found the idea of a bride and a serial killer incompatible, however, not after seeing all the rules and decisions and inane things that seemed to go along with trying to get married. There wasn't a page in the magazine about why you would want to get married, or what happened after you did, how sometimes it could be great and other times really hard. Nothing about marriage being a compromise, about balancing your work and the rest of your life, about raising a six-year-old by yourself and maybe not wanting to share her. About what happens if you get to marry the love of your life and he dies and you have to start over, but you're afraid.

About what to do if you're not even sure what you're afraid of.

Windy decided she was not destined to be a *Sophisticated Bride*. Maybe if there were a magazine called *Deadbeat Bride*, that might be more her style. Or maybe she would just stick to crime scene photos.

The clock on her desk showed a quarter to midnight. Almost Saturday. Was Eve out there somewhere, with her knife to another family's throat?

Only insane people asked questions like that before they went to bed, she told herself. Or people trying to make themselves insane. Cursing herself, she poured an inch of scotch in a tumbler and carried it up the stairs to her bedroom. She was going to sleep tonight. And then she was going to get up and go to Cate's soccer game and cheer like mad. And then, when Cate was at her slumber party and Bill was still en route, then she would think about killers. Not before, and not after. She hoped Bill wasn't on an afternoon flight.

As she fell asleep she wondered how you were supposed to plan your dream wedding, when all your dreams were about dead people.

CHAPTER 49

Strange shapes hunkered in the darkness of the demolition yard, shadows lit only by the light over the doorway outside. Every inch of Eve's body ached, but she reveled in it—dead people did not ache. The pain meant she was alive.

Her lips were chapped and her throat itched with dryness. In the half light she could see that she'd bled through the sweatshirt, and her legs were covered in dark gashes, some of them still glittering with pieces of glass. She did not know how long she had been there, but it had to be hours.

She had been jolted out of unconsciousness earlier by the sound of glass being smashed. Without thinking, she'd used all her strength to push down the backseat of the car from the trunk with her bound hands and crawl out the window opening. Jagged shards of glass had ripped at her skin and when she was almost out, her taped ankles had caught on them. Dangling there, she had looked up and seen the press coming down on top of her. *No!* she had wanted to scream. Not like this. I am not dying like this.

Only the reinforced roof of the car had kept her from being impaled right there. When the press lifted again, the tape on her ankles ripped and she fell to the ground. She had managed to stumble away and hide behind the front end of an old Ford before the steel plate crunched down and the roof supports of her car gave way. She lay there on the ground, trying to catch her breath, make sense of what she was seeing. When the noise stopped and the footsteps came closer, she had been sure they had seen her, that Harry was coming to get her, and she had no more strength.

But he hadn't. He just looked at the car, said something about the blood trail, then got on the phone. What had he said? Eve told herself to remember, but it was gone. God, she was so thirsty.

She had floated between consciousness and unconsciousness then, half aware of Harry talking with someone far away.

"I was hoping you could give me a ride home," he said. "It's worth two hundred dollars to me."

Another man's voice replied, "For that, I'll drive you any-where." Then footsteps, a clanging noise, and silence again.

She had slid into it, only to awake now. It had been light then but it was dark now, deep night. She willed herself to move. Her mind was hazy and her legs wobbled under her, but she knew she had to get out. She had to do something. Warn someone. Yes, that was it. But who? She could not remember.

She rubbed her bound wrists against the edge of the old Ford until the tape gave way, then clutched the side of the car and pulled herself to her feet. She had to bite back a moan at the stinging in her legs and head, forcing herself to look around. She was in a huge building, like an airplane hangar completely enclosed, filled with pieces of cars, ghoulish half-mangled silhouettes. She could see walls but no doors, no way out. Then she realized that one of the walls was a door, a pull-down door big enough to drive a car through. Of course. She stumbled toward it, trying to run, sighing at the pain, her dry tongue huge in her mouth, and looked for a way to open it. A button, a winch, something. She had to get out of here. She had to—

She found a lever and pushed it upward. Somewhere a motor

started to rumble, and she saw the door begin to lift. It climbed one centimeter, two, then stopped abruptly. The motor squealed and fell silent. The door was locked from the outside.

Lying down on the floor she peered as well as she could through the thin opening. She was looking into a street or alley. It was completely deserted. She was trapped. She had escaped being crushed only to die like this, on the floor of a garage.

She tried to scream but the only sound that came out was a dry rattle. She felt the coldness of the concrete floor against her, felt her strength drain away, and then felt nothing.

CHAPTER 50

"Mommy," Cate's voice said. "These have crust on them. I hate the crusts."

Over the sound of running water Windy answered, "You liked them last week."

Silverware clanged on the floor as Cate shouted, "I HATE THEM! I CAN'T STAND TO LOOK AT THEM."

The water got shut off and Windy's footsteps rushed across the room to comfort her daughter. Her voice was soothing as she said, "Shhh, honey. We'll cut them off. Okay? You're nervous about the game and that's normal, but you don't want to take it out on your toast. Hardly seems fair. It can't fight back."

Cate laughed and Windy laughed with her, crisis averted. Harry could almost hear her sigh with relief, he thought, as he rewound the tape and listened to it again. It had been a snap to install the audio surveillance equipment in the kitchen. She'd never even noticed the microphone in the oatmeal.

He listened to the tape from that morning as he drove to the park where Cate's soccer game was taking place.

"Don't forget the present for Lutece," Cate was saying on the tape now. It sounded like her mouth was full. Little girls were disgusting.

"I've already got it by the front door," Windy assured her. "Listen, this is your first slumber party. I remember the first time I went to a slumber party I got scar—I had trouble sleeping. If you have any problem falling asleep, or you want anything, just call me and I'll come get you."

A slumber party, Harry thought. That was very interesting. An entire house full of little girls. It would be a challenge for him. And it would certainly interest Windy. He'd need to get more tape, though.

Cate said, "I'm not scared, Mom."

"I didn't say you were. I just wanted you to know you could call me."

"We're going to have pizza."

Harry wondered how that made Windy feel, knowing that pizza could replace her love. He had waited for Cate and Windy to leave the house before picking up the tape so he was ten minutes behind them arriving at the soccer field. He saw Windy finding her seat in the stands, Cate, talking to her, then running off to join the other little girls.

Look at Windy, playing the good mother. She did it well, but she did not make it look easy, not the way the other mothers did. They would give their whole lives up for their kids. Windy was trying to do both.

She was distracted.

It was fun to watch her here, Harry thought as the game got underway. She got so into it, completely forgetting where she was, that it wasn't mature to scream so loud. Cheering like mad, jumping up and down when Cate just kicked the ball, didn't even get a goal. The other mothers looked at her from the corners of their eyes like they were thinking, didn't she know her daughter hadn't scored? But Windy was happy simply to see Cate out there trying. She was so proud of her. She couldn't think of anything else.

Harry knew the power of her complete attention. He knew the

way it felt to have her focused on you, her eyes seeing what your eyes left, her footsteps tracing yours, mimicking your movements, like a talented dancer performing a choreographed piece. To hold Windy's attention meant to control her. All it took, he knew, was to give her something interesting to look at.

And he knew he could be far more fascinating than some six-year-old's soccer game. As he took the tape of Windy and Cate out of his player and put in the other one, he weighed the pros and cons of the slumber party. It would definitely make an impression on Windy. But it might be overkill.

Plus, he knew Cate would come in handy later on.

CHAPTER 51

"Did you see, did you see? I kicked the ball! Hard!"

"I know!" Windy and Cate were both jumping up and down at the edge of the soccer field after the game. "You did great, honey. I'm so proud of you."

"I didn't make a goal."

"That's okay, maybe next time. I am just so impressed by how much your kicking has improved."

Cate smiled huge and Windy felt a sharp pang of sadness. She wished Evan were here to see this. His daughter, his wonderful daughter. She pulled Cate into her arms and smothered her.

"Mommmmy!" Cate squirmed and giggled until Windy let go. "You're weird."

"You bet. Now let's go get your other clothes and your bag out of the car so you can go to Lutece's."

"And the you-know-what."

"And the present."

Lutece's parents had rented a limo to take the girls from the soccer game to the pizza restaurant where the party would start, and Windy watched Cate pile into it, then re-emerge with her head out the sun roof, waving like a beauty pageant contestant. She was joined by four other girls as they pulled away, Windy resisting the urge to tell her to sit down and fasten her seat belt, resisting the urge to run after them and bring her home with her and keep her there forever.

Cate's first ever slumber party. She was growing up so fast, Windy thought, and realized that unfamiliar sensation was the prick of tears in her eyes. The last time she had felt this close to crying was on Cate's first day of pre-kindergarten. That day, watching Cate take her new teacher's hand and join a play circle without ever looking back, she had felt a kind of hollow aloneness she'd never imagined. She was feeling it again now.

Which was absurd, because she wasn't alone. There were tons of moms around, and she was engaged to a great man and had a great life. And still some immature part of her wished Cate hadn't wanted to go to the slumber party, had wanted to spend the day with her mom buying plants for the backyard or carving pumpkins or making lasagna. Even though she didn't know how to make lasagna.

She'd turned her work phone off during the game—Bill would be so proud of her—and when she turned it back on now the call log showed one message from a Vegas number she didn't recognize. Leaning against the side of her car, eyes closed, face in the sun, she pushed buttons, and listened.

"Hello," a woman's voice said. "My name is Kelly O'Connell. I am here with the Home Wrecker. I am going to die because I've been a bad girl. Thank you. And tell my husband Kurt that I wish—"

Silence.

CHAPTER 52

"I'm pretty sure it is scripted," Ash said, listening to the message for the fourth time as Jonah drove the task force SUV from the soccer field toward the address that matched the phone number the call had originated from. The patrol cars that arrived first had radioed in a 420, homicide, female. Their reaction left no question that it was the work of the Home Wrecker. The criminalistics van was meeting them there.

"If I hadn't turned my phone off, we might have gotten to her sooner. In time," Windy said from the backseat. It was noon now. The call had come through at ten thirty A.M.

"We don't know that," Ash said. "With the level of control Eve wields, I doubt she would have let that happen. And you are allowed to have your phone off. It's Saturday, Windy."

"I should have had it on."

Ash twisted around in his seat and stared at her until she met his eyes. "You're wrong, and later on I'll argue with you about it. Right now you need to let it go. This is probably exactly what she wants to do, debilitate you. You've got to move past it and pay attention to what the call can tell us."

"You're right." Windy was grateful for his support, and his reminder to refocus. There was no way she could do her job right if she let her personal feelings intrude. "Tell me why you think it's scripted."

"Did you hear that rustling in the background? Like Kelly was reading from something."

"That would be a sign of escalation. Increased domination to get her victims to say what she wants them to, even to the police. Of course, it could be Eve herself speaking, just pretending to be Kelly."

"I'm having Pete in audio compare the voice to the voice on the answering machine at her house and her café. So far he doesn't think so." He paused before adding, "This kind of escalation, along with the message for Kurt, seems to suggest that Eve is not just trying to emulate the men in the family, but to get their attention."

Windy's mind flipped to the sentence Kelly left unfinished, what she wanted to tell Kurt, the words she would have wanted to leave him with for all time. God, she knew how that felt, to have your relationship cut off in the middle of something. "This isn't just about attention. It's about punishment. Kurt is going to spend months filling in the blanks at the end of Kelly's last sentence, wondering what she would have said to him if she'd had the chance, writing and rewriting the history of their whole relationship through that one unfinished act." Some silences, Windy knew, were far worse than being yelled at.

She turned to stare out the window as the scenery raced by, normal people going about their normal Saturdays, none of them responsible for the death of a woman just because they'd turned their cell phones off.

God, she could not wait to get to the crime scene.

CHAPTER **53**

The first thing Windy noticed about the O'Connell house was how perfect it was. The O'Connells had only moved in two months earlier but Kelly, six months pregnant with their first child, had already almost finished organizing the nursery. Kurt O'Connell's sister Marie told Windy about that, after an officer had failed to stop Kurt on the front walkway of his house and he'd burst in, demanding what the hell right the cops had to—

Stopping dead at the sight of his wife's body.

An EMT had to empty an almost lethal quantity of tranquilizers into him before he would calm down.

Kurt worked for one of the larger casinos, the assistant to a man who brought in the big money gamblers. He had been away on a business trip in Taiwan for a week and just gotten in that afternoon. None of the daytime receptionists at his office remembered anyone calling to ask about his schedule, and Metro was still hunting down the other shifts.

Based on the evidence, there was no question that Kelly had been killed in her bedroom while kneeling by the side of the bed, her head severed by a butcher knife, just like the others, her killer wearing Kurt's shoes and shirt. There was an octagonal void in the blood spatter on the bureau, same dimensions as the ones at the Waterses' and the Johnsons'. Toast crumbs visible on her gums and un-

der one fingernail showed that she had also eaten breakfast. The
house was filled with the smell of Lysol. Kelly's wedding ring was
missing.

Kelly O'Connell had dedicated herself to making a home that
looked like an upscale catalogue shoot, a style Brandon called "PTA
chic." The sofa covered in a quietly patterned beige, the armchairs
in a complementary brown and green stripe, one of them with a
tiny needlepointed pillow telling everyone "This Is Not a Dress Re-
hearsal." In case the dead woman sprawled over the fake tiger rug
on the floor wasn't enough of a reminder, Windy thought.

Black and white photos of Paris, not taken by either of the
O'Connells Windy would bet, hung over the couch, fake ferns stood
in distressed white iron plant holders in the corners of the room,
the coffee table had what designers called "antique bronze-finish-
style" legs. Brandon had banned the introduction of any antique-
style objects into Windy's home. "Make it real or make it modern,
honey," was his motto.

Kelly and Kurt couldn't have afforded real if they had wanted to
on Kurt's single salary, but Kelly had done the best to make what
she pictured as a grown-up home, her sister-in-law told detectives,
doing all the decorating herself, taking meticulous care of everything. Vacuum lines on the rug in the hallway showed how Kelly had
spent her last free moments, a final memorial to housekeeping.

"Wife, homemaker, future mother. She was like an indictment
of everything Eve wasn't," Windy said to Ash.

"Maybe that is why Eve went a little nuts on her."

They had gotten a shock when they rolled Kelly's body over.
Unlike the other victims, Kelly had been brutally stabbed, hit, and
cut. There was a spot of blood on her big toe, otherwise clean. That
looked like an accidental drip mark but the other marks were deliberate. Windy kneeled and rubbed her fingers over Kelly's eyelashes.

She said, "She's not wearing mascara," like she was talking to
herself.

"Is that important?" Ash asked.

"It is just more confirmation that the shopping list we found yesterday was Eve's. There were traces of black mascara on the phone. If it wasn't from Kelly, it must have been from Eve."

"You sound unconvinced."

"No. I'm convinced. There is no way not to be, the evidence all links together. I guess I am just confused. And in the absence of children, people to use as leverage, I can't figure out how Eve would have made Kelly have breakfast with her while she was alive."

Windy stayed on her knees and moved to look at the lacerations on Kelly's arms, then carefully slid aside the robe the woman was wearing. A small knife—a butter knife, Windy discovered later—had been driven into her heart. Toothpicks had been driven into her eyes and her nose was missing. Windy shook her head. "All of these injuries to the body are postmortem."

"Kelly O'Connell was a bit younger, but of all the victims, she is the only one that looks anything like—" Ash's eyes went to Windy. "Like you. And Eve."

"What do you mean?" Windy asked. "That Eve is playing at killing *herself*?"

"Her ideal self. It's been there all along, violence against the women, the woman she couldn't be."

"So you are suggesting that her female victims could be her surrogates."

"Exactly. We've been focused on how the killings affect the man of the house, but maybe it does both. Maybe with each murder, she is directing more rage against herself."

"This could be what we discussed yesterday, a change in her methods. Have you been able to confirm that her family lived in this house?"

"Not yet. Why?"

"What if she is becoming less interested in families, the houses she used to live in, and is going to start targeting women? Like herself." Like me, Windy wanted to shout, struggling to keep her hands steady.

"That's an unpleasant thought."

Focus on the crime scene, she told herself. Keep it professional, don't let yourself get scared, don't let your guard down. She looked at Kelly O'Connell's mangled face and said, "I have another one for you. I think I just figured how she got Kelly to sit still for breakfast."

CHAPTER 54

Dr. Bob's first words in the warm examining room at five that evening confirmed what Windy had been thinking. The medical examiner pointed her gloved hand to marks on Kelly O'Connell's neck that became visible when the blood was cleaned off and said, "Choke chain was used to control the victim."

"Like you would use on a dog? Or in S&M?" Ash asked, wanting to make sure his detectives were on the right track.

"For S&M people usually prefer bigger links than this one. More dramatic effect. Anyway, the one used here was a pretty standard dog chain with an aluminum coating. I pulled a flake of it out of her hair."

"But she wasn't strangled with it, was she?" Windy asked.

"Oh no." Dr. Bob shook her head definitely. "She didn't die of that. Your killer just used it for discipline."

"You were right," Ash said to Windy. "Eve used it to make her do what she wanted."

"What was bad news for the victim is good news for you," Dr. Bob went on. "Some fibers got pressed into the skin. White satin. To the naked eye they match the ones from the other crime scene, but you'll want to have the lab look them over. And a hair. Not the victim's." She held two glassine envelopes out to Windy.

Windy wanted to take them and run them up to the lab, run

away, but she handed them off to a courier and made herself stay until the end of the autopsy. At one point Ash's phone rang and she looked at him with envy as he left the room. He was back after only a few minutes with the news that Nick Lee had been able to confirm through a connection at the water board that Eve's family had lived on Cottonwood Drive.

"At least we know she's sticking with her old houses," he said.

"Too bad Nick's connection can't tell us where she lived *before* she kills."

"Oh, he could. He offered to. Said it would take about six weeks."

Dr. Bob was moving around, weighing organs, making notations, while they talked. "Nice pink lungs. She must not have been in Vegas long. And this is interesting." She looked up at them. "Your victim seems to have had breakfast twice."

"Twice? Like a double portion?" Ash asked.

"No. Twice like on two separate occasions three to four hours apart. The last one was shortly before the time of death."

"Eve tortured her for that long," Ash said. "Long enough to get hungry twice."

"Or maybe it wasn't satisfying enough the first time," Windy said. "Maybe without anyone else to threaten, the thrill wasn't adequate."

"Can you give us a time of death?" Ash asked the pathologist.

Dr. Bob looked at the thermometers poking out of the piles of organs, and back at the body. "It's hard to say. It would depend on the temperature."

"The thermostat in the house was set at seventy-two degrees," Windy told her.

Dr. Bob shook her head. "Not that temperature. The temperature of the freezer where the body was stored."

"I'm sorry." Windy leaned forward as though maybe she had misheard. "Did you say *freezer*?"

"Yes. This woman was frozen. Probably for at least a day. I'll have to get the ice crystals on her heart under the microscope. Look at this—" The pathologist pointed at something, going on with the explanation, but neither Windy nor Ash were paying attention.

They were both wide awake now, their eyes meeting over the body, her saying, "The message on my voice mail must have been taped."

Him saying, "But what the hell was Eve doing in the house with a frozen dead body for twenty-four hours?"

"At least twenty-four hours," Dr. Bob corrected.

Windy was already moving to the door of the examining room, stripping off her gloves, almost gone when she said, "I don't know, but I am going to find out."

"Right behind you."

CHAPTER 55

Harry had just finished writing *Eve: Hair-pubic* on the envelope and was getting ready to go out when he saw the unmarked sedan pull to the curb in front of the O'Connells' and Windy get out, then saw Ash Laughton's sports car roll by and park in the other direction. What the hell were they doing here?

They were supposed to be long gone by now. He had spent the earlier part of the afternoon while they were next door catching up on cataloguing his samples—*Eve: Hair-head; Eve: Hair-arms; Eve: nail-big toe; Eve dental floss; Eve cigarette butts* in *lipstick, lip gloss,* or *plain*— but now he had things he wanted to do, and somewhere to be. He did not really care if any of the others noticed him near the house, he could pretend to be cutting through from an adjacent lot, thinking the house was empty, a million things. But he could not risk having Windy see him. That would ruin everything.

Windy started pulling equipment from her trunk, Ash joining her now, lifting out a big duffel bag and a black box, like they were planning to go back in and work the crime scene again. He did not like seeing them together. He wanted Windy in there on her own, just her, reconstructing the crime, looking just like Eve would have if she had been the one doing it. Ash was an annoyance, and a distraction for her. For both of them.

Harry wracked his brain, trying to think of anything he might have left out, any clue he hadn't wanted them to discover that he had left behind, but couldn't come up with anything. He had taken a risk spending more time with Kelly, experimenting on her, and he'd been a little nervous after Windy spent so much time in the kitchen earlier in the day, but he had told himself to cool it, stay calm. Now it wasn't so easy. Her looking so hard, so long—harder and longer than at the other crime scenes—made him feel like he must have missed something. He never should have taken Eve in there. Although the only thing she could have left behind were a few extra hairs, since she had barely been wearing any clothes.

That thought made him feel better, slightly. But he could not help feeling that Windy was going off on tangents. He'd left everything she needed in plain enough view, with a few surprises thrown in—he wondered how she'd liked learning the body was frozen. But what she was doing now was not what he wanted. She was being disobedient.

It was as though she were slipping away from him, just when he wanted to be tightening his control over her the most. Clearly he was going to have to do something. Something to upset her enough so that she would come straight to him. So that she would *need* him.

CHAPTER 56

Windy expected the officers in front of the O'Connell house to say "Who goes there?" they looked so serious and official when she and Ash came up the driveway at eight thirty that night.

"Its just us, Veronica," Ash said to Officer Franca. Calling her by her first name, Windy noticed, then kicked herself for noticing.

She had decided not to take Larry or Ned away from whatever their Saturday night plans were, partially out of compassion, and partially because she felt like she wanted to do this alone. Or mostly alone. She did not mind having Ash there.

They easily found the freezer where the body had been stored, in the back, behind the house, a big old model. Windy gave it a cursory glance, didn't see anything striking right off, and decided to leave it for Ned or Larry to go over the next day. She knew she was rushing things, but she wanted to get into the house. To figure out what Eve had been doing in there all that time.

"I'm afraid I've never been a CSI before," Ash told her as they stepped into the dark house. "You'll have to give me step by step instructions."

"Don't touch anything, don't lean against anything, don't move anything."

"Okay, that'll be a cinch."

Windy stood in the darkness, aware of him beside her in a way that was comforting, trying to figure out where to start.

Be Eve. What would Eve do.

"She cleans up the dishes after she's done the murder," Windy said, talking to herself, walking around. "I expect she did it right after, even here, because she'd want it to be taken care of. Erasing signs of breakfast is the most crucial and consistent part of her killings." Ash nodded, waiting for her to go on. "If she did, and if she wore latex, and if we are lucky, we might get some prints."

"Through gloves?"

"Soap degrades latex. But it's not even prints I am really interested in. It's more smudges. I want to know everything she touched."

"Are we looking for anything in particular?"

"A door. Figurative. Into Eve's past. There is something in this house she had to spend time with. Hopefully it will explain why she was so much more violent here too."

Windy had Ash start dusting in the living room, any surface that did not already have fingerprint powder on it, while she got to work in the hallway. Ash got a hit right off the bat with a nice set on the doorjamb, but given their location—near the floor—Windy was willing to guess that they belonged to one of the emergency workers who had been in the house. Still, you never knew when a killer who so far had left no prints might start, so they lifted them. As they worked they played "Name That Tune," until Ash stumped Windy on "MacArthur Park."

"That doesn't count, it doesn't start off at all like the song."

"And 'The Rainbow Connection' does?"

"I'm still impressed you know that one. I thought having *The Muppet Movie* be Cate's all-time favorite would at least have some advantage."

"I think Cate has great taste in movies," Ash said.

"She takes after her father. Anything with a sappy musical score. Evan's favorite thing to watch on TV was *Annie*. Except for National Geographic shows about windsurfing."

"*Annie* is okay, but I bet windsurfing is better. Have you done it?"

"A few times before Cate was born. After that it seemed too risky."

They dusted in silence for a while until Windy said, "Evan died windsurfing." Why was she telling him this? She did not talk about Evan with anyone.

Ash stopped what he was doing and went to the hallway. She was sitting on the floor, staring down at the beige carpeting. He came closer to her hesitantly, like he didn't want to overstep, didn't want to invade. He stayed two paces away, standing. "Windy, I'm so sorry. I can't imagine how that felt."

"When they found his body he was smiling. People kept telling me I should be happy. You know, because he looked happy. Had a good run."

"People can be idiots."

She swallowed back a lump and turned to Ash, his big hands dangling at his side, looking awkward as he just stood there but remembering not to lean against the doorjamb, eyes holding hers with warmth. He made her feel good when he looked at her, she realized, then told herself he probably had that effect on all women. She shrugged and said, "Anyway, it's over. That part of my life, anyway. But in the present, I think I found what I've been looking for."

I think I have too, Ash thought.

He looked around the hallway, seeing a line of iron-colored smudges along the freshly painted white wall in both directions. "Are these fingerprints?"

"Sort of. Eve was running her hands along here, looking for something but that is just window dressing. I was an idiot not to have thought of it sooner. The evidence was right here all the time."

Ash looked around. "Where?"

"This afternoon I noticed those vacuum marks on the carpet in the hallway but I was too busy being scared by the idea that Eve was going to come after me next that I stopped thinking like a criminalist. You should fire me."

"Too much paperwork. You stay. What do the vacuum marks tell you?"

"When the hallway was vacuumed. Do you see these drops of blood?" Windy pointed to rust-colored spots on the beige carpet. They still had numbers next to them from when the crime scene team was there earlier, taking photos and trying to establish a time line. "This one," she went to the one marked 3, "is smeared, like something went through it. The nail of Kelly's big toe on her left foot had a blood smear on it that we matched to this drop, which means we know Eve dragged the body from the bedroom into the living room."

"Like she did at the other crime scenes."

"Yes. But at this crime scene, there were no drag marks. The blood was smeared, but there were no marks on the carpeting. Only the vacuum trail. Which means the hallway was vacuumed after the body was moved. By Eve."

"Why?"

"To get rid of this." Windy ran her finger over the baseboard and showed it to Ash. It had white powder on it. "The house was painted before the O'Connells moved in, two months ago, and whoever did it used cheap paint. When Eve pulled up the carpet—"

"She pulled up the carpet?"

"Yes, and when she did, paint from the baseboard flaked off and left white powder. You can see the baseboards are slightly scuffed in that direction—" She pointed down the hallway, "But it stops about here." Where she was sitting. "This is where it is."

"What?"

Windy went to the end of the hall and tugged on the carpet. It came up easily, not hammered in any more, and she rolled it back to the place she had been sitting.

"This," she said, uncovering some beat-up, stained oak floor-boards, and a trap door. "This neighborhood was built in the 1950s and they included what every house needed then. A bomb shelter. In the seventies people sometimes converted them into basements or rec rooms." Four wood putty-filled holes and a rusty outline showed where hardware had once been fitted over the door, from the looks of it a substantial lock. Windy rested her fingers over those and said, "I'd say while Eve lived here this one was made into a prison of sorts."

The first thing Ash noticed when they flipped open the door was the smell, sickly sweet like overripe fruit and cotton candy.

"That is what the Lysol is for," Windy said, not bothering to keep the excitement out of her voice at the discovery. She leaned on her stomach into the hole to dust the ladder that led downward. "To cover this smell. It smells to me like diabetic kematosis, what happens when certain kinds of diabetics get their insulin dose wrong. Can you move the light a little to the left?"

Ash shifted left. "Does that mean Eve is diabetic?"

"Probably. It usually shows up more in obese people than anorexics, but her body chemistry must be really messed up. I'll bottle a sample for the lab." She handed him a capped glass vial, got busy with the fingerprint powder again, then reached her arm out and said, "Camera."

Ash gave it to her and waited until she was done shooting the dark-colored blob on the ladder rung to ask what it was.

"Footprint," she said. "Eve must have come down here barefoot. Not as good as a fingerprint because there's no national database, but it's the first piece of identifying evidence we've found at a scene. Maybe that means she was careless down here, figuring we'd never find this." Windy dangled a powerful flashlight into the bomb shelter, shining it on the four walls looking around. After only a few seconds, she sat up, jerking the light with her, and said, "Oh brother."

"What's down there?"

How to describe it, Windy asked herself. She shook her head and said, "I think you could call it the autobiography of a serial killer."

CHAPTER 57

"Something nuclear definitely happened here," Ash said when they were standing inside what they started calling "The Pit."

He held the light while Windy photographed the walls. They, like everything else down here, were covered in layers of dust and cobwebs, but the writing was still visible. *Fucking cunt piece of garbage horse's ass little fucker chicken shit piece of crap loser deadbeat fat pig fat fat fat disgusting bloated hussy bitch bitch bitch bitch fat bitch, I'll kill you I'll kill you I'll kill you, foul faced ass wipe crap head* showed in the circle of light Ash was holding, and every wall was covered with the same.

There was a wooden table off to one side of the room, with footprints in the dust showing Eve had gone to stand next to it, but she hadn't touched the chair, or the objects on the table. They sat just where she must have left them the last time she was down here decades ago, three decapitated Madam Alexander doll heads, staring at the chair. One of them had its nose sliced off.

"I wonder if this is where she got the idea for how to treat Kelly," Ash said.

"I hope not," Windy said, looking at the other two dolls. One of them had her eyes gouged out, and the other had been repeatedly hit with something that left round marks, like a hammer.

They followed Eve's footprints around the room to a boarded-up window. The board and nails were old, but when they pulled on it, it came away from the cinderblock wall instantly, as though it had just been propped there.

"Eve must have taken this out earlier today," Windy said. There were plants growing in front of it, which explained why they hadn't seen it from the outside, but when Windy pushed them aside, they could see the house next door. All the windows were dark.

"There are NO TRESPASSING and PRIVATE PROPERTY signs all over the front yard of that place, and during the canvass today the private security officer who patrols the neighborhood said the owner of that house is out of town. That would have made it easy for Eve to come in the side door without being spotted," Ash said.

Windy nodded. That house was set lower than the one they were in, so from where she stood she imagined that if it were lighter she would be able to see into the rooms on the facing side. Bedrooms probably.

"I bet Eve stood here all the time when she was locked up, looking at the outside world and envying it," Windy said.

"It could certainly make someone misanthropic," Ash agreed. She was right next to him as she stared out the window, giving him her profile, so close their arms were almost touching. They were at a crime scene, standing in some sort of torture chamber, and all he could think about was saying something he'd never said before, "I've fallen in love with you," not even caring what her response would be, just wanting her to know that someone felt that way about her. Okay, maybe he cared about her response a little, but it wasn't the main thing. The main thing was to let her know someone thought she was wonderful.

So what he said was, "Do you smell paint? Wet paint?"

Windy closed her eyes for a moment, sniffing, then opened them and said, "Yes. From over there." She pointed and he moved the light, showing up a part of the wall that told them they were *worthless pieces of fat assed fucked up garbage crap* but had a place below the words where the cobwebs had been pushed aside and there was a square of fresh beige paint.

"What could she have needed to paint over that was worse than any of this other stuff?" Ash asked.

Windy looked at it and shook her head. "We'll have to wait until tomorrow, until we can get someone in who can lift the top layer and leave the writing underneath."

"No way. I happen to know a little bit about paint, and if she used the paint from upstairs, I can get this off in a minute."

"Are you sure?"

"Yeah, I have a special technique." He took the clean cloth Windy handed him from the crime scene kit, spat into it, and started rubbing.

"Special technique," Windy muttered, standing behind him with her arms crossed, thinking this was a bad idea. She kept her eyes off the mess he was making of her crime scene, reading the words on the wall, *cocksucker, disgusting cunt faced pig,* until it was Ash's turn to say, "Oh brother."

Windy looked over his shoulder. An uneven heart that looked like it had been traced and retraced in pen hundreds of times surrounded the words *Eve + Harry* and then beneath the heart *Always.*

"Do you think it's the same Harry the assistant manager at the restaurant was talking about?" Windy asked.

"If it is, I think we have found our trigger. From the fact that this was painted over in the last forty-eight hours, I'd say that Eve was trying to erase Harry from her life. It looks like they had a nasty break-up."

CHAPTER 58

It was after ten P.M. when Windy and Ash finished with The Pit and closed up the O'Connell house. When they got outside they stood in the dark driveway for several minutes, drinking in the fresh air, both of them feeling like they'd just been through more than a crime scene.

"Tomorrow I will get someone at the school district to find the yearbooks of the schools Eve went to, check to see if there are any Harrys listed," Ash said. "That was a good idea."

"It's a long shot. I'll be interested to know what the lab makes of that air sample. If Eve does have diabetes or some other condition, we might be able to use it to trace her."

Ash dug his hands into his pockets like an awkward teenager on a date trying to decide if he should kiss the girl, his whole body saying "yes." Bringing his hands out now, extending them to Windy. "I almost forgot," he said, opening his palms to reveal four packages of cherry Pop Rocks. "These were for after the autopsy."

That earned him a smile. He reached out to give two of the envelopes to Windy and she reached out to take them, their fingers brushing for a split second.

Then she was tossing her head back and pouring the Pop Rocks down her throat. "Thank you, Ash. You've made my night." And she looked at him in this way that told him it might be okay to kiss her, maybe just on the cheek.

The duty officer materialized from behind them then, his polite "Sir, ma'am? I hope I'm not interrupting something," like an indictment of guilt for them both.

"No," Ash said. "We were just getting ready to leave."

Windy picked up her equipment, saying to Ash as they walked down the driveway, "If you ever get tired of your job you I might be able to pull some strings for you in criminalistics."

Ash laughed. "You'd throw your weight around for me like that with the boss?"

"You're a natural."

"There is something really exciting about seeing the crime come together that way."

"I know what you mean," Windy said. "It's why I do it. Not everyone gets that. To a lot of people it's just disturbing."

They were at the bottom of the driveway now. Windy had picked up one of the cars from criminalistics when she went to get equipment after the autopsy. It was parked to the left, Ash's to the right.

"Good night," Ash said. He didn't move.

"Good night." Windy stood on her toes, gave him a kiss on the cheek, and turned to walk to her car.

She was smiling to herself as she headed down the block. She felt giddy, a little light-headed.

Then she saw the man in the ski mask come out of the bushes toward her.

CHAPTER 59

Windy froze. She stood, immobile, as he pressed his gun against her heart and said, "Now it's your turn to die."

Stood there as he bent down, getting his masked face inches from hers and said, "Did you hear me, lady? You're going down."

Stood, unable to move, her mind zooming, thinking, this is Roddy Ruiz, he had a gun, he does not really want to kill me, all he wants is a response, some kind of response why the hell can't I move, what is wrong with me, *what is wrong with me?*

"You trying to say you're not afraid. Okay, lady. You not afraid. Now prepare to meet your maker."

Bad lines, she thought, such bad second-rate movie lines. She was not going to die with those lines why couldn't she move, just anything, just to let him know—

"LISTEN TO ME YOU STUPID BITCH I'M GOING TO KILL YOU RIGHT NOW."

He was crying through the mask, she could tell. He was as scared as she was. But he wasn't petrified. He could move. He could move his trigger finger.

"Roddy," a voice said. Not her voice, she was pretty sure.

Keeping the gun against her heart, Roddy looked up. Behind her.

"Roddy, take me."

Ash's voice. It was Ash whose footsteps she heard behind her. Ash coming to her rescue. Damn her for needing it. Damn her for being a coward.

"This ain't your business, *cabrón,*" Roddy said.

"Look. If you want to kill someone, kill me."

"What you mean if I *want* to. I'm gonna."

"Okay. I just thought, you know, maybe you were—never mind."

"Maybe I was what?"

"Well, I remember you from the station. You know? I watched your interrogation."

Roddy jammed the gun into Windy's heart again. "This damn bitch fucked me up."

"She was pretty slick," Ash admitted. "But so were you. That was really brave, what you were preparing to do. Stand in for your uncle in prison. That took a lot of guts."

"I woulda done it too if this *puta* hadn't stopped me."

"I know. And do you know why she did?"

"Because she's a tight ass bitch, that's why."

"Tight ass bitches are way too self-centered to get involved with something like this. No, it's because she thought you were smart."

"Right."

"She did. She could see why you'd want to take the fall for your uncle. But she also thought you could make more of yourself on the outside."

"What if I don't want to make more of myself?"

"That's bullshit, Roddy, and we both know it. By the time your uncle gets out, you could have finished school. You could make him proud of you. More proud than going to the joint."

"That's not me, man."

"I've seen the reports from your teachers. I know you do well in school."

"Bull. You're just saying stuff to get me not to hurt her."

"You're especially good in math."

Roddy wavered. "So I'm good in math. So what? You think I should become a stupid ass cop like you?"

"No way. Cops don't make enough. But you could become a doctor. You couldn't do that if you went to jail."

Roddy let go of Windy, pushing her away, and pointed the gun square at Ash. His voice was high pitched, angry. "Stop bullshitting me, man. You don't know nothing about me."

Ash kept his hands at his sides, his voice even. "I know you're brave. I know you're smart. I know you could shoot me dead right now if you wanted to."

Roddy's chin jutted out and he nodded furiously. "That's right, man. Fuck you up."

"But why would you want to?"

Roddy held the gun in front of him with both hands, staring at Ash.

"The way I see it—" Ash went on, smooth, slow, not scared, "—the way I see it, this can end one of two ways. You shoot me and go to prison for the rest of your life. Spend it inside, in a cell, with bars. Maybe an hour a day outside. Maybe you could study a few years, get your GED. Mostly you'd have to spend your time proving over and over again how tough you are."

"I got protection inside, man."

"Okay, sure. So you only have to prove yourself a few times. Or you could not shoot me. Stay out of prison. Go to school. Do something really cool with your life. Sure, it'd be harder outside. No one telling you what to do, how to think, where to be every hour. Maybe you think it would be too tough out here."

The gun had started to sag, almost imperceptibly, but Roddy straightened out his arms now. His eyes glared at Ash through the ski mask. "Like you care, man. You only talking to me because I'm pointing a gun at you. No gun, you wouldn't give a shit about me."

"To be perfectly honest, I'd rather talk to you without the gun."

"Shit man, stop joking. Why do you care about me?"

"Because I think you deserve a break. But maybe you're right. Maybe you can't do it. Make it on the straight." Ash put up his hands. "Okay, shoot me."

"Naw, man." Roddy bent his head to one side to rub his cheek against his shoulder, scratch an itch. "I can do it. I just don't want to."

"Then shoot me. Express ticket to prison, shooting a cop. Put you away for life. That's what you want, isn't it?"

"Come on, man. You're not listening to me. I could make it on the outside fine. I know how to dress myself and feed myself. Take care myself."

Ash kept his hands up. "But you don't want to. It's too much work. I hear you."

"It's not like that. I don't mind it. Sometimes I even like to cook, you know."

"But you'd rather have someone telling you when to do it. When to take a shower. Not have to organize your own schedule."

"No way, man. I can take care of my own self. I don't need no one reminding me to take a shit. I been getting myself to school by myself for five years. I don't need no cop telling me I don't want to take care of myself."

"Okay, I believe you. Do you want me to turn around? If you shoot me in the back, you'll get where you want to go even faster."

Roddy threw his hands up in exasperation, completely forgetting to point the gun at Ash. "Man, will you shut up with that. I don't want to shoot you."

"Why not?"

"Why not? Because you are a crazy ass dude. I don't shoot crazy people."

"Good rule. I told you that you were smart."

"Damn right, *hombre*." The gun hanging limp in his hand now.

"Where are you staying?"

All of a sudden, Roddy looked like a kid again. He shrugged. "I got a foster home."

"How is it?"

"It's okay. My foster mom? She makes pancakes for breakfast."

"Do you think you could stay there awhile?"

"Yeah, I think so. They're pretty cool. I should be getting back there." He looked at Ash. "You just going to let me walk away?"

Ash glanced at Windy, who nodded. "Yes," he said, "I think we are. Officially, we're going to pretend this didn't happen. But you'd better not do anything this stupid again. I mean it. If you do, I'll find out about it and I'll know I was wrong about you being smart."

"You bet I'm smart. Smarter than you."

"Maybe," Ash said, not challenging Roddy, but giving him something to aspire to. "Hey, before you go, can I have the mask and the gun?"

Roddy took the ski mask off and tossed it to Ash. His face was textured from the tight weave and he had red lines around his eyes and mouth, like a clown. Only he looked sad.

"The gun?" Ash repeated.

Roddy looked at it then at Ash.

"You don't need it," Ash told him. "Anyone can seem brave with a gun, but you don't need one. You're brave enough on your own."

"So why you got one?"

"I have to, it's a job regulation. But I've never used it."

"No?"

"And I never want to."

Roddy looked at the gun again. "This was one of my uncle's pieces."

"Then I can see why you don't want to give it up."

"Yeah."

"I can't let you keep it, Roddy. It'll end up getting you killed anyway. I'll hold it for you in my gun safe. You ever want to visit it, I'll give you my card, you can call me and set up an appointment."

Roddy shook his head at Ash. "I don't think I should give you a weapon. You are one *loco* cop."

Ash held out his business card. Roddy held out the gun. They traded.

"Hey, lady," Roddy said, turning to Windy. "I'm sorry about that. Before."

"It's okay."

"I didn't mean it. I wouldn't have hurt you. I just—I just wanted to talk. Only I was afraid you wouldn't let me without the gun."

"I think I understand."

"It's not your fault, you know. What happened to Mr. X, him going to prison and all that." Roddy glanced at Ash then looked back at her. "Maybe even it's a good thing."

"Maybe even."

"Well, bye," Roddy said and went.

CHAPTER 60

Windy watched Roddy walk down the street, not swaggering, not giving it any attitude. Just walking. She could move again, now, but she didn't want to. Didn't want to face Ash. She knew what he was going to say. That she had messed up. That she had to be more careful. How could she expect to do her job if her brain was going to stop working at the first hint of danger? How could he trust her in the field, or anyone with her?

She heard his footsteps behind her, then his voice. "Are you okay?"

"No."

"Look," he began and Windy thought, here it comes.

Ash went on, "I'm sorry I interfered. I just wanted you to know I was there to help. I didn't mean to take over. I can understand if you are upset with me. That was clumsy."

Windy turned slowly to face him. "That's not what happened."

"Then what is?"

"I had a panic attack. He came at me, and I froze. I screwed up and you saved my life."

"You think you screwed up because you were scared? It is a normal reaction to freeze when a man holds a gun to your heart point-blank. It is actually safer not to move."

"You didn't freeze."

"He wasn't aiming at me."

Windy shook her head. "If I can't be counted on to protect my-self, I can't do this job. I quit."

"No."

"I'm not kidding, Ash. I endanger everyone I work with."

"Nuts. Because a boy with a gun comes after you? How is that endangering anyone?"

"I have to know I can take care of myself. I have to know I'm not going to panic every time something scary happens."

"In the past week I have been with you when a half dozen scary things happened and you never even flinched."

"That's bullshit," Windy said. Then, "Wait, where are you going?"

Ash's jaw was tight and Windy realized he was genuinely an-gry. "I am not going to have this conversation with you. You're right. You froze. You're the only person who has ever done that and you are a danger to society."

"It won't work. You can't talk me down the way you did with Roddy."

"Don't worry. I only try that on people I'm pretty sure aren't going to shoot me."

"I don't have a gun."

"I'm certain you could find one."

Windy took a step closer to him. "You could give me yours."

He crossed his arms over his chest. "You wouldn't like it. It's not loaded."

"Oh. Well if I can't shoot you, can I take you out for a drink?"

Ash stared at Windy, trying to figure out where that flare of anger he felt had come from, realizing it was because seeing her with a gun to her heart had been maybe the worst moment of his life.

Maybe she *was* a danger to the people she worked with.

"So," she said, her head to one side, looking up at him, "can I buy you a drink to defuse some of the adrenaline?"

No, he thought. No I don't want to have a drink with you. I want to take you to my house and strip you out of your clothes and hold your body next to mine all night.

"A drink would be great," he said. At least he would be with her. Then he changed his mind. "Actually, I have a better idea. Roddy gave it to me."

She looked at him skeptically. "What?"

"Pancakes. We didn't eat dinner, and I'm starving. If you provide the facilities, I'll provide the know-how." Her house was safer. In her house he could not forget that she was engaged.

"You can cook?"

"I can make pancakes. From scratch."

"Okay." Windy gave him a big smile. "Pancakes."

"Why don't I drive and we can have someone pick up the criminalistics car tomorrow."

"You don't think I'm fit to drive?"

"I don't think you'll drive fast enough."

In the car on the way to her house, he felt her watching him. Differently than she had before. "What?"

"I was just wondering how you knew what to do with Roddy. What to say. Did you really look up his school file?"

"I like to know a little something about the people my team arrests. It seems only polite."

"That's not why you do it."

He shrugged. "It came in handy tonight."

She was still looking at him. "You were amazing to watch. So calm, saying all the right things. Have you had negotiation training?"

"I had training in being a fifteen-year-old boy who feels alone."

"Did something happen in your family when you were fifteen?

Did your parents divorce when you were a teenager?" She shook her head. "I'm sorry, that's none of my business. I don't mean to pry."

"It's okay. My parents were never married. My mother divorced a few times when I was growing up, though."

"A few? How many stepfathers did you have?"

Ash had never thought of it that way. He'd always thought of them as his mother's husbands. "Five, before I left high school. After that I stopped counting."

"Your mother was married and divorced five times when you were growing up?" Windy repeated, turning in her seat to face him.

"No," Ash assured her. "Only divorced three times. She killed two of them—not literally, at least I don't think so. My mother's list of desirable qualities in a man is short: old, rich, and emotionally distant. Or, as she would put it, emotionally self-sufficient."

"I like that. Very snappy."

"My mother has some great lines, although she doesn't know it. She can recite jokes, pretend, but in reality she doesn't have much of a sense of humor. She's a psychiatrist," he said, as if that explained everything. He could never remember having talked about his mother this much.

"What kind of relationship did you have with your stepfathers? Were you close to any of them?"

"I was more of a bystander in the lives of my mother and her husbands. I learned a lot from them indirectly, but there is only one I could really say I had a relationship with. Major Rice. He's the reason I became a cop."

"Was he a cop?"

"No," Ash laughed at the thought. "He was a con man. He tricked my mom by marrying her for her money, when she was marrying him for his. It turned out that they both had plenty, but not enough for either of their ambitions, so they divorced. But they were married for about six months when I was fifteen. That's what reminded me of Roddy. I started doing stupid stuff, and one time I boosted a car from the Hunts Mill Country Club parking lot. That night I drove the car back to the house of the guy it belonged to and parked it in his garage. It was a prank, to show how cool and brave I thought I was, you know? Boys do stuff like that. When I got home, Major Rice was sitting on my bed. He handed me his flask and said, 'Look, Ash, being a criminal is a pain in the ass. You're too smart for it.' When I pointed out to him that I'd returned the Mercedes, he just sighed and said, 'If you want to play that way, why not be a cop? All the fun of thinking like a criminal, with a pension.' "

Ash stopped there, not telling Windy the rest of the major's advice, the two of them sitting on Ash's bed, emptying the flask, the major saying, "You can always have affairs, go on dates, Ash, but take it from me, no woman worth being with is going to accept a short-term arrangement. You find one you like, you marry her. The older I get, the more I see the value of having someone to grow old with." The old sap. Some con man.

Windy's voice interrupted his thoughts. "So, is that really why you do this? Because you like thinking like a criminal?"

"You bet. That and never having to drive the speed limit."

Ash stepped on the gas and they blew by a patrol unit on Desert Inn Road. The officer behind the wheel waved but didn't move off the side of the road, knowing Ash's car by sight, figuring he was going to an emergency. Not knowing the emergency was the temptation to act like a fool in front of Windy, tell her that he'd used up all his green paint trying to get her off his mind, that he could make her happy if she would let him.

Twelve years a cop and still an idealistic idiot.

He glanced at her in the passenger seat and could tell by the way she was looking at him, eyes sparkling, laughing, not afraid, that she liked going fast. And that she had no idea how he felt.

Standing next to her at her front door as she fumbled with the lock, cursing her key for not working right, Ash could not stop himself from wondering what it would be like to do this every day. Come back from dinner and stand right here, with her. And then go inside and be at home.

The door opened before she got her key to work, a tall blond man filling it. She looked up, startled, then laughed. "Bill. I didn't realize you'd arrived."

"I just got in. I'm so glad to see you. I was starting to worry." The man gave them both a dazzling white smile. He was Ash's height, lean, wearing pressed chinos and a yellow cashmere sweater, loafers without socks. He looked really nice, and the way he gazed at Windy it was clear he was crazy about her. Ash hated him instantly.

"I'm sorry," Windy said. "I didn't know when your flight was getting here and then—never mind. Bill, this is Ash Laughton. My boss. Ash, Bill Henderson."

"Her fiancé," Bill put in.

Ash didn't even like his handshake. He said, "It's great to meet you. And I'm not her boss."

"Nice to meet you too. Thanks for bringing Windy home." Bill slipped his arm around her shoulders.

Windy looked from Bill back to Ash. "Do you want to come in?"

Ash smiled. "No. I've taken up enough of your night."

"But—"

"Really. I'll leave you two alone. You okay?"

"Yes." Windy nodded. Did she look disappointed or was that just his imagination?

Bill's face registered concern. "Did something happen?"

"No. Nothing," Windy answered. Too fast, Ash thought.

"Okay. Well, uh, good night," Bill said.

Ash realized that he wanted to punch Bill with the full force of the adrenaline and anger he'd kept from Roddy. He wanted to shake the man's arm off Windy and take her himself.

He was thinking like a caveman. He said, "Good night."

"Bye," Windy said. Then, holding his eyes, she mouthed the word "Sorry."

When the door was closed, Ash mouthed, "Me too."

He drove home wondering why, in a city where even the damn dry cleaners were open twenty-four hours a day, he couldn't get his hands on a lousy tube of green paint at midnight.

Windy stared at the place he had been, the man with five stepfathers who did not think her weak for freezing when she saw danger and who knew how to make pancakes from scratch and realized she had not even thanked him for saving her life.

"He seems nice," Bill said as he locked the deadbolt.

"Yes."

"Tough day?"

And he knew the songs from *The Muppet Movie*. "Long day. I don't want to talk about it."

Bill winked. "Your wish is my command."

He linked his fingers with hers and pulled her close to him, and she shut her eyes as his mouth covered hers. Her hands came up and tangled in his hair, deepening the kiss, holding on to him desperately until her body was burning up with desire and she couldn't take it any more. She whispered, "God, I want you."

And he said, "I haven't heard that in a long time."

Windy pulled away and gazed at him, shocked.

"What?" Bill asked.

Her hand went to her lips. "Nothing." How could she tell him that she thought she had been kissing a different man?

"Let's go upstairs."

"Yes. Okay. Let me just make sure the back door is locked."

"It's locked. Come on."

Her eyes moved to the scuff mark she'd made on the baseboard, twenty-one feet from the front door. Twenty-one feet, the safe distance. Ash hadn't even come in that far.

Following Bill up the stairs, she told herself that what she was feeling was simply the result of a long and harrowing night. She would be back to normal in the morning.

Ignoring the thought that maybe with some men there was no such thing as a safe distance.

CHAPTER 61

Harry lay in bed and thought about Eve. Making love to her had been like having a feather resting on your chest, she was so light and tiny. This little fragile creature. It wasn't at all like what he'd imagined, when he'd started imagining it years earlier.

The first time he really noticed her she was lying on her back, biting her nail, with a naked man on top of her. The complete lack of expression in her face fascinated him. Here was this man, pouring everything into her he had, and she couldn't care less.

When the man was done she gave him a little smile and showed him out the door. Then she returned to her room and stood naked at the window smoking a cigarette with one hand and furiously stroking herself with the other. When she came it was just a flicker on her face, nothing more.

After that he couldn't stop watching her. With her bony arms and legs and big eyes she reminded him more of an insect than a woman. He watched her everywhere she went, from home to school, and eventually school to the Yucca Motel. When her family moved he moved with them, becoming familiar with the back alleys and trees around their houses, so he could always see her. Always watch.

He read all the magazines she threw away to learn more about her. He knew that she was "Sassy but Smart" according to the "Rate Your Male IQ" quiz. Knew that she was "The Shy Girl" according to "What Kind of Friend Are You." And he learned other useful things, "How to Be Your Own Best Friend," "Who Girls Think Is Hot Now!," "What to Look for in a Perfect Boyfriend." He saved the articles she marked, notes she threw away, preserving her with the same care he had once lavished on his delicate models. Maybe if he got enough pieces, he would know all about her. And Charles could not take her away.

He saw the afternoon that her mama made her cry. That night he went through the entire Dumpster behind a florist shop to find the most perfect flower. He kept the yellow rose in water overnight and the next morning snuck out to put it on her windowsill.

She'd seen it when she got up. He watched her pick it up and smile. She smelled it then read the card. She cried a little. He was sure after that she'd thrown it in the trash. When he'd met her again at the opening of her restaurant, she said she had saved it. He knew she was lying but he didn't let it bother him.

As the months of watching her turned into a year, he decided she had to know he was out there. He was the only constant in her life, the only one who followed her everywhere, knew everything about her. He felt like she depended on him. Sometimes when she was with men in her room at the motel he saw her looking out the window, and knew she was looking for him. He would listen for the special way she went "oh yeah" or said the name of whoever she was with. She wrote the names on her palm so she could remember them at the right time.

Then one day he went to the Sun-Crest apartments in the morning, to walk with her to school—on the other side of the street, staying out of the way so she wouldn't notice him—and she never came down. He waited a half hour, then figured she was sick. But when she didn't come down for a whole week he asked a girl he went to school with who knew Eve, where she was. The girl told him Eve moved. Left town. Just like that, without saying anything to him.

He was heartbroken. He had been saving money to ask her to run away with him, and he took it and left, went up north. He got a job with a guy he'd been in school with working construction and he discovered he liked it. He started losing weight, gaining muscle. Feeling good about himself. He forgot all about Eve, dated other girls, slept with some of them. Saying "oh yeah" and their names the way Eve had.

And then, finally, he'd met Amanda. He saw her at a bar one night and his heart stopped. She wasn't the prettiest girl there, or the sexiest dressed. But he was in love instantly. She looked just like Eve.

He remembered the lessons from all the magazines of Eve's he'd read, all the soaps he had watched as a boy and he put them into play. Afraid she would say no if he asked for her number directly, he got her address from a mutual friend and showed up at her house unannounced, with a big bouquet of flowers.

The door, and then her heart, opened to him like magic. They were married seven months later. As he looked at his beautiful bride, his Eve, he had thought, this must be what happiness is like. And then she had become pregnant and he had discovered true bliss.

Harry had been the most joyful father in the world. *Look,* he would say to anyone who would listen. *Look, I am normal. I have a wife. A beautiful baby. I am a success.* He was going to school at night for his degree, working days in her father's security business. Security work. He was good at it. He'd honed his skills following Eve. He liked to know people's secrets. He always liked to know what went on in their heads.

One morning after he'd been up late studying he was feeding

Kyra breakfast and trying to get her ready for day care when she started to cry. Just started wailing as he was putting her sock on.

He hadn't heard Amanda come into the room but there she was, next to him. She snatched the sock out of his hand and said, "Harry, let me do it. You're a mess with her."

It was the strangest sensation, like being in two places at once. He was here in his house, and then at the same time he was back at his sister's crib when she was a baby.

"Don't touch my daughter," he heard Charles's voice overlaid with Amanda's.

He didn't feel anything inside him click, but his throat tightened and it got harder to breathe. "She is my goddamned daughter," he said.

Amanda stared at him, her eyes hard and confused. "Give her to me, Harry."

She reached out and he slapped her hard across the face. "She is mine. I will dress her." He dragged Kyra out of her chair and pressed her against his chest, holding out his hand. "Give me the sock."

Amanda did not move. Kyra wiggled and held her arms out for her mother, trying to get away from him. It infuriated him. He held her harder, and shouted, "Give me the goddamned sock. I can do this. *I can do it!*"

Amanda blinked at him, the sock dangling from her hand, like she did not understand what he was saying, what she was seeing. And he knew at that instant that she was going to leave him. Because he was a failure as a father. A failure as a husband. She was going to take Kyra and leave him and get a divorce and he would be alone and abandoned.

He wished he could just start over, rewind and begin again. Erase all of this so no one would know. And then he saw how he could do it. Make it so it never happened.

"You're going to leave me, aren't you?"

She was still staring at him with blank, stupid eyes. She shook her head slowly. "No."

"You lying bitch." He squeezed Kyra until she howled. "I don't believe you. Beg me for forgiveness."

Amanda came back to life. "Please, Harry, Please. Let her go. Give her to me."

Power surged through him like a lightning bolt. His mind raced with possibilities. So many things he could do. Clutching Kyra to him he walked toward his wife.

"Give me my baby," she moaned, backing up until she was against the counter. He closed the distance between them and she shrank into a corner. "Please," she said, reaching for the baby. "Let me have her." She was pinned against the dishwasher, looking at him with terror.

It was so easy. Too easy. Even at the moment he remembered thinking, *Next time I need to take it slower.*

He did not know how long it lasted, seven, maybe ten minutes. When it was all over, the room was incredibly quiet. He hadn't realized how noisy it had been but the peace that descended then was more than just silence. It was an incredible sensation of tranquillity that went deep into his bones. It was like the feeling he had when he took a good run, only even better. Because it did not make his bad knee hurt. It had been a lot easier than running.

Although he did work up a marathon appetite. He sat back down at his place at the head of the table and ate his toasts, then Amanda's, then the little squares she had cut for Kyra. Everything that passed his lips was ambrosia. Breakfast had never tasted so good.

And that was the problem. He'd been trying, here in Vegas, to recapture that taste, but he just couldn't get it. He knew from his research that it had something to do with his adrenaline, the chemicals in his body when he got excited. All he wanted was to experience that taste again, that perfect breakfast. Apparently he just hadn't gotten excited enough yet.

Certainly taking Mrs. Waters's head and trying it at home had not worked. The second breakfast with Kelly O'Connell had been better. He had almost killed her but then stopped, and as a result of this reprieve, Kelly was both more scared and more willing to believe him when he told her he would let her go if she just pretended that he was her husband, having breakfast with her, nice and normal. But it was still missing something. His overall diagnosis was that he had not yet been emotionally involved enough with his victims to get the same rush.

That would definitely not be a problem with Windy.

CHAPTER 62

Sunday was perfect. Windy had slept in and then she and Bill had a long, leisurely brunch before picking Cate up from her slumber party. Cate was bursting with half recalled ghost stories and the information that she had not been scared at all and was completely ready to do it all again next week on her class camping trip. They spent the day running errands, including driving by the gated development Bill was interested in, Falconview Falls, which Cate liked because there was a huge bronze bird perched on top of the guard house.

They wound up the day at Cate and Windy's favorite restaurant, the Rainforest Café at the MGM Grand, sitting surrounded by the fake trees and fake animals, Bill not even once murmuring that it wasn't very healthy. They played Count the Brides as one wedding party after another passed them, and Cate discovered that her name rhymed with "great" and made up a song commemorating it. It was a wonderful day, the three of them getting along beautifully as a family, even when they heard an advertisement on the radio for rooms that rented by the hour in case you wanted to have a quickie at lunchtime and Cate asked what a quickie was, Bill looking over at Windy like saying, "I told you Vegas wasn't a good place to raise a child"; even when Cate went on a little too long for everyone's comfort about how great Mom's friend Ash was and how much Bill would like him and maybe he could be Bill's friend too.

Windy spent the day doing everything she could to be the perfect mom, the perfect fiancée, working to prove to an internal judge that her life was everything she wanted. Doing anything to subdue the stomach-clenching feeling of guilt she had gone to bed with and woken up with and spent the day with. Even a chocolate milk shake couldn't quell it.

It was exhausting and after tucking Cate in at eight thirty she felt like she was ready for bed herself. But she still had a few more hours of quality time with Bill left this weekend, and the Perfect Fiancée was going to see that he enjoyed them. She poured them both drinks and went to join him on the sofa. She almost turned back around when she saw that he was flipping through the bridal magazine she'd bought on Friday.

He held it up with a big, happy smile. "I didn't know you bought anything like this, babe. Does that mean you changed your mind and decided you want a large wedding?"

"No. Oh no. Actually, I bought that for—" She stopped and changed course, "—for ideas." He looked so happy at the thought that she'd bought it for them, she could not bear to crush that by telling him the truth.

He took the glass of scotch she gave him and patted the couch next to him. "Sit down and show me what you were looking at in here so I can keep up."

She sat cupping her drink in both hands, leaning forward. "A lot of different things. Just to, um, get in the mood."

Bill was still beaming about the magazine. "I wasn't going to tell you this but your mother called me this week. She was worried that something happened between us because you don't call her back to talk about wedding plans. She said she thought she was more excited about us getting married than you are. I'm glad to see—" tapping the magazine, "—that's not the case."

"No. I've just been too busy to deal with it."

He put the magazine aside and turned on the couch to face her. "Why don't you tell me about this big case you're working on?"

That caught her off guard. "I'd love to. Well, not really love to, it's pretty horrible. But I can't. It's not like in Virginia. The confidentiality rules here are pretty strict. No discussions of active cases."

Bill nodded, his smile fading. "Guess I'm damned if I do, and damned if I don't."

"Damned how?"

"If I don't ask about your work, and if I do. I was just trying to learn what you are so caught up in. So I would understand why you can forget about me so easily when I can't ever seem to get you off my mind."

Windy thought her heart might break. "Bill, that is so nice. I'm sorry. I wish I could explain it to you. You just have to trust me that it's important."

He leaned back into the cushions of the couch, balancing the scotch on one thigh. "Is this what it is going to be like all the time, Windy? I don't want to put you on the spot, or make you defensive. I'm asking because I genuinely want to know."

"What do you mean?"

"Are you always going to be caught up mind, body, and soul in a world we can't talk about? Rushing off to check your cell phone every three minutes even on Sundays?" He lowered his eyes to look at her. "Don't deny it. I could tell you were doing it."

She had thought all day that she was being so careful. Damn damn damn. What else had he seen through?

Bill reached out with his finger and stroked her cheek. "Recently I've started having a fantasy. Do you want to hear it?"

No, Windy thought, in no mood for sharing fantasies. Said, "Of course."

"In my fantasy, you come home every day at five and we sit

down to dinner, you and me and Cate and the brothers and sisters
we give her. And we talk, and spend time together. And then when
the kids are in bed you and I talk, and spend time together. Like
normal people."

Windy stared at her lap.

He leaned toward her. "I just want you to enjoy what you have.
Enjoy being with your daughter. Enjoy being with me. Enjoy making babies with me soon. Do you understand? Instead of me always
having the impression that I am distraction from what you want to
be doing. I don't want to feel like asking you to take a day off is
some kind of pressure. I want it to be a pleasure. Something you
want to do."

It was the word "pressure" that brought it all home to Windy,
made her understand, *boom,* like snapping her fingers. She looked
up and was staring into Bill's handsome face, his eyes holding hers,
but she wasn't seeing him. She was seeing a ceiling fan in a hotel
room in Hawaii. Cate asleep in the adjoining room, the ceiling fan
spinning slowly around over the big bed she and Evan were sharing.
It was a fancy hotel, but there was a cobweb on the fan, she'd noticed it the first night but hadn't mentioned it. That kind of attention to detail, part of her training, drove Evan crazy. She had been
practicing what she wanted to say to Evan all day, working out different tones, different sentences. Different ways of saying that maybe
she needed more from him. Evan was out of bed, standing at the
glass door, watching the wind. She was lying on her side, watching
him. Finally she blurted it out to his reflection, too chicken to ask
him to turn around. But he did when she was done, looking confused, hurt, saying, "Why are you doing this? Putting all this pressure on me?"

Pressure: she asked him to spend the last day of their vacation
just with her and Cate, the three of them, instead of going off to *do*
something. She got to spend so little time with him between work
and being a mom, and it would mean so much to her if they could

have just that one day together. It had come out pretty well, she thought.

But not well enough. "You've never said anything about needing more time with me before," Evan had pointed out and she had wanted to say because I was afraid you would react this way, afraid it would make you scared, make you pull away. But she had backed down. Had said, You are right, everything is fine. Had lain awake, watching the fan spin the cobweb around as he asked could they talk about this later and went for a walk outside, to be by himself for a while.

Had smiled and waved him off when he went windsurfing the next day despite the clouds. Had lain on the beach wondering if she would ever be able to do anything to compete with the thrill of that, even though he'd done it a million times before. Had watched and waited for him to come back, through one day, then the next and the next. At least, she had told herself as she spent those sleepless nights in the black leatherette armchair of the coast guard's office biting her nails, she was not looking at that cobweb anymore.

She had hated identifying the body. Hated having to admit it was real. But she'd done it. Because she had to see proof.

Now here was the dialogue reversed, Bill wanting more time with her, wanting just to be with her. And she was the one pulling away, acting like a child. Bill was offering her everything she wanted, stability, maturity. Attention. He would never be happier away from her. He would never make her feel boring. These were the things that mattered in a relationship, the ones that would see you through long years together, give you a rudder, a future you could count on. She wanted to put as much distance as she could between herself and the feeling she had after Evan died. A voice inside her said she was running away from her feelings for Evan, but that wasn't it. Being a grown-up was about compromise. Evan had never learned that, but she knew it.

She shifted the strap on the white Maidenform bra she'd worn for Bill and said, "Maybe you're right. Maybe I need to let something go. At least cut down my hours at work. Do a better job balancing."

Bill gave her a huge grin and pulled her to her and said, "Good girl." Kissing the crown of her head, his hand moving down to her breast, feeling the cup of his favorite bra. "Very good girl."

She was not ready for that again, not yet. She put her hand over his. "I think—I think I'm going to go get some water." Gently sliding out from under his arms and standing up. "Do you want some?"

"No thanks." Bill got up too, heading for the stairs to the bedroom. He stood with his hand on the banister and a wicked smile on his face, looking in his monogrammed button down and "casual look" khakis like a catalogue model for Brooks Brothers, and said, "Don't take too long, babe. I'll be waiting for you."

Windy carried her water from the kitchen to Cate's room and sat on the spare bed, listening to her daughter sleep, watching the rainbow comforter move up and down with her breathing. She was getting so big so fast, changing every day, learning new ways to talk back. Becoming her own person.

Maybe Bill was right. Maybe she was losing out on too many important things. Maybe she needed a different job. Because that was what lurked under his words, she knew. He was too respectful to suggest it, but she knew that nothing in the world would make him happier than if she told him she would quit.

Cate opened her eyes and looked at her. "What are you doing over there, Mommy? Did you have a nightmare?"

Windy put the glass of water on the apple green night table between the beds. "Sort of."

"Maybe you need a hug."

"Maybe I do," Windy said, and slid onto Cate's bed, clinging to her like she was drowning. As they separated, she spotted a box in the corner of the room and said, "What's going on over there?"

"Those are my things for the pawn shop."

"What?"

"The things I don't want anymore. You said they go to the pawn shop."

Windy reached out and started lifting things from the pile. Cate's toothbrush, the cough medicine she took when she had the flu, a T-shirt, a brooch her grandmother had given her one Christmas. And then something that made Windy's throat go tight. A white terry cloth dog in blue chenille overalls. "Honey, Big Fred is in here."

"I don't want him anymore."

"But you love him. Your dad gave him to you." She still remembered Evan coming to the hospital after Cate was born, looking like a worn-out wreck. Then explaining he had spent two hours at the toy store, quizzing mothers and kids, to find the very best stuffed animal for his daughter. When he'd shown her the floppy dog, Windy had been skeptical, but as soon as she was able to, Cate had grasped it by one white paw and not let go for three years.

She wouldn't even look at it now. "He makes me sad."

Windy took the stuffed toy and slid up the bed toward her daughter, who was hunched with her arms crossed over her chest, her face set.

"You can't make me keep him," Cate said.

"Okay. But let's talk about this first. Why does he make you sad?"

"Because he reminds me of Daddy."

"It's okay to be sad sometimes, especially if it's because you miss someone you love. You have to be sad to be able to be happy."

"Looking at Big Fred makes me cry."

"That's okay too." Windy brushed the hair off Cate's forehead with her fingertips and tucked it behind her ear.

"You never cry."

Windy's fingers froze over Cate's ear. She looked at the box Cate had filled with things for the pawn shop and wondered how many bad memories she'd put in there, shoving them out of sight, just like her mom. What was she teaching her daughter? "I do cry, honey," she protested. She could not remember the last time she had really cried, but she was sure this wasn't a lie. "You just don't see it."

"I want to."

Now Windy laughed. "Okay. Next time I cry, I'll be sure to show you." She paused as if she were thinking. "What if you're not here?"

"You could take a picture," Cate said, dead serious.

"I sure could."

Cate sat up a little straighter. "Bill doesn't like to talk about Daddy, does he?"

Windy shook her head. "No."

"Why not?"

"I guess because he didn't know him. It's hard to talk about people you don't know."

"I talked about him with Ash. Did Ash know him?"

Windy paused. "No. What did Ash say?"

"I asked if he always wanted to be a policeman and he said no he wanted to be an artist when he was growing up and I told him I wanted to be an artist when I grew up too."

"I thought you wanted to be a monster truck driver."

"*And* an artist. Like Picasso."

Her daughter knew about Picasso? How had this happened without her knowing it? Bill's voice was in her head with the news flash that it was because she was always working, and she couldn't even object.

Cate was still in her story. She said, "So Ash asked if you or Daddy liked to do art and I told him that you were really bad at it, and how Brandon and I had to repaint the part of the cabinet you did—"

"That was because no one told me the lines had to be straight," Windy objected defensively.

"—and that I didn't know about Daddy. Did he do art?"

"Not really." Thinking of their time in Paris, the hours they spent at the Louvre, mainly posing like the decapitated and dismembered Greek statues and laughing so hard that they were escorted out by red-coated guards twice. "But he loved to look at it."

"Oh." There was a long pause, then Cate said, "How about since Bill doesn't like it, if you talk about Daddy with me?"

"That would be great."

"And then maybe we could cry."

"Maybe we could."

"Tell me one thing about him right now."

"He loved you very much."

"That's a boring thing," Cate said, giving a big yawn.

Windy wondered when she stopped thinking love was boring, and if she could get back to that place. She kissed Cate's forehead and said, "I think it's time for bed for both of us."

"All three of us," Cate said, reaching for Big Fred. She tucked him in next to her, pulled the covers under her nose, the way Evan used to, murmured, "If you have any more nightmares, just . . ." and was asleep.

Windy went to bed, careful not to wake Bill, telling herself she was very lucky. She had a wonderful daughter, a man who loved her. Why did life have to be more complicated than that?

Lying in bed and running her fingers over the red lines the bra left across her rib cage, telling herself that just meant it was the wrong size, she must be putting on weight. Wondering if she should try the "Beat That Bulge Before Your Big Day Diet" outlined on pages 32 and 33 of *Sophisticated Bride*.

CHAPTER 63

"Surprise" was one of those words like "accident" that made Windy's spine go tight. It was pretty hard to surprise her, she usually saw evidence of whatever was coming on a shirt cuff or the bottom of a shoe, the way a pen stuck out of a travel wallet, something like that, and she thought maybe part of the appeal of her job, at least now, was to be sure she wouldn't be surprised.

But in the car as she dropped him at the airport that morning, Bill had said that he was coming back on Friday afternoon, and he had a surprise for her.

"I don't like surprises," she reminded him and he said, "You'll like this one. Trust me."

The word seemed to be hanging around the air of the car like cheap air freshener as she drove to her office. In books and movies the idea of a surprise like that, where they were in their relationship, could only mean one thing. She thought back to how happy he had been to see *Sophisticated Bride* on her desk, and hoped she was wrong.

She loved Bill. She knew she did. Around four in the morning, she had realized that her fantasy about Ash on Saturday had more to do with the pressures of the investigation, trying to escape from them, than any real feelings on her part. It was natural to project all your insecurities onto someone that way, particularly someone she felt as comfortable with as she did with Ash. By six A.M. she really believed it. Sitting at a red light now a few blocks from her office, at nine-fifteen A.M., she reiterated it to herself. She had just been looking at it backward, taking everything too literally. Ash wasn't a romantic interest, he was a symbol of her work, of the tug of war she felt between that and her life with Bill.

Looking at it backward.

Brakes squealed and horns screamed as Windy stepped on the gas and zoomed through the intersection against the light. She'd got it. She had figured out why Eve had marked those pages in the bridal magazine. And what she had been bringing with her to the crime scenes.

Ash could smell her, the clean scent of her skin, before she burst into his office in her camel pantsuit, looking like the best thing in the world, her eyes shining the way they did when she got excited, and said, "Flowers."

He hung up the call he was dialing and let himself stare at her for a moment as he tried to figure out what she meant. "Flowers?"

Windy put three crime scene photos on his desk, three pictures of tables, each spattered with blood, each with a clean space of the same octagonal dimensions.

"Eve brought them all flowers when she came to kill them. In a vase with an octagonal base. That is why we keep finding the octagonal voids in the blood spatter near the killings."

"Like a memorial? The way people bring flowers to a funeral?"

"It could be. It would go with her making them kneel, to pray. But I think if they were intended as a funeral offering, she would leave them. Instead, it might tie in with the wedding magazine. There was a piece of paper in the magazine and I thought she was using it to hold her place but now I realize the magazine was holding it." She held up a plastic evidence bag with the rectangle of card stock in it. "It's a card from a florist shop."

"There's some connection between the anger she feels that makes her kill, and flowers, weddings. Romance. Is that what you are saying?"

"I think so. I had a friend in college who said that only good girls got flowers. Women who put out almost never did—although they got a lot of male attention. Maybe that is what this is about. If what we saw in The Pit really does mean that she was dating someone named Harry and they broke up, someone she knew from her childhood—before her bad girl days—maybe the flowers are a sign of her failure in the relationship. Symbolically representing what she couldn't be."

"So now she uses flowers in her revenge?"

"Yes. In fact," Windy was warming to this, "what if flowers are her key, the way she gets people to open their doors? Saying, these flowers are from your husband, he called and ordered them to be delivered. Using the idea of a loving marriage as her entry to destroy it. Romance as a cover for murder." That felt right to Windy. Right and scary.

Ash's expression got serious. "Dammit, we need to find Harry. Whoever he is. Finding out what went on between them might go a long way toward answering our questions."

"Nothing from her phone records?"

"No. We're pulling the ones from her restaurant but it's taking a lot longer. In the meantime, it looks like I'd better start tracking down where Eve is getting her flowers. And catch her before she buys them again."

"I might be wrong."

"You might be, but I doubt it."

She looked at him like he'd said something special rather than just saying the truth. "Thank you." Then, glancing at her watch, said, "I'm sorry to dump this in your lap, but I've got to run. I have a meeting at City Hall with Hank Logan."

"About Roddy and the other night?"

"Yes." He saw her swallow. "I'm sorry about that, how it—I didn't realize Bill was home and—I wasn't sure—"

Ash's toothpick tipped up. "I know you were just trying to escape from my pancakes. That's okay, I won't take it personally. How are you feeling?" Keeping his tone light, so she would not worry that he'd been upset.

"Fine. Surprisingly. I actually didn't think about what happened at all this weekend. Did you?"

"Nope." He shook his head. "Not about Roddy." It wasn't even a lie.

CHAPTER 64

"Welcome to City Hall," Hank Logan said as he ushered her through security in the lobby. "You'll notice that all the doors have sliding name plates on them. That's to make sure none of us gets too comfortable."

His office, on the seventh floor, was larger and newer than hers. Instead of dented steel filing cabinets and unsteady metal bookshelves, his were made of shiny pressed wood, and his desk had a fancy multiline phone on it. When it was first completed, the building at 400 Stewart Avenue that housed City Hall had won several awards for being the ugliest structure of the year, but Windy didn't think it was that bad, and she certainly liked Logan's view.

The window behind his desk faced west, giving him a view of the valley stretching for miles, and the hills beyond. It was a slightly hazy day so the mountains hovered in the distance, with a flat quality they only seemed to get here, like they had been cut out of paper and lowered by a movie crane.

"You should see it at night," Logan told her, following the direction of her gaze. "Lights going out for miles and then, boom, they stop. Anywhere else you'd think it was the ocean, but here it's just where the developers left off for the day."

"Do you work a lot of late nights?"

"Depends. I have a lot of sleepless nights, but that's not the same thing." Instead of moving behind his desk, he gestured her into an upholstered armchair, and took one facing hers, leaning forward earnestly. "Tell me how you are."

"Fine. What happened with Roddy really did not upset me too much."

"Okay. Good."

"You sound like you don't believe me."

Logan shrugged. "Well, most people who get held up at gunpoint are a little less sanguine about it. Maybe with everything you see in your work, you're inured."

"That could be it. Or crazy."

"Is it true that you don't want to press charges against Roddy?"

"Yes. But I am curious. Why do you think he came after me the other night?"

"Roddy hasn't had a lot of experience dealing with his own emotions. Most abused children are pretty numb on the inside. Because they don't recognize the emotions they get scared, and fear becomes anger. Anger can always find a good target."

"And he is angry at me because I destroyed his chances of spending his life in jail."

"Because you took away the only life he knew. The abuse, being bad, that was how he defined himself. To you and me, where he is now looks like an improvement and I think it will in time to him too, but for now he's on shaky ground."

"Poor Roddy. Can I ask you a hypothetical question about the results of abuse?"

"Sure."

"If a child were abused by being set on fire, for example, when they grew up, would they retaliate by setting other people on fire? Repeating the patterns of their abuse?"

Logan thought for a moment before answering. "It could happen that way, but it's not likely. Do you know the story of Bluebeard?"

"The legend?"

"More like a fairy tale. It's about a man who kept marrying beautiful women, each of whom would mysteriously disappear. Finally he marries one and tells her I'm going away but here are the keys to every room in the house, all I ask is that you not use this one little key which opens that one little door. But of course curiosity gets the better of her and she unlocks the door, only to find the heads of all his other wives there. When he comes home he figures out what she's done and cuts her head off."

"Punishing her for her curiosity."

"Yes, that and her disobedience. Being a bad girl. But I've always thought that the real reason he kills her is because she's seen his big secret. Abused kids are like that. They work hard to hide the evidence of their abuse."

By cutting people's heads off, Windy thought to herself. Could this be what Eve was doing? The woman in her gated community, her sterile house. Coming out only to behead her victims. Because they saw something in her she couldn't stand?

She said, "So they purposely mislead people about what happened to them?"

"They might pretend to love the abuser when in fact they really hate them. They'll acquire a hundred other psychoses to mask their real one. Anything to draw attention away from what the real problem is. Anything to keep people from seeing behind that door, getting their hands on the key."

"So you're saying Bluebeard had a bad childhood?"

Logan laughed. "Something like that."

"Doesn't everyone keep secrets? Have things they don't want other people to know about them?"

"Of course. In fact, there's a way in which the core of anyone, what drives them, is precisely what they are afraid of. And many so-called normal people do a modified version of the Bluebeard thing, keeping a box of old photos or a birthday candle from when they turned sixteen, things that trigger memories, both sad and happy. That trigger is the key to their secrets. With victims of abuse, what they've packed away is more volatile and so they have to work harder to keep the door closed, drawing attention away from it with other vices, or dodging detection by faking their feelings." He paused, gave a deriding laugh. "God, I must sound like a lecturing fool. Sorry for the long answer—sometimes when I get started talking about work, I forget to stop."

"It's fascinating," Windy said, a little uncomfortable. She felt like she heard a bit too much about herself in his description of people locking things away.

"Sure. Now that I've given you a tedious lecture about my work, maybe one day you can tell me a little about your job. Over lunch, for example. I've been thinking about maggots since I saw those pictures at your office."

"I've found that discussing my job over lunch usually leads to getting asked to leave a restaurant. Most people prefer to eat their Cobb salads without having to hear words like 'pubic hair.' "

"Maybe in Virginia, where you're from, but this is Vegas. Here people think you're odd if you're not commenting on someone's anatomy while you dine."

Windy started to laugh, then heard her cell phone ringing. "I'm really sorry. I need to take this call," she said, pulling it out of her bag.

"Windy Thomas."

"Windy? It's Trish. Eve's friend? I'm sorry to call you out of the blue like this but I thought of something. Can you hear me? I'm on my way to work."

"I can hear you great. What is it?" She fished in her bag for a pad of paper.

"Remember you asked me if Eve ever mentioned anyone named Harry or Barry and I said no? I couldn't stop thinking that maybe she did and I'd forgotten about it. And then last night, I remembered who it was. This guy who lived next door to her when we first met. We called him KS. That's why I didn't get it right away."

"Case?"

"No K-S, like the letters. For kitchen sink. Because he was so fat he looked like he'd eat anything—"

"—including the kitchen sink," Windy finished for her. "Nice."

"Yeah, we weren't really the most thoughtful people. I did not realize he and she were friends, but right after she left to live with her aunt in L.A. he came up to me at school and asked me if she was okay, if something had happened to her. I was surprised because her family had moved out of the house next door to his like two years earlier, but I guess they had stayed in touch. Eve was ever a woman of mystery where men were concerned. The idea that he could be the guy you were looking for kept bugging me, so I got out my old yearbook."

"We've already looked in her yearbooks."

"Eve and I didn't go to the same school. She went to the regular school and I went to a special magnet school for the arts, the Las Vegas Artistic Academy, you know, because I was going to be a world class painter." Trish snorted. "He went there too, in the music program. He was two years ahead of me, but I found his picture. His name is Harold Williams."

"Harold Williams, Las Vegas Artistic Academy," Windy repeated, cradling the phone between her ear and her shoulder and writing fast. "What year is the yearbook?"

"Nineteen eighty-five. He's on page seventy-eight. I'm on page twenty-three if you're interested."

"Do you think you would be able to recognize him if you saw him now?"

"I hope not for his sake," Trish told her. "You'll know what I mean when you see the picture."

Windy thanked Trish and hung up, gathering her things together.

"Was that a lead?" Logan asked.

"Yes. A big one." She stood up. "I apologize, but I have got to get back to the office."

"Good luck."

"Thanks."

They shook hands and then Windy nearly sprinted down the corridor to the elevator, her bag on one shoulder, her other cocked to hold her cell phone to her ear. Harry stood in the doorway of his office watching her go with his fingers on his wrist. His heart was racing, and that was without even doing anything, just hearing that she was on his case. Just hearing her say his name.

He went to the armchair she had been sitting on and carefully lifted two blond hairs from it and wrapped them in a sheet of memo paper. He would put them with the others in the envelope labeled *Windy: Hair-head* he had at home. His collection of Windy was not yet as extensive as his archive of Eve, but it was coming along.

Overall he could not remember when he had enjoyed spending time with a living person so much, but one part of the interview had been a disappointment. He had expected her to be upset by the encounter with Roddy. It had gotten her into his office, yes, but it did not seem to have shaken her confidence in her abilities at all. In fact, she hardly seemed to have noticed it.

He sighed. That meant he would just have to come up with something better next time. Something she would not be able to shrug off. Not scare her, this time. Terrify her.

To do that he would have to dig into his third collection. The one he thought of as an invisible choke chain, the one that would allow him to control Windy. It was labeled *Cate*.

CHAPTER 65

At a quarter after one Monday afternoon Jonah dropped a cardboard box filled with yearbooks on the conference room table, sneezed, and said, "Okay, now will you explain why I just had to do something I swore I would never do again once I graduated from high school?"

"Don't tell me that the man who told off the Los Angeles police commissioner is intimidated by a school librarian," Ash said.

"Watch it, Scamp. These weren't in the library, I had to go see the superintendent of schools. Of course I'm afraid. You can't honestly tell me you've never had that nightmare where you're back in high school, flunking out of history."

"French," Ash said. "My dreams are always about Mademoiselle Jacques."

"*Oui?*" Windy said, coming into the room then. "And what kind of dreams are those, *monsieur?*"

"I bet Windy speaks perfect French," Jonah said to Ash.

"No." Windy shook her head. "But I spent some time in France. A long time ago."

Ash saw something—pain?—flicker across her face, and changed the subject. "Jonah outdid himself. He got every 1985 yearbook from every high school."

"I was scared, man. Wanted to get out of there as fast as possible."

Windy laughed and riffled through the box of yearbooks until she found the Las Vegas Artistic Academy *Arcadian* from 1985. She pulled it, flipped the pages, and stopped at page seventy-eight.

"There," she said. Her finger was next to a grainy school photo. "That is Harry."

Harold Williams weighed three hundred pounds when the photo was taken, and looked into the camera like he was scared of it.

"Are you sure?" Ash asked.

"That's what Trish says."

They stared at the photo. It was hard to believe this boy could have grown into the man they had been searching for since they first heard of Eve. "He's not what I expected," Ash said.

"No. Given Eve's own weight issues, I wouldn't have thought she would get involved with someone so heavy," Windy agreed. "Of course, he probably looks different now, so this photo is more or less worthless."

"I put out an APB on Harry Williams when you called with the name and had Jonah begin checking all the databases."

"In process," Jonah said. "But you might be jumping the gun. I found eleven Harold Williamses already."

"That was fast. How?" Ash asked, impressed.

Jonah raised one eyebrow. "I looked him up in the phone book."

Windy sat with her feet propped on her garbage can and stared at the calendar hanging on the wall of her office and tried to clear her head. Five days from Saturday, the last time Eve had killed, was Wednesday. The day after next. And they were no closer to finding any of the other houses Eve had lived in, anyone who might know where to find her.

Her eyes moved from the days of the week to the photo above

them of the woman with the shiny lip gloss astride the golf club. The woman looked so serene sitting on that golf cart in her bikini, not caring that it wasn't proper golf attire. The photo was taken at the Turtle Egg Golf Course, a course notorious for not allowing women to play. Apparently the rules were different if they showed up in bikinis.

Her phone rang, startling her, and she knocked the receiver off with her elbow before answering it.

"Windy Thomas, Criminalistics," she managed to say breathlessly. There was no response, just some background noise and a faint sound like someone making an announcement on a PA system. "Hello? Is anyone there?" Windy heard a click, and the line went dead.

She scrolled back through the call log but it just showed "unknown number." Glancing at the calendar where she'd written Bill's flight information she thought maybe it was him, calling with a bad connection to say he had landed and—

Windy sat up so fast she almost launched herself out of her desk chair. Coming into her office at that moment, Ash took a step backward.

"Are you okay?"

"I think I figured out what the note means. The one you found. *Nadene Tues. 1230.* What if it is a flight number?"

"You could be on to something," Ash said, excited. "And if Eve wrote it down, maybe she was planning to meet the flight."

"Right. Could you trace something like this to a ticket record?"

"Not legally," Ash said, heading for the door.

"Don't get caught," Windy called after him.

"I haven't yet."

She got out of her chair and followed him. "Wait, what were you coming to tell me?"

Ash paused, already halfway to the exit. "We found Eve's florist. She put in a standing order for flowers, delivered to her at her restaurant on Mondays, three weeks ago. She paid a month in advance, in cash. But what I think you will find most interesting is that they come in an octagonal glass vase. And the assistant manager remembers commenting to Eve on the flowers Monday night, and noticing they were gone the next morning. Tuesday. The day the Waterses were found. Which brings me to the best part: the flowers have been coming for several months and everyone in the restaurant thought they were from her boyfriend, Harry. But as of at least three weeks ago, Eve was paying for them."

Three weeks ago, Windy thought. Three weeks ago Eve had started sending herself flowers, pretending they were from Harry. Windy was willing to wager that three weeks ago Eve and Harry had broken up. And one week later she had started killing.

CHAPTER 66

The chimes on the door jingled as Harry walked into the Mailboxes and So Much More! shop. It was the "So Much More!" that kept him coming back. You could get almost anything you needed to make yourself happy here. Well, if your needs were simple like his.

The girl behind the counter blew a bubble, popped it, and said, "Hello Harry."

She was skinny like Eve, with thick black eyeliner around her eyes, a pierced nose, and six earrings in her left ear. Her shoulder-length black hair was up in a perky ponytail at the crown of her head, making her look like a cheerleader from hell. She always smelled like Bazooka bubble gum.

He smiled at her. "Hi, Amy."

"Did you get to try out those keys I made for you last week yet? Did they work?"

"Perfectly," he assured her.

"Don't tell me you need more packing tape."

"I do."

"You must be sending hundreds of boxes to those poor orphans in Somalia."

He'd forgotten that was what he told her. "It's amazing the donations we are getting."

"I think it's wonderful that you do that. Use your talent to raise money for those less fortunate."

"Thank you."

She smiled and clicked her bubble gum as she rang the order up. Five rolls of packing tape. A box of envelopes. Three mini-cassettes. A do-it-yourself lamination kit. A box cutter. "You know, the packing tape and cutter combos are on sale," she told him, her fingers hovering over the keys of the cash register.

"I think I'll keep them separate, like this."

"Just wanted you to know. In case you want to save your money for other things."

"I can spring for both," he said, handing her cash for his purchase. He leaned closer. "You have any time?"

"Do I? It's the dead zone in here." She turned behind her. "Ralph? I'm going on break. Cover for me, okay?"

The voice known as Ralph said, "Yeah," from the back.

Harry went out the front door and Amy came out the back, meeting him at the side at his Camaro.

"It's been so long, baby," she teased, settling herself in the bucket seat of his car and pulling him to stand in front of her. "I haven't seen you since Friday." She took her gum out of her mouth with one hand. The other reached for his zipper and wrapped around his penis. "Look how happy he is to see me."

Harry stood with his back to the parking lot, hands resting on the warm roof of his car while she sucked on him. He liked it that way because he didn't have to look at her and he had a nice view of the mountains. He came here after each killing as a sort of celebration, and also as a release, a way to let off steam. He'd come today because he needed to relax after his meeting with Windy.

His mind went back to the first killing, the Johnsons'. Mrs. Johnson smiling at him when he came to the door, inviting him in, saying the children were in their rooms. Not knowing, not suspecting. Until he showed her the knife and her eyes got big, huge.

She had started to shake and collapse, could barely make her hands work to tape her ankles together, just whimpering on the floor. Her words were almost indistinguishable from her sobs when she begged for her life, he kept having to bend close to hear her.

Not that satisfying. Not like Claudia Waters. She had fought him like crazy. Claudia had been a woman of steel, not believing him when he said he would spare her life if she begged. She had refused to use the tape and he had been forced to have her daughter do it instead. It had been a risk but my, how it had paid off. He stood behind Minette with the knife over her head, out of the girl's vision but not the mother's, and watched as Claudia Waters sat and let her daughter immobilize her.

"Can you move, Mommy?"

"No, angel."

The little girl standing there, spinning the tape around on her finger. "Did I do a good job?"

Her mother, with tears pouring down her cheeks. "Yes, a very good job."

She had tried to reach for her, to hold her, but the girl didn't understand. She said, "I'm going to tape Martine now in our room. Bye."

Claudia had begged for her life after that. Begged better than any of them. That had been a thrill, breaking that woman. He made her tell him she loved him. Not because he wanted to hear it but because he could.

"I love you, Harry. I love you. Please, don't hurt my daughters. Please."

He heard it in Claudia's voice, then in another voice, seeing Windy on her knees, broken, terrified, begging him, "Please don't hurt my daughter. Please. I love you, Harry. Please."

"Ahhhhh!" he groaned involuntarily, shuddering at the strength of his climax. He jerked himself out of Amy's mouth and stood, dick exposed to the air, trying to get his breathing back under control.

"In*tense*," she said, putting her gum back in her mouth. "You've never done anything like that before."

He swallowed. "Yes." He fumbled with his pants then took fifty dollars from his pocket.

"Fifty! That's a raise. Thanks."

"It was worth it."

She started to go then turned around, cocking one hip to the side and wrapping her gum around her finger. "I hope I'm going to see you again soon," she said in a little girl voice.

"You will," he promised her. "Wednesday."

"Good. You know you're my favorite. I thought men with small feet were supposed to have small you-know-whats. But you're a full-size package."

"Flattery isn't going to get you more cash today."

She laughed and ran back toward the store. "Bye, lover."

He sat in the car gripping the steering wheel, amazed at what had happened. It had never felt like that before. Windy was going to be the best yet.

He took several more deep breaths, catching a whiff of bubble gum, and felt himself really starting to unwind. From the back, in her Catholic school uniform, Amy looked exactly like Eve.

CHAPTER 67

At two fifty-eight in the morning Windy awoke to the sound of Cate screaming.

"Mommy! *MOMMY!*"

She flew to Cate's room and found her daughter sitting up in bed, sobbing.

"Honey, I'm right here." She wrapped her arms around her and Cate began to tremble uncontrollably. "Cate, lovie, it's okay. I'm right here."

Brandon hovered in the doorway to make sure everything was okay, but Windy nodded him back to bed. "Shhh, honey, it's okay. I'm right here. Nothing is going to happen to you."

Slowly the crying and the shaking began to subside. Windy kissed the top of Cate's head and said, "Do you want to tell me about it?"

"It was a *really* scary dream," Cate said.

"If you talk about it, it might start to seem less scary."

Cate clung to her. "I don't want to talk about it."

"Okay, honey. No talking about it."

Cate pulled away and looked up. Her eyes were deep blue from crying. "Mommy, you aren't going to go away and leave me, are you?"

Windy smiled at her. "No way." She bent down so their fore-heads were touching. "I am going to be right here until you're forty-three."

"What happens when I am forty-three?"

"Then I might let you move out of the house. But until then, you and I are a team."

"Are you forty-three?"

"Not yet."

"When will I be forty-three?"

Windy decided that Cate's equilibrium was coming back. She said, "You know subtraction. You figure it out. What is six out of forty-three?"

"A lot." Cate wrinkled her nose. "When your face is so close like this, it looks like you only have one eye."

"How do you know I don't?"

"Eeeew," Cate squealed, and wiggled away from her.

Windy let out a big breath. Cate was fine. "Do you think you can try to go back to sleep?"

Cate stopped squealing and shook her head solemnly side to side. "No."

"What if I stay here and sleep with you?"

"No."

"Let's just try it, okay?"

"Okay."

She and Cate and Big Fred snuggled up together in Cate's twin bed until Cate's breathing grew deep and regular. Then Windy climbed out and went downstairs. The LED display on the oven told her it was three thirty-eight in the morning, but she knew there was no way she was getting back to sleep. She made herself a cup of Earl Grey tea, because a friend of hers had told her it would bring her good fortune, and sat cross-legged on the couch. She could use some good fortune, she thought, as she pulled the lab reports she had brought home from the office out of her bag. She could not shake the idea that she was doing the same thing with the case she had done with the wedding magazine, looking at it inside out, being so preoccupied with the pages that she had almost missed the florist's card.

The top report was the result from the bloody T-shirt they had found in the Dumpster, which turned out to be covered in dog blood, so she set that aside. Dogs were not in her jurisdiction.

The next report said that the hairs found in the lacerations on Kelly O'Connell's neck were a visual match to Eve's hairs, but could not be tested for DNA because they had no roots.

The fibers from the choke chain were microscopically matched to the white fibers found at the Johnson and Waters crime scenes, as well as on the roll of tape from Eve's house.

Best of all, the prints Ash had recovered from the doorjamb between the O'Connells' living room and their hallway matched the fingerprints from Eve's apartment. It was the first time Eve had left her prints at the scene, and although there was enough other evidence to place her at the crimes, fingerprints were something juries really liked when going for a conviction.

Everything present and accounted for, Windy said to herself. All the evidence pointed conclusively to Eve. Windy was still puzzled by what Eve would have been doing gripping the doorjamb close to the floor—had Kelly attacked her? If she had, why didn't Kelly have any defensive wounds?

The next item in Windy's stack was the rogue crime scene photo she had asked Ash about on Friday. She had brought it home to see if she could learn any more about it. When she was a sheriff in Virginia, other law enforcement agencies would send her their crime scene photos from time to time to see if she could help them with tough cases. It was one of the things she had promised Bill she would stop doing—she had been on the news once, and that made him worry that she could be a criminal target—but she figured that this one posed no threat. And there was something about it that had continued to nag at her from the first time she looked at it.

Initially she'd thought that whoever took the shot was simply a bad photographer, someone she would fire. When she realized what the problem actually was, she thought she should fire herself instead. Because it wasn't a crime scene photo at all. It had no scales in it to show the size of footprints, no numbers following blood drops, no markers of any kind, no crime scene tape. It was a photograph of a murder scene, but not a professional one taken by a criminalist. This was the work of an amateur. Someone who just wanted to document a job well done.

"What kind of amateur photographer takes pictures of dead bodies?" Erica, the visual imaging computer whiz, asked her the next morning when she brought the photograph to her desk.

"My guess is, a serial killer."

"Taking pictures of his kill before the police arrive. Way creepy. Well, what do you want me to do with this?"

"Can you enhance the footprints, the shadowy area off to this side, and the milk carton?"

"Why do you want the milk carton if you already know what it is?"

"Milk is one of the few commercial products with both regional and chronological characteristics. If you can pull any information off that carton at all, we should have the date and location of this photo."

Erica rubbed her hands together with excitement. "I'd been looking for an excuse to use that NASA software again."

"I'm not listening. Speaking of illegal activities, do you know where Ash is? I haven't been able to find him."

"Yeah." Erica turned to feed the photo into her scanner. "He's got his phone off."

"Where is he, Erica?"

"I could tell you, ma'am, but then I'd have to kill you," Erica said without looking up from the screen, then pointedly ignored Windy until she went away.

At four that evening a man who looked like Ash after being wrecked on a desert island appeared in her office, dropped a piece of paper on her desk, and said, "Nadene Brown's flight got in an hour ago. I had Jonah call her house but she wasn't in yet."

"Were you at this all night?"

"No. I also chased down some Harry Williamses—none of them our Harry Williams. Nadene is our best chance for information about Eve and Harry. Would you mind going? The way I look right now I would just scare her. Plus, you can go and seem less threatening. Maybe she won't ask why we're questioning her."

Windy's eyes narrowed. "Where have you been?"

"You don't want to know."

"Why does everyone keep telling me that?"

"Because if you don't know, then you won't have to lie to anyone."

"How illegal is what you were doing?"

"You should probably get going."

"I am not joking, Ash. Anything that requires you to practically go hide in a cave isn't a good idea. And I can't believe you didn't have your phone on."

"That would not have been advisable."

"What if something happened here?" Windy asked, sounding more upset then she'd intended. "What if Eve killed again and we needed to find you."

"I would have heard about it."

Windy stood up, smacking her desk with her open palm. "How? You are the head of the Violent Crimes Task Force. You can't just turn your phone off when you want to. What if something happened to you?"

He leaned toward her. "Believe me, Ms. Thomas, I am aware both of my job and of my responsibilities."

"Good."

"Good." His jaw tightened. He said, "I have my phone on now if you need anything," and ducked out the door.

Jonah was waiting for him in the hall. "That sounded ugly."

"Yes."

Jonah looked at Ash more closely. "You're smiling."

"No way."

"You think she yelled at you because she missed you today."

"You're putting words in my mouth," Ash said. But he was definitely smiling.

CHAPTER 68

Nadene Brown lived in a sprawling one-story house which looked like an English cottage that had been run through a play dough extruder and come out long and skinny. It was surrounded with a white picket fence, and between the fence and the house the front yard was a riot of colorful wildflowers.

Windy felt herself being watched as she slid through the gate and walked past the flowers to the door, a feeling confirmed when it opened almost before she pushed the bell. The woman standing behind the screen had piercing blue eyes, short silver hair, and incredible cheekbones. She made Windy think of Lauren Bacall, one of those women who are beautiful and ageless, then made Windy jump when she said, "Many people think I look like her. Lauren. But we met recently and there isn't really a resemblance. Don't be startled, I'm a bit of a mind reader. I'm Nadene Brown and you are Chicago Thomas."

"Yes," Windy said, holding out her card. She figured Ash had finally gotten through and told Nadene to expect her, but she would play along with the mind reading thing. "From Metro Criminalistics. May I come in?" Nadene led Windy into a white-and-blue silk covered living room that felt more Marie Antoinette than Vegas suburban. There were portraits on the wall, all of young women. Or the same young woman, Windy realized, looking from them to her hostess.

"I'm fifty-nine," Nadene told her as she settled herself into a blue chaise. Windy had never seen anyone look comfortable in one of those, but Nadene managed it. On the table in front of the chaise a Wedgwood tea service was set up. "You were trying to guess my age."

"You don't look fifty-nine."

"And you don't look like a policeman." She cocked her head to one side and ran her fingers over a necklace of thick lapis beads with an elaborate diamond clasp. "You look like her, you know. Eve."

Windy didn't feign surprise that Nadene knew why she was there, just said, "So I've been told."

Nadene began to pour tea, and Windy glanced around at photos in silver frames displayed on the sideboard and the top of the piano. There was one of Nadene and Gerald Keene, it looked like during his election bid for mayor. Windy's mind sent up a "be careful" flare.

Nadene was saying now, "It's something around the eyes that makes you two look alike. You're both a little haunted, in opposite ways, like mirror images. You should learn to let that go, Chicago America Thomas. You have nothing to reproach yourself for. I can see I've made you uncomfortable. I have a tendency to do that to people I like." She handed Windy a cup and saucer, saying, "But we were talking about Eve. She's lovely. You are wrong, you know— whatever you think she's done, she hasn't. But I have decided to help you anyway."

"Thank you." Windy went to add milk to her tea and realized that Nadene had already done it for her. She brought her eyes to the other woman's, which sparkled mischievously. "How do you know I think she's done something?"

"The police don't spend their afternoons making social calls on costume designers just to follow up missing persons cases," Nadene told her. "You thought I was going to say that I read your mind."

"I was curious. How did you know Eve?"

"Have you been to her restaurant?" Windy shook her head, and Nadene said, "You should go. I designed the outfits the waiters and waitresses wear. The wings. That is my specialty, designing angel wings."

Windy looked around the jewel-box room and Nadene laughed. "No, you can't support yourself on wings alone. I used to model, and then, years ago, I designed the costumes for the big shows on the Strip. Those feather headdresses and huge peacock skirts. But after a while every feathered and sequined can-can outfit begins to look just like every other feathered and sequined sailor outfit, or shepherdess outfit, or—the worst—swan outfit, and I wanted something with more clarity. So I turned to wings. I do tails, too, but only on special commission."

"And you and Eve became friends? While you were designing the outfits for her waitstaff?"

"Eve is an intensely private person with an intensely needy soul. I loved her instantly, and she confides in me."

"Do you know anything about Eve's past? Where she grew up?"

"Eve wanted to live in the here and now. It is an admirable goal, don't you think?"

Windy decided Nadene was not the only one who could play Dodge That Question. She said, "I know that you have been out of town. When was the last time you saw Eve?"

"It has to be about a month ago. She was very happy. In fact, she asked me if I would go wedding-dress shopping with her."

Windy sat forward. "Did you?"

"I didn't have time that week. We had to put it off."

"Was she marrying Harry? Harold Williams?"

"Of course."

The tone was wrong. Windy sat forward. "What happened between Eve and Harry?"

Nadene looked beyond Windy out the window toward her

swimming pool, where green vines trailed up white lattice work over a cabana.

Windy's cell phone began to ring. She said, "Please, Nadene. Anything you can tell me can help Eve."

"Don't you mean help you? Don't confuse the two, Chicago. They may not be the same thing." Windy's phone rang again and Nadene said, "Do you need to answer that?"

After the railing she had given Ash, Windy knew she had no choice. She pulled the phone out of her bag, saw from the caller ID it was Brandon's, and answered. "Hello?"

Cate's voice screamed, "Mommy!"

Windy stood up. "Cate? Is that you?"

"I WANT MY MOMMY. WHERE IS MY MOMMY?"

"Cate! I'm right here. What's—"

"MOMMY!"

The line went dead.

"Is something wrong?" Nadene asked, but Windy couldn't hear her. She hit redial to Brandon's phone and got bounced into his voice mail. Think, she told herself. Don't panic, think. She dialed again.

"Ash Laughton."

"Ash." She gulped air.

"Windy, are you okay?"

"Someone has Cate. Someone took Cate. I have to find Cate." Think. Explain. Don't waste time. "My phone rang. It was Brandon's number. When I answered Cate screamed 'I want my—my mommy.' Like she was scared. Like someone was hurting her. Then the phone cut out. Now there is no answer. Ash, you have got to help me get her back."

"We're on it."

"Anything. I don't know what I would do if something happened to her—"

"Jonah is already on the radio, scrambling all units. Brandon drives a blue VW bug, right?"

"Yes."

"I'll get a helicopter up. We'll find her, Windy. And I'm sending someone to pick you up."

"No. I'm going to help look."

"Windy, you could be in as much danger as Cate is."

"NO! I am helping. I am—"

"The best way for you to help would be to go home. Right now. We'll set up a command post at your house."

"I want to—"

"I don't have time to waste. Go home. That is an order. Just do it."

"Okay I—" She was about to hang up when she said, "Thank you. I'm sorry I yelled at you—"

"Windy, get to your house."

CHAPTER 69

Windy wished she had kept Ash on the phone with her, reassuring her, as she sped home, because all she could think about was that Eve had her daughter and was going to hurt her, going to make her play with tape, going to punish her, use her as a pawn.

She was going to quit her job, she was going to move with Cate into a monastery, please if Cate is alive, please just let Cate be alive.

She heard the sound of a helicopter overhead, approaching from the other side of town but converging with her toward her house. Don't let that mean they didn't find them. Don't let it mean that Brandon had an accident, that Eve hurt Brandon that—

She screeched past the patrol cars parked in front of her house into her driveway as the helicopter hovered over her roof. Brandon's car was at the curb. Brandon was standing at the door talking to two uniformed police officers and Ash.

Oh God, that meant he wasn't with Cate.

"Where is she?" She stood in front of them shaking. "Brandon, what happened to her?"

Brandon looked at Ash, who put his hands on her shoulders. His voice was calm and he held her eyes. "She is inside. Nothing happened. She and Brandon were home for an hour when this—" He gestured to the police cars and helicopter. "—happened. Brandon put in a video when the doorbell rang and she hasn't looked outside so she has no idea something is going on. Do you understand?"

Windy blinked at him. "Nothing? They are both fine?"

"Yes, and there is no reason to scare Cate."

Someone had been trying to manipulate her, playing a game with her, Windy realized, and that was worse. Because they had used her daughter.

Think about that later, she told herself. Ash was right. There was no reason Cate had to know what happened. No reason to frighten her.

"Thank you."

"Go inside. I'll take care of things out here and send Brandon in to you in a few minutes."

Windy nodded, not really listening, her mind repeating, don't scare Cate. Don't let on. She made herself walk calmly into her house, drop her bag in the middle of the entry hall like normal, and call out, "I'm home."

Cate rushed out of the living room to her, saying, "Mommy you should have seen it, you should have been there."

Windy got down on her knees and hugged her tight. Too tight, too long, but she couldn't stop it.

"Mom, you're squashing me."

Windy loosened her hold. "Sorry." She said, "Did you call me, sweetie? On Brandon's phone a little while ago?"

"No. I wanted to, but we couldn't find his phone. Why didn't you come?"

"Come where?"

"My game."

It was Tuesday. She had forgotten Cate's Tuesday soccer match. She had blown it. "How—how was it? Did you kick?"

Cate stepped away from her and Windy realized she was still wearing her soccer clothes. "Sort of," Cate said. A pause, then, "I scored two goals!"

Two goals. Cate had scored twice and she had missed it, off tracking a psychotic killer instead of being there to watch the biggest moment of her daughter's life. Great choice. "Oh honey, that is great. That is really great," Windy said, swallowing back a lump in her throat.

"Brandon had Mrs. Carlyle tape it for you, so you can see it."

"Thank you."

"But it won't be the same as if you were there."

"No. I'm so proud of you."

"I thought you were going to be there," Cate said and her voice was tense now.

"I'm sorry. I had to work, honey."

"Everyone else's mom was there. How come you work and everyone else's mom doesn't?"

"Someone else in their family works."

"Does that mean when you and Bill get married you won't work any more?"

Windy felt like a fist had hit her in the stomach. "No."

"Why not?" Cate asked, getting mad.

Windy shifted from kneeling to sitting on the floor. "I have to work. I have to catch the bad guys. It's my job."

"Why can't someone else's mom catch the bad guys? Why can't you just be a mom like the other moms?" Cate's little face got tight and she swatted a tear. "How come you work all the time and dress different than them and look different than them?"

"What do you mean?"

"You don't look like a real mom. You don't look like a grown-up. I want a real mom. I want a real mom and a real dad."

Cate stormed up to her room and slammed the door, then opened it, then slammed it again. Windy stared after her, frozen, her hand over her mouth. Then she went numbly to the couch, put the tape marked "Game" in the video recorder, watched the soccer game come on. And began to sob for the first time in over three years.

There was Cate, doing beautifully, kicking, working with the team, clapping for the other girls. And there were the moms in the stands, all wearing pastel-colored polo shirts with their sweaters tied over their shoulders and their perfect hair and nails. Windy didn't even own a pastel item of clothing. None of them talking on cell phones. None of them having bitten their nails down until they bled. None of them responsible for endangering the life of their own daughter. And missing her soccer game.

How had she let her life get so fucked up? How had she lost track of what was important?

The screen blurred in front of her as she cried harder. She heard Brandon's footsteps, felt his arm come around and hand her a white linen handkerchief. Brandon, probably the only person in Las Vegas to have cloth handkerchiefs, certainly the only one wearing Diesel jeans, Doc Martens, and a Clash T-shirt, his "punk" outfit. The idea made her smile through her tears.

"Thanks," she said, looking up.

"You need to remember that the Minx is six," he told her, rubbing her shoulder. "Six-year-olds are sadists."

Windy sniffled and wiped her eyes. "I know. It just hurts because she is right."

"About what?"

"I'm not a real mom. Not like the moms of her friends."

Brandon frowned. "You could look just like them if you wanted to." Casting a glance at the screen and wincing before adding, "Although I don't see why you would."

But Windy knew that wasn't the problem. She could maybe look like them, but she could never *be* like them. She could never be a real mom. A good enough mom. She was failing hard at everything.

Brandon said, "She doesn't mean it, honey. She's just being six."

Windy nodded and headed for the stairs, saying, "But maybe she has a point."

She knocked on Cate's door, ignored the DO NOT BUG ME sign

hanging on the knob, and went in. Cate was sitting on her bed with *The Little Prince* open in front of her. Windy sat down across from her.

"I watched the tape. You were so good, Cate. The way you kicked, but also the way you worked with the other girls on your team. The way you cheered Lutece on even when she let a goal slip through. You made me feel so proud."

Cate didn't look up from her book but Windy knew she wasn't reading. She said, "Thanks. You can't catch every goal. Even professional goalies miss sometimes." Sounding so wise, so cool.

"I could tell you've been working really hard on your kicking."

Cate shrugged. "It wasn't hard. I just did what Ash said."

"I think he would be impressed. Could I show him the tape?"

Cate shook her head. "He would just be bored. Soccer games are boring."

"No way. That didn't look boring at all. Besides, he could fast-forward through all the other parts, of all the people he didn't care about, and just watch the good part with you in it."

Cate almost looked up from the book, but remembered at the last minute she was giving Windy the cold treatment and kept her eyes down as she said, "You think he would like that?"

"You bet."

Still without looking at her mom, Cate slid off her bed and went to the easel that stood in the corner of her room. "I made this for Ash. It's a thank-you card." She held it out and Windy saw a crayon drawing of him and Cate holding hands, with a soccer ball between them. Below it, the word "TanK you" was written hesitantly in pencil. "I couldn't remember how to spell thank you. Could you help me?"

Windy went over to the easel and they sounded the word out together, then practiced writing the letter *h* in the right direction, and finally had it perfect.

Windy was kneeling next to Cate. She said, "I'm very sorry I missed your game, honey. I wish I could have been there."

"I made you this," Cate said, pulling out another sheet of paper. It had flowers drawn on the top, and lots of uneven squares. "It is a calendar. I thought we could fill it in with all the times of my soccer games and you could carry it with you and then you could come to them." She looked at Windy. "Please, Mommy."

For the first time Windy understood how scared Cate still was of being left behind, how deep-down insecure. She pulled her to her and said, "I will try, sweetheart. And if I can't come, I will call you and wish you good luck, so you will know that I am thinking about you."

"You mean like if there are bad guys to catch."

"Yes."

"Where do the bad guys come from?"

"Different places. But mostly I think it's because they never had anyone to love them. To pay attention to them."

"Don't they have moms?" Cate asked.

How to answer that? "Not really."

"Oh," Cate said. She thought about it for a long time. "That must be really lonely." Then she touched Windy's cheek. "You're crying, mom!"

"Yes. Because I'm sad that I missed your game. And I'm sorry I made you worry."

Cate tilted her head to one side. "You look funny when you cry."

Windy started to laugh. "Thanks."

Brandon tapped at the door then and put his head around. "There are some cookies just out of the oven in the kitchen for anyone who wants them."

Before he finished Cate and Windy were already racing each other out the bedroom.

"No running in the house, ladies," he called after them, shaking his head.

When they'd each burned the tops of their mouth devouring cookies too fast and sprayed crumbs laughing at how stupid they each looked with their mouths open going "hot hot hot," Cate leaned over to Windy and said, "I'm glad you aren't like a real mom."

Windy knew it was a compliment, but she still couldn't help feeling like she had failed.

CHAPTER 70

At nine thirty Windy was trying to decide between hot chocolate and her pajamas when the doorbell rang.

She opened it and saw Ash standing on the front stoop. "Hi," he said.

Her heart rate picked up. "Hi. Will you come in?"

"Are you up for visitors?"

"Yes." She closed the door behind him. "Can I offer you a drink?"

"I have to work tonight."

"Coffee? Hot chocolate? It's only instant, but it has mini marsh-mallows in it."

"Mini marshmallows. That I can't resist."

He followed her into the kitchen and leaned against the counter while she filled the kettle. "Is Cate all right?"

"Yes." She had been staring at the kettle but now her eyes came to him. "I'm mortified that I had you call out the National Guard for nothing."

"Not nothing. It was a clever manipulation. Someone was trying to scare you."

"They succeeded." She rubbed her upper arms with her palms. "What do you think happened?"

"I think someone recorded Cate asking for you, then lifted Brandon's cell phone and used it to call you when it was convenient."

"Convenient. Then you think someone didn't want me talking to Nadene."

"That is my guess."

"We've got to warn her. Protect her. Let's—"

"I've already got two officers at her house. No one gets in without us knowing."

"Good. I want to interview her again. She is fascinating although she has a bit of a problem answering questions."

"Did you learn anything talking to her?"

"Only that she and Eve had planned to go wedding dress shopping a month ago." The water started to boil and as she spoke she poured it into two mugs, mixing them with a Cinderella spoon. "Do you want the Evil Bunny mug—" Windy held up a mug with a fairly basic rendering of a rabbit with large pointy teeth. "—or Snappy the Happy Turtle?" A mug with a turtle wearing a feather boa and a tiara.

"Did Cate and Brandon make these?"

"Yes. Can you tell who did which?"

"I want the Evil Bunny."

She motioned for him to take one of the chairs at the light blue kitchen table and put the mug in front of him, seating herself opposite. "I'll let you have her, although she is my favorite, to atone for telling you how to do your job so many times today. I'm really sorry. You would think by now I would just get out of your way."

"I like the back-up." He slipped the toothpick out of his mouth, put it in his pocket, and took a sip from his mug. "Speaking of which, I also have two cars outside your house. I'm sorry, I know it will feel like an intrusion but—"

"No, I'm glad. Thank you." Windy blew on her hot chocolate for a while. "If the call was purposely timed to distract me from Nadene, that means it was Eve."

"Between the timing and using that MO again, taping someone and playing it back later, I'm thinking yes."

"So Nadene must know something important. Maybe I should go over there now."

"She is asleep. And you aren't leaving the house tonight."

"Is that an order?"

Ash sipped his hot chocolate. "Yep."

"If she taped Cate at her soccer game, someone might have seen her."

"We have asked around and come up with nothing. But Brandon said you have a tape. She might be on it."

"Of course. That's why you came," Windy said. "Just to get the tape. And I waylaid you with hot chocolate. I'll go get it." She had gotten up and was moving past him when he reached for her wrist. He gently pulled her into the chair close to him.

"No. That is not why I came. I came to see you." His voice was low and intimate. "I wanted to make sure that you were all right. What happened today—I can only imagine how you must have felt."

Windy stared at her knees. "It was unpleasant."

She heard him chuckle. "Be careful with those strong words, ma'am."

She started to laugh too and then she brought her hands up to her face and covered her eyes and whispered, "Oh, Ash, it was the worst feeling in the world. The absolute worst."

His arms came around her and she pressed her face into his chest and reveled in the sensation of absolutely perfect safety. She loved the way he felt around her. She loved the smell of his fabric softener. She loved the way his chin rested on the top of her head.

She said, "I think I might have to quit."

He pulled away so he could look at her. "I would respect that decision, if that is really how you feel. But if you give me a chance, I will try to change your mind."

"I—I can't put Cate in danger that way. It's not the right thing to do. That's not how a mother who loves her daughter behaves." It was true. It was logical. It was what Bill would say.

"You are conflating two things. You did not put Cate in danger. Eve put Cate in danger. Eve targeted Cate because of your job, that's true. But you did nothing to imperil your daughter."

She wanted to grasp onto his answer and say *Yes! It's not my fault.* But it was. Her decision. Her job. Still channeling Bill, she said, "If I weren't a criminalist, it would not have happened."

"If you weren't a criminalist, you would be a different person, and Cate would be a different person. It's useless to speculate about that. You *are* a criminalist. You are one of the best in the country. What you do saves lives and helps people."

"You can't know how much I want to believe that."

"Whether you choose to or not, there is one other thing you should consider making your decision. Eve has already targeted you and Cate. She isn't going to stop if you leave the case. She is just going to have more chances to hurt people. Because without you, our chances of stopping her soon are minuscule."

"Oh. Then I guess I have no choice but to stay on the job."

"Good." His voice changed, became lower and more playful. "But this is the second time in about four days you've tried to quit. Do you think you can wait until the case is over before you do it again?"

"I don't know. I like making you reflect on how much you want me."

"Don't worry," Ash said. "I have." For a moment their eyes met and Windy felt a jolt that ran from the top of her head to her heels, unlike anything she had ever experienced. Then he was pushing his chair away and standing up. "I should go and let you get some sleep. And don't say you could come to the office now, because you aren't going to. You're staying here."

She stood up too. "You know, you're getting pretty bossy for someone who says he's not my boss."

"Someone has got to make sure you take care of yourself."

Only half joking. And she didn't care. Because she knew he believed in her.

"Thank you for coming over. For making sure I was all right."

"Of course. That's what bosses do."

Walking up the stairs to her room, she wondered if he had felt it too, that electric charge. She was almost asleep before she realized she had forgotten to put the security chain on the front door after she let him out.

The officers in the black and white police car parked outside of Windy's house did not understand what they were hearing at first.

"But sir," Officer Franca protested, "you can't be our relief."

"I am," Ash assured her. "Ten P.M. to three A.M. shift."

"But this is a routine protection detail. No one would ever assign you to this."

"I assigned myself," Ash said. Not adding that there was nothing routine about it as far as he was concerned.

CHAPTER 71

Windy woke up five seconds before the phone rang at 6:06 on Wednesday morning, as though she knew what was about to happen. She picked it up on the first ring.

"Windy. I'm sorry to call like this," Ash said.

And Windy answered, "Where did they find Nadene's body?"

Ash had gone from Windy's house to his office early that morning. He was standing at the window now, seeing dark mountains outlined against the dark sky, hating this. "In her house. She's been strangled. From the looks of it, it could have been with a necklace. Round beads, maybe pearls."

"Lapis. She was wearing it when I was with her. Didn't she have it on?"

"No." He paused, watching the taillights of a car in the distance. "I'm so sorry, Windy. I know you liked her."

"Can you send a car with equipment to meet me out there?"

"Yes. There's just—one other thing."

Windy was already going through her underwear drawer, getting dressed. She stopped in the middle of pulling on a sock. "What?"

"It was called in. From a cell phone. We triangulated the position of the call."

At that moment Windy knew why she'd woken up. She had

heard a noise. She went to her window and looked down at her driveway and saw four extra police cruisers there.

"Where was it?" she asked.

"In the front seat of your car."

Cate was excited to have bodyguards at school, asking if they could help her with her spelling test, but Windy just felt ill. Brandon agreed, no problem, to skip his classes that day and stay at the house until the locksmith came to put new locks on. All Windy could guess was that the time she'd left her keys in the door of her car someone had lifted them and made copies.

All she would let herself guess.

She would not think about the fact that there had been police guarding her house and yet Eve somehow got into her car. Or that they had been guarding Nadene and yet Eve managed to kill her.

A Metro tow truck was just pulling her car out of her driveway to take it to the criminalistics garage for a thorough going over when the crime scene van pulled up. Ash was driving. He said, "I thought you could use a little company."

The truth was, he had no intention of letting her out of his sight for as long as he could manage it. The idea that she might be in danger, a target, hit him like a body punch. He had stayed outside her house even after his relief had come that morning, and it still wasn't enough.

They drove behind the truck pulling her car to the corner, where it went right and they went left. Windy took a deep breath and said, "I've been thinking that car isn't quite right for Vegas anyway. The cup holders especially. Maybe I should get a minivan."

Ash reached out and put his hand over hers. She held on to it all the way to Nadene's house.

———

She had Ned take the garage, Larry the back door through which Eve must have left. She took the kitchen where the body was found.

Nadene had been grabbed by her necklace, from behind, taken by surprise. Usually strangling victims die with their eyes open, but hers were closed. Windy looked around at the EMTs and officers who were staked out around the crime scene and said, "Did anyone touch the body?"

No one had. The killer had closed Nadene's eyes. It was a strange gesture, almost loving. Stark contrast with coming up behind your victim and twisting her necklace until she fell down dead, then taking the necklace with you. Windy said, "I want her eyelids printed at the lab."

Dusting the kitchen, Windy found Nadene's prints on the tile counter, on the front of the cabinet, and on the floor. Places she had grabbed on to when she fell.

Larry came in and studied the line of prints. "Do you think she struggled?"

Windy looked at Nadene's clenched hands and slipped paper bags over them to preserve anything inside them. "Yes."

Next to the prints on the kitchen counter stood the two teacups she and Nadene had used, the teapot beside them, its lid off, as though Eve struck right after Windy left, when Nadene was cleaning up.

Which meant Eve was either in the house when Windy was, or had arrived shortly afterward, sneaking in before the police came. They had been protecting the perimeter of the house, but the threat was already inside.

It meant Nadene's conversation with Windy had been her last.

Why hadn't Eve done the dishes this time? Why didn't she clean up? So that Windy could see that reminder of the two of them having tea and feel guilty?

It worked. Even knowing her own prints would be on the cup did not make it easier for Windy when she found them. Criminalists hated finding their own prints at crime scenes because it meant they had been careless, touched something without gloves on. Gotten someone killed by drinking tea with them.

Ned came in, hauling his gear. "No sign of a car. We got two Diet Coke cans from the garbage outside with prints on them. Get this—they were in the recycling bin."

"She's very tidy when she thinks about it."

"Yeah. There were also four cigarette butts, Marlboros, with traces of lipstick on them."

"That's Eve's brand but I don't smell smoke in here. Do you?"

"No. Maybe she only smokes outside. I mean, if she's environmentally minded enough to think about recycling."

Windy was frowning. "I guess. Was there anything else in the trash?"

"Two cotton pads soaked in what I am guessing is makeup remover, with smudges of black mascara. A Lean Cuisine wrapper. How about in here? Find anything?"

"Nothing unexpected. I think I'm done." She looked at the sink, at the place where the cups and teapot had stood, noticing the switch for the garbage disposal. Whether by intent or accident, she had forgotten to check it. She reached her hand inside, and went pale.

"Did you find another ring?" Ned asked. "Kelly O'Connell's?"

Windy brought her hand out and opened it. "I found two."

The two rings lying on her palm were badly beaten up, like someone had run them through the garbage disposal a dozen times. They were both plain gold bands, engraved on the inside, like thousands of other wedding bands, except for having been brutally mangled in a garbage disposal.

"It'll take the lab ages to pull any ID off of those," Ned said.

"Yes. I'm pretty sure one of them has to be Kelly's. And Nadene is still wearing her wedding ring." She took a big breath and exhaled it. "Which means there's another victim out there somewhere."

Ned made a growling noise. "You know what? I am sick and tired of this case. I want something straightforward and easy. I never thought I'd say this, but I'd give my next paycheck for a simple B & E, some old woman crying over her VCR being stolen. I wouldn't even be tempted to tell her that it was time to upgrade to a DVD. Just something that makes sense."

"I know the feeling."

Ned started loading equipment into the criminalistics car and Windy put her gear away. Before leaving, she took a walk around the outside of the house, periodically bending down to study the ground.

Ned was leaning against the car, waiting for her, when she finished. "Trying to get landscaping ideas?"

Windy said, "Something like that," and settled into silence for the ride to the autopsy, asking herself, if Eve smoked outside, why weren't there any ashes in the flower beds?

Asking herself who the other ring belonged to, and not liking the answer she came up with.

CHAPTER 72

Windy was already in the autopsy room with Dr. Bob and Nadene's body when Ash arrived.

"Sorry I'm late."

"That's okay, she's not going anywhere," Dr. Bob said, pulling on her mask. "Besides, you two are in my good graces today. This body is much nicer than the others you've been bringing me. So refreshing to have a head attached. Much easier to work with."

"We try to oblige," Windy said. "What can you tell us about her?"

"No question that cause of death was strangulation. Most likely with a round bead necklace. And not fast—I got skin and hairs from under the nails. She definitely fought."

"We knew that," Ash snapped. He shook his head at himself. "I'm sorry, I'm just a bit tense."

"Understandable. Here is something you might not know." The medical examiner reached for her black light and shined it on the edge of Nadene's neck. A series of circles popped out, like a glowing bead necklace, interrupted at one point by a crest shape.

"What is the dark spot?" Ash asked.

"The clasp of the necklace. The killer had to twist so hard to kill her that the pattern got impressed in her skin. She was a good fighter."

"Do you have a dental mirror?" Windy asked.

Dr. Bob handed her a mirror on a long handle. She held it over the bruise. "It's not a pattern, it's a monogram. NBL. The *B* was for her last name, so the *L* must be her middle name."

The autopsy ended three hours later at a little after one P.M. with no surprises, and no more useful information. Nadene Brown had been in good health when she died, and would have lived a lot more years if she had been given the chance.

"Have you made any progress tracking Harry?" Windy asked Ash as they walked toward their cars.

"We have been through a dozen Harold Williamses and none of them are our guy. This morning I decided we should try to track him from the past, starting from his school records and working to the present, so I've got Nick Lee on it."

Windy stared out at the street. "We found two rings in Nadene's garbage disposal."

"I heard. I also heard that they were pretty beat up. Hard to ID."

"They are. But it made me wonder if Harry was married."

"Now you are asking for information I can only dream about. Next you'll want to know what alias he is using here in Vegas since he clearly isn't living anywhere as Harold Williams. At this point," Ash was saying as his phone rang, "I would take proof that he ever existed outside a yearbook photo." He took the call and smiled when he hung up. "Nick Lee got a look at Harry's old school records and was able to confirm he was Eve's next-door neighbor on Cottonwood Drive. So he does exist."

"Did he find any family members? Any recent contacts?"

"There you go again with that moon and stars stuff. His mother is dead, but the guidance counselor from his high school still works there. He wouldn't talk to us, claimed patient-client privilege, but with a little coaxing from Nick Lee he did volunteer the name of Harry's piano teacher. I'm going to see her now."

"That sounds scary. Old music teachers." Windy shuddered. "Be careful."

"What are you going to do?"

"Go to my office and rip my hair out. Maybe see if I can rip anyone else's hair out too."

Ash got serious. "I know the investigation is frustrating but you can't beat yourself up. You have got to—why are you laughing?"

"I meant it literally. There's something about the way Nadene was clutching Eve's hair in her hand that is bothering me and I want to try it out." She smiled. "But thank you for making me laugh. The expression on your face—" She chuckled. "I feel much better."

Ash watched her walk to her car, still chuckling, and made a mental note never to fall in love with a criminalist again.

CHAPTER 73

As Windy walked into the visual imaging laboratory, Erica looked up and said, "I was just about to page you. I found something on your crime scene photo."

"I can't wait to see it. But first, stand up and get behind me."

"Why?"

"Just do it. Yes, right there."

"Ouch! Did you just pull my hair?"

Windy nodded, looking at the two short purple strands in her hand. They looked like the other strands she had pulled out of everyone in her department's head.

"Is this a hazing ritual?" Erica asked suspiciously, rubbing her head and sitting back down at her computer. "Those are illegal, you know."

"No, it's an experiment I'm doing. For a case. But I discovered that if I asked people ahead of time they wouldn't let me do it. Sorry." Windy slipped the hairs into her pocket. "What did you find?"

Erica hit keys and an image of the footprints at the crime scene came up. "First, I was able to enhance these. They appear to be tennis shoes. I haven't looked them up in a sole database yet."

"It would be better to do that once we figure out what year we're talking about. I'm guessing the shoes come from the mid-

1980s, but this pair is really worn in, so the photo could still be recent. And they're not tennis shoes, they are running shoes, men's size seven or women's size eight and a half." Eve's size, Windy's mind ticked off. "Whoever was wearing them shouldn't be running, though. Bad left knee."

"You are making that up."

"No. The treads are very old school, pre the Air and Gel cushioning, which means before the 1990s. Assuming that those are standard floor tiles, I can judge the shoe size. And look at the wear pattern. The right foot is flat, the left foot heavily pronated. That means the gait is uneven, which would put pressure on the knee. It wouldn't be noticeable, but they would feel pain running, unless they got orthotics."

Erica gaped at her.

Windy didn't notice. "What else did you find? Anything on the shadow in the lower right hand corner?"

"I saved that for last because it is going to be the easiest. I started working on your milk carton." Erica used her mouse to cut the image of the milk carton out of the larger photograph and paste it into an empty screen. Then she pushed a button and the screen filled with vertical and horizontal lines, the way it had with the surveillance tapes from the pawn shop, only this time what emerged was the corner of a milk carton. "We lucked out, because two sides are partially visible," Erica explained. "I was going to start by enlarging the front of the carton, but then I realized what was on the back and thought that might be better."

As Windy watched, the picture of a girl's face began to emerge, with the words MISSING above it, and beneath it

> Name: Marcie Blum—
> Last Sighting: 4/30/9—
> Last Location: Olymp—

"I couldn't get the other half of the information, but I ran a check on the name, and I think I found the missing girl. Marcie Blumfield. Kidnapped from her parents' home in Olympia, Washington, in 1996. Body found in Seattle, Washington, in October 1999. They would have pulled her off the milk carton when her body was found, which means our photo was taken between 1996 and 1999."

"Are the missing person listings regional?"

"Not always any more, but I looked it up on the web and in the 1990s the network was smaller. So the chances are, your photo was taken somewhere in Washington state."

"Amazing, Erica," Windy said. "This is super."

"Can you use it? Will it help with the Home Wrecker case?"

"I don't think it is involved in that case." Windy watched Erica's face fall. "But then again, it might be," she said, trying to sound optimistic.

Windy went back to her office and arranged all the hair samples she had taken on her desk on one side, and the lab reports about the hair found on Kelly O'Connell's neck and Nadene Brown's fingers on the other, and stared at them, seeing what she had known she would, not liking it.

Maybe everyone she worked with was just too well nourished, she told herself. Their hair was too healthy, held together better. Maybe Eve's anorexia made her hair so brittle that it never seemed to have a bulb on it when it got pulled it out, but everyone else's did. Maybe Eve just needed a better conditioner.

Or maybe she was wrong about something.

Her mind flipped back to the crime scene photo. Was there any chance that it did have something to do with the Home Wrecker case? Could Eve have sent it to her to taunt her? But that would mean that Eve had been in Washington state at some point in the 1990s and there was nothing in her biography about it.

She looked up the number for the homicide divisions in Olympia, Washington, and Seattle, called them both to ask about any brutal murders of a woman in her kitchen in the mid- to late-1990s. The Olympia bureau was small enough that they were able to tell her right away that there were no matches. The duty sergeant in Seattle said, "Sure sure, I'll ask around but we're pretty swamped up here."

Windy could tell he was barely paying attention. She said, "Anything you can find out, I'd appreciate. And of course, if this is an old murder and it gets solved, that would close a cold case for you. Help your statistics. Without you having to do anything but look up some files."

The sergeant snorted good-naturedly. "You're a woman who knows how to talk to a man, aren't you? Give me that information again." This time Windy heard the scrape of a pencil on a pad.

When she was done with Seattle, since she already had the phone out of the cradle, she called home for the eighth time that afternoon. "Hi, it's me. Is everything all right, Brandon?"

"Hmm. Let's see, honey. Not much has changed since ten minutes ago when you called."

"It was fifteen. What are you doing?"

"We're practicing sleeping in our sleeping bag for the class camping trip this weekend and trying to decide which outfits to take."

"I think she only needs two outfits. And I'm not sure I am going to let her go. It might not be safe."

"Well, I'm not going to be the one to tell her she can't take her red glitter mary janes camping, or that she might not get to camp at all. You're the mom."

"So everything is okay?"

"Everything is *fine*. And we have such nice men outside guarding us. Oh, speaking of guarding, Bill called and asked you to call him. You didn't tell him about yesterday, did you?"

"Why?"

"If you had, he would have been here packing boxes to move you back to Virginia."

Windy laughed. "Hey, will you do me a favor?"

"Of course, honey."

"Pull out a piece of your hair."

"No way. I'm already concerned about premature hair loss."

"Brandon."

"Ow. Okay, I did it."

"Is there a bulb on the end? A round part?"

"Yes. Why?"

"Never mind. I'll see you by six."

"I'll sure be looking forward to it, but I have a feeling I'll hear from you about a dozen times before then."

Erica poked her head around the corner of Windy's office as she was hanging up.

"I reduced the shadow in the corner of that photo," she said, handing Windy a print-out.

Windy glanced at it and looked away fast.

"I'm not sure," Erica said, "but I think it's a baby."

"Yes," Windy agreed. A baby in a pool of blood.

CHAPTER 74

The La Françoise School of Dance, Specializing in Ballet and Tap Instruction, was adding Tango-for-Tots! classes to its roster, Ash learned, reading the neon blue flyers tacked to the wall of the reception room while he waited for Miss Cordelia Kincade. She was the piano accompanist, presumably the one playing the snippets of music that could be heard over the hum of the air conditioner. The plastic chairs lining the walls were all filled with moms, Ash assumed, waiting for their children to come out of class. The woman closest to Ash had a baby in a car seat at her feet that she was rocking with one toe as she read *Madame Bovary* in French. Anyone who talked did it just loud enough to be heard over the piano coming from the other room.

The music stopped and the room got quiet, like the calm before the storm, and all the moms began to shift, gathering up purses and backpacks. Then the door to the back of the dance academy opened and tranquillity erupted into babble as a dozen pink-tutued little girls with their hair in buns spilled out, being bundled into jean jackets and sandals and sneakers and sweatshirts, some of them laughing, one getting carried out while complaining to her mother that her toes hurt. Ash stood to one side against the wall, fascinated and more ill at ease than at a shoot-out, watching the controlled chaos, until the last mother-daughter-stroller combination had gone out the door and he was alone again.

"You're not a parent, are you?" a woman said from near his elbow, and he looked down to see a tiny lady who appeared to be in her sixties.

"No," Ash said to the woman. "Is it that obvious?"

"Just the look of sheer terror on your face is all, dear." Giving him a smile and a once-over at the same time. "I'm Cordelia Kincade. I believe you are waiting for me."

The small woman had an air of authority that made Ash feel like he should pat down his hair, straighten his shirt collar. As he followed her into the academy, past a large room with a wood floor, a wall of mirrors, ballet bars at two heights, and a piano, he took the toothpick out of his mouth and put it in his pocket.

She turned in at a room marked LOUNGE. There were two women in their late thirties, both wearing black leotards, tight buns, and red lipstick, sitting on a gray-brown sofa smoking and speaking in what sounded to Ash like Russian. They paused to nod as he and Miss Kincade came in, then went back to their conversation. Miss Kincade sat down in an easy chair and pointed him into a straight-backed wooden chair next to a potted plant.

Feeling like he'd been caught cutting school, Ash sat down, knees together, hands in his lap.

"Now, what can I do for you, Detective Laughton?"

"I was hoping you could tell me a little about one of your former students. Harold Williams? You taught him at Las Vegas Artistic Academy. If you remember him."

"I'm not that old, Detective Laughton, and I'm certainly not senile. Of course I remember Harry. He was a doll and very charming when he wanted to be."

"The guidance counselor at the school said you and he had a particularly close relationship."

"Harry was a very driven student. A perfectionist. He would

stay very late to practice. I think music was a release for him. Since I was there when he was playing, I got to know him."

"Was he talented?"

"He was diligent. Technically accomplished. And dedicated. But his playing was always slightly unsatisfying. It sounds like a cliché, but to be a truly great musician, you put emotion into it. Harry was not very emotional."

"What can you tell me about his home life?"

"Very little. Once he had, well, a small problem at school. He started to steal things here and there, other student's lunches. I had his mother and his stepfather in for a conference, told them I was concerned. After that there were no more problems, so I assume everything worked out." A crease appeared on her forehead. "There was one strange thing. His mother and stepfather never came to any of his performances. I know he had a little sister, so perhaps they were at home with her."

"Harry had a sister? Do you know how much younger she was?"

"Perhaps ten years? I remember him telling me how when she was a baby, they got along so well, but as she got older it was harder to be with her. He loved babies. In fact, when he was talking about his sister, his playing was the best. The most emotional. Except— now I remember. Except for the last half of his senior year."

"What happened then?"

"He started dating that wonderful girl. What was her name? Something biblical. Judith, maybe, or Delilah."

"Eve?" Ash suggested.

"Yes, Eve. That was it."

"Did you meet her? See them together?"

"No, she didn't go to our school. But he talked about her often. About the things they did together, taking long walks, picnics. She must have been a very special girl to appreciate him. Their romance sounded like something from a storybook. And there was a decided change in his playing."

Ash was trying to picture Harry and Eve—the Harry and Eve he knew about—taking walks and having picnics, when Miss Kincade said, "I was sorry to learn it did not work out for them. He seemed very much in love with her. Of course, he was only eighteen. People change."

"Did he tell you they broke up?"

"No. But I got a wedding invitation from him, must have been six or seven years ago. The name of the woman he was marrying wasn't Eve. It was Amanda. I remember because that is my niece's name."

"Did you attend the wedding?"

"No, I couldn't. I don't really believe in airplanes."

"Where was it?"

"All the way in Seattle. But it was charming of Harry to remember me. If you see him, tell him I hope he is still playing."

Ash was on the phone to the Seattle police department before he reached his car. "Anything you have on Harold or Amanda Williams," he told the detective on the desk. "Going back maybe seven years."

"Doesn't ring a bell. I'll add it to the other information."

"What are you talking about?"

"You're from Vegas, right? One of your people already called asking about this. Crime scene photo from the mid- to late-nineties? Woman with her throat cut?"

Ash stared at his phone. "Do you remember the name of the person who called?"

"It was a woman. Chicago something. I told her we're busy but I'd look into it."

"Please do. It's urgent."

"Always is," the man assured him.

CHAPTER 75

Windy sat up expectantly as Jonah came into her office, but got dejected when she saw he was only carrying a folder.

"You don't happen to have one of Ash's Twinkies on you, do you? Or know where he keeps the key to his supply?"

"No way. One of the conditions of my employment is I don't have to touch those things. But I've brought nourishment for your mind." He held the folder out to her. "File on your Jane Doe from the desert the other day. The one who ate dirt? Just came in. I think you'll find it interesting."

"Daisy Graber AKA Daisy Deluxe. Deejay KRST," Windy read, then her eyes popped. "No. Oh no. The night before she died she did a monologue about the Home Wrecker?"

"Yep."

"Is there a transcript?"

"Two pages back. And a report by the officers who took the missing persons call. I'll leave you to your reading, I just wanted to be here for the good part."

Windy read the transcript, then flipped to the report by the officers who were assigned to check Daisy's house when she didn't show up for work.

"Front door ajar, but no sign of forced entry. Large quantity of dirt on back stairs, and leading inside house. Neighbors report that subject's dog, a large Great Dane, is also missing. Subject described as medium height, five-foot-five to five-foot-seven with short brown hair, almost always concealed with a wig."

Windy reached for her file on the evidence from the Dumpster.

Item 10: Yellow T-shirt, large quantity of blood; blood identified as canine.

Item 16: Blond wig, traces of type O blood inside consistent with a head wound.

Those listings convinced Windy that Daisy had been killed for her derision of the Home Wrecker. Which meant that in addition to the green Saab, Eve had a mid- to late-eighties Camaro IROC-Z, perhaps the most muscled-out muscle car of them all. She thought of the tire impressions, perfectly preserved gatorbacks, the kind of tires only a serious car buff would buy. And then she tried to place Eve behind the wheel.

She couldn't do it. Maybe Eve borrowed the car, she told herself. Maybe. But all the doubts she had been having came nagging back. Her eyes roamed over the notes all over her desk and kept coming back, over and over again, to Crest White Strips.

She sprinted from her office to Ash's flapping the file in front of her.

"If you're planning an armed assault on my Twinkies—" he started to say, but stopped.

She leaned over his desk, cheeks red, out of breath and said, "We've got it backwards. Eve Sebastian isn't the killer at all."

CHAPTER 76

Windy took three deep breaths and went on. "All the evidence is just window dressing, to make us notice the wrong things."

Ash eyed her skeptically. "You're saying we need to ignore the evidence? That's a new approach. Gerald will like it."

"Stop being snide. Not ignore it, but reinterpret it."

"How can you reinterpret away the fact that she was at all the murder scenes?"

"That's not a fact."

"We've got her hair, her cigarette butts, Diet Coke cans—why are you shaking your head?"

"The hair is phony. It's her hair, certainly, but none of the pieces, not one, has a bulb on it. That means it is all broken, the way hair is when it comes from a brush or comb, rather than pulled out, the way it is in a struggle."

"You think the killer collected and then dispersed Eve's hair."

"Yes. And I think he did the same thing with her cigarette butts. There were butts at Nadene's house, but no ashes. And there was no ashtray at Eve's."

"So your killer took the ashtray and is using the cigarette butts as plants. To make it seem like Eve was present."

"Exactly. The Diet Coke cans at Nadene's too. Those would be easy to take from Eve's house and easy to store for later use. But leaving them at Nadene's was actually a miscalculation on the part of the killer, because it's too obvious. While someone might bring Diet Coke with them when they go to murder, two cans is, well, overkill, and the chances of them chucking the cans and forgetting about possible prints on them when they haven't left prints anywhere else, is laughable. All of that is evidence that is a cinch to plant."

"What about the shopping list you found? Eve's prints were on that."

"Print, yes. Because she turned the page. She wrote Nadene's flight number on the next page. There is not enough writing for a really good comparison, but it's different than the writing on the shopping list. Which is different from the writing on the back of a photo Eve gave Trish."

"Eve wrote on that photo seventeen years ago."

"Sure. But the writing on the shopping list looks a lot like the writing on the walls in The Pit."

Ash nodded. "What else?"

"Eating toast with the victims doesn't make sense for Eve."

"Why?"

"She doesn't eat carbohydrates."

" 'Defense by Atkins Diet.' But we know irrefutably that she and her car were outside the houses. We know she lived in all of them. We know she had the tape used at the Waterses' murder. Motive, means, opportunity. Reinterpretation?"

"Yes she lived in the houses, and yes she sat outside them, for reasons we can only guess. But the tape was planted in her townhouse."

"How? By whom?"

"By the ex-boyfriend she ran to when she heard that the police were looking for green cars, I am guessing. The one who used to follow her from house to house when she was younger, and is now getting his revenge on her for some real or perceived slight, by framing her for murders he is committing."

"Harold Williams. You think Harry is the killer."

"Yes."

"Then where is Eve?"

"I thought that was obvious. Eve is dead."

"What?"

"You found the evidence. The fingerprints from the doorjamb at the O'Connells'. We know those are Eve's. Based on the place-ment and the intensity—someone was holding on very tight—I think she left them when she was fighting Harry off. I may be wrong, she may be alive, but that would put Harry in a difficult position."

"Why?"

"His whole plan depends on framing her. Shifting the blame for the crimes from him to her."

"So Harry lived in the O'Connell house, not Eve. Harry was the one who spent time in The Pit. And Harry hates Eve. Can you de-duce any more about him from the evidence?"

"He has white teeth."

Ash leaned back in his chair. "What if I told you he was married and living in Seattle during the mid- to late-1990s?"

Windy dropped into the seat opposite his, her eyes wide with amazement. "Then I could tell you quite a bit more. I think I could even tell you about his first murder."

When Ash told her that Harry had lived in Seattle, Windy's first thought was that Erica would be pleased, her work did have something to do with the Home Wrecker.

Ash said, "All I know is that according to his former piano teacher, Harry married a woman named Amanda in Seattle seven or eight years ago. Of course, she also told me that Harry and Eve enjoyed walking in the park and having picnics together."

"Sounds like Harry was in the active fantasy life category."

"Was and is. If that photo you have is actually of a crime Harry committed, let's say against his own wife—"

"And baby."

Ash exhaled sharply. "—and baby, then why did he send it to you? Doesn't it conflict with his policy of framing Eve?"

"Maybe he did not think we would connect it to the other killings. Maybe he just wanted to brag."

"Or maybe he secretly wants you to know all about him. Do you still think the killer brings flowers to get into the houses or have you reinterpreted that, too?"

"No," Windy said, laughing despite herself, "that stays. I'm not convinced that flowers alone would get a man into a woman's house at night, but I haven't thought of anything else yet. Why?"

"What if the crime scene photo is his special version of flowers, just for you? Half taunt, half gift."

"Can I return it for something I like better?"

"I think Harry is drawn to you, wanting your attention more than anyone else's, and at the same name, your attention is the most dangerous. Because you have the skills to spell out what he is doing. So he is confused. He calls out to you, literally. But then hides. Sort of like a teenager with a crush."

"And we know how well his last boyhood crush worked out," Windy said. It reminded her of *The Little Prince*, taming someone. Get closer and closer, but not too close.

"I need to ask you a bad question. If by some miracle we picked up Harold Williams tomorrow, could we hold him for the murders? Do we have any proof?"

Windy thought about it. "No. Well, possibly, if he has a 1985 Camaro IROC-Z28. But nothing that would hold up. Damn. Does that mean we have to proceed as though we're looking for Eve?"

"No, it means we're not going to tell anyone about our suspicions. But I'll get some more officers out looking for that car."

"That's probably wise. Right now, the only advantage we have against Harry, if it is Harry, is that he thinks we're looking for Eve. The two Diet Coke cans he left at Nadene's give me hope that he's starting to be less careful."

"You sound more optimistic than you did this afternoon."

"I am. There were starting to be too many tiny inconsistencies in the evidence that I didn't like. It's one thing for this killer to manipulate me and my life, and quite another for him to interfere in my evidence." She was trying to joke, but it was obvious that on some level she meant it.

"Let's hope we are on the right track now. Gerald made it clear earlier today that he's coming to suspect *I* am the Home Wrecker, trying to ruin his city's image and screw with his reelection bid next year."

Jonah poked his head into Ash's office. "The mayor is on line one for you again."

Ash sighed. "Me and my big mouth."

"I've got to go," Windy said, beating a hasty retreat. "I'll be at home if you need anything."

Ash said, "Coward."

"I'm going to reinterpret that to mean you're jealous."

Nick Lee and Bob Zorzi were waiting in Jonah's office when he got there.

"We didn't want to bother the boss," Nick Lee explained, wincing as Gerald Keene's voice could be heard giving Ash a royal chewing out.

"Good call. What do you have?"

"Information you wanted about Nadene Brown's car. It's a 2002 Lexus. The patrol cars stationed outside her house saw that one pulling out of the garage Tuesday night and figured she was just going for a drive. Flashed his lights at her for the 'okay' signal and she flashed right back."

"Except it was probably the killer," Nick Lee put in.

"Yeah, I got that. Fantastic," Jonah said, imagining what the mayor would make of that if he heard. "I'll radio the license plate to dispatch."

"The Lexus isn't the only car registered to her. She's also got a 1985 Camaro IROC Z. Kind of a weird car for an old lady."

CHAPTER 78

Windy picked up the message slips from her desk on her way out to the parking lot, flipped through them, saw one marked URGENT from Bill, and shoved the others in her pocket.

Then she realized she didn't have a car. This had been the longest day of her life, she thought, and it was only five thirty. As she walked to the street, wondering if she would be able to flag down a taxi, she returned Bill's call.

"What is urgent?" she asked him when he picked up. It sounded like he was watching television, probably a golf show.

"I forgot to tell you. For the surprise I am planning this weekend you need to pack an overnight bag. And pick out a fancy outfit."

Windy felt her shoulders sag. "What are we doing, Bill?"

"I'm taking care of you, and you are being surprised."

"I'm not sure this is a good weekend for it."

"Why not? Cate will be at her camp-out until Sunday. It's a great weekend for us to have some time together."

"Does it have to be fancy?"

"I'm afraid it does."

"I'm not sure I'm up for anything like that. I'm exhausted. And I might—I might have to work."

Now there was a long pause, Bill not sounding so happy. "What do you mean?"

"We are in the middle of a huge case. I might need to work this weekend. A little."

"When is this going to end, Windy?"

"When we catch the killer."

"Since when is your job to catch the killer? Isn't there a police force there? What are they doing?"

"They are working on it too. We all are."

"This guy must be pretty smart if everyone is working as hard as you are and you can't catch him."

"It's not that simple."

"Maybe you can explain it to me. This weekend. When we're together."

"I'll try, Bill," Windy told him, not sure if she was going to try to explain or try to get the time off.

A bus went by and he said, "Are you standing on the street?"

"Yes. Waiting for a ride."

"Where's the car?"

"In the garage." It was true. Just not the kind of garage he thought. She could not handle what he would say if he knew.

"What is wrong with it?"

"Well—"

"Did someone break into your car? I told you, you should start parking it in your garage, rather than in the driveway. That's what it's for."

"No one broke in. The door wasn't locking properly. And there is something in the garage at home."

A tan Lexus pulled up at the curb next to her and the window went down. "Are you taking some air or do you need a ride, pretty lady?"

Windy was ready to flip the guy off when she realized it was Hank Logan making a joke.

"Who is that?" Bill asked. "Is that Ash Laughton?"

"No. I've got to go, I'll call you later," she told Bill, and said to Logan, "A ride would be great."

"How are you?" Harry asked as she got into the car. He had to grip the steering wheel to keep his hands from shaking. His pulse rate was soaring.

"I'm okay. What are you doing over on this side of town?"

He was tempted to tell her. Well, I've been driving by your office telling myself that I can't kill you yet, even though I want to, because if I wait a little longer it will be that much more exciting. And then you appeared, standing at the curb. To test me.

He said, "I was coming to see you. I have a note for you from Roddy." He pretended to feel around the pocket of his slacks. "I thought it was here somewhere."

"Maybe in the glove compartment?" she asked, reaching for it.

Wouldn't that be something. Have her open it and watch the packing tape and the piece of Kelly O'Connell's nose he was keeping as a souvenir fall into her lap. "No, it's not in there. I must have left it at the office."

"Okay." Windy eased her hand away. "How are you doing?"

He smiled and said what was really on his mind. "Great, now that I have you in my car."

"That sounds menacing."

He laughed out loud. "You have a very suspicious mind, Windy Thomas." He started to signal a turn, the turn he'd make to go to her house, and stopped himself just in time. He wasn't supposed to know the way. "Do you want to tell me where you live, or do you want me to drive off into the sunset with you? Careful, I know it's a tough decision."

She shook her head. "My goodness, you know how to lay on the charm."

"Only thing I learned from my daddy, how to talk to girls."

She laughed at that, and he laughed with her, even though it was true. He had learned everything he knew about managing women from Charles.

They had a pleasant conversation, not talking about the investigation, until they reached her house. She turned to him and said, "Thank you for the ride." And then did the unthinkable. "Would you like to come in? You could meet Cate. She is always trying to make sure I have friends."

He thought about what that would be like. Sitting at her table, eating cookies with her and Cate in the kitchen like the two of them had the night before. Having Cate bind Windy's hands and feet with clear tape. Making Windy sit in a chair and watch as he played with Cate. All kinds of games. Games he hadn't played with the other girls. Taping Windy's eyes open if she wouldn't watch.

Then he would teach Cate about sitting in one place and counting to one hundred with her eyes closed and her fingers in her ears. And he would let Windy start begging. When it was over, he could collect the cassette from the tape recorder he'd installed outside their house, and listen to it as many times as he wanted.

He had the knife in the backseat under his coat, a corkscrew in his pocket, and the tape in the glove compartment. All he had to do was say yes. Yes, I would like to come in.

"I wish I could," he said to Windy. "Unfortunately, I have plans."

It was true. He had other plans for Windy.

Harry watched her walk up the front path to her house, turn to talk to the policeman who materialized from the side of the path, then go inside. He bet she felt really safe with all those police around. He bet she would sleep really well tonight.

His palms were sweating so much he could hardly hold the wheel to drive.

CHAPTER 79

Windy started her morning on Thursday engaged in a battle with Cate about why she had to wear her underwear inside her clothes, by the end of which Windy wasn't even sure.

"Super Friends wear them outside," Cate pointed out, and instead of objecting that they weren't underwear, they were costumes, Windy threw up her hands and said, "Do whatever you want." She wondered if letting your child go to school with their underwear outside was considered child abuse. Not to mention with three armed bodyguards.

It was a grayish day, the kind that anywhere but Vegas meant rain. Windy had just pulled into the parking lot in her rental car when Jonah flagged her down.

He said, "Ash was hoping for a word with you."

"He made you stand out in the parking lot waiting for me?"

"He would have come himself but he's on the phone getting yelled at by Gerald again."

Windy grabbed her bag and followed him toward the task force offices. "Has this been going on all night?"

"No, last night he was outside—" Jonah stopped himself. He wasn't sure Ash wanted her to know he'd been up all night guarding her house. "Ever since he got in this morning. It turns out that Kelly

O'Connell was talking to a phone psychic when the killer came calling, and the psychic called 911."

"Did she get a busy signal?"

"No, I think they about solved that problem. It's worse. Two officers were sent out about an hour later. Knocked on the door. Spoke to a woman inside. But she was—get this—making choking noises so they left."

Windy stopped walking and stared at him. "What?"

"They thought she had morning sickness."

For a moment Windy didn't know whether to laugh or scream. Harry had been within their grasp. But it wasn't the officers' fault. She could only imagine how awful they must be feeling.

How much Harry must have been enjoying himself.

"What does Ash want to see me about?"

"No idea. I just get these scrawled messages that he writes as he eats Twinkies and says 'yes sir.' "

Windy tiptoed into Ash's office and stood against the wall. On the speaker phone Gerald was saying, "Because if the Home Wrecker kills again, we are all going down."

Ash, looking tired, handed her a piece of paper. She read, *Harry Williams's half sister Misty—*

"Yes sir," Ash said, writing something fast.

—works at Stardust gets off at twelve thirty—

Gerald's voice boomed, "Which is why I think a public appeal is the only way."

"Yes sir."

We've been trying to find her for two days. I can't get off phone. Will you interview her please?

"You have got to go on television and beg the killer to surrender."

"Yes sir," Ash said. He sat up and shook his head. "I mean, no sir. Gerald, I am not going on television and begging a mass murderer to do anything. I told you that." Ash took the mayor off speaker phone and grabbed the receiver.

Windy nodded and inched into the hallway.

"I would stand a better chance of catching our killer if you would let me do my job, rather than forcing me to debate with you about press coverage," she heard Ash saying as the door of his office closed behind her.

Misty Williams worked in one of the change booths at the Stardust. Windy found her standing in front of the casino, just off her shift, waiting for a ride.

"I really don't have time to talk to you," Misty said, touching up her lip liner in a compact mirror. Men getting out of cars in the pull-through stopped to gape appreciatively at her figure laced into a black velvet corset and body-hugging black lace skirt. She was wearing platform pumps that made her two inches taller than Windy and had long platinum hair that fell almost to her bottom. She brought her black-lined eyes to Windy over the mirror and said, "Besides, I haven't seen Harold in more than fifteen years. He left like a year after he graduated high school."

Her skin was bad, sallow and covered with too much light-colored foundation. Still, with red lipstick on and about thirty coats of black mascara, she was striking. One guy walking by said loudly to his friend, "I'd like a piece of that," and she flipped him the finger, tough girl, saying, "Keep dreaming, Payless."

She said to her reflection in the mirror, "These men, they think they can have any girl. Like I'd ever do a guy who wore cheap shoes like that. You can tell if a man's got it by his shoes every time."

Windy didn't know what to say to that. She asked, "You must be much younger than your brother."

"Half brother," Misty corrected, wiping lipstick from her front teeth. "Uh-huh, I'm ten years younger. My mother was married to his father first. Big mistake."

"What happened to his dad?"

"All I know about him is, he gave my mom this ring." Holding

out a finger with a band that had two emerald chips and a small diamond. "And what that tells me is, he was a cheapskate. I mean, look
how small that diamond is. I only wear it when I'm going somewhere I don't really care what I look like."

What did she wear when she did care? "Do you know what he
did for a living? Why they got divorced?"

"He was a traveling something, repairman or salesman or something. Mom got tired of him, so she tossed him. Then she married my dad and they had me. Williams is my dad's last name. He
adopted Harold when they got married. Don't think he didn't regret it."

"Why?"

"Because Harold was like that."

"How was your relationship with him? Was he a good brother?"

"We didn't exactly hang out, if that is what you mean. I mean,
ten years is a big difference. Plus, he mostly hung out by himself in
his room. He was weird."

"Weird? What do you mean?"

"Like, you never knew what he was going to do. He scared me
and Mom too, something about him, and his size. I was just a little
girl but I remember it. So Mom made him stay in his room most of
the time. But even still, he was, like, freaky. No one wanted to live
with him." She snapped the compact closed and gave Windy her
eyes direct. "You want to know if he was a good brother? No. He
was a piece of shit, as a brother, and as a person. Every time things
were going good for us, Harold would do something to fuck it up.
He made my father leave. He was evil."

"Evil how?"

"Mean. He liked to hurt people. And have you seen him? He is
disgusting. No one wanted to admit they were related to him. My
mom and I, we were so glad when he finally left. We could get on
with our lives."

Windy looked at her, tapping her foot and waiting for a man to pick her up from her job, not looking especially happy, and wanted to ask what she'd gotten on with. Asked instead, "Why did he leave?"

"He just did and good riddance. Maybe Home Depot hired him. They'll take anyone. We didn't ask any questions."

Windy decided to change approaches. "Do you remember a girl named Eve?"

That got Misty's attention. She smiled, looking almost pretty, and said, "The bitch who lived next door to us?"

Almost pretty. "Yes."

"I don't remember her exactly, I was little when she moved, but I remember Harold talking about her. I asked him one time if she was his girlfriend, and he hit me. I think he was totally hot for her. This other time, when I was eight, I went to the mall with some friends and I saw her there, making out with this old guy. And then I looked around and I saw Harold. He was staring at them." Her eyes glittered with pure malice. "He was sweating like a pig. I swear he almost reached into his pants and jacked off right there. I know he did later at home."

Windy hoped that image was not going to haunt her dreams that night. She said, "Do you know of anyone else who might know where he is? Maybe any other relatives?"

"No way. My whole family hated him. I was worried he would show up for Mom's funeral, but he didn't."

"What about on his father's side?"

"Them? Sure, maybe one of them, but I never met any of them. They were freaks too, that's where he got it from, my mother said. We never saw them." She looked out at the street, at her watch, the street again. Then frowned, and came back to Windy. "Actually, you know what? I think he had an aunt somewhere in Vegas. Yeah, you know, she sent him presents on his birthday. His father's sister or whatever. She married some rich guy. She was a bitch."

"I thought you said you never met them."

"I didn't, but one time for his birthday she sent Harold a BB gun and he shot up my father's car with it. Used to aim it at me too. That was right before he went away."

"Who? Harold or your father?"

"Both of them. Look, has Harold done something? Because I don't want my name in the papers connected to him."

"I doubt it will be."

"Good. I'm just working here until my career takes off and I can't afford scandal." She tossed her hair, a studied gesture, and said, "I'm getting into modeling. Anyway, if you see him, will you tell him one thing for me?"

"Of course."

"Tell him he owes me $1,860 for our mother's funeral. I had to borrow the money. There is no reason he shouldn't have to pay half of that. Right?"

"Sure. You have no idea where he might be?"

"Try looking in the gutter," Misty said, making a joke. Her eyes scanned traffic again and she perked up, pushing her chest out, saying, "I gotta go."

"Just one more thing. Do you know his aunt's name? The one who gave him the BB gun."

"My mom called her something. Fucking Nadene, that was it. I guess her name was Nadene." Misty clutched her purse strap under her arm and said, "I don't like to talk about Harold, so don't come back here, okay?" then took off.

Windy watched Misty run over to a black Mitsubishi Diamante with chromed-out wheel rims, three fake bullet holes in the front by the driver's side and a purple neon license plate frame. The windows were down, so she heard the man in the driver's seat with the braided goatee say, "Where have you been, bitch? I been waiting here for you," and heard Misty whine, "I'm sorry, baby, I had to talk to that lady over there," before the car screeched out of the driveway with Misty's door still open, one platform pump hanging out.

"Fucking Nadene," Windy repeated to herself. So Nadene Brown was Harry's aunt.

She was heading back to her car, dialing Dr. Bob to ask her to send over a photo of the impression the clasp had made on Nadene's neck, when she saw Ash walking toward her.

That could only mean one thing. She closed her phone and ran to him. "What happened to Cate?"

"Nothing. She is fine. I just talked to her bodyguards."

"What are you doing here?"

"The lab came back with the rings. They were able to lift both engravings."

"And?"

"And the first one was Kelly O'Connell's. No question."

"The other one?" She did not like the look on his face at all. Her heart started to pound.

Ash took a deep breath, then held a photo out to her. "I think it is yours."

CHAPTER 80

Windy stared at the photograph he was showing her. It was of a ring, cut in half so you could see the writing inside. *EMKIII-CAT Toujours amie.*

Windy's throat went completely dry. "How did you know?"

"That's not important. It is your ring?"

"Yes. But, my God, Ash. How did he get it? I keep it in a box. Hidden in a box. I keep it—oh God. He has been in my house. All the way in."

Windy felt his hands on her shoulders. "The reason I came out here was because I thought you might want to go home. And you might not want to be alone."

"I should get back to work. Nadene Brown is Harry's aunt. Was Harry's aunt. I should—"

"Windy, I don't think you understand. Your home is a crime scene now too."

She looked up at him. "This means I'm next, doesn't it?"

She left her rental car in the free parking lot at the Stardust and climbed in next to Ash, glad to be with him, glad to be going fast, glad to be doing anything rather than thinking about what she had just seen.

"I'll double the officers around your house," Ash said.

Windy nodded. "I think I'll send Cate and Brandon to visit my parents in Chicago for a few days."

"Do you want to go with them?"

"Yes," Windy said. "But I'm not going to."

Ash looked over at her quickly but did not say anything. They drove in silence for a long stretch and then Windy broke it, asking, "What did you do about Gerald? How did you get off the phone?"

Ash wanted to tell her he was there for her, he would lay down his life to keep her safe. But he knew that wasn't what she needed to hear. He said, "Nothing. He's probably still talking on speaker phone."

She gaped at him. "You didn't."

"It was the easiest thing to do. When I saw—I had to get out of there fast."

"He could take away your job, Ash."

"You know, at this point, that doesn't really bother me."

"Why do you do this job, put yourself in danger, if you don't need the money?"

The question caught Ash unprepared. He shrugged. "Being rich was never something that mattered to me. It happened by accident, I developed something that a lot of people were willing to pay for. Basically what I realized is that having money is nice, but it doesn't give you a reason to get up every day." Being more honest than he'd intended.

They had turned off the Strip and were rolling to a stoplight on Sands Boulevard when a group of motorcycles, four Harley David-sons, one with a side car, roared up next to them. Ash looked over and was surprised to see Windy smile.

"Do you like motorcycles?"

"Yes." She looked far away. "My husband, Evan, Cate's dad, used to ride one. A Ducati F1-750. When we met."

They settled back into silence, until she looked over at him and gave him a half smile. "It's okay. You can ask whatever you want."

"Where did you meet?"

She went back to looking out the window. "Paris. We were both doing our junior year abroad."

"And then you stayed in touch when you got back to the States?"

"Sort of. I wrote to him. For four months I wrote to him and he never wrote back."

Ash frowned. "Why didn't you call?"

Windy turned away from the window to face him. "Nice girls don't call boys. My mother could tell you that. Besides, he'd said he wasn't sure of his phone number." She shook her head at herself, for being so stupid then, for talking about it now. She hadn't told anyone about this in ages, not since Evan died. But she kept going, saying, "I thought I had been an idiot, you know, falling in love with this guy. And then one day, I was home at my parents' house for spring break my senior year, and all of a sudden there's this terrible noise outside. It was Evan, roaring down the street on a custom soft-tail Harley Davidson."

She shook her head again. "My mother started crossing herself and found religion again as he pulled into the driveway. Parked his hog right next to her Buick. I thought she was going to faint when I answered the door."

"What happened?"

"He just stood there, covered in leather, dusty. He'd been riding for two days. He said, 'I'm not that good at letters. I can't ever get them to say what I want. So I thought I would just drop in.' "

"Drop in? He was coming from—"

"Connecticut."

"And you were in Chicago."

Windy smiled and nodded.

"What happened then?" Ash asked.

"I invited him in. My mother, falling back on etiquette, offered him something to drink. She went off to the kitchen—I have always suspected, to take the first shot of hard alcohol of her life, although she denies it—and he sat down next to me on the couch." She stopped talking, seemed to curl in on herself.

After a little while Ash said, "And?"

She swallowed. "He leaned over to me and whispered in my ear, 'Windy, will you marry me?' "

"That's how he proposed?"

She nodded.

"And you accepted."

"Of course not. I mean, I was going to, but not right away. Good girls do not immediately accept proposals, particularly not from men who talked them out of their virginity in a French garret and then didn't respond to their letters for months. I said I'd think about it."

"And what did he say?"

"He said, 'Can I use the bathroom? I've been riding nonstop for the past thirty-six hours.' "

Ash stared at her. "You're kidding."

She shook her head.

And they both cracked up. "I think I would have liked Evan," he said. "Not the part about making you wait four months, but the other part."

"I think you would have too," she said. Got very quiet.

Ash glanced at her. "Is it harder when people say that? When you talk about it?"

"No. Actually, it's nice. It's really nice. I haven't told anyone about that in a long time. A lot of people get uncomfortable talking about it." She looked out the window, slightly fogged, and drew a circle on it with her finger. "Tomorrow is Evan's birthday. He would have been thirty-five."

And all of a sudden she started to cry. Ash veered over to the curb, stopped the car, and put his arms around her, holding her tight as she sobbed into his sweater, clinging to him. He did it just as a friend. But it felt like something worth dying for.

"I'm sorry," she said, her faced pressed against his chest, not moving away. "I think everything is getting to me. I'm becoming a mess."

"Shh," he told her. "No apologies." His hand stroked her back, her hair, making her know it was okay.

A few minutes later she sat up and turned from him. "That is so embarrassing." She was fishing around her bag for a Kleenex, not looking at him.

"Not as embarrassing as finding a wad of these in my car," he said, handing her a stack of Krispy Kreme napkins.

She sniffled into one of them and dried her cheeks. "Thank you, Ash."

"You're welcome, Windy." Now their eyes met and wouldn't let go. Time stood still. She moved toward him and gently kissed him on the lips.

She pulled away first. Ash could not move. It was a stunning kiss. And it had lasted maybe two seconds.

She rested her hand on his cheek, staring at him. He opened his mouth to say something but she shook her head.

"Not today. Not yet. Okay?"

"Okay."

It felt like everything important got said anyway.

CHAPTER 81

Ash watched until Windy was in her house, counted the officers he'd stationed around the perimeter, then realized he'd lost track and counted them again. For the first time since becoming a cop he had to work to stay focused on a case, his mind wanting to replay what had just happened, and what it meant. When he and Windy got together, he wanted her to have no regrets and he was willing to wait as long as it took for her to get there. He was in this for the long haul.

Still, he wasn't concentrating as much as he should have been because he was halfway to the office before it all came together. It was the memory of a tan Lexus like the one registered to Nadene Brown parked a few blocks from Windy's that did it, made him see how they could find Harry. He dialed as he shifted into high gear, glad the afternoon traffic was light, and when he got Jonah on the phone said, "I want a list of all the property Nadene Brown owned."

Jonah handed it to him when he arrived. "Her lawyer's office faxed it over. Didn't even ask for a warrant."

"Must be our lucky day."

The list was extensive and impressive. Nadene Brown had invested well in real estate and owned several corners of the city that now had supermarkets and drug stores on them, as well as four houses and two apartment buildings.

"I want plainclothes officers to check out all of these for any kind of suspicious activity," Ash said. "Every building, every apartment, but low profile. If Harry is hiding in any of them, I don't want to alert him."

"What about that one?" Jonah asked, pointing to the address on the bottom of the list.

"I'll look at that one myself."

Windy had tried to sound calm with her mother, explaining that she just thought it would be good for Cate to see her grandparents for a few days, not wanting to give any hint of what was really going on, but at the end she'd lost it and had to beg.

"Please, Mom. I don't have time to answer questions. I'll explain it all next week. I'll come myself. Oh, and please don't call Bill."

Bill would be there the next day. She had already put off what she needed to say to him for too long. The least she could do was say it in person.

She put on a good face and told Cate about the exciting trip she was about to go on, giving in to everything her daughter wanted to take, rain boots and swimming goggles and her Soccer Barbie, working hard not to grab Cate and hug her every two minutes. She knew this was the right decision, to make Cate go and stay herself, but the thought of being separated from her made her ache. She was relieved to see that at least it did not seem to bother Cate, who spent the entire ride to the airport telling Brandon about all the great things they could do at her grandparents' house, "especially without Mom there to get in the way."

At the security checkpoint she discovered that Ash had called ahead, getting them whisked through. She stayed with Brandon and Cate until they boarded the eight-fifteen P.M. flight to Chicago, waving good-bye long after either of them could have seen her. Then she stood in the empty departure lounge, wondering where to go. Feeling alone and depressed. And scared.

She was making her way back to the parking garage to drive Brandon's blue VW bug home when her phone rang. Like an idiot, she felt her heart skip when she saw Ash's name on the caller ID, then skip again when he said, "I think we've found where Harry is staying. A year ago Nadene Brown bought a house on Cottonwood Drive. Twenty-two-oh-six—the one next door to the O'Connell house."

"Didn't some security patrol person say the place was empty?"

"Yes," Ash said. "And I'm beginning to think that person was Harry himself. I'm meeting the Metro SWAT team over there now."

CHAPTER 82

It was after nine o'clock when Windy got to the SWAT staging area, in the middle of the block just east of Harry's house. Ash was standing at the front of the police squadron, talking to the SWAT commander, both men looking military and alert and worried.

"We're pretty sure he's inside and we didn't want to give ourselves away," Ash explained as she joined them.

"How do you know it's the right house?"

"We can't be positive, but there's a Camaro IROC parked in the driveway and the neighbor across the street said there's been 'unusual activity' over there."

Unusual activity. That sounded bad to Windy. "What do we do now?" she asked, looking between the men.

"We wait until my operatives are organized and in position," the SWAT commander told her. "If he comes out during that time of his own free will, we grab him. If not, we make him come out unwillingly."

Two hours later they were ready to move on the house.

"We've got men in position around the house in case he tries to run for it," the SWAT commander reported. "Heat scans are picking up someone in the kitchen." He looked at Ash. "How do you want to play it? Call first or surprise him?"

"I don't know what we're dealing with." Ash turned to Windy. "Do you think he's suicidal?"

"I don't know. But I'd like to try talking to him. See if I can get him to surrender."

Ash shook his head. "Absolutely not."

"He has been targeting me," Windy said. "I would stand the best chance of getting him out."

"Or getting killed," Ash said.

Windy ignored him and turned to the SWAT commander. "Can your men cover me if I go in closer?"

"No," Ash said to both of them. "Under no—"

The SWAT commander's walkie talkie started hissing. "Subject on the move. Subject approaching window."

From beyond the perimeter, they heard the scraping of a window being raised, then a voice.

"What is happening?" Windy asked.

The voice on the walkie talkie said, "Subject is asking for Chicago Thomas. I repeat—"

"Copy that," the SWAT commander said. He looked at Ash and Windy. "You heard. He's asking for you."

Windy started down the street toward the house. Ash went after her.

"You can't go," he said. "This could be a trap."

"Or it could be our best chance to get him out." Windy ducked under a wood barrier, slid between two policemen and went to stand on the sidewalk opposite the house. The street was eerily deserted, the streetlights turned off. The only light came from the half moon.

"Is Windy Thomas here?" a voice yelled from a second floor. Windy could see the outline of a figure, but no face. "I want to talk to Windy Thomas."

Windy stepped forward. "Yes. I'm right here."

"Can you come closer? I can't see you."

"No," Ash growled from behind her.

Windy crossed to the middle of the street. "Is this better?"

"Closer."

"Who am I talking to?"

"Don't you know? It's me. Harry. Come closer."

Windy didn't move. "Harry, you need to come out of your house. You need to give yourself up."

"Is that what you want?"

"Yes."

"Okay." The shadowy form disappeared from the upstairs window.

"This is too easy," Ash muttered. "I don't like it."

Windy did not say anything, but she did not disagree either. On her right, she heard the SWAT commander tell his men to be on point. The street was silent.

A window on the lower floor of the house opened slowly. "Windy?" Harry's voice said. "Tell them not to hurt me."

"Don't hurt him," Windy said aloud.

"Promise you won't let them. I'll give up, but only to you."

"I promise."

"If you take one step, I'll take one step."

Ash growled behind her but did not say anything.

Windy took a step forward.

"Take another one."

"No, Harry. You need to come out now."

"I don't trust them."

"They don't trust you."

"Why did you stop believing me, Windy? Why did you stop believing it was Eve? Wasn't I good enough?"

"Yes, Harry. But it's impossible to be someone else all the time."

"I didn't want you to come here. This is not where I wanted it."

"What *did* you want?" Windy waited for him to answer but he didn't. "Harry, if you come out we can talk. You'll feel better."

"You are lying to me," the voice from the window said. "The way everyone lies. They said it was my fault. I never meant to hurt anyone. They made me."

"Who?"

"You don't understand. You'll never understand."

Behind her Windy heard the SWAT commander hiss, "Get ready to move on my order."

She said, "Help me to understand, Harry."

"I can't. It's hopeless. Good-bye, Windy."

"Alpha team in," the SWAT commander said into his walkie talkie and Windy watched as black-clothed operatives started to move like shadows toward the house.

"Harry," she said, "you need to come out now. Right now."

He did not respond. She could no longer tell if he was standing at the window. For five long seconds everything was completely still.

Then a voice inside the house screamed, "Get away from me! Get away!" sounding terrified and desperate, and a gun fired twice.

The SWAT commander's walkie talkie shrieked, "Operator down! Operator hit!"

Everything moved at once, the SWAT team swarming up the front walkway, breaking down the door, bursting through windows.

"Take cover!" the commander ordered, but Windy was up and running toward the house.

"No!" she shouted as Ash's arms came around her, dragging her down. "Let me go. Don't let them—"

For a split second Windy caught a glimpse of a man in a checked shirt in the living room staring out the door, staring at her. He was holding a huge rifle and as the SWAT operatives poured into the house he ran at them, waving it.

"Harry, no!" she screamed and tried to break free of Ash, but it was too late. She watched with horror as a barrage of shots went off and his body danced jerkily up and down and sideways, then crumbled to the floor.

Two beats of silence. The SWAT commander's walkie talkie saying, "Subject down. I repeat, subject down."

Windy felt as though she were seeing a movie. Numbly she observed the paramedics rushing on the house, one team going around the side to where the shot operative was lying in the dirt, the other running into the living room. She was aware of people moving all around her, ambulance lights flashing, but it was as though she were seeing it all with her peripheral vision, none of it in focus. Ash's face was in front of her now and he was saying something but she could not make herself listen to the words.

She was furious. It should not have ended this way. There was no justice in an ending like this, not for the dead families. Not for her. There were too many questions they all deserved answers to.

She pushed Ash's hands off her and headed for the house, ignoring him shouting her name behind her.

"Ma'am, we have not checked the premises for—" a SWAT officer said, trying to stop her, but she brushed by him. She was unaware of Ash behind her, telling the officer to stand down.

A group of men all in black with their night vision goggles still on was huddled around the body and the paramedics in the middle of the living room. As she joined them, she heard one of the medics say, "Time of death, eleven twenty-four P.M."

She stared hard at the dead man. Harry lay on his back on the floor where he had fallen as she watched. On one wrist he wore a medical bracelet advising paramedics that he had diabetes. A cluster of shots over his heart and neck showed the SWAT snipers were good at their job. His face still had an expression of surprise, his mouth open, his forehead furrowed. His arms stretched in front of him, as though he had been reaching out, and although Windy knew this was because he'd died holding a deer rifle, aiming it at the

SWAT officers, she could not help feeling like he had been reaching for help.

This man had threatened her. He had killed families. He was a monster.

And yet, she could not wish this death on him. She wanted him to stand trial. She wanted to know why. Why had he done it? Why had he chosen her? She was so damn tired of unanswered whys.

Windy did a solo walk through of the house as she waited for her team to arrive. The living room was riddled with bulletholes and covered with shattered glass and shards of broken furniture, but the rest of the house was intact. Two of the rooms, one on the ground floor and one on the second floor, had locks on the doors and DO NOT ENTER signs on them, making the SWAT commander worry that they were booby-trapped, so the bomb squad was called in and everyone else ordered out.

For forty minutes, Windy and her team remained outside the house while the squad worked, but when it was ascertained that the door of the downstairs room was not wired, she got impatient and went inside. She could feel Ash watching her, but he did not say anything and she would not have listened if he had.

She started her walk-through in the kitchen, looking in empty cabinets and an empty refrigerator. On the kitchen counter were two sets of keys, one on a Camaro key chain, the other on a keychain with a heart. She recognized those as her old house keys, the originals. He must have had a set copied and given those to her, which was why hers had been sticking. She wondered if knowing he had the ones that had been hers excited him, and the thought made her shudder. Once.

Next to the keys was a wallet containing credit cards in the name Harold Williams, a receipt from Mailboxes and So Much More, another from a florist shop, and a five dollar bill. A clear plastic sleeve contained a Washington State–issued driver's license in the name of Harold L. Williams. She slid it out of the holder and saw that it had a sticker on it that said he was an organ donor. She studied the photo for a long time.

Just before two in the morning, the bomb squad gave the all clear. In the end, there were no traps, no bombs. The two rooms were just rooms, the doors just locked doors. It made Windy think of what Logan had said, about abused children protecting their secrets at all costs. She suspected that whatever was most precious and personal to Harry would be behind those doors.

The keys on the Camaro keychain unlocked them. Windy went into the upstairs room first. It was almost monastic, a steel desk, an old-fashioned wood desk chair, and matte gray walls lined with file cabinets. One whole file cabinet was labeled EVE. It was filled with hanging files with labels like *Hair-pubic* and *q-tips, ears, bra-dirty, skin-elbow, saliva-morning, blood-menstrual, blood-regular, lollipop*. Other drawers had other names on them, some sharing several: DIANE/ GERALDINE/CANDY, MONA & TERRY, WINDY & CATE. Windy wanted to take everything out of her drawer and go home, hide it deep in a corner of her house so no one could see, but knew that was not right. She made herself stay cool, professional. Inside she found *Windy: condom-used (Bill)*, and *Cate: underwear—clean*.

Her hands started to shake. He had been in Cate's underwear drawer. He had been in her daughter's bedroom. He had touched—

Focus.

There was a closet filled with different uniforms: waiters, locksmith's, a mailman, security officer. In the middle of them was a white satin jumpsuit with wide lapels and rhinestones.

The other locked room was a mess, but it looked as though it had been untouched by time. Windy did not know if it was exactly as Eve had left it, but it was unmistakably a little girl's bedroom. It took her a moment to realize that the windows were covered with plywood, because they were hidden behind frilly gingham curtains. There was a canopy bed with a floral print ruffle and a Holly Hobby dresser. Posters of Madonna and Adam Ant hung on the wall. Prints from the room and hairs they pulled from the sheets and pillows matched the ones they took off Harry's dead body.

Windy left the job of checking the sheets for semen to Larry.

Outside, floodlights turned the early morning into bright dawn. Windy stood on the front stoop of the house for a moment, breathing the fresh air, watching the emergency personnel weave between the news crews and the growing number of curious neighbors emerging in their pajamas.

"I'm standing here in front of the scene of an exciting SWAT operation," five reporters were saying into five different cameras, almost the same words as Windy walked toward them. She pushed through the corridor of people, hearing the operation described as a "raging firefight," a "gun battle of Wild West proportions," and "a nightmare," before she found Ash. He stood at the front of the police lines and behind him, a female anchorwoman pressed as close to the scene as she could get. As Windy came over, she was saying, "And so it looks like the Home Wrecker has wrecked his last home."

It was weak, Windy thought, but she wouldn't have been able to do any better at this point.

She tugged on Ash's sleeve and he turned from his conversation with the SWAT commander. He smiled at her, hesitantly, and that made her feel worse.

"There is a pile of evidence inside to show he was harvesting samples of Eve's body to leave at the crime scenes. We also found this in a closet." She handed Ash an evidence bag with the white satin jumpsuit in it. "I'll have the lab see if it matches the fibers we found at the Johnsons', Waterses', and O'Connells'. If it does, I think we know how he was getting in."

"Looks like you were right about Vegas camouflage, just wrong about the type."

"Dressing up like Elvis, rather than wedding dresses," she agreed. "Who could resist that. It would explain the black mascara on the phone as well. Touching up his sideburns."

Ash wanted to take her and hold her, brush away her quiet stoicism which had to be costing. He said, "Okay."

"I think we were right about the flowers. I think he probably pretended to be delivering them, maybe doing a singing telegram, and that got the women to open their doors. I also think he was planning for another performance. Soon."

"What did you find?"

"In his wallet he had a receipt from a florist's shop, dated today, and there was a vase of flowers in the living room. It got shot at, but I am pretty sure it will reconstruct into an octagon. I found this next to it." Windy held out a clear plastic evidence envelope. Inside was a card, the kind that came from a florist. It read, *To Windy, with deepest admiration.*

Neither of them said anything. Windy looked up at the blue sky over the house. The sky in Vegas was a different color than in Virginia. Or Hawaii. Finally she said, "You were right to keep me from running in. He would have killed me. I'm sorry I fought against you, Ash."

"I'm sorry I made you feel like you had to."

"You know, I stared and stared at him. At his body and his driver's license photo. I would swear I have never seen that man in my life."

"I did the same thing," Ash told her. "With the same result. He looked so ordinary. He could have been anyone."

The anchorwoman appeared then, stretching the crime scene tape as far as it would go to get near them, her microphone out. She said, "I'm here with detective Ash Laughton and head of criminalistics Chicago Thomas. We've been told the man inside was the prime suspect in the Home Wrecker murders. Would it be safe to say that the Home Wrecker is dead?"

Ash looked at Windy, who nodded, and said, "It's not official but yes it would."

"You heard it here first, America."

Lucky America, Windy thought.

CHAPTER 83

At nine A.M., Windy ran out of adrenaline. The clouds that had moved into the Las Vegas Valley the day before hung lower, and it started to drizzle, sending the press crews scattering. Windy watched them go and knew she had to get out of there too. She was making mistakes, snapping at her team. Thinking too much. She caught Ned by the arm and said, "Can you take over?"

"Go home, boss," he told her. "We've got this."

She hitched a ride from one of the patrol cars. With Brandon and Cate in Chicago, she would have the house to herself. What she wanted more than anything in the world was to fill a glass with ice, pour a beer over it, take it into the bathtub and lay there for about three hours.

She spoke to the patrolman still stationed in front of her house, telling him he could go, the case was over, fumbled for her key, and just had it in the lock when Bill came up the path toward her.

"Next time you change the locks, would you mind telling me?" he said, his folding bag draped over his arm.

"Bill. Of course. I'm sorry. It's been a crazy week. I didn't realize you would be here so early."

"I got the feeling you weren't expecting me when the bulldog guard over there practically arrested me for trying to get into my own house."

She opened the door and said, "I'm sorry," again. Feeling as though her whole vocabulary consisted of those two words.

He peered at her. "What happened to you? You look exhausted. And what are you doing home now? After all your talk about work, I didn't expect to see you for hours."

Windy was assessing the chances of having a beer over ice in the bathtub now that Bill was here, and decided they were nil. She dropped her bag in the middle of the hallway and fell onto the couch, saying, "My case just ended. I worked all night."

Bill moved her bag, putting it on the hall table where it belonged, but he looked up when she said that. "That's great news."

Windy said, "I guess," closing her eyes and leaning back against the cushions. She felt Bill sit down next to her. He put his arm around her, making her shift her head, her stiff neck, pulling her toward him.

"This means you don't have to work this weekend, doesn't it?" he asked, tickling her ear with his finger.

She reached up to still his hand. "I suppose it does."

She felt him smile. He said, "Then my surprise will be perfect."

She wished she could do this any other way. She wished she were more rested. She opened her eyes and faced him. "I know what the surprise is and I can't. I can't marry you."

He was astonished. "How did you know?"

"I just did."

"Well, why not? Because Cate isn't here? I promise you, she won't mind. As long as we have a party, the three of us, when she gets back from camping. She won't even know she missed anything."

"Yes she will. And she's not camping." She shook her head. "That's not the reason."

Bill took her hands in his and smiled at her. "I understand. You have cold feet. After what happened with your first husband it makes sense. I know he hurt you when he left you, but I am not him. I won't treat you the way he did. I'm not leaving. Bad memories are no reason not to get on with your life. On with our life. They are the reason to start making good memories."

"This isn't about Cate or Evan or anyone else. It is about you and me. I can't be the woman you want me to be."

"What do you mean?"

"I'm not going to be home at five o'clock for dinner every night. I don't know if I want to have more children. I'll never be anyone's perfect picture of a wife, a mother. I'm not like that. I don't even want to be." She paused, then added, "And I hate plain white underwear."

"Okay."

"Okay?"

"Okay, wear whatever underwear you want."

"The underwear is just a symptom. The problem is that we don't want the same things."

"Yes we do. A nice house. A family." He looked at her. "Of course you want those things. You've always said you wanted them."

"You've always said *you* wanted them, and I went along because— because I didn't know how not to. But that isn't me. That isn't what I want."

"Well then, what do you want?"

"I want to stop feeling like I am living in a battleground between my work and my home life. I want to stop feeling guilty all the time, like I'm letting one or the other of them down, doing a bad job at both. It's not fair to either of us."

"We can make it work. We'll both change."

"How?"

"I could take up a hobby. And that way I wouldn't miss you so much, because I would be busy. And you could work less."

"That won't fix what is wrong."

"Why not? Windy, all I want in the world is to take care of you. Tell me how."

"That's the problem. Don't you see? I don't want to be taken care of. I want to take care of myself."

"But you need me. You're a mess without me."

"No. I'm a mess when I am trying to balance you with the other things in my life. I am tired of having to apologize for everything I want, everything I care about."

"Then don't apologize."

Windy shook her head. "I am not making this clear enough. What I am trying to say is that I am very fond of you, Bill, but I am not in love with you. And you're not in love with me. With who I really am."

"You don't know that."

"Yes, I do."

Bill's eyes narrowed. "This is about Ash Laughton, isn't it?"

Windy frowned. Was he listening to her? "This is about you and me."

"You're in love with him." He laughed. "You stupid fool, you've gone off and fallen for your boss."

Windy was having trouble recognizing Bill. "Even if that were true, it would not change the fact that you and I are not going to be able to make each other happy."

"Really? We made each other plenty happy the other night. Saturday. Remember that? Or were you fantasizing about him the whole time?"

"Please, don't do this. I care about you and I am sorry I am hurting you. Can't we end this amicably? This isn't about sex and it isn't about anyone else. It is just about the two of us."

"Bull. You wouldn't be moving on unless you thought you had something better in the works." Bill's model handsome face got ugly. "I feel bad for you, Windy. I don't know what he told you, but you're a fool if you think he'll take you. I've read about him in the paper. He's a local celebrity, he can have any woman he wants. He doesn't need to tie himself down to a thirty-four-year-old woman with a kid and a closet full of emotional baggage. Sorry to be so blunt about it, but you've always been interested in knowing the truth." He got up, grabbed his garment bag, and moved to the front door.

Windy followed him. "I'm sorry, Bill. Really sorry it had to end this way."

He sneered at her. "Not as sorry as you will be. You think you hurt me? You're the one who is going to be hurting. You're going to regret this for the rest of your life. I can do better than you, but you'll never do better than me."

She gently closed the door in his face.

She locked it, put on the security chain, and walked, not numb anymore, not shattered, not like she thought she would feel at all, into the living room. Mostly she was aware of feeling sorry. Sorry that she had treated Bill shabbily, not because of Ash but because she had never been honest with him. He could not really love her, because she'd never even let him see who she was. She hadn't let herself see. Until now. *A thirty-four-year-old woman with a kid and a closet full of emotional baggage.* He was right. That was what she was. And she was tired of pretending to be something else.

Tired of trying to do everything right and getting it all wrong.

On her hands and knees she pulled the brown cardboard box she still hadn't unpacked off the bottom shelf of the bookcase and opened it. It mostly contained papers, back taxes, the documents about Cate's money. But on top, Windy knew, would be the photos of her wedding to Evan.

She lifted the photos out, pictures jammed into an album but never glued in, because somehow she never had time, and then Evan died and she couldn't look at them. Hadn't in over three years. She opened the album now and saw two faces smiling up at her, faces she hardly recognized. Her and Evan, seven years ago. No, she corrected, nearly eight. Veteran's Day weekend. This year would have been their eighth anniversary, she realized. Coming up fast. But she had started to forget about it, as other dates—Cate's birthday, Brandon's birthday—other people, became more important.

In the photo, Evan is looking right into the camera, pointing and laughing. And she, beaming, is looking at him.

That one picture captured their whole relationship. Not that Evan hadn't loved her, he had, as much as he was capable of loving any living person. But he loved fun, loved being alive, loved experiences more.

After he died—*left her,* Bill was right about that, it was how it felt, like he'd made a choice—she had looked for the opposite of that, someone who would never give themselves up to anything wholly, who could always be counted on to keep their feet on the ground. She'd sought safety, started driving slower, talking quieter, stopped taking risks. She'd chosen Bill as the antidote to Evan, as if Evan had been some sort of poison that had to be driven out of her bloodstream by seriousness.

That had been her mistake, trying to drive Evan out. It was okay to still love him, love what they had had, and want something different. She had known it for weeks, but it had taken the past two days, this precise level of exhaustion and emotion, to make it all seem so clear.

Outside, it started to rain, the first real rain Las Vegas had gotten this year. Windy looked at the photos one by one, seeing a couple she didn't know, two people whose lives seemed to be disconnected to her own. She had changed in those eight years, but not the way she had thought. She thought she was growing up. What she'd actually done was hide.

At the bottom of the box she found a tiny Zip-loc envelope, the kind she used for evidence in her lab. It had Evan's wedding ring in it. It had once held hers, too.

No more hiding, working so hard to be a good girl. No more running away. No more trying to please someone else, be something she wasn't, and doing a lousy job of it. Windy went upstairs, took a quick shower, put on her favorite underwear and an outfit she had not worn in over three years. She sealed the thank-you note Cate had written to Ash in a watertight bag, went into the garage, and pulled the cover off the bright yellow 1995 Ducati 916 motorcycle that had been Evan's wedding present to her. Seeing the bike again, its gorgeous lines, was like running into a friend you hadn't seen in years. Not realizing how much you missed them until you were reunited. God, she loved that bike.

She didn't wonder if it would start, if there was gas in the tank. She just snapped on her helmet, pulled the bike out of the garage, and turned the key. It purred to life as though it had been waiting for her.

The cops watching her house turned to stare as she roared down the street, revving the engine as loud as it would go, drawing attention to herself, and not caring.

She had worked so hard to keep Evan's voice out of her head all those years out of fear and guilt. But she was done with that. Now she heard him say, "I think motorcycles are the most fun in the rain." And she said to herself, to him, "You know, honey, you might be right."

Harry watched Windy roar off, and then the officers who had been guarding her begin to gather their cups and get ready to go. Like a magician, *poof!,* Harry was making them disappear. He was letting Windy think she had been granted her life. Letting her think there was a reprieve, that he was gone, that she was safe. She looked relaxed, ready to believe that the nightmare was behind her. That the body she found was his, that the Home Wrecker was dead. Believe she could start the next week with only burglaries and car thefts, easy crimes. Believe she would see her daughter again, laugh again, eat pizza again.

"Enjoy it while you can, Windy," he said to himself. He would give her twenty-four hours to revel in it. Then he would be waiting to show her she was wrong and make her beg.

CHAPTER 84

Ash's address was in a part of town she hadn't been to, mostly industrial, and it took her a moment to realize that his place must be somewhere in the white brick warehouse she was standing in front of. There was an auto-body shop with two guys taking a cigarette break outside it, and a sign over a closed roll-down metal door that said FANTA-Z DESIGNS AND AIRBRUSH. She pushed the big lit-up button with the word LAUGHTON on it next to the industrial door. After a moment, she heard a click and pushed it open.

"Up here," Ash's voice said at the top of a steel staircase. "All the way at the top." He watched, spellbound, as she came up the last flight of stairs, wearing a tight black leather jacket, black leather pants, black boots, her helmet cradled under her arm. When he could talk he said, "You look like an action hero."

She did not stop when she got to the door but kept going, walking right into his house, right into his arms, no hesitation. She brought her mouth to his and kissed him hungrily on the lips, said, "I broke up with Bill this afternoon" and he said, "Marry me."

They kissed around the words, touching and smiling, wanting to make up for the time they lost, keeping their eyes open so they didn't miss anything, kissing instead of breathing, and better. Her jacket came off and his hands touched her hair, the back of her neck, the line of her jaw, her nipples through her T-shirt, and her hands clutched his forearms and she wrapped them around her.

He said, I've never been kissed like this before and she said, This is a hundred times better than I dreamed it would be, and he said, I'm a little nervous about competing with Evan and she said, Believe me don't be, this is the best kiss I ever had.

"Me too," Ash said.

Windy pulled her lips away and leaned her forehead against his. She wanted this to be forever, something she was inside of, not something she was watching. She wanted to be able to be her, no apologies. She wanted him to know what he was getting into. "There are things about me you don't know, Ash. Important things."

"Like what?"

"I toss and turn a lot in bed. Wake up at night."

He kissed her forehead, her cheek. "Me too. We can tell each other stories."

She said, "I eat cookies in bed and make crumbs."

"I sometimes stay up all night to finish a book."

"I fall asleep with my reading light on."

His hands slid through her hair, so damn soft, pulling her head back, exposing her neck to his mouth. He murmured, "I wear reading glasses."

"Really?"

Ash looked at her. "Yes. Want to see?"

There was something about that image that caught Windy, something solid and yet sexy, Ash in bed in his reading glasses, a future of sitting up at night with him, reading next to him, years spreading out like a landscape. She could see it, see herself in it, not from the outside but *there*. And she knew she wanted it.

Her hands went under his sweater, pulling it off, then catching her breath at the sight of him without a shirt on. She said, "Sometimes I use all the hot water when I shower."

"We'll have to get a larger hot water heater." He lifted her shirt over her head. The last barrier.

Their hands were everywhere now.

"Sometimes I can be immature."

"Sometimes Jonah and I put on Bike Patrol uniforms so we can ride up and down the steps in front of the Venetian hotel on our mountain bikes."

"You do not."

"About every six weeks."

"I sometimes leave my shoes in the middle of the floor."

"I sometimes forget to refold my towels."

"I forget to come home for dinner."

Ash saying, "Oh," as her fingers undid the top button of his jeans and her hands slid inside. "I, ah, know where you work. Cate and I can come find you. Even bring you tacos or Chinese food sometimes. Not on school nights, though."

"I'm selfish and moody."

"Me too."

"I'm absorbed in my work, and my daughter, and I have no time or energy for anything el—" His lips were on the edge of her nipple, gently kissing it.

His head came up, a finger going to her lips, and he said, "That's not true. You don't have time and energy for things that are separate from your work and your daughter, but that's not what I want to be. I want to be in there with you. I want all of it, not just the easy parts."

They stepped out of their pants, wearing nothing but their underwear now, Ash in white jockey shorts that hugged his body in a way that made him look like a sculpture, Windy thought. Windy in a rust-colored silk bra and panties with beige lace edging that Ash would have slain dragons to protect and wanted her out of almost as bad.

He slid his hands over her rib cage, down her waist, cradling her behind through the little silk panties, discovering a tiny bow on them at the base of her spine.

She pulled away. "Look at me, Ash. Really look. I am a thirty-four-year-old woman with a kid and a closet full of emotional baggage."

Ash said, "And I am a thirty-seven-year-old man who moved every year as a child and is really good at unpacking. And who loves you, Windy. Every part of you." He dragged her toward him and held her pressed against his body, hugged close. "You look like the best thing in the world to me."

She said, her last protest, "You have lines on your ankles from your socks."

"So do you."

"Make love to me, Ash."

And they tumbled together onto the wide chenille couch. Ash leaned on one elbow and pushed the cup of her delicate silk bra aside to kiss a birthmark he saw on her left breast. Windy said, "I can take that off if you want me to."

"I want you to do whatever makes you most comfortable. I think you look beautiful just like this."

Words Windy had been waiting more than fifteen years to hear. But words that made her scared again, scared she would disappoint him. "I know you've had a lot of experience and I'm afraid I'm not very good in bed."

That got Ash's attention. He said, "Then it's a good thing we're on a couch." And, serious, "Windy, you are all I want in the world. I've never done this before, made love to the woman I am in love with. Just having you here with me, like this, just being close to you, is better then anything that has ever happened to me. Okay?"

"Okay."

He kissed her on the lips, then on the stomach, his hand sliding under the silk of her panties and touching her there. She moaned and he stroked her harder, making her arch toward him, her hand coming over his to stop it.

She said, "You have to stop or I'm going to, um——" Was there a polite way to say this?

"Come," he supplied. "You are going to come. That is the point, sweetheart." And put his mouth where his hand was, and sucked her clitoris between his lips, and heard her shout his name. Her bitten nails dug into his shoulders as his teeth nipped at her and then dug in harder as he slid a finger inside of her. Windy looked at his handsome, angular face between her thighs, eyes closed, frowning in concentration the way she'd seen him at the office but now all of that ferocious energy focused on her, on her body, watched his lips pressing around clitoris, his tongue dart out and over her, and let go. Came.

She pushed her hips up, into him, and he felt her body tighten, then shudder, felt her climax on his tongue and heard her cries and then her hands were pulling him up her body, pulling his mouth to hers.

"Ash," she sighed his name, holding on to him, burying her face in his shoulder. "My goodness, Ash. Holy moley."

She felt him begin to shake, and realized he was laughing. "Holy moley," Ash repeated, laughing out loud. Laughing in a way he hadn't laughed since elementary school. "Windy, you are fantastic."

Now they were both laughing, until her hand went inside his briefs, slid up the length of him and she said, in a much more serious tone, "Holy moley." She pulled his underwear off and looked at him and Ash felt more insecure than he could ever remember feeling. She ran her palm from the base to the tip of his penis, cradling his balls in one hand and petting him with the other. "You are so beautiful. You take my breath away."

"Mine too," Ash moaned, her fingers circling around him, pressing him against the soft skin of her thigh.

"I want to feel this inside of me," she told him. Her eyes on her hands, watching the way his body moved when she touched him.

"I want that too," Ash assured her. "In a second." He tilted himself off the couch and went to rifle through the pockets of a jacket draped over the kitchen counter, coming back with a condom. He started to open it but she took the package from him, made him stand in front of her, pulled his jockey shorts off, cradled his penis in her hand, and rolled the condom on, slowly, with her fingers. She was meticulous and it was excruciating and the sexiest thing anyone had ever done to him, this woman who could make him want to explode just with birth control. She smoothed her hand over it, then kissed him on the tip, slid onto her knees on the furry white rug, and pulled him down on top of her.

"Now," she said, pushing her panties to one side. "I can't wait any longer."

Her legs came around his waist as he filled her, taking him in all at once. They made love like teenagers, hungry and clumsy and having the time of their lives, all over each other like they'd never done this before and had been dreaming of this moment forever. They threw themselves together, nothing off limits, touching and tasting, daring to whisper secret desires that got played out as realities, ending up somehow on the kitchen counter, neither of them sure how they got there.

Spent, entwined together, laughing as Windy, her head under a basil plant, said, "Wowie."

"Is that better or worse than 'holy moley'?" Ash asked.

They went into the bedroom and took a nap on top of the sheets and then started all over, using up Ash's supply of condoms, Windy asking why he kept them in a jacket pocket instead of in his bedroom or bathroom, and him explaining that he'd never had anyone to his house before like this.

"The kinds of relationships I had were more about hotels," he said. "Or actually, motels." Coming clean.

"Sounds kind of exciting."

"No," he told her. "Not like this."

They ate leftover Chinese food naked in bed out of the cartons and talked about nonsense and held each other. Windy made Ash model his reading glasses, him looking so good in them that her heart stopped beating.

Late at night, Windy made a plane reservation to go to Chicago the next day and then they fell asleep, forgetting to turn the lights off in the other room, forgetting about everything that was not the two of them.

CHAPTER 85

Ash honked twice to say good-bye as he turned left, heading to the office, and Windy turned right, going home. It was early and the streets she rode down were quiet, most people still in bed, the sky just starting to go blue. She felt a mixture of contentment and excitement she could not ever remember. Not with Bill. Not even with Evan. Waking up that morning, she had looked over at Ash, still asleep, and felt her heart beat the way it did when she looked at Cate, but not exactly for the same reason. The phrase *bad girls never sleep alone* had flashed through her mind, making her think of Eve, and she smiled a little sadly. She felt bad in the best way.

She pulled up to her house and waited for the garage door to open. The street was empty, no more patrol officers, no more guards, but she felt safer than she had when they were there. It was over. She could not wait to get Cate back, get everything back to normal.

Climbing the stairs to her bedroom she hummed to herself. She just had time to shower and pack before heading to the airport. She couldn't wait to hug Cate again. She was a little nervous about explaining everything to her parents, but that would be okay too. Everything was going to be okay.

She stripped off her clothes and got into the shower. As the water poured over her she thought of Ash, of the first moment that she knew she was falling in love with him. It had started earlier, but only when she watched him outside the O'Connells' house talk Roddy down had she allowed herself to understand what she felt. He had been without fear, but not without compassion. She had never seen anyone like that before.

She wondered how Roddy had been since that night. She wasn't sure she entirely understood why he had sought her out, what he had been hoping for. Or even how he had found her.

She froze with a palm full of shampoo halfway to her head.

Only the killer could have guessed where she would be. And only one person could have told Roddy. Her heart started to pound.

Harold L. Williams. Harry. Hank.

Hank Logan.

Not even turning off the water, she stepped out of the shower, reached for a towel, and jumped. There was a man in her bedroom, going through her purse.

Not a man, she realized. A police officer. Protection. Thank god.

"Officer," she said, gripping a towel around her. "Officer, get on your radio and—" Her voice caught as the man turned around. He was wearing a police uniform, but he was not a policeman.

Hank Logan walked into the bathroom and smiled at her. "Hi, Windy."

Windy backed away from him. "Hi, Logan."

"Please," he said, "call me Harry."

"We have a problem," Jonah said, bursting into Ash's office. "A big one. We ran the prints off the guy who was shot in the SWAT raid yesterday."

"Harry," Ash said.

"No. That's the problem. It's not Harry. His name is Dwight. He owns a demolition company in North Las Vegas, and he's been missing since Monday. But that's not all. His mother, who identified the body, says he's never been to Washington State. And if that wasn't enough, the way we got a print match is because he has a record—he spent 1991 to 1999 in prison in California on a robbery charge. The years that Harry was in Seattle. He can't be our guy."

Ash stared at Jonah, his mind racing. "He must have been keeping Dwight locked in the locked bedroom, where Windy found all the evidence that linked him to the house. No wonder the man was staggering around, confused and scared. I bet Harry shot at the SWAT operative himself, then pushed Dwight forward to take the fall." His jaw clenched. "I wouldn't be surprised if he dressed as a SWAT guy and just melted into the confusion."

"He probably faked the Washington state ID too. It wouldn't be hard with a home lamination kit."

Ash hit the top of his desk. "Harry set us up. Goddamn it, he set us up. I should have known it from the beginning. That list from the lawyer of Nadene's properties, I sensed it was too easy. And—" He reached for the phone and dialed Windy's home number, got the answering machine, and dialed her cell phone. It bounced into voice mail, as though it were turned off. He looked at Jonah and his voice changed. "Get every available patrol car to Windy's house right now. *NOW!*"

This means I'm next, he heard Windy's voice saying when they identified her wedding band. "No," he said aloud in his office. "Not if I can help it." He reached into his bottom drawer for ammunition, loaded two guns, and went to his car.

He almost hit Jonah when the man came running out of the building. He slammed on the brakes and skidded onto the walkway, leaving black tire marks. "What the hell is wrong with you?" he demanded, then saw the expression on Jonah's face. His blood went cold. "What happened?"

Jonah looked ill. "I scrambled the cars to go to Windy's but before anyone answered, the patrol officer stationed outside her house radioed in. He hasn't seen her all morning. She never came home." He paused to catch his breath. "She's not there, Ash."

NO! Ash wanted to yell. Wanted to pound his fist into the steering wheel and break things. But that would not help Windy. He backed the car into a parking place and got out, forcing himself to focus. "Harry must have grabbed her when she left my place. If she's not at home, we're just going to have to figure out where he would have taken her."

His tone was controlled, reasonable. But a muscle on the side of his jaw was throbbing and his hands were clenched into fists.

Harry, said, "Roger that, I'll hold my position," into the police radio, smiled at Windy, and smashed the handset against the tile bathroom counter. "We won't be needing that anymore, now that they know not to waste their time looking for you here."

Her last lifeline gone. When the call had come over it scrambling all cars to her address, she had almost fainted with relief. But she should have known better. Harry hadn't missed a beat, just signed on with a car number and told them that Windy wasn't anywhere near her house. He was right—they would have every unit assigned to look for her, and not a single one of them would find her.

"Now," he said, eyeing her. "Where were we?"

He was blocking the door of the bathroom, trapping her in the small space with him. She had tried to knock him down, and been punched in the stomach. She was now sitting on the edge of the bathtub, fighting back fear. She could not freeze. She had to keep thinking. She said, "Why are you here? Why did you choose me?"

He smiled. "You made me come."

"How?"

"I gave you a choice. I gave you the chance to live. To believe that Eve was a killer. Eventually, I would have given you a body for her and you could have closed your case. I have one all picked out. But then your curiosity got the better of you, didn't it?"

She swallowed hard. Maybe she could reason with him. Maybe there was another way out of this. "I was just doing my job."

"Your job. Just following the rules, like a good girl." He sneered. "You could have believed me, focused on the evidence I showed you, but you didn't. You started looking at things that were none of your business. Disobeying me. So now you have to die."

"Bluebeard." Windy exhaled slowly.

"Exactly."

She shook her head. "You know, you told that story wrong. It's not about the dangers of curiosity. It's about a serial killer shifting blame from himself to his victims. The real criminal is not the person who looks, it's the murderer."

"Really? What about Nadene? She died because of your curiosity. Your disobedience to me. You never should have talked to her. And so did Dwight, the man whose body you found at my house yesterday. If you had just believed Eve was the killer, if you hadn't meddled and sent the SWAT team there, he would still be alive."

Windy stood up and went toward him. "No. You set me up. You wanted me to look for you. Practically forced me to by sending over the photo of your crime scene from Seattle. You wanted me to discover Eve wasn't the killer. You are trying to move the guilt for what you have done away from yourself, just like you do in your killings. But you did fool us about one thing: you didn't kill because you hate families or leave the fathers alive to punish them. You left the fathers alive to show them that they could not protect their perfect families from a monster any better than you could. The difference is, you *are* the monster."

"You are a lying bitch." Harry changed instantaneously. His face went red and his eyes got glassy. He shoved her backward, hard, then leaned over her, breathing heavily. Circles of sweat showed on his uniform. "Don't ever call me that. I tried to be good. I was good. Say you are sorry."

Windy stared at him, for a moment more fascinated than scared. "What happened to you, Harry?"

He gripped her by the shoulders and shook her and screamed, *"Say you are sorry!"*

Fear took over now. She shrank away from him and he let go of her shoulders. His eyes went over her body, making her clutch the towel around herself more tightly.

He smiled. Gently, deliberately, he took one of her hands in his. "You are sorry, aren't you?"

His tone, his expression, made her mouth dry. "Yes."

"Say it louder."

"Yes."

His smile turned to a sneer. He said, "You are lying," and slowly began pushing her pinkie backward. "You are so bad, you are going to make me hurt you."

"I'm not lying," Windy protested, but he wasn't hearing her. She tried to pull her hand away and he forced the finger back harder.

"Please stop," she said, tensing against the ache. "Please."

"Why? Are you going to tell on me?" he asked, then twisted until the bone snapped.

Windy moaned involuntarily as pain screamed through her body.

Harry let go and smiled. "That is what happens when you are bad," he said. "You get hurt. Now are you going to be good? Going to obey?"

"Yes," Windy said, clutching her aching hand against her body.

"Good." He leaned his face close to hers, breathing with his mouth open. "Then get on your knees and beg for your life."

Through the throbbing in her finger Windy realized what that command meant. It explained why all the victims had been kneeling when they died. Not because they were praying. They had been pleading for their lives.

She said, "Never. Because it won't work. You are just going to kill me anyway. The way you did with all the others."

"How do you know I won't change my mind this time? Won't let you go? Isn't it worth the chance?"

"No. You can hurt me as much as you'd like and I won't beg."

Instead of getting angry, Harry looked amused. "Oh, let's not think about your pain right now. Let's think about Cate's. About the pain your death will cause her. All alone, an orphan. Or, better, about how much pain I am going to inflict on her when you are gone."

Fury swept through her. She tried to stand up but he pushed her down. "Do not talk about my daughter."

"You don't like me talking about her? Perhaps you would prefer to see her." He reached into his jacket uniform and pulled out a stack of color photographs. "Here is one of her at the supermarket," he said, holding up a picture of Cate with her nose in a stack of grapefruits, as Brandon, distracted, checked the shopping list. He flipped to another one, this time showing Cate standing just apart from her school group on a school field trip, the teacher looking in the opposite direction. The next photo showed Cate with her nose pressed against the glass of the lion habitat at the MGM Grand as Windy stared at the ground while Bill kissed her ear. The final one was Cate asleep in her bed.

"How did you get this?" Windy demanded. She was shaking.

Harry ignored her, looking at the photo. "She's very independent, isn't she? Spunky. I bet she is curious. Looks all kinds of places she isn't supposed to. Like her mom." He smiled at her. "If it was this easy for me to get close to her when you were around, just imagine what I can do when you are gone."

"You will never lay a hand on my daughter."

He tapped the finger he had broken, making Windy wince. "You've seen what we do to disobedient girls. Did you happen to check Minette Waters's fingers? I think you'll find that three of them were fractured. I don't know if they can tell these things from the autopsy, but I did it when she was alive. Those little fingers, like twigs, but with more of a jolt. Much better than grown-ups. The sound they make is intoxicating."

Windy lunged at him now, grabbing him around the neck. "Stop it!"

"You know," he said, peeling her fingers off his throat, starting with the pinkie. She was strong but he was stronger. He held her hands in his as she struggled against him, crushing the broken one hard. "Now that I think of it, I've never had a virgin before."

"*STOP!*" Windy launched herself at him, sending them both crashing out of the bathroom and into the door of the closet. She was oblivious to the pain in her hand, oblivious to everything except her need to escape. They fell to the ground and they rolled together toward the bed. She clawed at him, drawing blood, aiming for his eyes. He caught her hand and squeezed the wrists together until she wanted to scream. There were tears streaming down her face. She started kicking then but he flipped her over onto her stomach, and pinned her under him. With her arm twisted behind her and his knee in the small of her back he said, "Are you ready to beg?"

He was sweating massively and she felt his pulse pounding through his grip. He was reveling in her pain, her struggle. She said, "I will never beg anything from you, you bastard."

"Really? Think about this. I'm going to get away with all of this. And I'm going to get Cate, too. You'll never get to see her graduate from first grade, or college for that matter. Never meet the man she is going to marry. Never plan her wedding. If I decide to let her have one." He bent over and whispered in her ear, "I might keep her for myself."

Windy fought him with everything she had. The pain in her finger had spread to her arm but she ignored it, bucking hard, turning to get him off of her, kicking her legs. She felt him shift and thought she might have done it, and then his knee came down on her neck, making her choke for air.

When she stopped moving he said, "You don't like that idea, do you? If you were alive, there might be something you could do about it. If you beg, I might let you live."

Windy was sobbing. At that moment, she would have begged if she believed it would have worked, but she knew it wouldn't. The only victory she could have in her death was the knowledge that she had denied him that pleasure. She rasped, "I hate you."

"Very well. I am disappointed that it had to end this way, but you have only yourself to blame." He stood up and grabbed her by the hair, dragging her to her knees. Her body felt like a rag, her strength, her will, gone. He jerked her head back toward him, so her neck was exposed. Looking up, she saw the blade of a knife catching the light.

This was it. There was nothing she could do. Game over.

"Windy Thomas, you've been a very bad girl. Now you will die."

She closed her eyes.

A quiet voice somewhere near the door of the room said, "No, Harry. That's not actually how the Bluebeard story ends. What happens is the wife's twin sister rides in and saves her. You can look it up."

Windy opened her eyes. Harry was gaping at the stick-thin woman wearing a faded T-shirt two sizes too big for her and a tattered pair of jeans, who stood on the threshold of the bedroom. She looked like she had been through a war and although they'd never met, Windy knew immediately who she was.

Harry said, "What the hell are you doing here, Eve?"

And she said, "Making sure the story ends right." Then she rushed at the arm holding the knife.

For a split second, Harry's grip on Windy loosened. She ducked away from him, just in time to see him get his arm around Eve's neck.

Eve kicked, fighting him off, but he held her in front of him, her back to his chest, her legs flailing into space. Sounding amused, he said, "You did not really think you could overcome me, did you, Eve?"

Eve was not listening to him. She looked at Windy and said, "Go!"

Harry laughed and held the knife at Eve's throat. "Yes, Windy. Go. If you take a step toward the door, I'll kill her."

"This is between you and me, Harry," Eve said. "You told me that I made you the sick monster you are when I ignored you all those years ago. So now fight me." Her expression pled with Windy to leave.

Windy struggled to her feet, leaning into the mattress for support.

Harry spoke to Windy. "I won't kill her fast, either. I'll do it slowly, so it hurts the most. And it will be your fault." He dug the tip of the knife into Eve's neck deep enough to draw blood and Eve flinched. "Like this."

Windy stood up, her hands behind her. "No," she said. "That isn't going to happen. Because I'm going to kill you first, you bastard. I am going to make you pay for every word you said about my daughter." She brought the gun she'd taken from under the mattress around and aimed.

"No!" Eve screamed.

Harry was unfazed. "After I kill her, and you, I'll start working on Cate."

Windy cocked the gun

Eve shook her head violently. "Don't kill him. This is not how you want it to end."

Harry dug the knife into her throat deeper. "It's you or me, Windy."

Windy fired.

Harry staggered sideways, and fell down. He stared at his left kneecap, blossoming with blood, then at Windy. "You shot me."

"I'll do it again."

He started crawling toward her. "You bitch, you shot me."

Windy took aim. "Stay where you are."

He pulled himself closer. "I'm going to kill you."

"No, Windy—" Eve shouted, but her words were lost.

Windy fired again.

Harry jerked sideways, wove drunkenly for a moment, then kept coming. He said, "You are going to die."

Windy shot him one more time and as he collapsed onto his stomach the house shook with the sound of a dozen men pounding up the stairs. Ash burst into the room at the head of the SWAT team, and looked from Windy to the man writhing at her feet.

"He needs paramedics but he's not dead," she said in the flattest voice he had ever heard. Then she dropped the gun and walked out of the room.

CHAPTER 86

Harry was taken to the prison hospital. Windy had shot with precision, one to his bad knee and two in the arm. None of the shots would be fatal. He would recover and stand trial.

Alone in Cate's room, Windy could not stop shaking. She had put on sweatpants and a sweater but she still felt naked, exposed. Cold.

She had let the paramedics bandage her finger, then come in here to separate herself from the crime scene in her bedroom. She was sitting on the bed, clutching Big Fred, staring into space. She knew Ash came by every few minutes to check on her, but she was not ready to face him yet. She was not ready to face herself.

There was a knock on the door, and Eve poked her head around. She was still wearing her too big clothes, now with a blanket the paramedics had given her wrapped around her shoulders.

"Hi," she said, shyly.

Windy stood up. "Hi."

The two women looked at each other for a long time, then Windy hugged Eve.

"Thank you," Windy said. "You saved my life."

"I thought you saved mine. Shooting down the man with the knife."

Windy shook her head. "That's not what I mean."

Eve reached over with the corner of her blanket to dry a tear off Windy's face. "I figured that I did not survive being almost beaten and crushed to death, crawling through a doggie door, and spending three days in a hospital being treated for a concussion and dehydration just to stand back and let someone ruin their life."

"I am so glad you made it."

"Me too. But I think I'm going to have to make a lot of changes about how I live." Eve paused. "One of the detectives let me use his phone and I called Trish. She thinks you're great."

"She thinks you're pretty great as well."

Eve bit her lip. "I have some making up to do as a friend. Speaking of pretty great, there's someone outside who wants to see you." She leaned closer to whisper, "He's been hanging around the hallway for an hour waiting until you were ready. I'm glad your taste in men seems to be better than mine."

Windy looked past her and saw Ash on the threshold of the room. He said, "I can come back if you two want to be alone."

"No," Eve said. "I'm leaving. I have a lot of statements to give, and about three years of sleep to catch up on. And I wouldn't mind getting into my own clothes." She looked at Windy. "I'll see you soon."

Windy nodded, watching her pat Ash on the arm as she left. She had been okay with Eve, but she couldn't meet Ash's eyes.

He stepped closer to her, but not close enough to touch. It was quiet until he said, "I like this room. The rainbows are great." Making small talk to cover the awkwardness.

"Cate and Brandon decorated it."

"I figured."

Silence. Then Windy blurted, "I wanted to kill him, Ash."

He nodded. "Of course you did."

"I was so close." She looked at her hands. "I would have done it. Done just what he wanted. Denied Mr. Johnson and Dr. Waters and

Kurt O'Connell the possibility of closure. I wasn't even thinking of them."

"But you didn't."

"Because Eve stopped me."

"That's not what stopped you, Windy. You stopped yourself."

"How do you know?"

"Because you value life—everyone's life—too much. It's why you do your job. And why you are good at it."

"I thought so. Now I don't know if I believe that."

He stood right in front of her. "That's okay, I believe it enough for both of us."

"Thank you." She wasn't ready hear that yet. She felt numb, the way her tongue did after she drank coffee too hot. As though she were all scar tissue. She changed the subject. "How did you know to come here? I heard him say into the police radio that the house was empty."

"You had told me to call off the guards yesterday. Which meant that there wouldn't have been one to see you come home. And that someone was trying to mislead us. About your house, and about Harry being dead."

Her jaw clenched. "I can't believe I fell for that."

"We all did."

"But I should have—"

Ash raked a hand through his hair. "Dammit, Windy, stop it. From now on, you are not allowed to beat yourself up over things that are outside your control. You'll just have to live with the fact that you are not bionic or a mind reader."

"Why are you yelling at me?"

"Because I almost lost you and it was the worst feeling in the entire world and I'm not dealing with it as well as I want to be."

Just saying it, letting it be out there. Windy let it sink in for a little while then said, "What happens now?"

"What do you want to happen?"

She thought about it long enough for Ash to start getting nervous. Finally she said, "I want to go to Chicago and get Cate." She looked up at him. "And I want you to come with me."

Late that night Windy tiptoed from her childhood bedroom into the guest room that her mother had made up for Ash, and slid under the covers with him.

"Are you awake?" she asked.

"No." He reached out and turned on the duck decoy lamp that stood on the bedside table. "Yes. Is something wrong?"

She looked up at him, his hair messy, his eyes heavy with sleep, the man who would protect her but never coddle her. "I just realized there is something I haven't told you. I love you, Ash."

"I know." He smiled. "But it wouldn't hurt if you said it about a million more times."

CHAPTER 87

I DO, I DO TOO

BY STORM LARKE

EXCLUSIVE TO THE REVIEW-JOURNAL

The mayor's race is heating up with former boss of the
Violent Crimes Task force going head-to-head with the in-
cumbent, Gerald Keene. After stirring up talk with his
unconventional Vote For My Dad billboards featuring drawings by his fiancée's daughter, Cate, Ash Laughton grabbed
the spotlight this weekend with his quiet wedding and not
so quiet reception. The bride and groom had planned to
celebrate by taking the bride's 7-year-old daughter to a
monster truck rally, but their friends had other ideas.
When they went home to change after their private ceremony, they were kidnapped by campaign manager Jonah
Priestly and whisked away by minivan to Eve Sebastian's
rechristened Paradise Found Café, the perfect setting to celebrate this match made in heaven. Two hundred fifty guests,
the writer included, dined and danced into the dawn hours.
A surprise late-night appearance by the band Chicago, who
stopped in after their show at the Stardust and played a double set, nearly brought the roof down. The groom's mother
sent her congratulations from Río where she is recovering

from surgery on the estate of her new husband, Dr. Gabriele Nildo. The bride's mother, Magda Thomas, said she was delighted and hoped that now her daughter would settle down and make a family. Little chance of that since Chicago Thomas has just been named the new head of the Violent Crimes Task Force, replacing her husband as the person charged with keeping our streets safe. All the best to this celestial couple.

Not to be upstaged, Gerald Keene will marry his press secretary in an elaborate private ceremony with 1000 of their friends at the Bellagio this coming Thursday. The wedding will be carried live on a special edition of the 10 o'clock nightly news.

Windy folded down the paper and looked across the breakfast table to the yard. Ash and Cate were outside, building something that might have been a bookcase if any of its pieces were at right angles to one another. Brandon stood off to one side, hands on his hips, shaking his head. As she watched, Ash glanced up, saw her, winked and mouthed the words "I love you."

This was it. This was her life now. And she felt good.

Bluebeard

This door you might not open, and you did;
So enter now, and see for what slight thing
You are betrayed. Here is no treasure hid,
 No cauldron, no clear crystal mirroring
The sought-for truth, no heads of women slain
 For greed like yours, no writhings of distress,
But only what you see. Look yet again—
 An empty room, cobwebbed and comfortless.
Yet this alone out of my life I kept
 Unto myself, lest any know me quite;
And you did so profane me when you crept
 Unto the threshold of this room to-night
That I must never more behold your face.
 This now is yours. I seek another place.

—Edna St. Vincent Millay
Sonnet IV

ACKNOWLEDGMENTS

Like any bad girl, this one has a lot of sordid history, and I have wracked up huge debts in her creation. I would like to thank: Lisa Faber of the NYPD Crime Laboratory and Debbie McCracken, David LeMaster, and the "A-Team" at the Las Vegas Metropolitan Police Department Criminalistics Bureau, for generously sharing not only their expertise, but also their insights and experiences with me; Susie Phillips and Meg Cabot, who provided critical insights when critical insights were needed, and tolerated me when I was definitely intolerable; Linda Francis Lee, who went above and beyond any call of duty or friendship helping me revise the manuscript; my publishing posse, Susan Ginsburg, Linda Marrow, and Gina Centrello for never giving up on me; and my friends and family. Every bad girl should be so lucky.

Anything good in the book is all their doing. Everything else I take full credit for.

ABOUT THE AUTHOR

Michele Jaffe holds a Ph.D. in Comparative Literature from Harvard University. She is the author of *The Stargazer* and *The Water Nymph*, as well as *Lady Killer* and *Secret Admirer*. She lives in Las Vegas. Please visit the author's Web site at www.michelejaffe.com.